THE COLONEL WHO COULDN'T REMEMBER

ORLA
KELLY
PUBLISHING

Marc Mc Donald

Pour Camille

Acknowledgements

Many people helped and guided me in writing this novel. Some helped without knowing it. To everyone – my sincere gratitude.

Above all, I am indebted to Clive Margolis, a brilliant and committed content-editor. I am also indebted to John Hobbs, Willie Lawrence, Gerry Dunne, Sean Costello, Damhnait Mac Domhnaill.

Thanks also to Maxime for important help at different times. Frédérique was incredibly supportive with practical assistance and encouragement.

Finally, I am grateful to Orla Kelly of Orla Kelly Publishing and Jean O'Sullivan of Red Pen Edits for helping turn a manuscript into a novel.

PART 1

Chapter 1

Waiting for Boris

Staring out the kitchen window at the long narrow garden, deep-green grass, dense purple foliage of the prunus tree, weighty branches of grey-barked beech trees. All chilled by the first sour winds of Autumn. Didn't want to be staring at them. Wanting to see Boris instead, his glorious rustiness and flinty infinity eyes to lighten a moody day.

Always felt this way on the monthly anniversary. Strange, because getting out had been so joyous, like frisky bubbles frothing inside me.

Tapping the glass with impatient fingers, drumming from little fingers inwards until I had to stop – no left thumb to complete the beat. Don't remember when it left me. Never had the chance to say goodbye. Except for moments like this, didn't think much about it either. Never thinking about how it was coping on its own. But, then, it probably never thought about me and how I was coping.

Gave it a good lick, tongue slithering over wrinkly folds. A lick of quick love. Love helped me get used to the scarred flesh. Amazingly, the pain eased once I left hospital, got to my own place. Head and pain sorting things out between them. Often wondered about that, the difference having my own place made, pain going AWOL when the head was happy. Click, pluf, gone. I don't know. Gave it another loving lick.

Two blackbirds perched on the wooden fence along the left side of the garden, big-bellied, grey-beaked, looked around, squawked, flew off. Reminding me of the Terrorists, Termites, Terminators – or whatever I called them during my time there – coming into my room, squawk-talking.

"The way you actively compensate proves you once knew how to do things with a left thumb. Therefore, you must have some residue of pre-trauma memory somewhere. From whence," the long-faced, long-winded Chief Hospital Terrorist said, taking a quick breath in case he might expire without it, "the difficulty arose. Find the key to that, Dominic," wagging a skeletal finger at me, not his left thumb, "and … voila."

Voila what? Fireworks in the sky? In my head? Become a lug of a dry dope like him?

Buzzy buzz. A droning kamikaze fly zooming around the kitchen, speeding up to attack the glass. If it survives, next time it'll do the same. Flies just don't get it. No memory, that's their problem. They're the ones who really need counselling. Guffawing loudly, 'where'd I hear that before?'

Just as the fly hit the glass again, the front door opened, closed faintly. Listening keenly. No Brat-bang and he never entered the house without making sure I knew. Could be behind his mother, following her in. No, unlikely. He couldn't stay quiet that long, it would kill him. Turned my head slightly to pick up signature footsteps. It wasn't the Politician. Always came in from her place next door via the gap in the garden wall that looked like it had been specially made. Must be her daughter, the Brat's mother, the not-so-young young woman she called Joan, who claimed – incorrectly I stress, to be my daughter. All of them had keys and bloody-well used them far too often. Definitely wasn't Irena. She didn't have a key, but did expect to be let in, and once inside moved everything around as if cleaning, but I suspected she was looking for something.

"Hi, Dad, it's me!" a soft, calming voice called out.

Fake cheeriness. Snorting. Never had any time for that. First 'Dad' of the day. No point sighing.

"Anyone home?"

"No," I growled at the glass, stayed where I was. Knew she was frowning down at the pile of post on the polished light brown wooden floor under the letterbox, tut-tutting like an auld one, picking it up with a shake of her head.

Made sure I was sitting at the kitchen table when she came in. Hands flat on the red tablecloth, perpendicular to the white stripes and green band, in a studied pose of patience.

5

Always easy on the eye though. Gentle face, blue eyes, a real smile I didn't see much of. Past the first flush of womanhood. No weight to talk about or throw around. Never painted herself because she's a gardener or something like it. Fine straight brown hair sometimes tied back with a bandana. Didn't like me staring at her.

"Uf!" she exclaimed as she heaved a bag of groceries onto the kitchen island. Where did she get that figure? Her mother was built like a horse. Never met the father. Didn't try to help her because she shouldn't be buying the stuff. Haven't they noticed I can easily do all that myself? Like, I can take money out of the ATM at the busy bank on the main road, buy a shirt, follow the news, be worried about global warming because the bloody rain kept me indoors so much. Hmmm, not worth picking a fight over.

"Sorry I'm late." She paused to look me over, checking had I grown a second nose she could tell the Shrinkage about. Brief dutiful smile, came over to the table, leaned down and rested her head on my shoulder. Quite nice. Sensed she wanted me to put an arm around her shoulders. My arm had its own ideas. Only worth doing if the Brat was there. Drove him nuts.

"How are you, Dad?" she asked standing back.

"Fine. I'm always fine. I can't be anything but fine." Not gracious, I know, but I was struggling. Teaching myself to let more and more 'Dad's' pass wasn't easy. She was fixated on that bloody word, and then went all sad if I reminded her – for her own sake, not mine, that I wasn't her Dad. She wasn't my daughter – period. Didn't matter she was kind, certainly as good as any of the nurses in the hospital.

"I was out helping Mam with the last canvass," her voice in brittle-mode, as if it didn't want to be used. "And got these on the way back." Started unpacking the groceries, putting them away. Stopped after a moment, studied me, as if checking in case she missed something the first time. "You know it's the last night, don't you?"

"What? The end of the world?"

"Haha." Fake laugh. "And she's always nervous before the voting. She's convinced she won't get in. Again." She nodded philosophically. "She's always like this before polling day."

Didn't put one thing in the wrong place. Knew where everything went. Dried fruit out of the packet into the jar on the shelf beside the porridge. Bananas and apples on the wooden platter on the window ledge going down to the basement. Olive oil in the pull-out larder. Tins in the bottom drawer under the oven. Knew it as well as I did.

"Here," she said, coming over, handing me a letter.

"This is for me?" I tried handing it back. As far as I was concerned, I didn't get letters from anyone because I didn't send letters to anyone.

"No, no." She was insistent, pressing it back at me. "It's for you."

"No. Take it back. I don't want it."

"It's your voting card, silly. Look," she pointed at the writing on the card. "There's your name and number and that's the polling station." Whiff of lemony soap or perfume off her as she leaned over me. Pleasant.

"It's in the girl's school, beside the church. Voting is tomorrow."

"Is it?" I asked, looking up at her.

"It's the General Election."

How had I forgotten? Every bloody pole was creaking with the posters.

"You are going to vote, aren't you, Dad? Everyone should vote. And don't forget to bring the card with you and your passport or driving licence. You could be challenged if you don't have ID with you."

I didn't have a driving licence because I didn't drive, though I was sure I could drive if I had to. Buses suited me fine.

"Remember, Mam is running. You'll see her name on the list." She went back to flitting around the place like a buttery butterfly with skinny arms. "Won't you give her your number one?" she cried as she stretched up to put teabags in a jar.

"What? Give that woman my number one? Are you mad?"

"Oh, Dad, don't be like that. You're being … personal now, not political. Think about it that way. Can you give me one good political reason why not?"

Looked away, hoping Boris would appear, save me from this. Absolutely no point to this conversation, as she well knew. Looked like she thought so too, until she came out with this.

"I know you don't like me bringing it up... but I can never understand why."

Noisily blowing air out of my mouth. Even if she was right, it was tiresome, always talking about the bloody Politician. Of course, it was personal. Damn well personal. What's more personal than some fool claiming she's married to you? The Politician was the most irritating interferer of them all, and there were quite a few contenders for that title. She'd even made a grab for Harry. More than once. You don't forget that sort of thing in a hurry. Anyway, I had no political views that I knew about, though I could always invent some if I had to.

"She's not my wife," I said tetchily. Final word.

This frustrated her, as usual. In the silence for some unknown reason, I felt sort of sorry for her. She could be so sensitive about this kind of thing, even though she'd heard me say it many times.

"Look," I said, friendly-serious, "seeing pictures of me," holding up fingers for inverted commas, "and her together doesn't mean I remember anything... and anyway it isn't me," I added, waving at the pictures they'd put on the wall, in case she said it was. Noticed someone had turned them around again after I had made them all face the wall. Christ, I knew all their tricks. If I saw the photos often enough they thought I'd start believing them. How stupid did they think I was? Think it was the Brat they got to do it. Opportunity, motive, malice.

"I can't believe something like that just because you all say it." Sounded like I was pleading. I don't do pleading.

Quick change of tone to assertive. "I have to feel it here." Pointed at my gut where my instincts lived like chortling geese.

"Well, Dad, give her your number two vote then, won't you? Who will you give your number one to?"

Had no idea. "I haven't decided yet."

Almost a full smile as if she knew. "You see, Dad, that's my point."

Shot her a warning look. That was enough 'Dads' for one day. Her delusion was tolerable only to a point. Drummed my fingers on the table, shuffled my feet, thinking about my non-thumb, and looked at the pictures on the wall. Could they possibly turn by themselves? She placed a second card in front of me.

"You can take this one too," I said, brusquely pushing a postcard she'd also put in front of me, straight back at her. "It's nothing to do with me."

She picked it up, giving me *that* look. "It's from Uncle Terry in Argentina." She read it. "He's wishing Mam the best of luck. Isn't that nice?" She examined the picture. "It's from a place called... Salta, I think."

Salta, Yalta, Malta, I said to myself massaging the skin under my chin. Surprised I knew names like that. No matter, often happened. She put the card back on the table. "Great timing, isn't it? Mam will be pleased."

To be agreeable I picked up the bloody thing and looked at it. A church like an overgrown cauliflower wedged into a tight corner beside traffic lights. "He's put the wrong address on it," I complained, tone definitive, handing the card back to her. "He put down twelve in-stead of thirteen."

A common mistake. I'd spoken to the postman about it a few times, but he'd stopped listening to me, insisting bloodymindedly he was right and continued putting them in my letterbox. I put up a sign on the door saying, "She doesn't live here" which soon disap-peared. When I threatened to put the sign up again, the young woman told me to stop being ridiculous. Did I want to look ridiculous in front of the whole neigh-bourhood? I knew better than to answer. She didn't know, but an irritating shrink once told me I was like a teenager, thinking I was the centre of the universe and no one else mattered. Never thought that at all, but when there are two worlds, yours and the Onslaught, where else could I be but in the centre of mine?

She put a plastic bag on the table in front of me. This was getting like Christmas.

"More surprises?"

She rolled her eyes like I was in for a big surprise. Up-ended the bag. Seven pairs of socks tied together tumbled onto the table, same dark blue.

"Look," she said enthusiastically. "The days of the week are on the top. See?"

I thumbed through them. She was right. The days were written in white, yellow, purple, green, blue, red and orange.

"Neat, isn't it? Now you'll always know what day it is. You just look at your socks." She looked down at my feet. "Look at that hole. You can't go out like that."

Fawn socks and leather sandals suited me fine. Didn't see anything wrong with the protruding left big toe. Nail well clipped, too. Smiled at it. It hadn't left me. Loyalty.

"No, Dad, I'm serious." She prodded my sandals with her dark ankle boot. "No one wears socks and sandals these days."

"Huh." What does she know? Studied the socks on the table. Saw lots of problems straight away. Making sure to wear the right socks on the right day, not mixing them up, would be a challenge. Would I have to organise a second sock drawer, arrange the socks according to the calendar in order to make sure the days always matched... What would happen if I wore Tuesday socks on a Sunday?

"Anyway, we don't have time for that now," she said, finishing putting the groceries away. "We have to get going."

"Going? Going where?'" Couldn't find any blasted instruction sheet. What if I stayed up after midnight, what would I do? Keep the same socks? Put on a new pair? Or even mix them up, left foot up to midnight, right foot after midnight? Or, vice versa? She didn't realise it was a lot more complex than it looked.

"I don't know where I'll stand in these socks," I complained, hoping for credit for the accidental pun.

"Dad! Come on. Up you get." She was hauling me to my feet.

"Where are we going?" Never like being hustled.

"We're visiting Granny in hospital."

"Whose Granny?"

"We can talk about that in the car. Come on." She picked up her handbag and car keys and hustled me into my coat and hat and out the door. Just as she was closing the door, she remembered. "God, Dad, your feet." She dashed upstairs for shoes, insisted I change on the doorstep.

"Maureen rang Mam last night," she said when the car was moving down the hill.

There was a Maureen somewhere, I knew that, and I knew I didn't like her. Called her Beetroot Woman. "Uncle John brought Granny into hospital on Wednesday night. She wasn't feeling well. Her breathing, I think. She seemed run down and, well, you know…" She sighed at the windscreen. "Poor Granny."

When I was in hospital myself, I remembered being visited by an auld one who claimed to be my mother. Very unpleasant. This shrunken-headed, grey-haired, wrinkle-faced death mask had peered around the room door scrutinising me, like she'd elbowed the undertaker out of the way, sizing me up. She'd been followed by Beetroot Woman – younger, purple-faced, prim and properly ugly, who wasn't quite so grim. Neither introduced themselves, both stood in the doorway with such solemn expressions I wondered was I already dead.

"Nurse!" I roared, thinking it might be another Shrinkage-trick, masquerading as helpers of one kind or another. Even then they were always trying to catch me out. Some of them didn't believe I didn't know stuff they thought I should know. In hospital they buzzed around me like flies over a carcass, trying to get inside my head. What they didn't want to know was there was only room for me in there. No one else, especially not them. Anyway, if my condition really was as rare as they claimed, it stood to reason they'd invent scenarios to study me in. Made the mistake once of mentioning this to one of them who immediately used it against me.

"Shrinks out!" I shouted at the top of my voice at the two statues in the doorway. Just in case. Neither moved. Were they deaf?

"Nurse!" I roared again. When no one came, I told the two women to go, pointing down the corridor. When they still didn't move, I suspected they were foreigners. "No here," I said really slowly. "Other ward. More bodies there, plenty, plenty." The older one started sobbing, and Beetroot Woman's eyes got bigger, and she hugged the auld one. "Not my turn," I shouted. Beginning to get hoarse. "Wrong fuckin' ward. It's next door you want. Goodbye, ladies, come back next month."

Grim Reaper renewed her dry sobbing, but Beetroot Woman was trying to stifle a giggle. Before she left, the auld one came over to my bed, grabbed my hand, threw her face on it like I was the Pope. "Oh Dominic," she moaned over and over. "What did they do to you?"

Couldn't push her away so gave her a papal blessing and told her to go in peace, her sins were forgiven, which she eventually did, looking sternly at her companion who hadn't stopped giggling. Told her too her sins were forgiven, so too were the doctors who were fine and not to worry about them.

What made that visit even more farcical was that it happened at a time I was actually getting better, much better. The pain from my non-thumb and in my head had eased. I wasn't as stuffed with drugs as I had been, had started going for walks in the hospital grounds, was eating and sleeping better. But just a few minutes in the same room with that awful woman left a lasting impression. Not bad for someone who's supposed to have no memory. So, naturally I wasn't too keen on a repeat, even if she was now the one in hospital.

Chapter 2

Visiting Auld One in Hospital

She turned right, right, right again, then another right – so many ruddy rights my body took to leaning left – straining against the seatbelt, fearing bad luck. Squeezed into the impatient flow of southbound traffic. All the lamp-posts and traffic poles along the way festooned with election posters.

"There!" my driver cried, pointing to a succession of identical posters. "You see Mam's?" She was examining each pole. "They've left them alone," she noted with a nod of approval. Switching lanes to turn left, almost felt like cheering. "You know they sometimes move them just a little, a nudge, or loosen the plastic so that after a while with the rain and wind they slip a little or slide down. It gives a terrible impression of the candidate. Who'd vote for someone who looked at you sideways or upside down?"

Thought about that, decided I would. If they were all like the Politician what was there to lose?

Met one of the Politician's colleagues once. Sitting on the grass in the front garden watching time pass, when this big snotty car pulls up exactly in front my house. Knew immediately it was for her, so why didn't it park in front of her house? Plenty of space there. Was up and over at the railings, glaring at the short-legged, pot-bellied, creased suit who got out of the back.

"I wouldn't leave it there if I were you. Not safe. Cars are broken into around here all the time." He's about to answer when she comes charging out as if the house was on fire, down the steps and practically puts a hand over my mouth. To distract me she introduces me to pot-belly man – dark-eyed Kevin. Shook my hand without asking permission. Sensed his high opinion of himself. Said he'd been in the cabinet as well. Looked him up and down, didn't take long. Undecided whether to ignore him. His hand didn't seem the hand of a cabinet-maker.

"You don't have the hands of a cabinet-maker," I said, leaning towards him across the railings.

He blinked. "Hoho! You got me there," puffy-laugh, head back, belly out. He glanced a question at the Politician who put on her stoic face.

"Do you have strangers calling to your house asking you to do favours for them?" I asked him.

"Of course, Dominic," he answered like we'd been friends all my life. Picked up the vibe he was doing me a favour talking like this. "How do you think we would get elected? Hoho!"

"Come on, Kevin, let's go in," she butted in, sensing worse to come. "Everyone in the street will be out in a minute, if we stay here."

Seeing the Politician's face on every pole looking down at me was not pleasant. Bad enough living beside her without feeling she was watching me when I went out of the house. Of course, on the posters she'd been tarted up. Serious, charming, friendly, distant, progressive, predictable, humane, tough. All things to all voters. Which wasn't at all my impression of her. She acted like she owned the bloody place, refused to knock on the front door before coming in, poked around in my stuff, made comments like, "Why do you keep wearing that awful cardigan?" Warned me never to talk to journalists, queried me about who I'd been talking to on the street, what I said to them. As if I spent the whole day doing nothing but talking about her to anyone I met. And she dismissed my complaints about weirdos calling at my door looking for her and treating me like a fool.

"Looks good, doesn't she?" her daughter said in an absent-minded way. I conceded the quality of the photo, no more. I was concentrating on finding a poster that was upside-down or sideways. A few streets on spotted one in front of a petrol station.

"Stop!" I shouted. A poster sitting on the ground at the bottom of a pole. "There's one. I want to see it." She managed to pull in and stop the car more or less beside the footpath. Out like a rabbit, leaving car door open, over to the pole. Had to get down on my hunkers, then my knees, to examine the picture for trustworthiness. Am not good at reading upside down so had to twist my neck around to look up.

First time I keeled over. Second time read that the candidate's name, Hospital Gaffney, a 'Non-Party Hospital Candidate'. 'Hospital' was written in large bold capitals so assumed it was his first name. But no. It obviously meant he was either in hospital or just out of it, possibly still ill in it and rather proud of it, or wanted to go back in and couldn't, so was running for election instead. Overall, good enough for me to vote for him.

"I'll give the Politician my number two," I said to my driver as a reward for her patience when I got back in the car. She said nothing, but I could tell she'd been worried a photographer might come along and take a photo of me sprawled on the footpath, looking up at the sky.

My unease grew as she drove down the narrow ramp into the darkness of the hospital car park. "What's after this?" I asked.

She glanced at me, turned off the engine, released her seatbelt. "Just your school reunion and a dinner if Mam wins. But she'll probably have one anyway. She'll have a separate one for her election team and…" she lifted her chin, slightly narrowing her eyes. "Oh, and maybe another visit to Doctor Papp, but I'm not sure about that."

I nodded dubiously. A long list. "I don't think I'll have time for all that." A school reunion? I'd no idea what schools I'd been to. "What's the school thing for? I can read and write. Oh, it's a refresher course, is it?"

A little smile that said she thought I was trying to be funny. I accepted laughs like that from her, but no one else.

A smarmy young shrink with fat cheeks and a small mouth once speculated openly that my lack of school memory might be 'exaggerated'. He got his answer when I grabbed him by the collar and said into his suddenly pale face, "Some people can't remember their grandparent's names or what they had for breakfast. I don't remember what school I went to. Big deal." It wasn't the first or last time I had to be forceful with the Shrinkage. I released him quickly because I didn't want to end up in restraints like some of the other patients in the hospital. I smiled nicely at his astonishment, and said sorry, smoothing his tie and collar. Could've been the same guy after I left hospital who asked me why I called the Brat 'Brat' and the Politician 'The Politician'. "Can you not guess?" I answered, tying and untying my shoelaces because I knew it intrigued them. Looking up I said, "Because that's what they are."

Waiting at the door of the lift. Just the two of us. "Is this reunion the Shrinkage's idea?" I asked in a low voice. An auld one in a wheelchair wheeled herself up to wait and kept looking at me. Looked back at her as hard as she looked at me, impressed by the effort going into her stare. "That's a healthy stare you have there, missus," I said to her when the lift door opened. Didn't answer, tried to roll the small wheels of her wheelchair over my foot.

"Of course not," the young woman whispered in the lift as we stared forward at the shiny grey door, listened to the whirring of the moving lift. "What are you talking about? I've told you before there's no such thing as the Shrinkage."

"There is. I know there is," I hissed, unwilling to concede the point under any circumstances. She came as far as the ward door with me, refused to come in. "She's your mother and it's you she wants to see. I was in earlier. So, in you go."

"She's not my..." Waste of breath. The young woman was gone, walking away along the narrow corridor.

Well, in fact when I'm faced with a situation I can't avoid, I force myself. Prepared a big smile, looked around the door, beamed determinedly at the auld one lying in a narrow bed across from the door. White sheet drawn up to her shoulders, limp arm lying on the sheet. Not hooked up to any machines, staring at the wall. The other bed had curtains drawn around it. About to check it out when the auld one came alive, her eyes sort of sucked me over to her. Had no idea what to say. Motioned with a jerky hand towards a chair, watched me bring it to the left side of the bed. Box of paper hankies on the bedside table. Grabbed it, put it on the bed between us, felt like a poker player showing the others how much money he has to lose.

"Do you think I'm going to die?" she asked in a raspy voice, getting straight to the point.

"So am I." Might as well tell her the truth. Took one out of the hankie box, held it ready.

"What's wrong with you?" she asked almost resentfully, showing unexpected vigour. "Have you got pneumonia?"

"Me? No, nothing. Why are you asking me that?" I slid my non-thumb hand out of sight. "We all live forever," I changed tack, suddenly afraid she might die in front of me and therefore had to keep her alive.

"That's true. We live forever with God." But she didn't seem quite happy with that. "I don't want to die," she said after a while, her arm doing a quick little spasm on its own. "But I know the man upstairs is calling me. He's waiting."

Cocked my ear up at the ceiling, listening. Maybe I was keeping her from an appointment? Stood up to go, but she motioned impatiently for me to sit down again. "No, stay. God is good."

Brainwave. Maybe she thought I was a priest? Dark jacket, tie-less grey shirt, clean-shaven, earnest face, slow-moving manner. In hospital myself, used to get visits from a chaplain dressed like that whose job was to put the fear of God into patients who already had plenty of it in them. I leaned forward, whispered some words into her ear.

"What's that you're saying?" she demanded aggressively, turning her head towards me on the pillow. "Speak up. I can't hear you."

"It's Latin," I lied.

She looked away. "You were good at Latin in school. Say something else in Latin."

I muttered a few hics, hocs, ibids and nominems. I'd no idea where they came from.

"Eh... what school was that?"

"Ssshh." I whispered, not wanting her to get excited and be blamed for killing her. "You'll wake the others up."

"They don't pray," she said accusingly, started muttering prayers to herself, maybe in Latin. "I can't remember your brother's name," she declared. "I want to know it before I die."

"You're not going to die."

"Course I am. What do you know? Are you a doctor? What was his name?"

Panic. Looked around for a nurse but this seemed to be a nurse-less hospital. The old woman stared at me expecting an answer. She might have been dying but she was well able to put up a hard stare.

I leaned forward. "Latin or English?"

That flummoxed her and she seemed to forget the question.

"Did you pray in..." Burst of dry coughing and wheezing. I gave her the hankie, took out another. "...Lourdes?"

"Lourdes?"

"Are you deaf? That's what I said. Lourdes." Closed her eyes, but her breathing was regular.

No idea what or who Lourdes is, but spotted a plastic bottle full of water with a blue cap on her locker. 'Lourdes Holy Water' on it. I poured half a glass for her, held it to her lips.

Eyes open again. "Lourdes," she said dreamily, "where the BVM appeared to the three little girls."

She's raving now, I thought, pressing the glass to her lips. She sipped a little. So afraid she was losing it and I'd be blamed, I repeated what I'd heard someone say during a phone-in. "Death is a full stop at the end of a life sentence."

Her eyes flashed open, fixed me with that grim stare like she was about to accuse me of being an imposter. Her mouth opened, lips bumped into each other until words emerged. "It's not death. It's a birth, a birth into God's kingdom."

"Exactly, that's what it is. Well said. Here, have some holy water. It's good for you.'

"What?" she gasped in horror, trying to sit up. "Sacrilege! Nurse, he's giving me holy water. He's committing sacrilege." I looked around guiltily, expecting nurses to come running. But she couldn't say anymore when I held the glass to her mouth and she had another sip.

"God forgive you," she complained, snaky tongue licking her lips. "Go straight to confession, you hear me?" She raised a couple of fingers and motioned with her hand.

Gave her the other paper hankie but she dropped it, sighing with impatience. Motioned again, gave her my hand, sat like that until I felt she was asleep or having her visa checked by St Peter. Put her hand back on the sheet, stood up, was backing slowly out of the room, very content with myself, heard a voice croak from behind the curtain beside me, "Dominic, is that you? Dominic?"

Deepened my voice. "No, Missus, it's Father Ward. I'll be into you in a minute."

"Dominic," the weak voice was pushing itself. "I know it's you. Come over to me, son."

Chapter 3

Voting

F oul looking, low clouds. A wall of white, grey airlessness. Like the planet stopped moving and no one noticed. Weather that sad, meant anything could happen. Stop staring at the dumb clouds, already barely missed thumping into plump street lamppost. Needlessly pushed dark blue hat further down on ears. On up the hill, right then left, ready for the one thing that looked unlikely, rain. Fast walking. Open raincoat flapping like a swan taking off. Along wide tree-lined, convent-walled footpath, nowhere special in mind, letting legs gear up into long strides, avoiding street-crossing. Ah, the pleasure of free-flowing legs.

Mrs Hand thirty metres ahead, what good luck. Ever impressive wide shoulders, old-fashioned three-quarter length tweed coat. A real ally. Never had to explain the Onslaught to her. Understood instinctively, being beyond the Onslaught, beyond the lows and highs of life. Something different about her today, though. Yep, that's it, not carrying usual two laden shopping bags. Practically sewn to her hands, they were. Never seen her without them. Intriguing. Didn't change her gait, still heaving herself along as if she had them. Sped up. Chance to chat with my favourite auld one, no matter how brief, not to be missed. Provided more umpf than twenty sessions with dreary Shrinkage. Where's she going without bags? Usually only met her passing my house or on the car-infested main road near the shops – no idea where she lived. Woah, boys, legs aching to run up to her.

"Mrs Hand, hello," cheery voice, little breathlessness, slapped disobedient legs as I fell into step beside her.

"Is it yourself?" she replied, low-voiced, not effusive, just how I liked it. Glanced briefly at me, noting hat and coat. She knew all about my rain-phobia, called rain God's own whiskey. "Grand weather for voting."

"Sure is." Voting? *Mon dieu*, completely forgot about it. Quick recovery. "You all set? I'm all set, even picked my candidate." Didn't tell her who because we didn't exchange intimacies.

"Will there be a big turnout?" she wondered as we skirted the tree in the middle of the footpath.

"That's a good question," I replied, pleased this was the kind of answer she'd give herself. Was impolite to disagree with Mrs Hand. Not that she'd react badly if I did. Just wouldn't have felt right.

"They're spending a lot on it, aren't they?" she said, looking at the poster-festooned poles on the far side of the street. A certain political face prominent on every bloody pole, serenely promising a new direction, meaning constant interference and pestering.

"Some people have no shame," I said, appalled by the ego-fest. "Oops, sorry." Accidentally rubbed shoulders, unused to walking alongside her. Sturdy woman, didn't seem to notice.

Round the corner onto Crawford Avenue. Primary school cum polling station. More damn posters. Steady trickle in and out of school, cars dropping off, picking up, few canvassers ahead, good distance from school gate. Quick check every pole, where's Hospital Gaffney? Couldn't see him and no upside-down posters. Good man, not wasting his money. Could be still in hospital.

"Thank God we only have to do this every five years," Mrs Hand muttered. Looking at the marauding canvassers ahead.

"Definitely."

"Or four," she continued, "if they can't wait."

"Indeed."

"Or three."

Nodded, ready to go down to one.

Spotted the Brat at the school gate. Beige, oversized hoodie, dark hair too long. His mother let's him away with everything. By God, what's he doing? Handing out election leaflets. Cheeky grin. Heard him say to an auld fella with a cap, "Sure, she's my Granny, so you'll give her your number one, won't you?" What's he playing at? Should be in school. Looked around for a guard to report him. Two other ill-proportioned waifs beside him, doing nothing, exchanging embarrassed looks. Stopped when he saw me, keeping wary eye as Colonel Thunderclap approached. Will he do a runner? Evil smile. Great, him taking off and me not chasing him. Not in front of Mrs Hand. Wouldn't catch him anyway. Mrs Hand sailed on into the school as I stopped in front of the Brat.

"Aha!" I glared down at him, small but vicious, beefing up the ominous, "Caught you, didn't I?" Never lose an opportunity because he won't. "I'm going to tell your mother you're skipping school." Nodded vehement agreement with myself, obviously expecting back-chat. Brat could be fierce impudent in public. "You're in big trouble."

"Nah," blithe Brat brushed it off, looking for new targets. "School's closed today for the election. Day off," he added, grinning smugly at his big-eyed mates.

"Don't believe you."

"It's true guys, isn't it? Ask anyone."

Disliked that word. In hospital remember asking a nurse where was this Mr Inywan the porters were always talking about. Didn't ask again. Sighed impatiently. Definitely not getting into public row with Brat. "Well then, em, you can't vote so…" Wasn't listening, handing out leaflets to two auld ones I'd never seen before.

"Oh thank you, young man," they cooed gratefully. What are they doing here? Knew all the auld ones around here. Could be illegal. Keep an eye on them.

"OK, quick," I ordered the Brat, "give me one for Hospital Gaffney."

"Who?" he guffawed. "Guys, who's Hospital Gaffney?"

About to swot him dead with withering repost when someone touched my arm from behind. Swung around so fast random woman shrank back two steps.

"Colonel Corley?" foreign voice asked, sticking a strange-shaped furry can up to my nose as if snot-catching.

Batted it away with my hand. Sniffled, was she one of those people my grand snoozer sometimes intimidates? Noticed sneaky camerawoman hovering behind, zooming camera in on me.

"It's a microphone," foreign woman whispered, shoving it back at me.

"Fine, and this is my snoozer," I replied, stroking it, feeling obliged to make an introduction. Never know who or what you're dealing with. Studied her, elephant scarf around her neck meaning no neck, made-up face like she'd just come out of a tanning salon, bundle of brown hair swaying on her head. Serious eyes, though.

"Ve are from Slovenia television. Can you comment on…"

"Slovenia? Where's that?" Colonel Curiosity asked.

"It vas part of the former Yugoslavia vere you served…"

"Served?" Fake laugh. "Was I a waiter?"

"Hehe, can ve ask you a few kvestions?"

Noted she dressed better than the journalists who followed the Politician around, sometimes trying their luck with me. Didn't mean she was any better at minding her own business.

"Vhat empact vill the election here hafe on the Irish government's attitude to Slovenia joining the European Union?"

Crazy questions not allowed distract me, but she kept up with me as I turned abruptly, walked off without answering. "I am not a colonel," I corrected her. Journalists are as bad as chickens, happy to feed on anything. "I am a private citizen, expert at minding my own business," I added stiffly. "It's a good policy. You should try it."

"Pardon Colonel, the opinion polls…"

Noticed the Brat listening and loitering with intent, every word would be reported back. Stopped, hauled him out in front of me. "Here," I thrust him at elephant-scarf woman, "the Brat will tell you anything you want to know. Goodbye." Shoved him towards her and hurried off into the school, fearing it was too late to challenge the two dubious auld ones. Heard him begin, "Well, eh, first, eh, you're welcome, eh, and sorry for that, he's always narky…"

Mrs Hand coming out. Double damn. Post-voting retribution glow. "How'd it go?" I asked, wondering who she'd taken revenge on. Also wanted to ask how it's done, not having voted before. Do you shout it out like at an auction, or go up to a top table in front of everyone and whisper into someone's ear? Probably a pad of some sort.

"For all the good it'll do," she said, sanguine to the point of death, hiking up imperial shoulders. "But we have to do it all the same, don't we?"

"Absolutely. Yes, it's our duty."

"If we didn't, someone else would vote for us, wouldn't they?"

"For sure. I'll be giving my number one to Hospital Gaffney."

"Will you now?" Slightest nod, expression as always encompass all possible reactions. "Suppose they all start off with good intentions and then it's downhill all the way."

"Which finger did you use?"

"All of them, I suppose, if you want to."

That's how I found out. You vote five times with different fingers, twice. "Hah…" I grinned, "I'll do that." Suppose you start with the right thumb, work from there. Supposed they could tell which fingers from which. Fingerprints must be different. I'd have only nine votes. So what?

School hall was cleared. Sports equipment, chairs piled at the back. Coat racks along the wall. Green clothed desks for staff, three voting booths over by the windows. Went straight over to nearest, stood behind guy hunched over narrow ledge in booth. Taking his time, making low grunting noises. Clearly painful choices. None of my business, didn't offer help. Sensing someone behind, he straightened up, looked around with screwed up face.

"Wha're ya lukin' ah?" he demanded.

Looked away, up at high ceiling, out the window, modelling imperturbability. Hadn't come here to have argy-bargy with a slow-voter with issues.

"Ger ourra here," he croaked, "An stop lukin' ar me." Went back to his ledge of indecision, sticking out his backside to force me backwards. Resisted giving it good kick but checking out the angles when interrupted.

"Sir?" swanky female voice from behind desk. "Sir, can I help you? Do you want to vote?"

"Yes, what else would I be doing here?" Grumpy, I know, but slow-voters fault.

"Come over here, please, over here." Hauls carcass over to her desk. Looked up at me with nice smile when I gave her my name, address, date of birth and favourite salad. Dark curls, heavy rimmed glasses, probably blue eyes if I could see them. She glanced at her colleagues, drew a line through my name and address on her big page, gave me a sheet as long as a toilet roll with endless list of names and boxes.

"Oi wanna see hiss Oi D," Slow-voter comes barging over, stands beside me, pointing finger at swanky-voice.

"Made up your mind?" I asked cheerfully.

"Fuck off. Shoew sum Oi D." Bald as a coot, pale-skin, sharp angled small snoozer, pumping up indignation. "Oi'm challengin' dis geeza. He can't vowte without Oi D," he said loudly. Slow-to-rouse policeman at back of room, coming forward to listen.

"Sir, do you have you poling card or other ID?" slightly frazzled swanky-voice asked, glancing uneasily at slow voter.

"Don't need to carry it with me, I know who I am. Just told you," answered amicably. "No problem there." Looked meaningfully at slow-voter, noting un-ironed curled-up ends of faded denim jacket.

"Ye can't le'r him vowte. Oi now de law."

Random voices behind me chipping in.

"Come on, hurry up."

"Let him vote."

"Everyone knows who he is."

"He's Colonel Corley. Man married to yer one."

"What her name?" Big laugh.

"True, all true," Colonel Opportunist agreed opportunistically. "That's what they call me." Quite happy to assume the dreary role of the Onslaught when it suited. Colonel Corley straightened up, shoulders back, military bearing. Slow-voter not budging.

"Oi down't care if he's Jaysus Chroist himself."

More back and forth, officials muffled consultations, decision. I was who they said I was.

Armed with toilet-roll list marched over to the voting booth, arms swinging. Inside, half-inside really, no curtain behind me, leaned on unpolished plywood ledge, held up lengthy sheet. Hm, counted sixteen names. Depressing, all preening fools wanting to be like the Politician. Must be a common character defect. Grimaced at third name, drew sharp line through it, carried on. No Hospital Gaffney, only Ernest Gaffney. Would have to do.

Looked for the pad, right thumb itching to make its mark on Gaffney's box. No pad, only a butty pencil tied with short string. Stood back a moment. Weird, how did the others do it? Booths beside me empty. Did they all just go in and pretend to vote, just writing whatever they fancied? Beckoned swanky-voice over. Double quick arrival accompanied by fat-faced male side-kick.

"Yes, Colonel?" tetchy voice, wondering what is it now. Most of the room watching.

"Madam, in the name of the Blessed Beloved, how am I to vote when there is no…"

Stopped me dead with firm head-shake. "Sir," inching closer, voice low to spare Colonel Numbskull's blushes. "It's the pencil. You use the pencil to mark the boxes one, two, three as far as you want." Pulling the upper part of the toilet roll up from the gap it had slid into, between narrow ledge and the back of the booth, pointing at the stupid instructions at the top. Stood back, studied me for further signs of imbecility, returned swiftly to her desk.

"Hm, I see," I said to fat-faced side-kick still there. "Well, fine, fine. Erm… thank you." Gazing suspiciously at the mean pencil. Yes, well, really just a different way of doing it, that's all.

Democratic work swiftly executed. Gaffney number one. Nothing else, drew second line through Politician's name, then a line through everyone else.

Chapter 4

Politician's Important Phone Call

T he back of the garden at night was a happy place. Perfect for foutering around. Wasn't only that I occupied myself with useless tasks, I did them on my own out in the open, hidden from view. The private fecklessness of a man, without the likes of the Politician bothering him. Any stuff on the ground, I'd pick up. If there wasn't, I'd break off a few twigs, poke at the soil on the small bank with my foot, scatter the earth around. "Aha," something needed tidying up. I'd say to myself, 'What a mess'. Look for a brush, start sweeping or picking up. Doing a bad job, but know I could, if I wanted, do a better one.

Also, the best for foutering, unlike the rest of the garden. Hemmed in by old brown brick walls, I was forever sticking my fingers in between the bricks to see what was loose, another way of counting time passing. Plenty of grass, deceased flowerbeds, thanks to the Brat. A few mature trees clipped back with branches that had no sense of direction. Impossible to climb even with ten fingers, though I still tried with nine. Agile Brat could do it, though. Two other younger trees were lanky with disciplined branches that grew out a short distance, got bored and shot fearlessly upwards. Couldn't climb them either, though the Brat did it last week for some reason. Remember wishing him unkind thoughts, as well as being jealous. Trees were tree-happy when jettisoning leaves, twigs, small, big branches, wind or no wind. Excellent for foutering.

Mild September night verging on warm. Midnight burst of energy. Over-snoozing in the afternoon sent me out to the back garden. Found myself tending respectfully to dead leaves and detritus of the day's now departed wind. Didn't have to create work for myself, all done for me. Only asking to be tidied up if I could see it, which I just about could. When I finished the sweeping, leaned on the brush admiring the neat pile ready for the brown wheelie bin which I pulled up behind me. Well-earned break. Checking how much of my weight I could put on the long-poled brush when a malicious gust of wind scattered half the pile.

Reflecting on the malign wind, heard soft sounds like a hushed foot stepping gingerly on grass. Look through the gap in the boundary wall into next door. Could just make out the shape, then face, of the Politician, leaning against the wall of her outdoor toilet. Short scratching noise, quick burst of light, cigarette smoke drifting across on the soft breeze.

Nodded to myself, unsurprised. She'd sworn to her daughter, told everyone, she'd given them up. Course she knew I was there but pretended not to. Just to be absolutely sure, I hit the wheelie-bin a good whack with the brush. Realising too late it sounded like I was trying to get her attention. Definitely the last thing I wanted. But I also didn't want her thinking I was hiding from her. Hit the wheelie-bin a second whack for good measure. The leading agent of the Onslaught, their top spy, provoking me again. Her delusion that we were married and once lived together, had sex and a daughter, was, as I've said, an intense affront to a man like me. The Shrinkage thought that living beside me was a great idea. Just meant I had to constantly keep her at arms' length, rarely smiled at her in case she misconstrued it, agreed with most things she said, and avoided her as much as I could.

What I should have done then was go straight inside my house and lock the door. Except, I hadn't spoken to anyone that day, which usually didn't bother me, but for some reason it did then. Carried on with my newly important task, brushing the ground like an over-enthusiastic barber, annoyed and enticed by the trespassing silky smell of smoke. Next time I sneaked a look, she was staring right back at me, ever so coolly with a look that said, 'I've been watching you, boyo.'

"I've had a tough day," she said, slightly hoarse tense voice. "I've been waiting all day for a phone call which hasn't come... Mightn't come... ever. And this," she held up the cigarette. "I need this. Look, I've almost eaten my nails away." The red tip of the cigarette glowed as she sucked in the smoke. "God, please make him ring me," she said, sounding suddenly desperate. "Please." She held out the packet. "Do you want one?"

I cleared my throat to tell her I never touched the filthy things when a mobile phone rang, its melodious pings alarming the midnight silence. Seemed to be coming from the front folds of her long skirt. She froze, dropped the cigarette carelessly on the ground. Some of the hot ash fell on her skirt. "Shit," she muttered as she stepped sideways to brush it off, fumbled in her skirt's folds for the deep pocket for the phone. Eventually got it out, held it the wrong way around, pressed the wrong button and cut off the caller.

"Fuck, fuck, fuck!" she cried, stamping her foot on the ground, rapidly pressing the caller's number on the screen. Glanced at me, chewed whatever nails were left, and waited.

"Hello! Hello, I just missed a call from this number," spoke with an urgency that didn't suit the time or place, confirming once again how unstable she was. Faint sound of a male voice, unsurprised, speaking slowly.

"Yes, it is. That's me… Yes, yes, I'll wait… Thank you." Wide-eyed, she looked over at me, held up two crossed fingers. Hand over the phone. "It's Kevin. I didn't recognise the number."

Didn't know what I was supposed to say or do. Were we in a conversation or not? Looked blankly at her.

"Kevin," she mouthed impatiently, "the new Taoiseach."

I blinked twice, once because I actually knew who he was. Second because I realised what a government we'd be getting. Pity, I liked his name. On the positive side though, they'd now have to take down the election posters. I could go out without her staring at me from every bloody pole in the place.

"Yes? Kevin, congratulations," she said, suddenly gushy, grovelling. "Brilliant, wasn't it... Yes, marathon count... Oh, thank you! ...but worth waiting for... Yes... Yes, I do feel so sorry for him... What? Of course, and absolutely... We need to... Pardon? ...Taoiseach, yes? I am, of course... I am honoured... Yes, of course... Defence? Em, great... Of course, yes... No, no, that's no problem... Wow, I am so.... Your trust will not be misplaced... Will he? OK, thank you, Taoiseach. Thank you. Good night and... to Angela, of course, give her my best wishes and to the children. She must be so proud of you and... Goodnight."

After pressing the red button on her phone, she looked into the black night, eyes aflame with excitement, absorbed in absorption. Made fists of her hands. "Yes!" She jumped three, four times with joy. "Yes. Yes, yes. I've done it. Urgh."

Sounded like she was dragging a crow out of her throat. Quite a sight. Alarmed too by the animal squeaks coming from her puckered lips, wondered how the guineas pigs would sound with the same dark-blood lipstick.

Now, she's walking in circles like she's looking for something. "You heard that?" she stopped. "I'm in the new cabinet. He's given me Defence." Her voice kept wanting to rise and she was forcing it back down again.

I know. I should've congratulated her, wished her well, even God help us, pecked her on the cheek. But I can't like someone for only a few seconds, even just to wish them well, then go back to disliking them. I'm not built that way. Besides, it was a big mistake trusting her with any job. Did they not know what she was like? All she was really interested in was having her photo on every pole and lamppost in the country, people looking for favours from her, having a free car and driver to swan around in. And, interfering in her neighbours' lives. Needless to say, lots of things needing fixing that were never fixed. Putting manners on drivers of illegally parked cars, chopping down the bloody forest of poles stuck into every footpath that auld ones, blinders and me sometimes walk into, all because some idiot in an office thinks that ten is better than one.

"You'll have to learn how to march," I pointed out to her.

"You can teach me," she replied with matching sarcasm.

"I know nothing about marching."

"Bah," she grunted. "Look at yourself walking sometime. You're like a moving statue with swinging arms."

Ignored the insult, realised something more important. "Does this mean you'll have to... do a lot of travelling?" Ever hopeful of peace.

She didn't hear me. Walking in circles again, muttering, "Brilliant, brilliant, brilliant."

Watched her, impressed she didn't fall, walk into the wall. I went back to my own business, found a rake by the wall, started raking.

"Don't go, stay, please," she said, still circling. "I just need to go inside for a second. Won't be long. I'll be right back."

Raking while waiting for someone is not the same as raking on its own. Besides, it seemed to have gotten darker, and raking in the dark is a skill I didn't have. Threw the rake into the corner, listened to the sounds of late-night traffic in the distance. A never-ending soft whooshing, comforting to listen to so late at night in the garden. Sigh of frustration. The Politician was always telling me about her life, making me think about it, sometimes more than about my own. And here I was at it again, worried for the sake of the country, how big a mistake this guy Kevin was making. I wouldn't trust her with a boat in a bath. Next thing the place will be plastered with photos of her on a tank, giving medals to goats, addressing troops going off to risk their lives.

Frightening thoughts. I'd seen it on the telly. I knew what she'd be like. All the same, if it meant she'd be away…

She was back, holding two glasses of champagne. "I thought we'd celebrate, and I just had to phone a few friends." She offered me a glass.

I hesitated. Whenever she offered me alcohol, my suspicions were aroused.

"Go on, take it. It's not poison."

I took it.

She clinked my glass and raised hers to her lips.

"Ah, against all the odds!" she declared, moistening her lips, and drinking half the glass. "Mm, nicely chilled." I copied her. "I had it in the fridge, just in case. I think I'd have opened it anyway." She took another sip, not much left in her glass, and put a finger on the tip of her nose. "Now, why did he give me Defence? I don't know much about Defence. It didn't figure in the campaign... but there are plans for some big spending, I know that... so that might be interesting. I heard the last Minister very seldom brought anything to Cabinet. I think it was only discussed six or seven times in two years. Hm, yes, there was some talk about amalgamating it with... Still, beggars can't be choosers." Last cheerful gulp and started sniggering, "You might be able to help me, Colonel. Sir." Attempted a salute and hit her nose. "Ouch," more giggling, dabbing a finger against her lips. "I forgot to ask. Who did you vote for? No, I shouldn't ask. It's none of my business."

"Ask away. I voted for the upside-down candidate."

"The what?"

"The guy in hospital, eh, Hospital Gaffney."

Gave me one of her it's-not-worth-it looks before resuming her monologue.

"Probably a bit of a demotion, really. Maybe he's hoping I'll make a mess of it or it'll blow up in my face. That's what the papers will say anyway."

This would go on and on if I stayed. All she needed was a face in front of her.

"Suppose they'll expect me to be all ballsy," loud guffaw. Not surprised the drink was taking control. I'd seen it before, couldn't hold water. "And I'm the one who doesn't have any." Champagne sniggles, shoulders heaving.

Noted she was moving closer to me. I backed away, banged into the wheelie bin, stuck to me like a fretful child. Turned on it, gave it a good kick.

"Jesus, it was close."

"No," I corrected her. "I hit it on purpose."

"No, not that." She lowered her voice. "I thought I wouldn't get anything, that it would be the end, you know... But I wasn't going without a fight." Shook her head defiantly. "Fuck it, I'm not the pretty one they trot out like a filly for the media. It's me they want when they have to defend the indefensible." Sly smile across her face. "Know what I did?" Looked hastily away in case she thought I was listening. Had absolutely no effect on her. Carried on regardless.

"I had Martina – thank God for that girl! I had her on the phone. I had her texting, emailing, following them around, spreading the word I wouldn't be appointed. She even got it on the nine o'clock news last night. Did you see it? It was brilliant." She put on a serious face mimicking a female TV newsreader. "There is growing speculation that there will be no woman in the new government to be announced tomorrow." She looked at me. "Wasn't that great?" She punched the air which brought her even closer to me. I was beginning to feel cornered. She was carrying on as if she wasn't aware what she was doing. "You know, they like Martina," she said in a confidential tone, taking my half full glass out of my hand, giving me her empty one. "She's so fresh, even if she's no great looker. Actually, it's better that way," she said, fondling the neck of the glass. "And, Dominic, listen to this. Some of them reckon the party got a sympathy vote because of you." I sniffed at the insinuation. "Can you believe that?"

I couldn't and I could. Didn't like her tone.

"Should be worth something with the generals… I bet they won't be too keen on saluting a boss with tits." Snorts of giggles, bubbles around her teeth.

"I have to go," I announced. Wallflower-duty over.

"What?" She looked alarmed. "No, wait. Are you rushing off somewhere?" Suggestive disbelieving tone. "I want to talk to you about something." Suddenly sounding almost serious. "I know it's not the best time to bring it up, well, it hasn't been for a long time."

Using the tip of my shoe, tried dislodging some earth onto the path to have something to do. Wobbled a bit, grabbed an overhanging branch to steady myself. Branch broke and I crashed into the wheelie-bin but didn't fall. Annoyed with myself, I growled, "Want a slap with this branch?"

"Maybe later, darling," she cooed. "But listen..."

Unbelievably, this provoked Harry into sitting up, full of unattainable hope. "You've made me want to piss," I lied. That should keep her away.

"Go ahead," she smirked. "Be my guest. I haven't seen Harry for a long time."

"What?" I spluttered. "How do you know Harry's name?"

"Ssshh!" She put her hands out as if to put a finger on my lips.

"Stay where you are," I shouted in a commanding voice, pointing at the white line on the ground I'd redrawn with fresh paint the other day along the gap. Realising I was on the wrong side and hastily stepped back. "That's the line. Stay on your side and there'll be no trouble."

She pouted. "How's poor Harry these days?"

"It's Harry the Hermit," I answered nonchalantly.

She sighed. "Poor Harry. It used to be Harry the Conqueror. He conquered me so many times."

Wasn't having any of this nonsense. "Are you finished now? I want to go to bed."

"He could be a hero again."

I remembered the last visit she made to my bedroom. Without any invitation, she sneaked into the house, climbed the stairs, opened my bedroom door, got into my bed, had her hand on Harry before I woke up and almost strangled her. She'd been holding a full glass of red wine which spilled on Harry, the sheets and the ridiculous red and black skimpy outfit she was wearing. "Yes! Yes!" she panted, near expiring, when I let go of her throat. Leering at me. "*Monsieur est servi*," she announced, leaning across my lap and tapping her backside. Awful, truly awful. She was like a horse trussed up in fancy dress. She got off the bed, stood in front of me, grinning like a crocodile, tried to take off the bra part, failed, farted, flounced about the place, flailing her arms like she was listening to music. Made another lunge for Harry, managed to grab him, spent ages choking him to death and when she finally got a response out of him, she floundered about on top of me like a dying fish.

That was not going to happen again. "The doctor says it's not good for me."

She wiped some drops off her lips. "Stop it," she said brusquely. "That's not true. He said no such thing. I know what he said."

I couldn't help smirking. "How do you know?"

"It's no joke, you know," her voice now resentful and tired. "I'm, I'm… I know it's something to do with what happened to you… there. Not there, I mean, where you were… God," her voice faltered. "I'm so exhausted and I should be celebrating, not… this." She stared down at the ground, moved backwards, finished the last drop in my glass, turned and walked back to her kitchen, leaving me holding the branch and her empty glass, annoyed it wasn't me doing the walking away.

She looked back when she was near her kitchen door, the light showing a broad, tired figure, lifeless arms by her sides.

"I forgot," she said in a loud whisper. "They'll be putting a hut in the front garden for security in the next few days. It won't be there long. I told him I didn't want it, but he said I had to have it."

"A hut? For what?"

"Security."

"What'll he be doing?" Suspicious and curious.

"Please, Dominic. Be nice to him or her. It might be a her," she laughed dryly and was gone, kitchen door clicking shut, light switched off.

I stepped through the gap in the wall, undid my zip, shuffled over to where she'd been standing, sprayed all around hoping I was hitting the cigarette ash. Took my precautions that night. Placed a row of empty bottles across the kitchen floor where it gets narrow. Tied a string across the stairs, halfway up. Took the hurley to bed with me.

Chapter 5

Constituent and Jean McBabe Call

"**I**'m looking for the Minister." The man at the front door declared. Straight up. Just like that.

"Grand. I'm not." I replied.

"Eh... eh..."

Blunt, yes, but all the world's tree-pruners, raffle-ticket sellers, charity-fundraisers, new window-installers, window-cleaners and the like, as well as the Politician's customers, were forever beating a well-worn path to my door. The latter were the worst. They damn well acted like they had a right to be listened to, always looking for something for nothing, and calling to the wrong bloody house.

This one, guy in his late twenties, thin face, meek eyes, rough-looking, frowned under my what'll-he-say-next gaze. Shifted his feet. He didn't move, his stance signalling I had a duty to help him.

"I'm looking for Minister Corley, the TD," he said, thinking maybe I hadn't heard him the first time.

I said nothing, reminding myself not to be rude straight away. But resolve was crumbling. "Do you think I'm hiding her?"

"Eh… eh, no, but…" He looked around again, wondering did he have the right address. "Is this… last time I was here…"

"What do you want her for?" I sighed.

"Eh… well, it's… eh, a private matter." How much to tell me to get me on his side. "I want her to write a letter for me."

"Can't you write it yourself?" Remembered too late some people can't write. "Em," cleared rusty throat, "didn't mean…"

"No," he blurted indignantly. "Course I can feckin' write." Cheeks getting red. "What are you asking me that for? Who are you?"

Impertinence. On my own doorstep. Should've slammed the door in his face "You tell me," I replied, quite seriously. The answer stumped him. He stared at me, scratched his chest, unable to figure anything out.

After I finally got rid of him, I was only back in the kitchen when the front doorbell started ringing again.

"Christ!" I cursed, banging the fridge door shut. "I'll show him no mercy. No mercy at all."

Went and stood right behind the frosted glass, letting him see I was there and wasn't answering. Only when it sounded like his finger was glued to the buzzer did I open the door, ignoring him, and put my finger on buzzer, checked if it was stuck. About to close door again when a female voice said, "Dominic?"

What, a woman? Scratched behind my ear. "Did he tell you I was deaf?"

"Good heavens, no," she tittered. Middle-to-late aged matronly-type full of self-assurance. A stone-melter? Not with me.

"I thought you might be in the garden. It's such a lovely autumn day, isn't it?"

Snort. "How do you know I have a garden?"

"I don't." Withering female chirpiness. "Just guessed." Fake contrition, "Sorree."

Looked her up and down. What's she selling? Weren't usually that well-dressed. Still, all past tense for her. Might have been a looker once. Now pale, pink, buxom, self-confidence replacing looks. Shrinkage? Maybe. Hospital-nurse checking why I'd missed my appointments?

"Dominic?"

I'm not falling for that. "What's my second name?"

"Thomas," she said without hesitation.

Hm, well briefed, or a lucky guess. Monster handbag dangling from her arm. Why was it so big? What was in it?

"You look like the photos in the paper," she said.

"Do I now? Do I know you?"

"Well, in the past, yes. Almost forty years ago, I think. Golly, doesn't time fly?"

Trying to fix me with that stare, the one the Politician used to find the softer inner me. Does exist, but off-bounds.

"It's Jean, Jean McCabe from Cavan."

That moved me as much as the plight of the snails in the desert.

"You used to call me Jean McBabe. I read about what happened to you and... your... condition and I, well, I thought I might be able to help." She started searching the monster bag for something.

"Where?"

"In the paper, the Tribune."

"Recently?" No one told me about it.

"No, about a year and a half ago. I couldn't find it. I knew I had it somewhere and only found it again recently."

"Photo?" I sighed, looked up at the sky. Should have guessed. Selling photos. Started closing the door.

"No, no, wait," she cried, suddenly flustered. "I have it here. It's in my bag. I'll find it. Just a minute."

For all I knew she could've been searching for a gun, a knife or a suicide vest. Put a hand on hers to stop her rooting. "Look, Missus, it's all right. Leave it."

"No, no. It's here somewhere. I know." Realising the urgency of the situation she knelt down on the stone step and started emptying her bag, putting stuff all over the place like she was offering it for sale.

Startled, I looked around to see if any neighbours or passers-by were watching. This was farcical. Bent down, started putting the stuff back in the bag as she was taking it out. "Are you losing it woman? Stop this nonsense or I'll get the guards."

"Here, here it is," she exclaimed, raising her head so suddenly she almost de-nosed me. "Ow!" I hollered, holding it, damn sore without blood. Ignoring my discomfort, she shoved a small square photo into my non-thumb hand. Bag refilled, she stood up, pushing a stray grey hair away from her face. "Sorry... You can keep it. It's a copy, original size."

I too stood up, leaning against the door. Best chance of getting rid of her was to look at the damn thing. "It was taken in Donegal, in the Gaeltacht. In Ranafast."

I held it at a distance to signal my disinterest. Simple scene, boy and girl, twelve, thirteen, bit older than the Brat, walking along a country lane, low hedges, mountains behind, smiles for the camera. He's frisky looking, she's tentative in white skirt starting just above smooth kneecaps, slim legs in knee length white socks. Curious, I turned it over in my head. Girl looked happy, lad big messer's grin, looking kind of satisfied with himself. Probably first girlfriend. Cords of an anorak tied around his neck.

Hopeful expression on the woman's face. Don't know why I said it, but I said, "Come on in," and stood aside. 'You sure you're not a journalist?' I almost forgot to ask when she was sitting in the front room.

"Lord, no!" The idea seemed to amuse her.

"Or the Shrinkage? Or a hospital nurse?"

She looked puzzled, shook her head. "But if you're unsure my husband is out in the car... if you want to ask him." She went over and pointed out the window at a car parked up the street. Could see hubby-outline behind the steering wheel.

Sitting down again, she gestured towards the photo. "Please, look at it again."

I did, attracted maybe by the simplicity of the scene and the emotions. Naughty eyes went straight for the girl's legs, notably slim, not yet stout in the upper thighs. Stole glance at the ample trousered thighs on the chair, closed together. If this was the same person, who wouldn't feel sad at what time had done to her figure? She shifted position as if guessing my thoughts.

Studied the lad again. Readable face, felt sentimental for him, no matter who he was. A lively feckless lad, barely beyond childhood, probably bewildered by his dick, his feelings for her.

"Almost twelve, thirteen?"

She nodded. "It's you," she spoke in a quiet voice.

"So you say." Couldn't nod back, unsure what it would say. Obviously the photo meant nothing to me, but I did feel something for time-lost kids. "No," I said firmly, shaking my head, naughty eyes back on the girl's legs. Quite striking really. Bad boy Harry wondering what lay underneath immaculate skirt. Did the young fella have any luck? Shook the photo to rid myself of naughty thoughts.

"What is it?" she asked, sensing a maybe. Then she began her story. "We were in the Gaeltacht, in the same class but different houses. It was my first time away from home."

"You were a pretty girl."

"Thank you." She looked around the room. "You kept telling me that." Shy smile. "Do you …?"

"Sorry?"

"Would you like to hear more about the photo?"

Began wondering for whose benefit all this was.

"It was a Sunday morning. We walked near the sea. We were going home that day on the buses. It was the end of the course. You asked me to dress like that for you... actually, you pestered me to." Memory-smile.

"Did I? Why did I do that?"

"Oh," she nodded vaguely. "You told me you had an image of me."

"I see." Even if it wasn't me, I was curious.

"You were my first... boyfriend."

"Did we...?"

"On the walk? No, Good heavens no." Prim madam. "Certainly not." If she's insulted, she'll get up and go. Instead, she reflected for a moment, light laugh. "At that age? I was only twelve, just twelve. You were the same. What did we know?"

Felt sorry for the virgin lad.

"But you were like a fly buzzing around me." Regretful eyes. "It was the first time I dressed up for a boy. It was... special. I remember it like it was yesterday."

Had to defend the lad. "It was a short skirt?"

"I know, probably too short. I'm glad my mother didn't see me." Face back to Mrs Proper. "I have two girls myself. Twins."

"Yes? About the same age as the girl here?" I asked, directional-nod at photo.

"Why, yes." Uneasy voice. Like the thought had never occurred to her before. Whereas lovelorn Dominic understood amazingly well. An insight I probably wouldn't have had only weeks ago. Good feeling. Stood up. Enough is enough. Handed the photo back to Mrs Memory-lane.

Surprised, disconcerted. "I just thought that showing it to you might mean something to you. Maybe help bring something back." She held the photo face down on her knees as if admitting defeat. Her voice now slightly plaintive. Sensed we were getting to the climax.

"Help me?"

"You told me often enough what I meant to you and you kept wanting to…"

Her hands were smoothing her clothes.

"Wanting to what?"

"It's nothing."

"Wanting what?" Commanding voice of Colonel Insistence, suspecting she wanted to be commanded.

Her hesitation told me she'd been preparing herself for this moment.

"When you look at me in the photo," she held it up again, "well, what comes into a boy's head?"

Devilment made me shake my head.

"You asked me often enough. You were very embarrassing and… nice, as well, but I couldn't tell you."

"What?" Mixed impatience. Get to the point Missus, and go. "What you were wearing underneath? Is that what he was asking?"

Eyes dip, but not for long. "Yes." No blushing maid now. Even seemed relieved. "I'm glad you guessed. That's good, isn't it?" She looked around the room. Light outside fading. Darkness creeping out of the corners. Still standing, but not moving. "You kept asking me."

Reckoned lonely hubby freezing in the car didn't know about this.

"And I wouldn't tell you. I couldn't... I would have died of embarrassment."

I sighed at the slow pace of revelation. "Did I want to know what colour they were?"

"Every time I sat down or got up you were trying to see. It was very tiring being so careful. I think once you might have."

Aha, a reward for the luckless lad. Harry, lazy sod, finally waking up, wanted a scenario. Let me imagine... choosing a spot in a field to sit, ever so carefully folding her bright skirt underneath, demurely drawing legs together sideways. Flustered air, looking away towards the distant sea, perhaps seagull squawking, or crashing wave. Realises time has flown by, bus could be missed, must rush, run, last time together, maybe forever, unfocused eyes as if body separates from mind, sitting back, legs separate to get up, skirt rises just enough for fleeting glimpse of white.

Unexpectedly, Harry's daisy-dream helped me figure out what was really going on. It wasn't only about the colour of her knickers maybe triggering a memory for me. It was mainly about the age of her kids bringing it alive again for her and needing to tell someone. For whatever reason, the memory was still haunting her and I, long-standing Shrinkage-customer, with no past and a non-thumb, was supposed to exorcise this? Perfectly understood why patient hubby was left out in cold car.

"I am flabbergasted," I declared emphatically.

Her face suddenly hopeful, misinterpreting my words, had the look of a saint waiting to be thanked for saving a sinner.

"Photos!" I exploded, surprising both of us by my vehemence. Walked over to her. "Damn photos!" I repeated, helping her to her feet. "Do you know," I said, politely taking her elbow, "how many times people have shown me photos to try to make me remember who I am *not*, who they *think* I am?"

Wordless fluster-face.

"Exactly. I could fill albums with meaningless photos that have been shown to me. I have been shown films which I was told were me at my wedding, me at my daughter's birth, me as child, me as teenager, me getting a commission, me and my brothers, me here, me fucking everywhere…" I turned to face her, not caring what she thought. She just had to listen. "And you know what, Missus?" I let out a hollow laugh. "It's not about me at all. It's about you, them, them all coping with what you think is a problem." Shaking my head. "And I don't. If photos could do it, they'd have done it a long time ago."

Got her as far as the door before she cut loose from my grip, gathered her wits. Stopped for her last stand.

"I'm so sorry, Dominic. I just thought, you know, first love and all that. It's such a sacred thing. Part of it stays with you forever." Drew her bag closer as if hoping to gain strength from its size, while I was briefly side-tracked thinking first-love must be one hell of a power-ful drama. "I was hoping that seeing it would…" Her voice faded. "Well, I tried. Even if you don't remember, I do and I always will."

Well said, if a little vengeful. Was she, could she still be smitten? Had to get her out of the house quick.

"You were pretty gone on me." Hurt brown eyes bor-ing into me. "I could tell that."

"I suppose," I said, trying to soften her disappoint-ment, "any young lad would have liked to know."

Got the front door open. Gust of wind blew her hair over her face. Pushing it back, she had more to say. "I never told you. It was all so new, boys," she forced a wry smile. "It could never really have worked between us. We were too young, we lived too far apart. We rarely saw each other…"

By the time she ended, had manoeuvred her onto the footpath. She closed the gate carefully, as the guilty al-ways do.

At that very moment – what timing! Who should hap-pen to come sauntering along but the Brat, head in a grey hoodie, walking fast, bag swinging on his back, desperate as always to get to the toilet in time. Ignored her as if she wasn't there until he saw me standing at the door watching him. Stopped, looked behind at her, then at me. Would she say anything, maybe ask him his name, maybe show him the photo, ask who the boy was? Looked again at me, boring adults, hurried past me, dropped bag, up the stairs.

"He's lovely," she said from the footpath.

I didn't have to say it, but I did. "Neighbour's child, comes here after school."

She nodded, came back, closed the gate after the Brat, and went off to tell nothing to lonely hubby in the car.

PART 11

Chapter 6

The Park and Glasshouses

S ometimes I forget to leave the house. It would hit me coming up from the basement, why am't I outside in the fresh air? I remember often running out of the place, nearly always heading for the park. Cabin fever would creep up on me, thousands of barely noticeable pinpricks all over. I'd just about remember, no matter the weather, to grab a hat and coat before slamming the door behind me.

Entering the local park was a liberation movement. The world moved out of my head into the vastness of the park's open spaces, mingling with the richness of its life, the boundlessness of its skies, its birds propelling me along. The exhilaration of being commanded by nature to do, be, nothing but awestruck. I knew every detail of the place, its bushes, trees, flowerbeds, trimmed grass, neat edging, stout trunks of its aging poplars along the riverbanks, its two footbridges, the children's playground and the thirty-three metal benches scattered around.

The river had two courses, one meandering, the other canal-like, designed by inspired engineers. Felt so small I almost forgot myself.

Its daily rhythms were its life. In the morning the park was empty, except for dog-walkers, pram-pushers and loner-joggers. Early afternoon, waves of boisterous children passed through homewards from school, younger ones with parents, grandparents or minders gravitated towards the playground. From then on it was a tranquillity-free zone. Sometimes, in good weather, youngsters waded into the shallow river to get a football, wet a dog or chase a duck.

I loved being on first name terms with Cecil, park superintendent. Third generation council worker, widower, authority-figure, proud beyond measure of his park. Patrolled in a small white van which I happily made way for on the narrow paths. Had I been dictator, Cecil would have been Minister for Parks, Paths and Open Spaces. Every town would have had a park like ours and a superintendent like Cecil. Noisy kids controlled themselves when they saw Cecil's little van trundling along.

Cecil was one of only two people I told about my fear of rain. Caught in a sudden downpour during treasonous weather, running like a chicken being chased by a housewife in my sandals from tree to tree when Cecil came along in his van, offering me a lift. No questions from Cecil, not his style, but I felt obliged to explain myself.

"It stresses me out, Cecil," I said, fiercely rubbing my hair, trying to think of a non-alarmist way of putting it.

Cecil didn't look like he was listening. His eyes were scanning his domain for signs it was being swept away. When the river flooded a few years back, big sloping earthen banks had been constructed afterwards. So, I understood Cecil's preoccupation.

"It's not getting wet that bothers me, or it's the… it's…" I had to get it out. "And it's not the rain falling either. Well, it's partly that. But it's… it's the… randomness of it. You know what I mean, Cecil? You never really know whether it's going to start or stop raining, or where it will fall." Watched him closely. What Cecil thought mattered, but his eyes were relishing the free soaking his park was getting.

"Don't get me wrong, I like rain. Well, sort of. It's great for the park… I just prefer to watch it from inside."

The rain eased off and he switched off his wipers. "Look, I think it's ended," he said, stopping the van to let me out.

Too early today to go back to the house. Still sifting the memory of this unexpected confession in my head, I went on to my other favourite park, also created to reward good citizenship. More problematic though. Botanic Gardens were cluttered, over-occupied, stuffed with enough bushes and foliage to feed Noah's Arc for eternity. So little open space, grace, vistas or orderliness.

However, all was more than compensated for by two crowning glories which lifted the place and my soul out of the mundane into the sublime. Its two glass palaces. One squat, bulky. The other linear, curvaceous, graceful as a maharajah's tented summer palace.

That mid-October morning, patchy-coloured leaves clinging on for dear life in typically unpredictable breezes, I stood in front of the two glass palaces, overawed by their magnificence. Feeling an urge to do something to repay the pleasure they gave me. Eyes swept up the cliff-face panes of the big bulky one, over its curved glass roof. My breath unexpectedly held itself for a brainwave. I would count every pane of glass in each palace, methodically and carefully, taking my time. I would circulate the information to the glass makers, cutters, installers in the Yellow Pages. They would take great pride in the information. The glass palaces were monuments to their professional forefathers.

Certainly ambitious, but I was determined. Started there and then, having pen and paper in my coat pocket. Started modestly counting the vertical wall panes of the bulky glass palace up to where the glass roof curved inwards and where there were more panes to be counted later. Counted the panes at the front first, then the sides, but not the ones that curved over the low-rise annexes stuck out on each side, also for later. Allowing no distinction between big and small panes. Sure, if I had been a big pane, this was unjust. But all glass panes are created equal in their glassiness, entitled to be treated equally. Reminded myself, each pane of glass had its own story, part of the lost civilisation of botanical glassmaking which I also wanted to pay homage to.

Full of enthusiasm, returning home, made my usual salad, got to work. The tasks were manifold – add up the numbers from the different sections which I had counted, make a tentative list of glass makers and glass cutters and glass installers, imagine the hidden lives behind the glass panes. This gave me another idea. Write a short history of an individual pane from its start, as grains of sand in a sand pit somewhere like Morocco on its journey to the glass furnace, to its transportation and inauguration in the glass palace. I would be both witness to and narrator of its battles with the elements through the decades. Would have to return soon to the Gardens to select the lucky pane. Wasn't sure how I'd do that, except it would have to resonate with me in some way. A drawing as well, or a photograph of the pane. Could I give it a name? Plenty of time to decide.

By early afternoon, had made good progress. Added up the numbers visible from the front of the five-sided glass structure. Counting from the left 60, 60, 121 at the front, including 13 for the door, and on the right 60, 60. Giving a total of 361. A fine figure. Would be higher if I included the panes from the sneaky low-rise annexes on either side. Decide later. Was prompted to get up from the kitchen table, go up to the top of the house and count every external pane of glass in the house. Counting the double-glazed windows as one came to a paltry 61. Also completed a list of glass companies using current and out-of-date Yellow Pages. Older editions, found in a box in the basement, the catch was older companies may have gone out of business. Couldn't leave them out. Listened to radio as I worked, waiting for phone-in to start.

Brat arrived just after phone-in began. Heard him dump his school bag on the hall floor, waited for the heavy pounding up the stairs to the middle toilet. No, wrong. Kitchen door pushed open. In he comes, usual mess, looks briefly at me, walks around the kitchen like it was his, trailing filthy fingers behind him on the worktop. Health hazards for all the flies on the planet. Comes over to the table, covered with directories, notes, pages of drawings of glass panes. Looks at me, looks at the drawings and wisely says nothing. Goes over to the fridge, rummages in it, door left open, like a dog sniffing food. Finally door closed, stood there, asking, "Wha' ya doen?"

Told him in case he was deaf, I was listening to the radio.

"Wha'?" That was just a teaser to get a rise out of me, which he got. Made as if to get up. He duly vamoosed out the door.

Afternoons listening to phone-in radio were precious. It was how I kept in touch with the world. Papers demanded too much, television too little. Not one of the Shrinkage ever suggested I listen to phone-ins. Shows how much they knew. One had suggested I listen to the news, but that was way below my pay grade. He said it could help re-acquaint me with the world, but when I realised what the world consisted of – people like the Politician and Kevin. I said no. By then I had discovered phone-ins. No exaggeration to say there I found another home. True it's the opposite of silence, and I like to hear myself think. One time a Finn rang in to say people in his country only talked when they really needed to. Then he went silent. The presenter didn't know if he was still on the line or if this was some kind of test.

So much can be learned from phone-ins. One day was Unhappy-Mother's Day. They phoned in in droves moaning about their under-twenty-five-driver sons being targeted by police 'for no reason', being given parking tickets or being stopped for speeding when over-twenty-fives were 'sailing past way over the limit'. Wasn't that a disgrace? Of course it was. They were right to have a good moan. I always kept the phone beside me in case I wanted to ring in myself.

Got through once to a live show about infidelity. Callers were stridently against it. Bad for marriage, bad for families, bad for children, bad for society. I was having none of it. The Brat had just come in. Suppose I was showing off a bit. I called them blasphemers. Infidelity was the saviour of civilisation. I was parroting stuff I'd picked up somewhere. Said we wouldn't be here today without it, that Jesus himself preached it. Really got them worked up, went at me hammer and tongs, accusing me of profanity and every mortal sin.

The presenter kept egging me on, great for ratings, asking me to clarify my extreme assertions. Then, slyly siding with the mob, asking me, "Where did I get the right to insult so many listeners?" and "We should all keep calm." More calls came in. Had to keep shushing the Brat. He'd run into the front room, all doors open. The sod hadn't been door-trained yet, listening to the radio up there, and was whooping and hollering. The presenter announced the lines were jammed. They wouldn't be taking any more calls. It ended when some bright spark asked me what I meant by infidelity – "Christianity of course, the name Muslims give it". Presenter then apologised to his listeners. My few minutes of fame were over. Think the Brat admired me for about five minutes afterwards.

Chapter 7

Brat Spying on Toilet Next Door

Switched off the radio – can't remember what the day's phone-in was about. Heard the Brat clumping down the stairs. Not the usual thudding. Appeared wearing a metal helmet I'd never seen before, way too big for him, covering half his face. He put a finger to his lips, approached the table, even coming within swipe-range. Brave indeed. So I did nothing. Leaning close to my ear, borderline reckless, whispered, "I was spying on the guys putting up the camera."

"What camera?"

"The one outside. At the end of Granny's garden."

No idea what he was talking about, but impressed by his clear diction, being used to unscrambling his mumblings. "Well, go back and spy on it a bit more in case it moves."

Didn't budge. "I watched them from 3:47 to 4:11. They only spent five minutes at the camera. Seven minutes talking in the garden. Four minutes in the lane."

Only half-listening. "Who are 'they'?"

"How do I know?"

Where was this leading? Couldn't help counting. "That's only sixteen minutes."

"Eh, and wait till you hear this. They went into the toilet. Together. That's where they were for ten minutes!"

I looked at him. Does he know about such things? Wasn't grinning or smirking or blushing, so I guess he wasn't making it up.

"Were they on my side of the wall?"

He nodded but looked unsure. I looked closer for signs of a fib. Lately he'd been getting better at keeping a straight face. "Right." Slammed my hands on the table. Got up. "Stay here," I said, going to the hallstand to get the other hurley, went out into the back garden. Brat followed me, looking worried.

"They didn't take anything. They were just, just looking."

I stopped. "Looking? Looking at what?"

"Eh, dunno."

"You dunno?"

"I dunno."

"Are you having me on? If you're having me on..."

"No, I swear. I'm not. I'm not."

Red-faced, so I half-believed him. At the end of the garden I threw open the door to the lane. The usual clutter of distressed toys, a metal crowd-control barrier, a clutch of wheelie bins huddled together. Spikey gate at the end of the lane to the road locked. No one there. Turned to go back inside, almost fell over the Brat, he was that close behind me.

"Out of the way," I commanded.

"They *were* here," he over-insisted. "They were." He was like a puppy yelping at my heels. "They must have gone through Granny's house."

"For God's sake, will you stop calling her that! I don't know whose Granny she is," I said, closing the lane door, going over to the gap in the wall.

"Not here," he said, going through the gap. "They weren't here." He went on a bit. "They were here." Stood at the door of her outside toilet, stamped the ground. "Here," he almost shouted, as if he thought I was deaf.

Stayed on my side of the line.

The toilet was at the boundary wall end of a shed built against her lane wall. The shed door looked solid, but the black paint on the toilet door had largely peeled off and the door was loosely held in place by three rusty hinges. Looking at it reminded me of another phobia I had. I couldn't abide leg-hugging toilets when the door was closed and locked. The walls heaved inwards over me, I'd break out in a sweat, my hands clamped themselves on the walls to push back. Sometimes the walls pushed back as well and I had to bang them. Mostly I just about coped and only remember once when I didn't and started shouting. Had to explain myself to the startled security guard who came running.

There had been one rogue toilet like that in my house when I moved in first. The middle one, but I dealt swiftly with that, removing the door, replacing it with a thick large brown blanket. The other two toilets, downstairs and in the bathroom at the top of the house, had plenty of space. Wasn't obvious that putting up a blanket would work, but it did, giving me a wonderful feeling to know I could banish any creepy phobia by just sweeping the blanket aside. At the beginning, did this once as the Brat was heading up to the attic. Needless to say, he complained to his mother. I had to be extra careful from then on. Astonishingly – the Brat was very prudish. After a few weeks he decided he liked the new arrangement. In fact, liked it so much he organised tours of the house to show it off to his friends after school. All thought it was dead cool. Tried to get the Brat to use the downstairs toilet instead, promising he could have it all to himself. I put a stack of comics I found in the basement in there for him. Total waste of time. Brat was barely literate, would only read if his life depended on it.

His mother and her mother, the Politician, thought the whole thing was indecent, barbaric, swore they'd never use it themselves. Of course, they told the Shrinkage which at the next session led to attempts to probe my non-existent childhood toilet-training.

"There, there, look." The Brat was pulling my sleeve, jabbing his finger towards the toilet door. He'd come over and was trying to push me towards it.

"I can see. Stop jabbering and stop pushing," not at all keen on going into that sardine toilet. Examined the door from a distance. If it was locked, I reckoned the door could be forced and the Brat could go in to investigate. There wouldn't be much left of the door. Noise might bring out the neighbours.

"They were in there for ten minutes."

"What were they doing?" I examined his expression again, rubbing my chin, still open to the possibility he was having me on. He made a face, didn't want to answer. "Maybe they're plumbers as well," I suggested.

"Plumbers?" he repeated incredulously. "You're mad. I know what they were. They weren't plumbers. They were homos."

"Humus?"

"Homos!" he shouted so loud I expected to hear neighbours' doors banging open.

"Homos?" Where had he learned that word?

He was scrutinising me with his trademark expression, mixture of pity and contempt. "Stands to reason," he added, sure of himself.

"They could've been having a chat or a smoke or doing a crap."

"Huh?"

"And what is a homo? Do you know?"

"It's gays… queers… They… they like each other." He made a face. "They kiss," he said, stepping back, looking around for an escape in case he'd gone too far. He'd seen the look on my face but couldn't stop himself. "You don't know? God, you're…"

For his own sake I cut him off. "Are all plumbers' homos?"

He wondered if that was a serious question. "I dunno. Maybe. Could be." He had a second thought. "Well, maybe… no. One girl in my class, her dad's a plumber… I dunno."

"Go on and look in the toilet and shut up," I said, losing patience. "Maybe they're still in there, having a good laugh at us, no, at you."

He stopped at the door, looked back at me. "Me? Why me?"

"Have a good look and tell me what they're doing."

"They're gone!" he shouted.

"Well, go in anyway and have a look. Do a pee if you want, it's free. I don't mind."

"No, you do it. I'm only a kid. You're the adult. There might be something inside."

"More homos?"

"F- Feck off, will ya." Then he noticed I was still on my side of the wall. "Come on in," he said impatiently, beckoning me over.

"Can't." I mimicked a child's voice. "Not allowed." Pointed at the line on the ground. "There's a barring order against me." I'd heard about them on a phone-in.

I could see he was thinking there's nothing as stupid as an adult pretending to be a child. "Go on," I urged him before he chickened out. "Bet you're too scared to do it. Yeah, that's it. Scaredy-cat. I'm gonna tell what's-his-name, next time he's here."

Brat approached the door like it might explode in his face and leaned his ear against it.

"Do you hear ticking?"

"No," he answered, then caught himself. "Cut it out, will ya?"

"I'll keep an eye out for you," I whispered. "She could be back any minute." Ducked down behind the wall. "Go on. You're very brave." Popped my head up, smiling encouragingly at him.

"There's no noise."

"Try the door."

He put his hand on the rounded handle with a keyhole in the middle, tried turning it.

"It won't move. It's locked."

"Push it again."

"It's no use. It's locked."

"Doesn't she have a key?"

"Dunno."

"Probably lost. You probably lost it."

"I did not, you f…" He knew if he used the f-word I'd hit him. Our eyes locked in combat. He was trying to think up some new insult. "You're a, an… arsehole."

That was OK.

"Come on back," I said. "We need another strategy."

He didn't move.

"Bet you couldn't kick it in," he jeered, "like in Kung Fu." He made a fast sideways kick at an imaginary enemy.

Stupidly I retorted. "Course I could. Dead easy." Not for the first time I was infected by Brat-bravado, and made a surprisingly swift, neat sideways kick, followed by a hard downwards chopping move with my right hand. Where did that come from? We stared at each other, both astonished. Had no idea I could do that. "That good enough for you, huh?"

His eyes bulged, a sure sign he was overawed.

"Yeah, you didn't expect that, did you?" I sneered.

"Bet ya couldn't do it on the door," he taunted back and backing further away from me in case I turned vicious. "Bet ya couldn't, bet ya couldn't, bet ya..."

"Shut up, you twerp." Rush of blood to the head. Against all common sense, decided I'd show him. Stepping over the line, strode over to the door, examined it, judging how hard it would be, how much force would be needed, where best to apply it.

"Shut up and let me think." Staring at the door and then at him. "Come over here."

He watched me like a hawk.

"If you want me to do it, come here."

Approaching me cautiously. When he was close enough, I grabbed him by the shoulder and gave him a light clip on the ear.

"Ouch!" he cried, suddenly all red. "What was that for? You can't hit me. You've no right."

"Shut up and listen. That was for that. Now, listen."

Face puckered up as if he was going to cry, but he kept it in.

"Stop pretending you're going to cry. Listen. If I try this you must promise not to tell anyone, you hear me. Anyone. You know absolutely nothing about this. OK?"

Couldn't speak so he nodded, still befuddled by my hard-cop, soft-cop approach.

"Right, stand back." Positioning myself in front of the door, making a few practice swings with my right foot, stood a good while in silence, concentrating on getting all my power into the single strike. Without any command, arms started moving in slow circles. I let out a roar and in an instant, swung my right leg and crashed the side of the foot into the door just below the handle. Kkk... Crack. The wrenching sound of fixed wood splintering. The door heaved inwards. I quickly pushed hard at it with my shoulder. It gave way, two of the hinges breaking, the door hanging loose by the third.

"Wow," the Brat cried, jumping with excitement. "Look a' tha'!"

The damn foot hurt. I overstretched my inside-thigh muscles. Hobbling away from the door, I gestured to him to go in.

"Well?"

"There's nothing here," he announced from inside in that tiny squeaky voice he sometimes can't help using.

"Leave it then, come on. We've wasted enough time here."

Chapter 8

Brat Gives Him a Fright

Hobbling back to the house in puzzled silence, astonishment and pain jeered each other. The Brat went up to the front room to pretend to do homework. Staring at the window for a while, then got the Yellow Pages and found a locksmith.

Thought about doing some ironing to calm myself. A pile of towels, dish clothes started the other day and abandoned. Guinea pigs in the kitchen squealing for cucumber. Amazing hearing. They could hear me from the garden, start skeltering around their cage like mad yokes. Won't stop until I give in. Without doubt the stupidest creatures I ever liked.

Skimming through the Yellow Pages 1994 for glass replacers, heard a soft noise behind me, then this horrendous roar right behind me.

"Aaaaghhh…." It went straight through me, ringing my eardrums like a dentist's drill going into my head, staying there. Practically jumped out of the chair. The roar stopped as quickly as it started. Turned around. Saw the Brat's head, stationary for an instant, before it disappeared behind the door, his feet pounding the stairs like his life depended on it. Which, at that moment, it most certainly did. If he thought it was a joke to frighten the living' daylight out of me, I'd show him what a joke was.

"Awweeoowaagh!" An unknown, unnerving, strangulated roar emerged from my throat. The chair fell back behind me as I took off after him, shouting, "You stupid Brat, I'll... I'll... just wait 'til I get my hands on you, you idiot. What do you think...?"

Nimble Brat flew up the four flights to the attic and the safety of the only locked door in the house, knowing I couldn't kick that door down. Clambered up heavily after him, one, two, sometimes three steps at a time, rushing at the steps so furiously kept hitting the risers and stumbling. Drove myself on, fully intending serious harm to him.

"You little fucker... I'll kill you when I get you. Who the hell do you..." Couldn't finish a sentence. By the time I reached the landing before the fourth flight of stairs I was exhausted, breathless, woozy. Slumped down on the landing, strength vanishing from my legs, shouting up at him, "You better not come out of there because if I see you, you're in for it Big Time. You've really done it this time."

Secretly though I was relieved I hadn't caught him. Afraid I wouldn't have regained control until I had hurt him.

Total silence after a sudden commotion is inner noise. Heart had moved up to my ears, lungs didn't know if they were full or empty, legs turned to spaghetti. Sat very still, stuck hands over my ears, hollow echoing. Stretched out on the floor, rolled onto my stomach, searching for a good position, fell asleep or dozed because I had the sensation of lying on bare earth, holding something like a rifle firmly, aimed at something. Couldn't tell what or where, just felt familiar, sharp. Elbows tucked well into my body, angled legs slightly apart, steady grip, focused mind. As I grew more aware where I was, checking for wooziness, said to myself this must be another of these… strange awareness's I get from time to time, weird stuff, no big deal, but don't tell the Shrinkage. Looking up, now sure where I was.

Brat now sitting on the top step of the attic stairs, door open behind him, spindly legs incongruous in white football shorts, fiddling with an old remote control, looking intently at me.

"How long am I here?" I asked in a tired voice as I heaved myself upright against the wall.

"Dunno. Are ya having a fit?"

I looked away, my nose picking up a stray whiff of polished wood. "Why did you do that?" I eventually asked, not looking at him.

"Everyone does it."

"Who's everyone?"

"In school."

"Everyone in school does it," I repeated, unable to get my head around such idiocy.

"Do you not realise… Do you not think…?" Couldn't finish, but often with the Brat unfinished sentences were smarter than finished ones. He wisely said nothing, knowing the wrong word or gesture could, despite everything, start me again.

Evening gloom spread up the stairwell, diluting not dissipating the tension. Brat had moved down three steps, fiddling with bits and pieces on the step. The front door opened. Our eyes crossed. The Brat immediately stood up, clattered down the steps, confidently stepped past me. Siege lifted.

Round table set for three. Meaning no matter where I sat, I was opposite the Brat, His mother, when she did sit down, in the middle. Never had an itch to sit at the head of a table, another of my failings in the Brat's eyes. The one time he mentioned it, I told him bluntly he only said that because he had no father. Cruel, I know, but war is war.

Watching him eat was like watching a human compactor at work. He fed himself like a lazy farmer with a pitchfork. The bigger the amount, the fewer the forklifts. Not caring how long it took to get the hanging bits of salad into his mouth. Mostly eating open-mouthed as if trying to tempt flies in as well. Couldn't blame his mother for his ignorance because she didn't eat like him. No, it all had to be because he didn't have a father, but I couldn't say much about that, being fatherless myself. At times, the way his mother and the Politician carried on, it was as if they were trying to make me a substitute father for his sake or even mine.

No doubt a Shrinkage plan, but once I figured that out, I pulled back. Even if, in his own way, he had an occasional sneering regard for me. His many failings were not my responsibility.

The young woman had finished work early and thought it would be nice to have a 'family' tea together. "So, Mammy got Defence," she said pleasantly when she sat down, while the Brat and I glared at each other, and she didn't want to be depressed by the silent hostility. "Isn't that great?"

I shrugged my shoulders, the Brat lost somewhere inside his impenetrable skull.

"She's talking about the Politician," I explained to the Brat. "The country has so many enemies they put her in charge. We're safe now."

"Huh?" Brazen head looked up. "What?" Fortunately, his mouth was empty, so I only got an eyeful of two lines of uneven teeth.

"Boys, please...." She looked disappointed. "Be nice, please." Clearly wanting one of those happy-family-meals we were so good at not having.

"Mammy said you made a scene when you voted," the Brat jabbered.

"Did she? Was she there?" No answer. "And who made a show of the country on Slovenian TV?"

"You did," bully Brat shot back quick as a pickpocket.

"No, no, it was you!"

"No, you!"

"No."

"Thomas," his mother intervened, "you'll help with clearing up, won't you, dear?"

Gave him a triumphant look.

"Why doesn't he do anything?" the Brat complained. "I'm always…" He was silenced by his mother's stern look.

"I'm not well," I groaned.

"Balls," he mouthed at me when his mother wasn't looking.

Maybe she was too young when the Brat was born. That was the problem. "What age are you?" I asked her.

"Dad, you know my age."

Course I do, that's why I'm asking you. For God's sake. Looked at the Brat. "What age am I?"

"Who cares?"

"Haha, you don't know, do you? You can't remember."

"Course I do. You're fifty… fifty…"

"Ah, that's right," I jeered. "I'm fifty fifty, a new age."

"You… you can't remember anything, anyway. You're… you're empty," he declared, tapping the side of his head.

Let him have his little victory. Didn't have many.

He helped his mother while I gazed out the window. Top branches were swaying in the breeze, while the bottom ones were still. No idea how this happened, and realised I liked that. Sometimes it was good to not know. No sign of Boris. Wrong time of course. Hadn't seen him all day which made it seem like it would be a long evening.

In the hallway as they were going, the young woman gave me a hug. Gave her one back, a good squeeze. Only for the fact she thought we were related, I'd have suspected she was flirting with me. I wasn't averse to a bit of that. There were only auld ones around here. She had a fine figure for a slim one, easy to get my arms around, shiny hair that usually smelt lemony. I acted it up a bit because the Brat was watching us like a jealous hawk. When I drew away from her, I made as if to give him one too. Brat was out the door like a rocket, telling his mother to hurry up.

Chapter 9

Politician Visits

Two loud bangs on the kitchen door woke me up. Echoes like muffled explosions, reverberating inside my head. What in God's name is going on? Opening eyes, saw a bloated face peering in at me like a goldfish looking out. Squinting against the harsh dawn light, hoping it was playing tricks on me. No such luck. Fully dressed, looking like she meant business. Sat up slowly, checking I was decent, couldn't be too careful, my wilful grey blanket having played its usual will-I-or-won't-I cover him. Six fifteen.

What in God's name was she doing bothering me at this time? Gave me her election-poster smile which I had been injected against. Yawned, stretched, rubbed my face, trying to figure out what she was going to complain about now. There was plenty. The damage to her toilet door, to my toilet door, to the Brat, to his mother, the state of the house, the state of me, the state of... whatever. Another big yawn as I stood up. Why was I sleeping on the kitchen sofa? No idea. Still glanced behind her to see if, by any chance, Boris was around. Hoped he hadn't changed his habits and I was no longer high on his circuit. Yeah, that's what I'll say if she asks why was I sleeping in the kitchen. None of her business, but that's never stopped her.

Just as I was moving to open the door, she gestured she'd be back in five minutes. Christ, there's a woman sure of herself.

Almost the whole end of the kitchen was glass. They said it had been extended when I was in hospital to make it more cheerful for me to live in. A brighter, lighter place would be good for my moods. Who were they fooling? They were making it easier to spy on me. Bet you the Shrinkage will find some sly way to bring it up at the next appointment. Must remember to forget to go. Some visitors said the glass brought the garden into the kitchen. If that was true, why didn't I walk into the glass like the cats did when eyeing up the guinea pigs for dinner? Yep, that's what they did. Boris was the only one who wasn't that stupid. I'd seen them doing it. They'd spot or smell the guinea pigs in their cage inside the big window. Creep up to it, study the guinea pigs for ages, go into pounce-mode, pounce, smack the glass, tumble backward onto the grass. Boris always sensed there was something there and put out a precautionary paw first. Just more proof he was a superior cat who could probably run the country better than the Politician.

Let her in when she came back without any fuss, dived back under the blanket, wanting to believe that, if I couldn't see her, she wasn't there.

"I couldn't sleep," she exclaimed to the blanket, far too cheerfully. "I'm so excited. It's the big day and I'm so excited. It's a great feeling. The best."

I turned in towards the wall, muttering, "You woke me up."

She sat on the sofa, forcing me to move right against the upright.

"Morning, Colonel Corley," she purred in a smarmy voice, reaching out a hand to scratch my head.

"Why don't you use the front door like everyone else?" I said pulling the blanket over my head.

Mock tut-tutting. "Stop being a grouch. You're supposed to be nice to me today. Say 'Morning, Catherine, what's the big day?'"

"Morning Missus, what's the big deal?"

That didn't suit her. "But, if you want to be grumpy… Well, why did you kick in the toilet door?"

"I kicked it in?"

"Thomas said you did. You couldn't get to the toilet in the house on time."

Sitting straight up, facing her. "He said that?" Fair fucks to you, Brat. But couldn't let him away with it. "No, no." I shook my head slowly. "That's what he would say. No, it was the other way around. He was the one who had to rush to the toilet. You know kids, always waiting until the last minute." Twist the dagger. "He had to take a shower afterwards. Terrible smell," I snorted. "I don't have emergencies."

Usually this would puzzle her, but not today. "Anyway, I didn't come here about that. You will fix it, won't you? You can manage that, can't you?"

"The locksmith's coming today… or tomorrow." Still staggered by the Brat's audaciousness. "The fibber. He'd say anything to get out of trouble."

"Good, excellent. Well, I have other things on my mind today."

She paused for me to ask what. I glanced quickly out the window. Was there movement at the end of the garden? When I looked back, she was looking around the kitchen, noting everything in that notebook-memory of hers, developed from trying to run my life and the lives of every fool who called to the house looking for favours. Expected her to say, 'You'd never guess we pay someone to come in and clean the place.' But she seemed determined to be nice. "Besides the locksmith, what else are you doing?"

"This and that."

"Well, if you look at the telly around half ten, we have the vote to ratify the Taoiseach's nominees and then it's off to The Park for our seal of office from the President. Joan and Thomas are coming with me."

"Excellent." I lay back. Maybe she'll go if I say something nice. "The country will be in safe hands then."

"Why thank you, Dominic. Not sure if that's genuine, but I'll take it. And this evening we have our celebration dinner and… you're invited," she announced.

"Am I?" First I heard of it. I scratched my stubble, unsure what to make of this.

"Because you helped as well." She went over to some shirts hanging over the blocked-up fireplace, talking to herself, "Now, which one goes best with the…" She held a striped shirt against her chest. "Will you wear this one tonight with that dicky bow, you know, the one with the dots? I'll put it out for you." Took the other shirts, headed out of the kitchen up the stairs, carrying the shirts like booty.

"Hey," I shouted after her. "Leave them alone. They're mine. You've got your own."

She heard me. "Don't worry. They're too big for me. I've worn them before."

Jesus, that woman knew how to irritate me. I could hear her going into my bedroom, opening the wardrobe, drawers. "When did you wear my clothes?" I shouted up at her. "I never said you could." No answer. OK, I said to myself. That's enough. There's a simple solution. Get the blasted locksmith to change the blasted locks in my bedroom as well.

Boris, Oh Boris, where are you? In my hour of need. No point trying to go back to sleep. Just got up, blanket wrapped around me, standing on my favourite tile, arms stiff as goalposts, staring trance-like at the garden. Could he really have changed his routine? He generally had some wander-scavenging to do before he arrived in my garden. Neither I nor my garden were number one on his play-list, that was OK, we were still on it. That was the main thing.

Something brushed against me, startling me.

"Dominic?" She was back, right beside me, elbow touching mine. "Dominic, I've been planning to talk to you about something." Sounded too meek, like she was trying to disarm me.

Shuffled sideways away from prodding elbow, still watching the garden.

"Dominic, I have to talk to you... and... this is the time. I've been putting it off too long." She went and sat on the sofa. "Will you come and sit down, please? I can't talk to your back."

"But, I'm..." I reluctantly sat on the sofa but kept my eyes on the garden. She was fiddling with a bracelet on her left wrist.

"This... this is not easy for me to talk about and," held up her hand, "before you say anything," she noticed that look on my face, the one that said this is not a good time and, anyway, it has nothing to do with me, "before you... What I want to say is... before your, well, we had a life, you know, together, and... and sex. We had sex and now it's this." She flapped her hands helplessly on the sofa, palms up. "Sometimes, you make me feel like a... like a... nothing."

I'm not a brute. I listened. This was difficult for her, whatever it was. So, I turned, facing her completely so she knew she had my full attention.

"Dominic... Dominic, don't stare at me like that."

I shifted my eyes back to the garden. Can't win with this woman.

"I've thought about this a lot and I want to tell you, I know you act like you don't care. That's obvious, but I... I think you do care... in your own way, so, I have to tell you."

I guessed where this was going and hoped she'd get there sooner rather than later. Boris could appear any moment.

"I... I haven't been with anyone for such a long time and it's been, well... frustrating." She smiled shyly. "Dominic, I want you to know if... if, and I don't know if it will happen, but if something – someone comes along, I mightn't be able to... mightn't want to... you know."

Out of the kindness of my heart I refrained from telling her it made no difference to me who or what she slept with.

"I will be very, very discreet if anything..." She looked at her hands as if surprised they'd been folding themselves in each other. "I promise you that and certainly, now that I'm..."

I nodded, mouth firmly closed, my attention distracted by movement on top of the wall at the end of the garden.

"There he is," I cried, half standing up. "There's Boris." I waved at him. Sent by God to save a sinner. Of course, Boris being Boris barely looked at me, hardly stopped when he saw my wave, which delighted me even more. Boris ignoring me was part of the thrill. I could never guess what route he would take once he appeared on the wall. Some days he appeared on the wall to the left of the lane door and stayed there for ages surveying the world. Other days he had something on his mind and jumped either straight onto the ground or, if a wheelie bin was nearby, he jumped onto that. Still other days he went straight onto the narrow wooden fence separating me from the other next door which I was told was empty but had been occupied by an auld one who had long since gone somewhere else.

Aha, today, it's the narrow wooden fence. Walking along it with consummate balance and grace, better than a tightrope walker, placing deliberate paw in front of delicate paw. Such a model cat-walker, he could have given lessons in deportment to the other lumbering cats, most of whom were clumsy, overweight or too impatient. But Boris wasn't a nonchalant poser. He didn't need to put it on. The grace was in his bones. Even when he was on the narrow fence, he didn't move his head sideways to look for prey or danger. He could see both sides at the same time, and watch me, a lot of me. Above all, Boris was a birdwatcher and my garden was the best place in the area for him because it had the most trees. Boris didn't need binoculars to watch the birds. I am sure his knowledge of birds, their habits and habitats, was encyclopaedic. He could have, probably did, give lessons to the other cats in birdwatching.

An elbow nudged me in the side. For an instant I half thought Boris had sprouted an elbow.

"Dominic, are you listening to me? Dominic?"

"Sorry." Focus. Listen to her, this is her big day. Stop thinking that Boris would make a better Minister for Defence. Try to be nice.

"Will you go?" she asked.

"Go where?"

"What I've been telling you for the last five minutes. Your school reunion."

"Sure," anything to get rid of her. My good deed for the day. Now, back to Boris. I moved away from the prodding elbow. Boris was now on the grass exactly where I'd put the guinea pigs yesterday. Lots of smelling, examining, which he did with great thoroughness.

Glance at her. She was studying me, surprised I suspect by my agreeableness. Noticed she had no make-up on. Shoulders still too wide. Should I remind her about the make-up? Would she mis-interpret it?

"Stop staring at me with that stupid look," she turned away, strangely vulnerable, I thought. Then, just as quickly that moment was gone, back to herself. "Joan will bring you. Tonight is the victory family dinner."

"Don't you have to get ready for your big day?" I was getting cold with no trousers on and it wasn't a good idea to stay like that in front of her.

She glanced at me, stiffly holding onto the blanket around my waist – was she thinking of pulling it down? Then she looked at her watch, surprise on her face. "Oh, I'm late. I have to go." At the sliding door, she said, "Don't forget tonight. Joan is picking you up at seven. Please be ready and make an effort, Dominic. I've put out your grey suit. It's on the bed."

When she opened the door, Boris scampered. That was the last I saw of him for the rest of the day.

Chapter 10

Locksmith Calls

"**Y**ou rang me, Colonel," the locksmith announced, accusingly, making it sound like I spent my time bringing him all the way out here for no good reason. Short, chubby chap, balding, likable enough when he knew his place. Grey and white check shirt straining to keep his stomach in place. I waved my hand dismissively. No point getting into a useless argument before he'd done anything. Besides, I'd noticed his moustache and was resisting telling him my firm view – it didn't suit him. And it wasn't brushed, hairs sprouting in all directions.

"Hm, did I?" I ran my fingers over my clean-shaven lips.

"Maybe it was circled in the phone book?" he suggested with a glinty eye like he was playing with me.

"Oh." Possible.

"Every time I come here," he said as he practically forced his way past me, heavy wooden box and all, into the house, "it's the same. Always the same."

Closed the door, impressed by his self-assurance, still unsure why he was here, but confident it would come back to me. Was that a smell of pickled cucumber?

He looked around. "What's it this time, Colonel?" No answer. "Here, Colonel." He handed me a small card which read, 'Felix Delahunty, Academy of Keys'.

Took my time reading it, his eyes on me the way people do when they think I'm half-stupid. As well as wondering has the dodgy memory gotten worse.

"Mr Delahunty, Felix," I declared. "I've been demoted. It's Captain now."

"Captain?" He looked at me slyly, broke into a broad grin. "Oh no, it's not," he declared theatrically, thinking I was ready for Christmas-panto malarkey. Scowled at him.

"But it was in the papers," he insisted. "You were made a full Colonel. They said the government didn't want the opposition benefiting because of, you know, eh, your wife." His voice tailed off like a dying engine.

"She's not my blasted wife," I bellowed at him, no need to hold back with a looney locksmith I was paying for. "And if you want any more business here."

"OK, OK." Held up his hands, "You don't have to shout. She's not your wife, not now, not ever."

Would've gone on if I hadn't cut him off. "Enough."

Put his box down in the hallway, ran his hand over the few strands of hair he still had. "So, which lock do you want changed this time?"

Might tolerate eccentricity in a locksmith, but not condescension. I placed my hands on his shoulders, turned him around, facing the stairs and barked, "Up there."

In the bedroom pointed at the chest of drawers. "There and there," I said moving to the wardrobe, "and there and in the toilet outside."

"Righteo," he said slowly, opening drawers, examining the locks. It didn't bother me what he saw in there. Nor did it bother him. Just shoved anything in the way to the back of the drawer with pudgy fingers. He looked puzzled.

"But… I think I replaced this last year."

He went over to the wardrobe, bent down to look at the lock.

"What's the problem, Colonel? These look…"

"Security breach."

"What? Someone broke into your house?"

"Em… not exactly. Almost."

"Where are the keys?"

"The keys?"

"The keys."

Insolent tone reminded me of the Brat whenever he tried explaining something to me.

"Look, Colonel, it makes no sense to replace these locks." He wiped his hands. "They're all new and they're fine. I can get you some new keys if that's what you want. You'll save yourself a few bob. Or," he turned theatrically, went over to the bedroom door and examined the lock, "I could replace this and… rig up an electronic lock and keypad like the one I did in the basement." He studied the door frame. "How's the basement working?"

Shook my head dismissively, decided I would have to find another way to keep the bloody Politician out of my bedroom.

"Right, next job," I said and led him downstairs, through kitchen and out into the garden.

"Haven't been out here before," he said, looking around. "Big gardens."

Followed me through the gap in the wall. I pointed at the damaged toilet door. "I need you to fix that. Take off the old lock, put on a new one," I said briskly, smacking my hands together. "Can you do that for me?"

He went down on one knee, examined the door. "Nice bit of damage here," he concluded. "Someone give it a right kicking?"

I felt only pride. "Don't know who did it. Must have been really dying for a crap."

"Hmm. Terrible what people do these days. In some-one else's back garden as well. No shame." He scratched his head, looked around. "You'll be getting the door fixed first, won't you? No point fixing the lock with the door like that."

"You fix it."

"What? Me? Locksmiths don't fix wood. We fix locks."

Tiresome nonsense I was prepared for. "Course you can fix it. It's only bloody wood. I'd do it myself except for this." Held up my non-thumb, gave him a good view of the mess. Didn't often try to exploit it. He didn't look at it as long as I wanted. Must have tried it on him before. "Last time," I said, "you told me you came to locks through doors, haha. Said it was easier money."

"No, did I say that?"

"Yeah." I lied. "That's what you said. It was so witty I remembered it."

He still looked dubious. He glanced around the garden like he just noticed where he was. "Is this your place, Colonel? I mean, look." He pointed at the gap and the back of the Politician's house.

More impertinence. "What do you mean?"

"I can't put a lock on someone else's property."

"It's not someone else's property. It's mine. It's just a... tenant here."

"A tenant? Ah, Colonel, come on. I know who lives here and she's..."

I cut him off. "Look," I said, forcing a civil tone. "She is a tenant, my damn tenant, God have pity on me, and she agrees. She asked me to organise it for her because she's too busy herself. You know about her, she's apparently..." Couldn't bring myself to say it. Giving her that job was such a mistake. "Obviously, I'll pay you for it."

Still hesitated.

"Well, if you don't want to do it, I can always..."

Held up a hand. "No. No, I can do it. If you say she asked you and, you are saying that, aren't you? Well, yeah, then no, that's OK." He was twiddling his stumpy fingers as he said this.

"She has."

He opened his toolbox. "It's OK, you don't have to stay. I'm grand."

Stayed anyway. When he had the door off its hinges, I had a good look inside. There wasn't much to see. Stained toilet bowl, no seat or cover, cistern high up on the back wall, long dangling chain, empty toilet-roll holder. No radiator, no wash-hand basin.

"Looks like it hasn't been used in years, eh?" the locksmith said as if reading my mind. He fiddled around in his box, took out a power screwdriver. "Any idea how old these houses are? Must be 1890s or something."

"Are you thinking of buying one?"

He didn't hear me, finished drilling. He had to go back to his van to get new hinges and pieces of wood, tubes of paste. He could only do a patch-up job. The Politician would need a new door, anyway. When the door was up, swinging on the new hinges he said, "It's a simple lock, you want? You don't want anything fancy, do you?" He stretched his hand up and flicked the toilet light. Surprisingly, it worked. "I'll have this finished in a jiffy."

Could see better now. There was really only room in there for one person. So, what was the Brat saying about two? The locksmith was kneeling on the small floor of the toilet working on the lock from the inside. Ignoring my narrow-toilet phobia, I said, "Just a minute, please," prised open the door, lifted a leg over him, squeezing past him inside.

"What the...?" The locksmith tried to stand up, couldn't fully, looking up at me looming over him. "Jesus, can you not wait or use..."

Pushed myself further into the toilet, pressing one arm against the wall and pulling the door closed with the other. The locksmith shoved himself more upright, trying to get out. Look of panic on his face.

"Wait! No, stay. Stay where you are, please. I want you to stay." I turned sideways to ease the pressure. "This won't take a second." Our stomachs were pressing against each other over the bowl.

"Colonel, what the hell are you doing?" he yelled. "Fuck it, I want to get out!"

"I'm not going to do anything to you." How could he even think that? "Felix, I'm really sorry, I just need to check something. It won't take a sec. I need to see if two people can fit in here."

"Are you fucking mad? For God's sake why do you need to know that? Isn't it..."

"Zzzzz." Something vibrating against my thigh. "Aaaa-gh," I shouted in fright. His drill had gone off. "Turn it off," I roared into his ear.

"Jesus, it just went off on its own." He was pushing and shoving for space to get his hand down to stop the drill. "Umf, umh, it's wedged below my stomach. Need to get my hand..." Heavy breathing as he struggled. Finally, it was off. "Christ that was close."

Was obvious two men couldn't do much in there without being right up against each other. Only space for moving hands was above the head. Had an idea. Leaned up, ran my hands along the cistern, noting no cobwebs. Heavy lid of the cistern wasn't fully flush with its sides. Curious! Ledge on one side overhung by a few millimetres. Someone, sometime had taken the lid off, not put it back on properly. On my toes, using both hands to gently lift the lid on one side, run my fingers inside it.

"Almost there, just another two seconds."

Pushed one hand into the cold water, half expecting to touch something goey and dead. Immediately felt something like the shape of a lengthy slim plastic package. Wow, something hidden. Wanted to shout, "Eureka." Ran my fingers over it again to be doubly sure.

"Right," I said, extracting my hand, releasing the door and replacing the lid as I'd found it. "That's grand. Thank you very much, Felix. Sorry for all the bother."

Felix staggered out, wide-eyed, bent over, breathing deep, looking like a miner just released after being trapped for days. Rubbing his forehead, blinking, taking deep breaths, looking at me like I was a total looper.

"Colonel, you're a spacer, you know that? A spacer. What was that about?" shook his head, went straight back to work, keen to be finished and gone as quick as possible.

"Hi." The squeaky voice of the Brat. Looked at each other like we'd been caught. Came from my garden. Of course, it was that time of the afternoon. "Where's everyone?"

"Quick," I whispered, grabbing his elbow. "That's the Brat. Ssshh, don't tell him I'm here." Rushed back inside the toilet, switched off the light, closed the door behind me, slid bolt closed. In my excitement, I forgot what I was doing. How long could I survive in there?

"Hi!" The Brat was closer this time, his voice acquiring an extra shy-squeak. "Wha' ya doen?"

"What does it look like?" Cheers for the gruff locksmith. That's the way to speak to the Brat. "Can you move away? I'm almost finished." Door rattled as he worked on the new handle.

"I didn't know you polished locks," the Brat said. "Why's Granny changing the lock?" The Brat didn't wait for the answer. "Oh, yeah. I remember. Did you see the old guy who lives in there?" he asked full of himself, his voice fading as his head turned.

"What? Who? Who're you talking about?"

"He's big and old, bald, and... narky... He has a big nose like de Gaulle."

"Who's de Gaulle?"

"Eh, dunno... That's what they say."

"The old guy has a big nose, eh?"

"Like this."

Muffled laughter. Locksmith was playing his role well, maybe too well, but I guessed he figured on getting a big tip if he did. Already I was beginning to feel hot and clammy in there. Clamping my hands on the walls to keep them apart. It always took a while for the walls to start moving. Kept looking up at the cistern trying to distract myself, be patient.

"Wha' ya doen now?" the Brat asked.

Same answer. "What's it look like?"

"You're putting on a new lock and fixing the door. I didn't know locksmiths fixed doors."

Heard a loud groan. "We don't."

"Well, why?"

"Look, kiddo, I just want to finish and get out of here and you're wasting my time."

Silence for five seconds.

"How'd ya get in?" The Brat was finally thinking.

"I'm a locksmith."

"I know that. Are you one of the guys who were fixing the toilet?"

"What guys? I'm not a plumber."

"OK."

Shaking of the door getting violent.

"You weren't here before?"

Locksmith banged the handle like a cry for help.

"This is my second, no third time here and…"

"Ah, so you were here before. You could be one of them."

"Sonny, move back from that box. Why don't you go off and play like a good lad, before you annoy me." The locksmith couldn't take any more.

Time to take him out of his misery.

"Christ!" I roared from inside, "Can't a guy have a crap in peace around here without a crowd gathering outside?"

Pulled the flush chain, drew back the bolt, pushed the door open. The locksmith had no warning and it sent him flying.

"Now, look what you've done," I accused the gaping Brat while helping the bewildered locksmith to his feet.

"I'm so sorry he's bothering you. Has no father."

The Brat still so astonished, his small lips pout wordlessly.

"Jesus," the locksmith muttered. "Never a dull moment around here."

"Yeah," I jeered at the Brat, pointed at my nose. "Old big nose himself."

The Brat was looking from me to the locksmith, backing away from both of us. I saw the suspicion building in his eyes. Were the locksmith and I in the gay plumbers' club? And, more importantly, was I going to hit him?

Negotiating the locksmith's fee and tip took longer than expected. He seemed to think he should get locksmith's fee, carpenter's fee and actor's fee. We settled on seventy percent of what he wanted. I even got a five percent discount for entertainment value. Entrusted three keys to me on the express understanding I would give them all to the Politician. Fat chance of that.

Chapter 11

Politician's Celebration Dinner

T he Politician's dinner, where else but a grand hotel on the edge of the city centre. Entrance looked like a giant stool rammed up against the front of the building. For fun, cars had to drive under it. Foyer so vast it hurt my eyes to look at it. A low-ceilinged, over-arm-chaired, marble prairie dotted with tropical greenery that tried to catch me as I walked by. Complained loudly about it to the Brat who loved it when I went on like that, making a fool of myself, getting into trouble.

The Politician stopped to chat with another table as we were shown to our own in a discreet alcove against a big draped window looking out onto a lit-up courtyard with a mermaid in a small trickly fountain. Put my hand on the glass to block the Brat's view of the naked trans-specimen. "Stop looking at her boobies," I said.

"I'm not," he replied vehemently. "I'm… You're a f…"

Nodding encouragingly and mouthing the words, hoping he'd lose control and say it.

"Dad, leave him alone. Thomas, don't mind him. Look at whatever you want."

Making a special effort, the Brat merely tweaked his nose in disgust at me.

"It's nice and quiet here, isn't it?" the Politician said when she returned. "We can celebrate in peace, away from snooping journalists and," in a lower voice, "envious constituents. I've had enough of that now for another five years, hopefully." She glanced over at the table she'd been at. "Joan, you know who that was?"

The young woman shook her head.

"It's Ray Tucker. Remember him? A junior minister in the last government, in different departments. They're celebrating not being in government. Imagine. I suppose that'll be us in five years' time... or sooner. Five years? God, what year will Thomas be in then?"

"Fifth year," the Brat answered without hesitation. I didn't even know he'd been listening. I don't know, sometimes he could surprise me. I'd think he was away in the clouds and he'd come out with something like that.

The Politician bestowed a thoughtful look on him. The Brat had moved on to frowning at the three knives and three forks in front of him as if trying to make them move on their own.

"They assume you'll knock one on the ground," I explained. "Steal the second and still have one to use. Neat, isn't it?"

"Don't mind him," the Politician said. "Thomas, what would you like to be when you grow up?"

Lowered my menu to look and listen. If she'd asked me, I'd have said, "He'll never get that far. I'll have murdered him before then."

The Brat took his time, pretending to be thinking.

"Maybe a helicopter pilot," she suggested, "or an archaeologist discovering lost civilisations or, how about a computer whiz kid?"

"A hacker?" his mother smiled. The two women chortled.

The Brat astonished us all. "I'd like to be like you, Granny," he decided.

"You want to be a woman?!" I almost shouted, shocked into standing up.

"Stop, Dad! Sit down." His mother to the rescue. "And keep your voice down."

The Politician was also taken aback and then beamed at him. "Thomas, what a clever answer and I like the way you thought about it first before answering. That's what politicians should always do. But," her face grew artfully grave, "it's what so few of us manage." She rooted in her bag as if searching for a reward-lollipop or hankie to wet unshed sentimental tears. She took out her mobile phone and switched it off. "It's a hard life, Thomas. Harder for a woman, and you need to be very tough."

The Brat was glowing under the praise and couldn't help himself. Sat up straighter in his seat. "I want to see pictures of myself everywhere, just like Granny," he explained, bouncing a little. That quenched their enthusiasm and they glared at me as if I was to blame.

The Politician perked up when the shaven-headed waiter came to take the order. When he saw who she was, his face lit up with a big smile. He bowed his broad shoulders, exclaiming in a Polish accent, "Ah, *Madame*, congratulations. Ve hafe not seen you for a vhile."

The Politician's cheeks bloomed. "We missed you too, Piotr," she replied with almost equal enthusiasm. "Were you away?"

"You vere sad vhen I vas gone?" he said, suggestively. "Good. Now, you vill be sad no more."

They were both so pleased to see each other, I wondered was this the guy she might weaken for. Besides being loud like her, he was a couple of inches shorter than her and that could be important for a politician. Surprisingly high voice, unsuited to his frame, which he seemed to rather enjoy. She could have him.

"You were on holidays?"

"Yes, *Madame*, in my country."

"Where's that?" the Brat butted in.

"You know Poland?"

"Yes," his mother answered. "Do you like Chopin?"

"Chopin?" he sighed, suddenly dreamy. "Eat ease alvays complex vith Chopin. Sometimes makes me happy." Waiter tilted his head one way. "Sometimes makes me sad." Head tilted the other. "And vas nought sure how Polish he vas. Like all of us."

I whispered into the Brat's ear, "Was he one of the plumbers?"

He pushed me away.

The Politician was reading the drinks menu. "Last time I was here the Bloody Mary had too much relish in it," she said, looking up at him.

"*Madame*, you may punish me." He looked at her so frankly the two women started tittering. Even the Brat who was frowning, looked like he might have understood. "And to drink?" Piotr asked briskly after taking the meal orders.

The Politician didn't think champagne appropriate, after the campaign had focused on wasteful government spending. She ordered sparkling Italian white instead.

Following Piotr's departure, I'd nothing better to do than wait for the Brat to do something, anything, to kill my boredom. Battling to give them nothing to report back to the Shrinkage. He was spreading his hands in ever-widening circles over the smooth white tablecloth. Any minute now with luck he'd hit one of the mile-high wine glasses and knock it over. I inched one of them towards him.

"Mam, do you know what you want to do as Minister?" her daughter asked, taking a sip of water from a cavernous glass. I threw my eyes to heaven, wishing she wouldn't be so insipid. Have a double vodka, I thought. Live a little. Has she ever been drunk?

"You mean what will I be allowed to do? Well, I'll get some new outfits and, then... do nothing, keep listening to Martina, not get sacked and see why he gave me the job.

You don't do anything until you know that and who you're going to offend." Normal, matter-of-fact tone.

I was off on my own cloud thinking about glasshouses when the Politician turned to me. "And I owe part of my victory to you, dear." My hand was lying carelessly on the table, an alien touch resting briefly on it. Too much on guard to spoil it.

"Why?" the Brat demanded, like his ears only picked up things that made him jealous. "He did nothing. He was in the house in bed all the time or just… walking." The greatest sin of all. "And anyway, he's–"

"Thomas," his mother warned. He reluctantly shut his mouth.

"The opinion polls, Thomas," his Granny's voice was gentle. "You know the ones we did just in our own constituency? Well, they all showed that what your grandfather did could influence some voters. It was Martina's idea to put the question in. I wouldn't have thought of it, or even dared suggest it. It was also Martina's idea not to use Dominic in public. That would have seemed… exploitative." She smiled apologetically at me, but it didn't fool me.

"That's why you were so worried about the photo, wasn't it?" the young woman asked.

"Yes, Joan, that's right." The Politician was looking around for Piotr and the drinks.

For once I knew what they were talking about. Out walking, minding my own business, except for talking to auld ones who enjoyed my company, avoiding looking at posters of her. Passing the local supermarket where the

Politician was canvassing surrounded by shoppers, shop-lifters, bums, beggars and journalists. Too late to cross the busy road so pulled down my hat, and pressed on, hoping no one would notice me. Thought I was safe, almost past, when someone called out my name. Foolishly stopped, as you do, looked around. The crowd moved toward me, I backed away, cameras were clicking. I remember blinking. Then some fool clapped, others joined in, all looking at me with happy faces. I have to say, if people are happy for any reason, it's good. I glanced over at the Politician. After a moment, she shamelessly started clapping as well. No idea what they were clapping about, but since they were happy and it felt like a unique moment, I clapped as well, which they loved even more. Few cheers as well. But enough is enough, I smiled again, turned, walked off. Puzzled, of course. Buzzing too from inspiring random happiness. Later, when the young woman showed me the photo in the newspaper, the camera had caught me looking at the Politician with the caption, 'The Colonel of Drumcondra bumps into his wife on the canvass.'

Tucking into my fish – the Brat was being let away with chips and chicken nuggets, noticed the antics of a small girl in jeans at the other politician's table. Couldn't sit still, she was either bouncing on her seat or standing up and walking around the table like she couldn't decide who she wanted to be near. At one point she got under the table, had to be hauled out by her father. At least the Brat was beyond that.

On my way to the toilet I passed her table. Standing with her back to her seat, she watched me approaching. Her small eyes glued themselves on to mine, didn't let go, were so ferocious and direct, they brought me to a halt near her table. I couldn't move. Stood there like a statue on Easter Island, unable to break the stare. Whereas she, holding my eyes captive, sidled closer to her mother, put her arms around her mother's neck. Mother turned to look at me, conversation at the table quickly died away. Very conscious they were all looking at me.

"Eh, can I help you?" the other politician sitting across from the mother asked in a friend-or-foe tone. Ignored him, concentrated on not being the one to break the stare. A test of wills I had to win. But, the sanctuary of her mother's neck seemed to embolden the insolent kid, make her equally determined. The five people at the table were exchanging glances. One of the women asked, "Is there a problem, sir?" Ignored her too.

Then, I felt a small hand insert itself into mine, a child's voice said, "I'll show you where the toilet is, Granddad." And I was led off.

"Don't know what happened there," muttered to myself. Looked at the Brat. "Smart move that. Jesus, she is a little bitch."

Chapter 12

Guinea Pigs Speak

Night blacker than ink. Not a single starry-dot in the heavens. Feeble streetlights dimly reflecting pale car roofs. Street, footpath, redbrick houses, old-fashioned railings, sharing the nightly gloom. Occasional car hurries quietly by.

Couldn't sleep, still kidnapped by soft-faced, bully-doll. Unbelievable at her age, younger than the Brat. Funny, unfunny word, kidnapped, true in this case. Tapped my upper lip against the cold glass of the bedroom window, thinking hard. I've heard it before. Yeeeess, I know. The damn Onslaught when I was in hospital. Spun a yarn I'd been kidnapped somewhere foreign where I'd lost my thumb. Didn't believe a word of it.

Flicked a coin. Hot bath or concrete therapy on the basement floor? Useless thing rolled under the bed. Left it there. Think I saw heads. Don't often take baths, too comfortable. Soaked in warm, fragrant, bubbly water, big toes like peaks on an ocean island. Mind refused to empty itself, doggedly and fruitlessly pursuing wisdom about doll/Brat thuggery. Punching the water, "God-damn it!" I shouted at the pink soap sailing around my fist, the sheer brazenness of weaponising her eyes, attacking me when I was off-guard, coyly retreating into little girl-land. Should I have hit her? Yeah, no, couldn't do that nowadays, talk radio said so. Should be an exception for doll/Brat thuggery. Threw empty plastic bubble-bath bottle at the wall, foamy water splashed everywhere. Had to admit I was wrong thinking Brat experience meant I knew all about kids. Much maggoty carry-on still beyond me.

Recalled time I saw two street-performers in a city festival, no idea when or where, dipping long sticks into a basin of soapy water, slowly pulling up amazing shaped giant delicate bubbles that wobbled delightfully as they floated upwards. Awesome stuff, big hit with kids. Dense crowd around them, kids to the front, excited, gleeful. But all they wanted to do was jump on the bubbles, smashing them into nothingness. Disturbing. Had to stop myself intervening. Inane parents smiling, doting on their tiny barbarians. Couldn't fathom it. Reckoned if I'd been one of those kids, I wouldn't have done that, might even have stopped them. But couldn't really say, could I? Not having any childhood memory to make it easier to understand how kids looked at the world. Irritated feet started splashing getting-cold-quick water onto the tiled floor. Colonel Numbskull dumb as a dog chasing its tail.

Before dawn, minus sleep, standing on comfort tile, third in front, right side of the big kitchen window. Rain battering glass, dissipating into shivering droplets, streamlets. Daylight advancing hesitantly. Too early and wet for Boris, probably won't appear at all, doesn't like rain. Mood suited only brainlessness. Rain-staring, mesmerised by transparency of water. Socked feet caressing tile, tracing tile-edges, wanted the wear-and-tear of standing there to show itself, prove I had a past as well as a present. Zoomed in on that, realised like in the bath, it was all about proof of past.

Caught myself biting knuckles. Gave them a kindly licking instead as I slow-walked back and forth between front room and kitchen, afraid of hovering black mood while I stared at un-Christian rain. Guinea pigs too subdued by weather and life. Unusually quiet, inert, waiting. Only function of windows now was to bring dreary day into the house. Panes-of-glass project in abeyance.

Out of nowhere, it happened, came to me. Not a rumbling earthquake. Both hands resting on the kitchen island worktop, soliciting wisdom from wood.

"This can't go on," I said out loud, deep voiced. The guinea pigs weren't listening. Repeated myself, adding, "I've said to lots of people I can live like this, without a past, but now… Now I know I can't. It's getting too hard living without a childhood. And an adulthood. Can't have one without the other. Can't know how to handle kids if I've no childhood. Can't know how to handle rain if I've no rain-memories from childhood, right? Amn't I entitled to a childhood like everyone else? And an adulthood? The works."

Stood over the guinea pigs' cage.

"What would you do in my place?" I asked Maximus, eyeing her profusion of cows-licks as she came out from under the upturned box in the cage, scurried back in again. Box moved.

"Create your own past," thought I heard her say.

"What do you mean?"

Box moved again.

"Get a new identity. Become a new person," a voice speaking on behalf of Maximus said.

"What? Say that again."

Box moved again.

"Wow, yes," I whispered, intrigued. "I understand." Incipient tremors of excitement leaping like start-up flames. Put my hand to my mouth. "That's a bloody good idea." Stamped my foot on the ground like a soldier standing to attention. So loud, box went silent.

"That's exactly what I need to do. So obvious, why didn't I think of that before now." Went over to the fridge, tingling all over like I'd boozed up on energy-drinks, got a huge reward-chunk of cucumber, hurled it at the wise lions in their den.

Mood now firmly in positive territory. Walked in circles around the kitchen, excitedly thinking radical thoughts, daring to explore fantastical ideas. A new name, new birthday, new parents, new address, new school, new childhood, new everything. But no military codology. Had enough of that. A new civilian persona. Would I have to have, erm… emigrated? Yeah, and be dead, of course. No brothers, sisters. All dead. Maybe a bachelor or spinster third cousin somewhere, lost contact with. Maybe a priest on the missions in Africa, gone native, shacked up in the jungle.

Sat down at kitchen table with sober thoughts. How will I do all this on my own? At the start will definitely need help. Yeah, that's as clear as the post-downpour light, now foxing up the kitchen, celebrating with me. Obviously can't tell the Politician or anyone. Mrs Hand? Doubtful, but possible. Do I know anyone trustworthy and bribe-able? Someone who knows how to find things, to investigate?

PART 111

Chapter 13

Hut Arrives

Truck engine heaving, gears clanking under my bedroom window. Sleep impossible. What's it doing? Reversing downhill? That's mad. Definitely not rubbish truck. Maybe some disgruntled citizen come to ram his truck into the Politician's house. Better not mistake my house for hers like the others do. She'll have to pay for it if he does.

Heaved my carcass out of bed, shuffled over to the window, remembering no full frontals. Angry seagulls screeched at the truck, good birds. Pulled back the side of the blind, dazzling sunshine, delightful sun warmth. Stood back, raised the blind two-thirds, eyes adjusting as light transformed the room from morning gloom to morning glory. Harry purred in the heat.

Giant hydraulic arm connected to the back of a truck was hovering over the front garden. Swaying rectangular brown wooden hut, with slightly pitched roof, two windows, a door, hung from taut cables. Big arm slowly passed over the railings and hedge next door, to set its load down on planks. I leaned nearer the window, scrutinising where they'd put the hut. No railing between gardens, but boundary line clear from different railing paints. Hmm. was some of the hut's back on my side?

Operator of the big arm, standing beside the truck, re-alised his mistake. Hut lifted again, helper on the ground pushing it towards her side as it was re-lowered. No use. Cretins still left it partly on my side.

Glanced at the bedside clock. Six fifty-one. If I go down now, I'll start an almighty row. No one allowed at any time to invade my property. Looked across the street for support. Not a sinner stirred, not one winking curtain or brazen blind along the entire length of the seven-house terrace.

Tried putting the irritation out of my head for now but fully intended declaration of war if necessary. Went about my morning routine. Failure to catch the Brat on the attic-stairs had stirred me into a fitness regime: twenty minutes of pull-ups, push- ups, toe-tipping, wind milling. Listened to myself listing nice things about myself – chatting to all-comers, especially auld ones of the female va-riety; following blinders to keep an eye on them; love of animals, well, certain ones; great humanity and humour in the face of the Onslaught. Also went over what happened yesterday in case anyone asked. Didn't like being caught out. Finished by kissing my non-thumb.

The truck was gone when I went out to look. Yes, no doubt about it, definitely trespassing on my side. Made no difference that the hut was positioned behind her high, uncut hedge, its door half a metre from her path and steps up to her door. Its rear, maybe a tenth of a metre on my side. Obviously, measuring tape confirmed my estimate. Noticed through the side window, the big head of the hut's uniformed, hatless occupant watching me as I walked around the hut, tape in hand. Ninety-two millimetres of invasion. Tapped the hut window.

Hatted Guard came out. Swarthy, late-thirties, large man with simple face, looked me direct in the eye, sized me up, disappointed I wasn't smaller than him. Sensed he was used to being taller than most, and uneasy when not. I got straight to the point.

"You know," pointed at the offending rear of the hut, struggling between sociability and irritability, settling for factual, "That… thing is ninety-two millimetres on my side of the boundary of my property."

Calmly followed me around to the back of the hut, studying the situation without a word.

"Ninety-two millimetres," he repeated. "You know, you could be right."

'Course I'm bloody right, you dope,' growled to myself. Guess he had his own way of dealing with things. Probably a country lad. Waited for him to say more. They usually do, but this one seemed to have run out of words. He nodded a few times agreeing with himself. To be agreeable, I nodded as well.

"Do you want to measure it yourself?" I asked when the nodding stopped.

He bent down, put his shoulder to the back of the hut and pushed. Didn't budge.

"I'll give you a hand."

Together we pushed and heaved. Enjoyed the camaraderie of joint hut-heaving, but damn thing didn't move.

"It's too heavy," he conceded, standing back on my land, breathing heavily, but not red in the face like me. Readied myself for another bout of nodding, keen to join in from the off, show solidarity, build buddy-ness, but he was shooting glances at a heavy-shouldered auld one carrying two shopping bags who'd stopped to watch us.

"Hello, Mrs Hand," I greeted her, thrilled she'd stopped. Usual grey tweed coat, big buttons, large lapels.

"It'll get woodworm behind that hedge," she said in that rich Monaghan accent, getting straight to the point as usual, like myself.

"You could be right there," I agreed more than happily with her.

"Want to meet our new neighbour?" I gestured towards the Guard.

"Hello, Guard," she said neutrally. Could be like that with strangers, cautious, needed time to warm to them.

"Hello Missus."

"It's Mrs Hand," I told him.

"Mrs Hand," he agreed, nodded only once. I nodded too, she didn't. They were examining each other the way country people do. Making fast judgements that could last a lifetime. Mrs Hand must have taken umbrage because, without a word, she picked up her shopping bags, and took off up the hill, around the corner, out of sight. Never one to hang about if she felt negative vibes, but this was too abrupt. Something was amiss.

"Do you know her?" I asked him as we surveyed the street.

"Never saw her in my life."

"Well, you'll have to tell whoever put that thing there, it's got to go. It can't stay there. I want it off my property."

"I'll speak to the sergeant."

"You do that," I said firmly.

Guard still looking up the street where Mrs Hand had gone, as if suspecting she might return with a machine gun.

"If you don't mind me saying so, Guard, I think you put her off stopping for a chat."

He looked at me like I was the problem, not her.

"I know Mrs Hand well. She always stops for a chat."

He nodded. This time, I think, in disagreement. Interesting nuance, disagreement-nodding.

I offered some advice. "You'll get yourself a reputation like that. There's lots of auld ones around here. They're up and down the street all day. They'll all be talking about you and it mightn't be good."

I gazed up at the sky. "Nothing to do but walk and talk, walk and talk."

The Guard's expression told me he wasn't having the quiet time he expected.

"Want to know something surprising about them?"

"What?"

"They all believe in mercy killing."

"Do they now?" He nodded, this time to show he was postponing judgement. Hard work learning this nuance-nodding.

"Are you married?"

"What?"

"They'll want to know. If you're not you'd better have an excuse ready or be doing a steady line with some young one."

"I suppose there'd be no point telling them to mind their own business."

Followed him back to the front of the hut. "What exactly will you be doing here?"

"Security."

"Good God!" I exclaimed. "Is she that dangerous? Oh, the country's in a bad way, alright. You know, all she wants is her picture up on every pole? The Russians could be invading, and she'd be doing her hair for a photo."

No nodding. Just a curious look.

Sudden gust of wind blew my front door shut. "Fuck!" I shouted, rushing over too late, fumbling in my pocket for the key I knew I didn't have.

"You're grand," the Guard called out after me. "It's on the latch."

He was right. I stared at him, gob open. "How'd you know that?" I asked, foot firmly in the doorway.

"I saw you put it on the latch."

"How did you see that?"

"That's my job," he said, sounding pleased with himself. "I'm supposed to notice everything."

Super-impressed. "At this rate, you'll soon know us all."

"Ah, I do already." A slow smirk crept across his face.

Felt I was beginning to make a new friend.

"Oh, you do, do you?" I smirked at him. "Well... who lives there, then?" Pointed across the road at the mid-terrace house, two doors up.

"That's Tom McCarthy and his sister, they're both retired."

I didn't know Tom's surname. "And where does Tom go every morning and evening?"

He didn't answer. "Aha! And down there?" pointed three doors down, on our side of the street.

Strained his head to look. "That's Grace. Lives alone with a blind dog. Retired teacher."

"But what kind of teacher?"

He hesitated.

"Have you there, don't I?"

"All right," he said getting grumpy with me winning the game. "You tell me."

Had no idea either. "Physical education."

"You're having me on. She's..."

Waited for his answer, but he'd reached the limit of his patience. I nodded a few times to encourage him to nod back. No luck. Maybe there's no nod for 'I've had enough'.

"Look," he said. "I'm busy. I have a job to do. Nice talking to you." He walked over to the Politician's gate, busied himself checking the rooftops for snipers.

Went back inside, got pen and paper, wrote: 'Neighbour insists trespassing hut is moved off HIS land. PRONTO. Otherwise…' Didn't specify threat because wasn't sure who or what it was. Early days, not yet sure what I was dealing with. Stood up to go out and give it to the Guard, when struck by a magnificent thought. Instantly bunched up note, threw it where the rubbish bin should have been, rushed back up to the front room, via hop-skip-and-jump, stood in the bay window gazing longingly and fondly at my new best friend sitting lonesome in the now rain-soaked wooden box.

"Courage, Colonel Coward," I ordered to myself, "You've got to do it." Put on hat, long raincoat, opened umbrella, licked my non-thumb, threw open front door, took my life in my hands, and dashed over the glistening grass to the hut. Banged on the door like my life depended on it. No response. Peered inside window. Inert, inscrutable lug watching me watching him. Gestured. He reluctantly signalled he'd come over when his shift finished.

Chapter 14

Asks for Help

Grass was still glistening from the polishing the rain gave it. But sun warmth had sweated the footpath dry. I had the front door open before the Guard had time to knock. The long wait was over.

"I told them you wanted it moved," he began defensively as I ushered him in. Diminished, I thought, without guard-jacket, wearing a plain light grey anorak. "The sergeant says he'll look into it."

"Come in, come in," I urged, enthusiastically grabbing his elbow, steering him towards the front room. The hut's yesterday's news, depending. For now.

He hesitated as he stepped over the letters, flyers, leaflets scattered on the hall floor, looked at me. "There might be something important there," he muttered, badly hiding his disapproval.

My shoulders shrugged themselves. "There isn't."

The Guard bent down, like most visitors, picked up the junk, gave it to me. If I hadn't wanted a favour, I'd have thrown them back on the floor. Which was where they ended up when he left. Moved the hats on the hall-table to make room for them. Sat him in the armchair in the bay window, framed in light, hoping it would make him more amenable to helping me. Still frowning, though.

"Do you not realise…" he began in an earnest tone.

"Enough!" I shouted. "Leave it. It annoys me talking about it."

He blinked, shivered.

"Do you not get used to the cold?" I asked, mildly disapproving of sturdy men shivering.

"You never get used to that. There's no heat in the hut."

"Would you like a stiff one?"

"A what?"

"A whiskey." Went to the cabinet, took out the good bottle, poured two glasses. Handed him the larger one. He hesitated, looked at his watch, out the window, took a sup.

Some way into the detail of what I wanted him to do for me, he leaned forward, shock-eyed, and interrupted. "Hold on a minute. Stop." Looked uncomfortable. "I can't do that, and I can't be listening to you either." He put the glass on a small side-table, stood up to go. "What you're talking about is illegal."

"Course it's effin' illegal." Vexed hearing this from a guard. Quite unnecessary. "That's why I'm asking you. To make it legal. Sit down there and let me finish. Here, have another one." Filled his barely touched glass to the brim before he knew it. Trust it into his hand. Practically shoved him back into his seat.

"You'll be able to make it legal. That's why I'm asking you. I don't want you to do anything illegal. You'll be able to do it the right way."

Dubious look on big head. Tried appealing to his emotions. Told him how hard it was not having a childhood, or a past, about all the problems this caused me on a daily basis, how tiring it was always fighting the Onslaught and the Explanation on my own. First time I used 'Onslaught' with him. Calculated gamble. Didn't say what it meant, seemed to understand. Laid the misery on thick and heavy, stopped frequently, cited Doctors Papp, Canoe. Everyone except him sympathised with me.

"Look," he said firmly. There was no moving him. "I don't want to hear another word of this. It's more than my job's worth."

"Well then," I slapping my thighs, "you tell me what I'm supposed to do? Jump in front of a train?" Swift as the Brat, I reached back for the letter-opener lying above on mantelpiece, grabbed it, drove it firmly into the small table between us. Shocked silent, watching the quivering knife.

He gulped, big Adam's apple sinking and rising in his neck, professional bearing struggling with sudden fright. Began to understand that, with him, all depended on how you asked the question.

"If it was me," he said finally, sober-toned, eyeballing the quivering knife, "well… wait, look, I shouldn't even be…" He sighed, glanced out the window as if watching his career and conscience running down the hill. Took a quick sip of whiskey to stop them. "You didn't hear this from me, right?"

Nodded so slowly I invented a new deliberative-hypnotic nod. He hadn't nodded once since he came in. An outdoors-only nodder?

"What you need," he said, taking another guilty gulp, "is… a retired detective. Someone no longer in the force, but knows what to do, how to go about it. With the contacts. You know, contacts?"

I know what contacts are, you big lug. "Excellent."

"I know a man who's looking for some work now. Retired a few months ago. Doesn't need it, the wife still works, and he has two houses in bed-sits, but he likes to stay active."

"Two? Impressive." Envious nodding. Owning bed-sits was the dream.

"And he's good," he added, as if he thought I thought a two-house retired detective mightn't be reliable. "Worked on some big murder cases."

"Solved ones?"

"Of course."

"Excellent. You're sure he can work quietly? You know, erm…" I cleared my throat. "Next door? Very nosey. I don't want people to know."

"Sure, hasn't he been doing that all his life. You can tell him yourself."

Shoved stray unopened envelope and pen at him to write down a name, phone number.

"I'll tell him you'll be ringing him."

Gulped down the rest of his whiskey, and left in great haste, like a wicked thought fleeing a church before confession.

Chapter 15

Finding the Package

Raw air, sun-feeble, long shadows. Nature unlocking winter. Me unlocking secrets. True, hadn't rushed to find out what was in the Package. Rather enjoyed anticipating it.

Mug of tea in hand, strolled through the gap in the garden wall. Checked her back door, windows for spotters. Security camera nose down, limp as Harry. Tapped toilet door out of politeness. New lock shining in fading light, turned smoothly, as expected. Inside, cool, no more nervous than if using anyone else's toilet without permission. Closed, locked the door. Didn't switch on the light. Placed the mug on the ground, let adrenaline take over. Hands knew what to do without instructions. Lifted the lid off the cistern, placed it against the door, probed the cold water, lifted the Package out holding its narrow end. Counted to twenty, pressed the flush. Worked. Dripping Package didn't feel full, not hard. Decided, after cursing myself for not bringing a towel to wrap the Package in, to put it under my cardigan. Guessed the contents were probably compacted paper of some sort. Replaced cistern lid exactly as before. Knew it wouldn't stop them – whoever they were, discovering it was missing, but at least they'd know it was a neat job. Flushed the toilet again for good measure.

Dried Package lying in a towel on the kitchen draining board. Instinct warned me to wait a while, do something else. A clear head will be needed for the task.

The ideal distraction. Pile of clothes asking to be ironed on a table beside ironing board in back downstairs room. Verified all were washed – have ironed dirty clothes before. Have become a fastidious ironer. Ironing was more than having presentable clothes. It was my contribution to the global war on creases and wrinkles. Reality should, I believe, where possible, be smooth, crease-free because creases were blips, distortion in the cosmos. Not many agreed with me, nor were active in the cause. Didn't matter. The ironing board was one of two battlegrounds I fought on daily. The other, my bed, where rebellious sheets creased themselves as I slept. Was forever smoothing them out and remaking the bed. Wasn't far off changing sheets every day.

Usual routine. Began with shirts, non-button side first, working around to button-side, watching magic flow from the iron. Underpants? Big sigh. An unsolved problem in the global war. Impossible to iron into submission. Creases always remained. Was only waiting for the day the subject came up on talk-radio. Would have plenty to say on that subject. Would also raise the question of sheet-ironing. How to iron wide sheets on narrow ironing board?

Still, these were small irritants compared to the nuclear pleasure of watching the iron gliding over cranky creases and wretched wrinkles, magically smoothing them out of existence, restoring smooth nature and warm serenity. Binged on ironing that evening. Ironed t-shirts, folded sheets, towels mounted in unsteady piles.

Checked all external doors, windows were locked. Turned off all lights before bringing the Package down to the basement. Paused before the basement door, listening to the night's groans and growls. Locked the door. Centred the Package on the small worktable. Took photos. Package too well wrapped to be opened and closed without it being noticed. A no-going-back, crashing-through moment.

Quickly took a sharp knife, carefully slit-slashed the plastic wrapping. Two further, lighter plastic wrappings, tightly sealed with more tape. Slit-slashed these too. Fingers finished the job.

Six white envelopes tightly bound by thick elastic bands now lying on the table. More photos. Slid the contents of the first envelope onto the table. Counted twenty machine-stacked five-hundred-euro notes inside. When all six envelopes were open, sixty thousand euro sat on the table winking at me.

Stroked my chin. More surprised by the amount than the fact that it was money. Standing up, moved away from table, leaned against the wall, stared.

Big questions, little questions. Big questions too big to answer, but not to ask. Who did the money belong to? Why was it there? A bribe? A set-up? What did the plumbers have to do with it? Did the Politician know about it? Did she put it there?

Only two things clear. It wasn't for me, and I wasn't supposed to find it. Felt miffed about that. Sort of a personal affront.

Little questions weren't any easier. Why sixty thousand? A percentage? Of what? Why five-hundred notes? Why white envelopes? Why an outside toilet? Did she/they not trust inside toilets? And why a toilet?

Two things clear, though. There hadn't been any spider webs around the top of the cistern which meant the lid had been moved recently. Probably the Brat's plumbers, meaning it was all about the Politician and her new job. Secondly, new unique dilemma. Expose or protect the Politician? Or yeah, why not? Keep the money, say nothing, see what happens. Tremendously exciting. Scary too, but exciting scary. Someone would come looking for the money and wouldn't be polite asking for it. Felt a kind of strange thrill. Life had grown predictable. Yeah, missed having a real challenge. Surely a sign I was moving on, getting better, seeking more. Boy, wouldn't the Shrinkage love to know all this? Rewarded myself by popping an old pocket-mint into my mouth. Sucked with relish.

Turning it over in my head, another surprising realisation. The money was already putting down roots.

Ownerless money is never homeless. Even the Brat knew that. No stray coins ever survived long in this house.

Popped a second stale mint into my mouth. Fresh mouth, fresh mind. What would I spend it on? No shortage of worthy causes. Pay for expensive boarding school for the Brat? Excellent idea. Pay for his mother to find a husband? Less excellent, still good. Pay for a new identity for myself? Best so far. Pay for a quickie euthanasia for the two auld ones in hospital? Moderately good idea. Pay to fill in the gap in the wall? Also, excellent. Pay, no bribe, the Shrinkage to leave me alone? Beyond excellent but mightn't work. Maybe, even pay for a warmer hut for the Guard? Only good idea if it's fully on her side. Re-wrapped, re-sealed the Package, water-boarded it in a basin of water, survived. Brought it up to curtained toilet, fitted neatly into cistern there.

Coming back downstairs, only minutes later, couldn't believe my eyes. The outline of a figure behind the frosted glass of the front door. Knocker clanged three times, thumping the door like a policeman's baton hitting a wooden head. Christ, sure sign of a stranger with malevolent intent. Amazed they could be that quick. Just coming down the stairs, planning to go to the pet shop on a special mission.

Froze. Brain going into awestruck. Commanded myself to think. Jesus, think faster. Blew air into the fist. Only chance is to act really fast. Yeah, that's it. Best way to confront aggressor is with even greater aggression and surprise. Use resulting confusion to seize control of the situation, see if escape is necessary.

Crouched low up to the door, quiet as the Brat on the prowl, reached up for the door-handle, twisted it, stood up, threw the door open, about to roar, 'Fire, fire!' as loud as possible, when... Irena? Irena standing there, deadpan demure as only she can be, hand frozen in the act of banging the knocker again. Absolutely no reaction on her face. No surprise, no shock, nothing. Could've been starkers with a feather sticking out of my bum for all the difference it would've made. She lowered her eyes, briefly glanced up at me. Remembered, she could never look me in the face.

"Irena," my mouth spat out as the roar sinkholed. Blond, slim, peachy-skinned Irena. Desirable to all Harry's, except mine, even when she ironed, correction, tried ironing, underpants. Someone somewhere had given that girl those eyes. Hoped fervently they were suffering for it.

Stood aside meekly, guessing she was back because the Brat's mother or the Politician told her to. I'd told her I could manage on my own, she needn't come any more. Real reason? She ironed too much, too well, tidying away unfindably. Took it extremely well, helped by generous tip.

Closing the door behind her, noticed Guard's big country mug filling the hut's side window. Know well what you're thinking, bucko.

Irena hung up her jacket and bag, went to the kitchen to fetch the cleaning things. Me, stuck in hallway-shock, pondering who hadn't and who had just entered my house. Enigma Irena, never-smiling, Irena smirked instead. Like the Guard's nod, smirk was adaptable, suiting most occasions. Never asked her about it because all she'd do was smirk back at me. Her smirking could even be contagious. I'd feel pressure building on one side of mouth, bottom lip trembling, as it attempted to copy her. Smirking and nodding, two new skills I was honing. As long as I remembered not to try talking to her, we got along fine.

"The middle toilet needs a good clean," I said to her artfully as I put on my coat and hat to go out. Free security check for the you-know-what in the cistern. She'd clean, flush, and this would be the test. Will find out when back from the pet shop.

Chapter 16

The Tortoise

Tortoise rental is not common in the pet shop trade, as the shopkeeper kept repeating. Still, he agreed to rent one to me once I'd bought tortoise insurance. The tortoise came in a box with holes in the sides. Between food, box, rental, insurance, I could've bought the bloody creature.

On the bus home opened the box to study his ugliness. Bulbous eyes, deadbeat attitude, terrific study in self-pity. Even if it couldn't move in the small box, it still managed to give the impression it wasn't bothered. Woman beside me also studied it.

"It's lovely, isn't it?" she said.

Said nothing, angled the box to give her a better view.

"My daughter had one, years ago, looked after it and all, loved it, really loved it, but, you know, they've no feelings. They're not very affectionate." Glanced at me. Ramrod straight, knees to attention. "Is it a present for a little one?"

"It's rented for a party."

"Oh." She made a face. "Do they do that now? I never heard of that."

"Yes," I lied. "It's big in Japan. They rent everything over there." Was about to long-list shocking things they rented in Japan, but thought no, it's a short bus trip.

"And what name have you given it? Are you allowed give it a name?"

"Insurance."

"Oh." She looked away, unsure if I was joking "My daughter called hers Letitia because it liked lettuce."

"Sprinter."

"Pardon?"

"That would have been a better name. Too late now."

"Oh, I see."

"It's a racing tortoise. The Japanese breed them. Tortoises are very big in Japan."

"Do they now?" she murmured dubiously, the conversation getting too bizarre for her taste. She organised herself to get up. "It takes all sorts, doesn't it? This is my stop. Best of luck with Sprinter, I mean Insurance."

Got up to let her out.

Back to base, Irena gone. No worries. Package safe. Went straight to the Politician's outdoor toilet, freeing Insurance in a corner on the concrete floor. Scattering bits of greenery, brownery and foodery around it. Put two bits of the box on the ground to block the tortoise from escaping. Gathered a pile of leaves, twigs, pulled a few weeds and threw the lot into the tortoise's corner. Closed door. Creature would be safe at least until the Brat discovered it.

Just back in the kitchen, making a cup of tea when front door burst open, the Brat and a clatter of school-clones fall into the hall, laughing, jeering, shoving. Ordinarily, a provocation, but had been forewarned. Brat-mother left a note saying he would be bringing some friends back to the house before being collected to go to someone's birthday party. Colonel Thoughtful had bought a big bottle of Coke for them.

Dull thuds as schoolbags hit the hall floor. Unkindly hoping they'd all knock each other out. Heavy stair-pounding up to inspect amazing curtained toilet and agree old geezer was mad. But mad geezer quite pleased. Another free security check. Guffaws, snort-laughter, pee-silences. Colonel Flush listening for missed bowl pee-sounds. No flushes. Disappointing.

Wildebeest charge back downstairs. Ends abruptly when they spot old geezer at the bottom of the stairs, grinning like a hungry Dracula. Clearly forewarned by the Brat what to expect.

"Hello boys," I greeted them as mordantly as I could, licking my lips.

"Granddad," hypocrite-Brat cooed in nice-boy tone he put on when pretending we were happy-families, but his expression pleaded for leniency, to play along.

Looked them over. Four specimens fidgeting under Colonel Coke's gaze. Smiled inanely, showing more teeth than I usually do. All perfectly gooky, mousey, ill-formed.

Any optimism about the future of mankind badly misplaced.

"We're just here 'til Dan's mam picks us up. We're going to Chris' party." Pause. "OK?" Turned to his goons. "Come on, guys, into the front room, close the door."

Impressive pile of school bags, coats, monster jackets on the hall floor. Must all be taught this in school. Could hear teacher getting them to repeat, 'Floors are good. Hooks are bad. Floors are...' No surprise none of them knew how to say hello, let alone introduce themselves.

Back in the kitchen, prepared five big tumblers of fizzing coke, brought the tray to the hall. Behind the front room door all manner of squeals, grunts, scuffles, giggles, music, breathless competitive talking which stopped abruptly when I knocked on the door.

Brat positioned himself at barely opened door, blocking entry, squinting at me with his usual pity-contempt expression, which changed to suspicion when he saw the five big tumblers of Coke.

"Yeah?" he asked, greed and suspicion struggling for mastery.

"It's not poison," I said, barging in, forcing him aside.

Three of them on the ground in the middle of a wrestling or rugby scrum. One was sitting on the sofa and looking fearful of being dragged into the melee.

"Ah, boys," I said brightly. "A drink for thirsty work?"

They gathered around, silently taking their tumblers. One said thank you. To show my appreciation, I asked, "What's your name?"

"Eh…" Throat sounds, but no words. Had he forgotten it? He looked at the Brat for help. Obviously, the Brat had terrified them about the house-owner.

Put the sardine at ease. Went down on my hunkers to be at his level. "You don't have to answer if you don't want to. I only ask because you're the only one who said thank you, which in my book is good. Thank you," I said emphatically.

"Barry," he blurted out in a whiney voice.

One by one the others then said, "Thank you." and drank noisily, glancing at the Brat for leadership.

"Anyone ever see a wild tortoise?" I asked.

Silence. Oh, no, did I get it wrong? Weren't all kids curious? Then the one with matted hair and pale skin said, "My cousin has one."

"My sister had one but it died."

"My mam hates them."

"Yeah, they've got big shark teeth," another said. All giggled.

Looked at the only one who hadn't spoken. Another shoulder-less waif with an odd nose which I felt a kinship with. Spotted me staring at it, blushed.

"Thanks for the coke, Grandad," the Brat jumped in, slamming the empty tumbler on the tray I was still holding, his expression saying clear off.

Turned to wide-eyed Barry, still not recovered from the shock of introducing himself. "Don't mind him," I said in a confidential tone. "I'm not anyone's Grandad. He's mad."

"Eh ..." Brat-hand on my arm. Dangerous. "We have to... do some homework now... eh, a group project before Dan's Mam calls. Isn't that right, guys?"

"There's one out in the toilet in the garden next door," I said innocently. "Saw it there this morning. Amazing looking creature. I put a box around it to keep it from going. Thought you might like to see it. It's very rare to see one around here," I added. "Probably escaped from the zoo. Think it's a Japanese tortoise."

Brat led the charge out the door. "Where's the key?" he shouted back at me.

"It's not locked!" I shouted back. "Be gentle with it. And show it to the kids in the lane." There were always kids in the lane. "They'd love to see it too."

Went up to the back bedroom at the top of the house to watch. Few leaves on the trees so I could see. They crowded around the toilet door. The miserable creature was poked, prodded, passed from hand to hand with fascinated disgust. Even some stroking, except for Barry who refused to touch it. They insisted, pushed it at him, he recoiled. Back and forth, jeering, cheering, laughing. Poor tortoise had a rough few moments. Barry scarred for life. Then the Brat brought it out to the lane for the smaller lane-kids to look at it. While out there the others went into the toilet, one by one, closing the door. Just what I wanted. Thank the Lord for prudishness.

Brat returned, followed by two small girls and smaller boy, all standing around the tortoise-toilet. Was certain they'd all end up using it. Bell ringing with insistence. Cheery mummy at the door, gushing gratitude, gave me a headache. Left Insurance in the kitchen overnight to make friends with Maximus and Annabella as a reward. Nice plan, Colonel Strategic.

Chapter 17

First Meeting with Retired Detective

P ancake restaurant on quiet side street off the main road. Nice nothing-street, one house at this end, empty parking spaces. His suggestion. Afterwards regretted agreeing. Turned out Retired Detective Fahy was a pancake addict. Physique in transition from police-plump to senior-sagging. Suspect he used our meetings as cover to indulge his habit. Never saw him eat anything else.

Every time the door opened a mid-December wind tried blowing footpath leaves and cold into the restaurant. Bitty clouds chasing each other across imperious blue sky having too much fun to care about chilly customers.

Retired Detective, sitting at table near the toilet door, far end, well away from door, quiet enough for secretive quasi-criminal discussion. Already stuffing his face.

"Colonel Corley," he said without standing up, smiling, nor showing any enthusiasm. Inner sigh, another title-nerd.

"Fahy," I greeted him, shoving hand so far at him he had to drop his fork to shake it. Day's special half-finished. Smoked salmon pancake, maybe. Shameless at being caught eating in front of first-time potential new client. Gestured me to sit down, carried on eating. Neatly placed my coat and hat on the empty chair beside me.

"You like hats?" gruff voice asked, as if picking on obtuse subject was how retired policemen always opened conversations, giving early proof of observation and interrogation skills.

"I do," I replied briskly, wanting to show a healthy man could wear a hat without shame. "I'm told you own property," I said to move the small chat away from me.

"Don't believe everything you hear," grumpy voice, shifting posterior, chair groaning.

Sphinx-nod. "Don't worry, I don't." First feeling I was a suspect in some investigation. Did all retired detectives assume, on a first meeting, client had something to hide? My coffee arrived, good taste. Crutch as I waited patiently until he finished the bloody pancake.

"I hear you want something," he said as last fork hovered between plate and gob.

"And you'll tell me what's possible and what isn't?"

"That I will, that I will."

"Good." So, told him what I wanted and why, highlighting non-experience of first-love, childhood. Bull-eyes, closed-mouth, good listener. Advised me to lower my voice. Silence when I finished, so assumed he wanted to hear about money. Gave him my terms. No daily rate or expenses, job fee only. Give me a choice between two or three identities, I would select one, forty percent then, balance when presented with full biographical details and necessary papers.

Saw him staring at non-thumb. "What happened to your thumb?"

Lifted it for free viewing. "It deserted me."

"Did it?" He thought about that. "Is it sore?"

"Sometimes."

He pursed his lips. Does he want more?

"It's just like... I never had it. You get used to it. Not great for swinging out of trees."

No smile.

"OK," he said, leaning elbows on table, getting business-like. "You're serious about this?"

"Is anything more serious than deadly serious?"

Gravedigger-nod. "That's what I'm afraid of."

"Why's that?"

Pulled in his stomach, took solemn breath, putting his empty plate on a different table. "Your wife is a good reason. She's a government minister and you're well-known yourself." He glanced around. "People in here, I've seen them looking at you. You can't just invent a new identity like that."

Didn't bother me, why should it bother him? "You don't have to worry about that. It won't be your problem."

Hard stare. "Yeah? Assuming you get this new identity, what will you do with it?"

"Use it. I intend to become someone else, another person with my own childhood, my own past..." Didn't welcome his doubts. I leaned forward too, forcing him to sit back, and whispered for effect. "Now, are you going to help me or not?"

Waitress arrived. He ordered a banana and chocolate pancake.

"Oh, I'll help you," he said matter-of-factly, sounding like he'd already decided and would be keeping an eye on me, as well. First hint of customer care, I thought. "This is what I can do for you. I will get you the information you need and when you make your choice, I can fill in the details. I will not – I repeat, will not forge any documents and I will not – I repeat, will not do anything illegal. But," he paused ominously, "I can give you the name of someone you can approach to see about getting documents, but that will be none of my business. As far as I'm concerned, I am providing you with a research service for personal purposes."

Only then noticed how tense he'd become, eyeballing me like he still wasn't sure I wasn't a suspect in an investigation.

"You understand me? What you do with it is none of my business. And I don't want my name mentioned to anyone about this, ever, and that includes your wife and family... OK?"

I was as emphatic as he was. "I have no wife." His eyes didn't flicker, so he knew, good.

"Are we clear about this? Because that's the way it has to be."

Nodded. "You're sure these associates of yours are reliable?"

"They'll be as reliable as your money," he answered without a trace of irony, "if they're paid on time. They're not exactly people you'd bring home to your mother... but you'll have no problems with them if you stick to your side of the bargain. And all that business will be separate from my fee."

Sat back feeling deflated. Should have felt happy after all this. Excited. Realising a dream. First steps towards a new life. Instead, felt gloomy, like I was being dragged along an unapproved road, with a grubby, greedy, untrustworthy taxi driver.

"You don't seem to have enjoyed your job," I said, wanting to inflict minor social injury. Just shrugged his shoulders. "Any preference where you want these guys to come from?"

I brushed that aside. More important, "There has to be a first-love story in it," I said, deciding if his wasn't good enough, I'd use Jean McBabe's.

Chapter 18

Before School Reunion

Brat-mother, young woman, was the only person I occasionally confided in. Mrs Hand as well, of course, though possibly she didn't see it as a confidence, being so adept at taking all of life the same way, phlegmatically. Confided in the young woman – not that young, the Brat was nine, ten or eleven – over tea and scones on a day the enigmas of life needed sharing, about Jean McBabe. Showed her the picture.

Thin-faced, tight-hair, gardener's jersey, scrawny figure. She listens sympathetically, even if she'd gab about it to the Shrinkage. But, sometimes, even that didn't matter. I needed defusing. All these encounters took something away and left something behind.

"That will go with her to the grave," she said sitting across from me, drinking black tea from a green metal teapot with collapsible handle she'd just bought for no good reason. Spoke without hesitation, with uncharacteristic assurance. Her self-assurance surprised, pleased me. She needed more of that, especially with the Brat who got his way far too often.

"The only way she could've gotten over it was if she'd had another fling just after you and she obviously didn't."

Correction. After someone not me. Anyway, interesting observation. Scrutinized her face over rim of effeminate dainty flowers mug, trying to see where that came from.

"Dad, stop looking at me like I've said something weird." She held her mug tightly between her hands. "That was her mistake."

"How do you know that?" Inner female mind, foreign territory to me.

"All women know that," she asserted, hinting at sacred sisterhood. Turned her head to stop me staring at her. Her look meant she feared the conversation was heading where it often did – the origin of the Brat. Bugged me I knew nothing about the Brat's father, and she didn't like me bringing it up.

"Bitter experience," she said, guessing what I was thinking. Drank her tea, tight-mouthed.

Surge of unexpected pride in her fortitude. Almost got up to give her a hug. But hugging was problematic, even if she was quite huggable.

Photo still lying on the table between us. She picked it up again.

"Even if it's not you, I think it looks a bit like you. Don't you think?" Troublemaking look on her face.

"Amazing, isn't it? There's definitely a resemblance with Thomas. Mam will want to see it."

Cleared my throat. God, save me from interfering women. Convivial tea-mood rapidly vanishing.

"Anyway, we've got to get you ready." She finished her tea, stood up.

"What?" Go where? I didn't like the sound of that. "What for? You can forget it if you think I'm going to that bloody hospital again."

Apparently, I'd already agreed to go to some school reunion. Why would I agree to such an absurd idea? Vague recollection of some kind of discussion about it, though. And I hadn't had much company the last few days. Let myself be hustled into clean shirt, sports jacket, polished shoes, and car. All happened swiftly only remember wondering if this was what going to school for the first time was like? Felt I had to complain.

"I won't know anyone," I muttered as she drove downhill and waited to turn right. "And I've no idea where I went to school."

Shook her head dismissively. High on self-delusion, she had me well under control. "Doesn't matter. They know you and they all know what happened so..."

"That's what I'm worried about. All smug faces thinking they know more about me than I do, and I won't know a thing about them. It's not fair," I said in my best whinny Brat-imitation.

"Arragh whist, will you?"

I stared at her. Guessing that was exactly how Mrs Hand would speak if she was really annoyed, which I'd never seen. "They'll all be very understanding. Just wait and see. You'll have a great time."

"Hm… I suppose I could pretend I know them all."

Laughed. "Isn't that what you do all the time, Dad? You're great at it." She tapped my knee. "Have some fun, relax. You're young."

Glanced sharply at her, wondering had she let the mask slip?

Pulled in at a taxi rank in front of the hotel on the quays. Time and traffic hadn't been kind to the building, beaten into three-star submission. Young woman leaned across, undid my seat belt, opened the door and pushed me out. "In you go," she said.

"Are you not coming in with me?"

"Sorry, no girls allowed. Boys only."

Gathered guts, instincts, wits, courage into a tight ball in the lift up to the third floor. When it's unavoidable, I make a decision. I can stand around, drink, chat about nothing with non-auld ones as good as the next man. Reminded myself I wasn't the only person in the world fighting the Onslaught. There could be millions of Onslaught-warriors going through what I'm going through right now. Might even spot one or two tonight. What will they look like? Faced the dimly lit lift mirror. Like you, you fool. Get in there.

The Delvin Room.

Scatterings of suited, jacketed, generally bony-faced, pot-bellied, emaciated, grey-haired, balding men. Standing, leaning, lounging near a long bar in a low-ceilinged function room. Drinking, chatting, joking, sizing up the changes. Empty comfy armchairs in small lounge area over to the bar's left.

"There's Dommo!" a voice called out. Some heads turned, others didn't. Here and there hello's, brief lulls in conversations. Strode boldly over to nearest group, smiled, introduced myself, shook hands with everyone, including a woman, looked them in the eye to forestall glances, questions. Keen to make a good impression. Asked about their health, happiness. Told them I was grand, enjoying life. Smiles, gracious engagements, muted bemusement. A good start.

Warmest smile from the woman. Swimmer's shoulders, dark-rimmed glasses, constantly taking off, putting back on. Standing beside round-faced, bald, husband. Impressive hands, strong grip when we shook. Clatter of jangly bangles on her wrists.

"You like them," she asked me, coquettish tone.

"Hurumpf.' How would she feel if I wore bells around my neck? Husband quiet, only talked when spoken to.

Odd. Wasn't it supposed to be boys-only? Not that it mattered. All-comers, all circumstances. Shrinkage-survivors can handle it all. Vibe between woman, husband, two others, felt odd. Polite standoffishness wasn't all because of me. And she kept patting husband's arm as if afraid he'd disappear.

Studied her while husband answered question about tax case last year. Good heavens, big. Then it hit me. Big shock. Not a woman at all, couldn't be. She was a man, dressed as a woman. No doubt about it. Face too long, too bony, too craggy, body all bulk, no shapeliness, big feet. Next thought, I swear – what a great pity Brat not here to see what he'd be like if he wanted to be like the Politician.

Fair dues to her. Presented well. Plucked eyebrows, impressive eyelashes, eyeliner, powdered face, elegant attire. Dark tweedy skirt down to ankles, dark auburn blouse, glistening gold broach, beaded necklace. Dark curl-profusion hair to neck. When she swung her head, a wave of scented air wafted into my face.

What in the name of holy bread baskets is going on here? Clear gender-traitor or *agent-provocateur* from the Shrinkage in new absurd experiment. Mentioned she'd consulted 'counsellors' (code for Shrinkage) before coming or a genuine case of gender-transfer.

"Yes, indeed," artful demure smile on her face, eyes round, earnest tone. "After the final operation… two years ago, yes almost two, phew," hand caressing brow. "The end of a long journey. Snip, snip, boys, you know." Jokey smile, scissors-fingers. "Anyway …" Now fingering her throat. "Which actually began in boarding school. I mean the dawning, didn't it, Brian? You remember?" Tapped his arm. "Of course, you do. Anyway, my counsellor said, 'Pat, you should definitely go tonight, not as Patrick Twomey, but as Patricia Twomey… as yourself, not as someone they think you were or should be'." She gazed hopefully at the frozen faces in front of her, "Ain't I entitled to be here?" Slightly harder tone. Fleeting glance in my direction. "As entitled as anyone else!" Finished her black pint, cheeks slightly flushed. "I have to say I am really proud of you all for welcoming me…" Another tap on Brian's arm. "Especially you. Dominic, so brave and famous now, looking fit and healthy in civvies, isn't he, boys?"

Fake smiles all around. Why did she keep glancing at me? Did she think she knew me, aside from this reunion thing?

Time to speak up, Shrinkage-suspicions to the fore, determined not to be fooled again in front of these strangers. Shrinkage could be checking my attitude to gender-transfer. Why not? They'd tried everything else.

"Splendid, Patricia, so important to be yourself, your *true* self – once, eh, you know who you are." Quizzical looks on mute faces. Question time. "Where is it now?" I asked, friendly-like. "Do you know?"

"Pardon?" Elegant surprise. "Where is what?" she asked.

Leaning forward, whispered. Her mouth dropping, shocked eyes. A few moments before she could speak.

"No one knows where my thumb is either," I said to ease her discomfort. "I asked lots of people, but they couldn't tell me. If I'd been given the choice, I don't think I'd have said cut it off. And not want to have kept it or know where it is. I mean, how many thumbs do we have?" Studied her reaction closely. Shrinkage trained its stooges well, usually prepared for many scenarios, but they couldn't have predicted this. So, her reaction would tell me a lot. Staring at the parquet floor, speechless. Possibly positive sign wasn't Shrinkage but needed to be sure. "What's your counsellor's name?"

Her Adams' apple bopped up and down. Put up a defensive hand. "My counsellor? Why? Why do you want to know that?" Incredulity building in voice. "Do you think… he has it?"

Possibility-nod. "Wouldn't surprise me. They are not normal people… but I guess you know that." Quick look around faces. "Stands to reason." I stood back, drank some of my black stuff. Guy stroking his cheek with a thumb, stopped when he saw me looking at it. Brian looked mortified.

"But I don't miss it," she insisted loudly, stamping a foot on the ground. "God, are you trying to… That's gross, Dominic, utterly gross." She had a hankie in her hand, dabbing her neck. "I'm so disappointed in you. Really, what a…"

"Is it Doctor Canoe? He's well-known." The faintest glimmer in her eyes would be enough. "Or Papp. Do you know him?"

Nervous laugh into hankie, hand touching dark curls. "No," she said firmly. Drank more stout. "Darling, this is tiring," she said to Brian. "Let's move to another group."

Chapter 19

School Reunion

More or less left alone after that. Patricia was in more demand than I. All I had to do, as groups merged and scattered, was look at old photos passed around, listen to stories, laugh at how people looked after all those years. Only after the meal, speeches, plenty of pints consumed, and more to come, that attention turned to me.

My table had died, run out of words. Listless expressions all around. About to leave, when loud-mouth Ted, chief buffoonist during the speeches, barrelled over, banging the table, thumping me on the back.

"Dominic!" he cried into my ear, drink making him think I was deaf. "Come on over here to some real guys and tell us what's going on." Grabbing my arm, almost dragged me off to a new group crowded around armchairs, two long low tables covered in black and white pints. Eight guys, numbers increasing all the time. Ted bulldozed into the middle, pulled me down into a seat beside him, put a pint in my hand, tapped glasses, arm around my shoulders. Stared back at him. Who on earth was this bald, hollow-cheeked, ravaged looking guy? No idea, but drink kept him going at a roaring pace all evening.

"Now, come on, you auld bollix," he grinned red-faced at me. "I know this is all a big con. There's nothing wrong with you. Jesus, look at you." Leering into my face. "Fuck sake, it's me, Ted, you wanker. Best mates for years." To reinforce the point he released my shoulders, leaned sideway, gave me a good thump on the back. Guffawed, took another swig of his pint, nudged me to do the same and studied my neutral expression. "I can't fucking believe it. Look at you, the same old scrawny long-legged bollocks with a big snoozer." Grabbed it before I could stop him, tweaked it like a door-handle. "There," he sniggered as if that would surely bring me back to whatever. "Jesus, you remember the time Banjo hit Rooney on the face in class?" Clapped his hands fiercely, turned towards me, slapped me on both cheeks. Loud fish-smacking sound. Gasps all around. Stung like blazes. Some peals of laughter.

Three assaults in a couple of minutes. Must've been brutal school. If I didn't do something soon, I'd be black and blue in half an hour. Readied myself to deliver a lesson to this heart-on-sleeve buffoon. Minutes later, Ted turned away to belittle a small guy named Titch. Grabbed the legs of his stool, gave it a good yank.

"Caaawww!" Like a seagull falling into the sea. Toppled backwards, sprawled amid legs, wooden and human. Loud comeuppance cheer.

"Fight, fight!" chorus began. Ted got up, uninjured, embarrassed, breathless, went to throw a pint over me. Frightened crowd pushed back to get away. Chaos. Drink spilled on clothes, floor. Ted said not worth wasting good drink on a nutter. If he had, the whole place could have started throwing prize pints. Might suit Brat.

Madness abated after a while, random face squeezed behind two others, asked, "What's it like in there, Dommo?" tapping the front of his forehead, not the side. Big difference. "Must be ..."

"Yeah, go on, Dommo. Tell us," more drink-filled voices. Eager, animated faces, bleary-eyed now. Wasn't used to such direct honest curiosity. Hubbub died away. Ted belching like a cow.

"It's like... it's like..." Booze rushing around inside the brain urging skittishness. No. I insisted on proper answer. "...trying to remember something from before you were born."

"Atta boy!"

"That's great."

"Good man."

Crowd still laughing when Ted's voice outshouted all others. "Do you know what they did to you, Dommo?" Malicious question.

"Ssshh!"

"That's going too far, Ted."

"Ciúnas!"

Wrong. The question didn't bother me at all. As long as it didn't come loaded with the Shrinkage brand on it.

Before I could answer, commotion broke out behind me. Patricia arrived, worse for drink, dragging, not Brian, but a chair behind her. "Shove over, out of my way," kept calling out. Voice deeper, mouth and eyes agape, necklace back to front, broach hanging loose like it had been tugged at, front of jacket pushed back either side of bosom, legs straining against tight skirt, curls slightly askew, enough to suspect a wig. This the same Patricia? Muscled her way un-ladylike into the middle of raucous crowd, forcing general realignment of bodies, pints.

"Ah, you fuckin' idiot, Pat."

"The women's army has arrived."

"You're a right bitch."

"Get off me."

"Only lads here."

"Patricia the striper," Ted roared. "Strip! Strip!"

Patricia didn't mind a bit. Settled herself in front of the table diagonally across from me. Two pints put themselves in front of her. Waved a dismissive hand at baying crowd, friendly-voiced, "Ah, yis are all a load of wankers, lads."

No one demurred, but almost-sober Dommo can't believe the change before his eyes. Didn't she know who, what she looked like now, what she was? Like the Retired Detective said, once you do it, you can't go back. Hmm, suspicious again. Was this a twist to new Shrinkage-experiment? Switch back, see how patient reacts? Booze-shortened period of reflection. Impetuous decision to meet all challenges, show them, even with booze, I remained a formidable opponent. Mob still demanding I speak.

"Come on Dommo, tell us."

"Don't be stupid. He doesn't remember."

"Course he does."

Booze now in command. Sat me up, straightened jacket, outstretched arms, exclaiming, "You want the Explanation?" Pause, repeated myself for the cheering booze-deaf who'd cheer at passing flies if they saw them.

"Ssshh!" Glasses tapped for silence. Sneaky glance across at blissful Patricia. I stood up suddenly, stretched to full height, even tippy-toes, pulled up belt, loosened arms, spread legs, hands on hips, raised left arm, slowly pointed accusing finger at Patricia.

"Ask her," bellowed Colonel Fluttered. "She knows everything. She'll give you the Shrinkage Explanation." Self-nodding head felt strong, powerful, invincible. 'Get yourself out of that, Ms Patricia Shrinkage,' I said to myself.

Don't understand what happened next.

"Yeah, Pat," random voices jeered. "You tell us. Weren't you in Bosnia as well?"

"Different unit, wasn't it?"

"Don't try denying it."

What are they ranting about?

"Yah, he's right. Go on Pat, tell us what happened." Global head-nodding, global sniggering, global readiness to pick on anyone.

"He ran away," Ted roared. "She doesn't know anything. The inside story and no bullshit, ye hear me," Ted roared again.

I was lost.

Well past womanhood, manhood, some new in-between state. Patricia was rubbing her face with new-gender impatience, unaware she was taking smudges of make-up off each time. Aligning her pints of stout in orderly parade-ground line. Face streaked with red-Indian war-paint.

"The explanation!" she shouted, hands shaking in front of her. "Ye want the explanation? I'll... give ye the fuckin' explanation... and you, Ted, shut your gob or I'll shut it for you."

Cheers, boss. Patricia working through a pint first. Random voices still at her.

"Weren't they mad with him?"

"Found the graves in the forest."

"Dommo had the photos."

"Shut up, all of ye," Patricia shouted. "If ye want the real story, shut up and let me talk, will ye?" Voice now at ninety percent masculine.

She looked around, as if distracted, by a moment of clarity, patted the hair, dabbed paper hankie on war-paint, removed lippy stout-foam.

Colonel Fool, still not understanding turn of events, getting back to grinning, nodding in agreement with everyone and everything. Downing pints as they appeared magically, rapidly catching up with him. Said in my head, 'Yeah, Patricia, go on, tell us what the Colonel did.' Would be funny to hear non-Shrinkage version. Could've sworn I was speaking to myself, but crowd around me erupted, heaving with manic laughter. Dismayed how sound travels, never trust beery air.

"Jaysus, that's brilliant, Dommo."

"Dommo in Alice in Wonderland."

"What'd he say? What'd he say?"

"Ya wanker, Dommo!" Ted roared, delighted with any incomprehensibility.

Should've left then. Should've shouted, 'Enough. I've had enough of these drunks. Gormless wasters and watermelons, the lot of ye!' Should've kicked something or someone on way out, while preparing lecture for Brat on the evils of school reunions. But, no longer myself, replaced by grinning idiot happy among idiots, and for one simple reason. The drunken mob treating me like one of them, like I belonged. A waster among wasters, and that didn't happen often.

"Want to see something?" I exclaimed, standing up again.

Groans, cheers. My God, half them think I'm going to show them Harry. Cretins. Held up non-thumb, turned slowly three hundred and sixty degrees. "Absent without leave," I declared, hoping for more laughs. Only shock, dismay.

"Jaysus, Dommo. Put it away."

"Ah fuck! Sit down."

"He's boasting."

Sat down, drink-happy, two-second chastened.

Patricia finishing lady-looks-reset.

"Get on with it, you gobdaw, before he starts again. We don't have all night."

"Put away the paint-stripper."

"Haha! Patricia the paint-stripper!" Foot-stamping chorus. "Patricia the…"

"OK, lads, OK. Ye asked for it. *Ciúnas*. It's a long story." Held up empty glass, shook it like a beggar looking for pennies. "I can't keep talking with an empty glass, lads."

"You're bleeding gorgeous, paint-stripper."

Leaned down over the low table in front of her like a field commander setting out battle-plans. "Now, this is how Corley set it up."

"Ja, mein General!"

Crowd surged forward expectantly, almost collapsing over the table like a rugby scrum, laughing heads bent low over the table.

"Move back, ye gobshites!" Patricia roared in exasperated *á la carte* voice. "I can't see meself… and clear those glasses away. Get me a pen and paper, and a pint. Then I'll show you what Dommo here did. The feckin' brilliance of it."

I stood up, squinting into the glare of the few spotlights in the ceiling, looking for the toilet sign. Long overdue relief. A hand tried to pull me back down, shook it off.

"Pee," I barked. "I've ordered a pee."

Overheard Patricia begin, "Pay attention, boys. There was a small convoy bringing supplies from the base camp. It was a transport detail, some explosives and a French explosives engineer…" Remember thinking hadn't heard that before.

Peed forever in unloved, white-tiled, wet-floored toilet. Didn't go back. Suspicions of Shrinkage trickery resurfaced. Wits regained control. Fell into the blissful silent taxi.

Chapter 20

Meeting Mrs Hand on the Street

I n the back garden the western sky was lifeless, whereas in the front garden the eastern sky was alive with promise and new-born light. Standing in the front garden, after a wasted hour in the kitchen waiting for Boris the elusive or the owners of the Package to appear. Frankly, the lack of interest by the owners of the Package in their property was shocking. The longer it nestled upstairs in the comfort of its own cistern, as innocent as the guinea pigs, the more attached to it I became. Dangerous, sure, but you have to work at being frightened by danger you can't see.

Ignoring the hut and its occupant – another crafty-eyed guard I wasn't curious about – I stood beside the silver birch with its slim branches and few nervous leaves. Looking askance at their fallen unburied comrades, shaking even without wind. Leaned over the black railing, looked up and down the street. Few cars lower end of the street. No auld ones. The auld ones who couldn't sleep and could tolerate mild cold had come and gone, drawn out of their homes by the magic of light and the hopefulness of hopelessness. Killing time before time killed them. Our little hill put off only the most infirm. A challenge most felt they should not ignore if they wanted to consider themselves still alive. If they couldn't manage our hill, they were ready. Packed bag, clean ironed souls or not. A near-windless, mid-morning to inspire apathy.

Cupped hands spied on the white-geese clouds sown into the blue sky. I described the habit of sky-staring to one of the Shrinkage – did ask what I was looking for. Thought it better I do it in the back garden. But she didn't understand the difference between eastern and western light, between light being born and dying light.

It used to bother me. The uncupped eye could see, and ignore, so much in a single ungrateful glance. While the cupped eye had to contend with narrow field of vision, to work for the little it saw. Always hungry for more. Felt freer sky-watching with cupped eyes, knowing there was more to be seen. Having the freedom to see it if I wanted. Unlike prisoners in the nearby jail who looked up from their cell windows and saw the same sky-patch every day. For this, I believed they deserved a discount on their sentence. Not being able to see more was already serious punishment.

Grass under the granite ledge of the bay window was winter-matted. Removed hands from face. Closed eyes for next thought. Blinders. I am especially attentive to blinders. Any age, any class, any blindness who regularly appear on our street, some training to be blind, others fully trained. Our neighbourhood, blinder-city: blinder homes, institutions, schools, training centres. When a blinder passes by, I pay tribute by closing my eyes, imagining what it's like to be blind. Often walked behind them to study how they cope. If I bump into one, I apologise, tell them I too am blind. Did this simply because blinders are notoriously intolerant of the sighted bumping into them. Especially admired their belief in invisibility. They didn't need to see the world to know it was there. Wasn't it a bit like that for me? Only in reverse. My world was not invisible, but it was to everyone else and I had to navigate daily between the two. Forced by the Onslaught every day to see myself in a world they saw, but I didn't. Lucky Blinders had their white canes. I only had my guts and instincts.

"I see she's back in business."

Opened my eyes. Mrs Hand on the footpath, holding onto the railing, taking a breather, as well she might, her supermarket foraging in her usual wheat-coloured bags on the ground beside her. Looked like she was in the mood for a chat.

Immediately stood up. Mrs Hand always exceptionally pleasing, elliptical way of talking, acceptance of the world and me as I am, never interfering, never offering advice. For the moment, shoulders still up to the job of transporting heavy bosoms. And an engaging rural dignity

I was secretly jealous of. The only person I was ever jealous of, not counting people who remembered their childhood. Hadn't chatted since the Guard was disagreeable to her.

"Yes," I said gleefully, approaching the railing, not too close. Wondering should I apologise for the Guard's boorishness last time.

"We're being overrun with politicians," Mrs Hand said.

"I suppose we are." Sometimes found myself using her expressions.

"There's one of them on the main road and one on Lindsay Road, and an ex one around there." She pointed to the street at the top of the hill. "And one here," she nodded at next door. Unlike the pesky postman, she never got the house wrong.

"You're absolutely right." What I also liked was that she understood everything, especially the distance I insisted on keeping between the Politician and myself.

"And are any of them any use?" she wondered.

"Are they ever?"

She thought about this a moment. "What are they all in it for?"

"Gosh, you're asking the wrong man," I replied, thinking afterwards she probably thought I *was* the right man to ask. Looking at me, perhaps wondering was I being evasive. Or, maybe 'gosh' had disorientated her. Don't think she'd heard me use it before. "Maybe power," I suggested. "And ego." The Politician's was like a shadow that hung over the whole area, especially at election time. Now, if

Boris had run for election, I'd have voted for him. Just looking into his eyes and you'd know what to do.

"That too."

"And they love having their picture taken."

"There's no beating them."

"And who did you vote for the other day?" I boldly asked, breaking new ground.

"Oh, they're all the same."

"Who did your husband vote for?"

"He passed away ten years ago."

"Oh, sorry to hear that."

Stared at the ground, shuffled her feet. "I can't remember. I think he voted for whoever I voted for."

"A wise man. And who was that?"

"Can't remember." Tone was matter-of-fact. "Maybe herself," she nodded towards next door.

"Has she been around that long?"

Then, out of the blue... "I was at a school reunion the other night."

"Were you now?"

"The drinking was brutal. Never seen anything like it. Grown men with families falling over themselves all night."

"Oh, aye! The country produces them all right."

"There was a woman there who'd been a man who'd been in the army. And she was talking about me... or said she was." More new ground. Being totally reckless.

Mrs Hand didn't even blink. "I suppose they have to talk about something." I nodded.

"Sure, wouldn't we all die if we didn't have something to talk about?" she added, nodding at her feet and looking like she was thinking what she'd say next.

"She kept forgetting she was a woman. Do you think is that possible?"

"They're all God's own creatures, like the rest of us."

Couldn't think of an answer to that. After a moment I looked up at the sky. "Do you think it will rain?"

"You never know," she wisely answered under a by now blue sky with not a cloud in sight.

Chapter 21

Communing Boris

Back inside, no right to expect Boris to appear this late. He was, I suppose, a function of his master as much as most people are. Boris' master, neighbour Maurice, on wife Dora's orders sometimes tied a bell around Boris' neck. They considered Boris shouldn't try to catch birds even though Maurice once told me Boris was an exceptional bird-catcher but didn't like eating them. Could believe it. The thrill would be in the hunt, not the kill. Killing was quick, easy. Hunting took skill. If Boris had gotten at the guinea pigs, he would probably have lifted one up in his mouth to see what it felt like, carried it off to a quiet place to study it. The guinea pig would probably have died, but Boris wouldn't have intended murder. Hardly a murderer. More a connoisseur.

Amazed me Dora could be a bird and cat lover at the same time. She had other causes too, but none like Boris. It showed such poor understanding of Boris's nature. More than once, I wanted to ask her, "How would you like it if I put a great big bloody bell around your neck?"

Anyway, the trees in my garden were the best around for birds. Maurice said when we were in my garden looking up at the trees, "The reason Boris is so interested in your garden is the birds the trees attract." Fortunately, Maurice didn't see the hurt his remark caused me. But Maurice didn't know the depth of my feelings for Boris until later when it was too late.

"You know, Dominic, I have an idea," he said later that day when I bumped into him on opening the lane door. "What about putting a recorder up there in that tree," pointing up near the top of the prunus tree, "and tape the bird singing. Dora would love that. She loves their singing." Maurice's lifeless eyes, pale face, showed an unusual flicker of excitement.

What a mad idea.

"Of course, Maurice, great idea. No problem," I added, looking up at the leafless tree wondering who's going to climb it.

Maurice even gave me a remote control to use with sheet of instructions for Colonel Moron on how to press the ON button, written in perfect handwriting by Dora. Climbed the tree himself, set it up, recorder wrapped in plastic, promised to replace tapes, batteries. No idea how this worked out because the stupid TV sometimes came on when I was trying to record the birds. Think the pesky Brat had something to do with it.

Remarkable thing, going back to the damn bell, was that Boris didn't scratch and meow in protest. Noble creature that he was, he accepted it. Went on with life. Took the bell off once, put it on the ground beside him to see what he'd done. Didn't do much. Didn't jump on it, scratch it, run around it excitedly meowing, 'Freedom', or jump for joy, like I would have if the Onslaught's bell around my neck was lifted. Looked at it a while, poked it with different paws, got the twinkly sound, looked at it again, walked off, came back in case it had moved. Once sure it hadn't, he walked off again. No prizes for guessing I was in total awe of this.

Desperate times, desperate measures. Even if it was way too late, put cage with scattily-rushing guinea pigs out on the grass in front of kitchen window, waited inside on favourite tile, third in front from the left. Distract myself, tried thinking why owner of the Package hadn't come looking for it, and what I'd do when he did. The longer it remained in my house the more ownership roots grew in me.

Suddenly, tinkle, tinkle. Singular hollow sound of small thin metal bell coming from the lane behind the wall. Nearer, yes, definitely nearer. Excitement rocketing. A happy Christian bell announcing a providential arrival. Rubbed hands in glee, struggled to contain myself. Stood in perfect stillness. Of course, it only meant Boris was in the lane or maybe moving onto someone else's wall, not that he was coming into my garden. Bell sounding very close, the strength of my will drawing him in.

Yes! Lo and behold, there he was. On top of the wall, glorious, graceful, indifferent, self-serving, cautious. The perfect picture of rusty intelligence. Aloof, alone, alert, wise beyond his DNA. Soft paw in front of elegant paw, picking his way along the narrow wall, as I pick my way every day along my own wall, trying to minimise the tinkle tinkle. Too much for me. I burst into applause, hopping up and down.

Boris saw me. Stopped, studied my rapture with knock-out detachment. I bowed, gestured like a courtesan. What was mine was his. He had the freedom of the garden and the guinea pigs in the cage waiting for him, and the birds and me.

Boris didn't check to see if there was a dog hiding in the bushes. Already knew. Lightly dropped from the back wall onto the green wheelie bin placed there for him. On the ground, went into wander-mode. Except, we both knew where he would end up. Reappeared from behind the bushes, moving sideways, casual, disinterested. Cat-craft at its best. There was a way to stalk guinea pigs that were protected in a cage. It was the same as if there was no cage, and he was going to do it the right way. Perfectionist at work. A lesson for us all. Boris duly completed his diversionary tactics. Checking any threatening smells, flies, grass causing his bell to tinkle only once.

None of this had the remotest effect on his prey, happily gambolling about under the boxes in the cage. Jittery-fashion, grazing like butterflies. Boris switched to the other side of the garden, closer, almost gliding over the grass, pausing, sniffing, sensing.

Finally arriving at his destination, Boris stared at the guinea pigs a long time through the slim metal grille, mesmerising eyes, getting the creatures in the mood for death. For their part, if they knew any of this, they did a good job hiding it. Continued mowing the grass like organic lawnmowers.

Guinea pigs duly mesmerised, Boris extended an exploratory paw testing the mettle of the metal, caressing it, maybe hoping the bars would melt under his touch. Bell tinkled a few times. Although behind the window, I could sense Boris' frustration. He walked around the cage, looking for ways in. A few times I'd seen him jump on top of the cage, checking for weak spots, but not today.

Eventually Boris got bored, wandered off to try his luck elsewhere. No matter. Later than usual, I'd had my philosophy lesson.

Chapter 22

Trip to Sligo

Something building up inside. Over the days, sensed a gathering disturbance in the hidden hinterland. Doubly strange because I had reasons to be happy. New identity in-train. Politician frequently out of the country, interfering somewhere else, posing for pictures. Saw Mrs Hand, other auld ones and Boris quite regularly. And nothing of the Brat, probably on school holidays or in hospital after breaking a leg.

Foreboding at its edgiest if I spent too long staring out the front or back windows. Same garden, same thoughts. Began wondering. Hard to believe. Was I falling out of love with the house? Not a divorce. Not enemies. Not even a row. Just a cooling of ardour, the beginnings of silent hostility? Unthinkable, unsettling. Remember, this was the tree which held me fast to where I belonged, to what I was sure of. Because if I lost it, or it lost me, how would I know who or what I was? And, at the back of all this, even if the Shrinkage never threatened me, I knew they'd be ready to send me back to hospital. *That* was unthinkable.

Test to see was I falling out of love. Short trip away from the house on my own. Took a bus to the northwest of the country. February sun low in the sky, angled wintery rays flashing in and out of the side of my eyes as bus rattled along. Dusk hitting the streets as we arrived in Sligo.

Next morning, walked out of the town along wide, slow-moving river, lulled by heavy rural tranquillity seeping from hilly banks, grey shades playing on the water. Sat on a bench near a canoe club, watching sleek arrows gliding through water, leaping oars like fingers playing a watery-piano. Thought about many things – new identity, new life, leaving Onslaught and Explanation behind.

Kids shouting, playing hurling further up in sloping field that ran down to the river. Moved closer to watch. Hitting small welted leather ball back and forth without apparent boredom. Until one of them asked me why I was staring at them.

"You're great hurlers, lads," Colonel Patronising said. Glanced a dare at each other. Droopy Eyelids – how could he even see the ball? Offered me his hurley.

"Let's see what you can do, mister. Here!" aggressively pressing hurley into my hand. "Go on."

I hesitated. "Are you sure?" The stick looked and felt so fragile in my nine-fingers. "I don't want to break it," I guffawed, trying to give it back, but they'd moved away to watch.

"Aha ha! You're afraid!" Droopy Eyelid goading me. "Go on, try it."

Tiny handle, wrapped in black masking tape, wide flat curved base. Would make a good fly-swatter or Brat-threatener. They were sniggering to each other, waiting, for me to make a fool of myself and give them a good laugh.

"What happened your hand, mister?" the other, Double Cows-Lick, asked when he saw my hand.

"Fell off."

Looked at each other. Yeah, definitely day release from the local madhouse.

Suddenly, Droopy-Eyelids threw the ball at me. "Hit the sliotar, mister," he yelled. "Go on, hit it." That's what they called it. Liked it the moment I heard it. Nice slithery ring. An easy throw which I missed. They didn't laugh. Some things too stupid to laugh at. "Use your two hands," Double Cowslick shouted.

"Throw again," I commanded, throwing the sliotar back at him. Missed again, but not by much. Small snorts. Practised a few more wind-swings. "OK, try again," I called out. "Stand back. This one's sailing to America." Widened my legs, shifted slightly sideways, told myself to concentrate hard. As the sliotar approached, strange form of muscle-memory seemed to kick in. Instinctively took a wide but nimble swing at the sliotar. The hurley connected perfectly and launched that saucy brute high into the air at rapid speed. Not far, but good, good feeling. Boys staring at each other in disbelief at the incredible piece of skill.

"And again." I hit every single one after that, even the sly awkward ones when they got fed up haring around the field after the sliotar like demented hens. Boy, I sent that beauty soaring in stunning glory-arcs in all directions. Wow, wouldn't have believed it if hadn't done it myself. Would've done even better with two thumbs and a proper hurley.

"Who'd you play for? Did you play county?" Double Cows-Lick asked, as he came running back with the ball, touch of awe in his voice. "No idea," I grinned, short of breath, long on happy buzzing. "Who do you play for?"

"He plays for Kevin's under-twelves," Double Cows-Lick shouted, "and I…"

"He's a sub," Droopy Eyelids interjected in case his friend gave inaccurate information.

Gave back the hurley and sliotar. Double Cows-Lick piped up, "I'd say you played for Kilkenny."

"That's stupid," Droopy objected forcefully. "He wouldn't be good enough."

"Then, maybe Leitrim?" Double guessed, enjoying the challenge, adding gleefully. "Do they play hurling?"

Left them still buzzing like a fizzy tablet in a glass of water. Jogged some of the way back into the town. Unbuttoned long coat flapping in the wind. Hat in hand. Did someone at the reunion say I wasn't bad at hurling? Wouldn't believe it anyway. All drunk. But wasn't it curious there was always two hurleys in the house? Adult ones too. Had never questioned why or who brought them there. Just like the furniture. You don't ask furniture where it comes from, do you?

Had to admit a genuine conundrum which, for once, wasn't dismissible with a simple, 'no'. Instincts said they didn't recognise what I'd felt or if I knew anything about hurling, while muscles said otherwise.

By the time I got on the bus to go home, I was wondering could something strange have happened out there in the field. Original purpose of trip completely forgotten, superseded by hurling enigma.

Chapter 23

First Security Visit

Three strangers walking around the Politician's back garden. Talking, looking as if they had something specific in mind. Slid open the kitchen door to hear what they were saying, heard only voices, not words. Tried peering over the wall but could only see the tops of their heads.

Straight out to the Guard in the hut, noticed an unmarked dark green van parked across the road. Guard out of his hut, cap on – sure sign something was up – looking busy doing nothing.

"Who are the guys in her back garden?" I demanded without preliminaries.

His expression told me he didn't want any trouble from me today. "Military, doing a security check."

"But you're here, aren't you? Why can't you do it?"

No answer, just curt exasperation-nod. Hadn't seen that before. "I was just told to let them in."

"Did they show any ID?"

Instant disdain. "Course they did." Resented the slur on his professionalism. "You don't have to worry. They won't be going into your house."

"Yeah? Well, they better not."

Back inside rushed upstairs to the top back bedroom. Never liked that room. Irena didn't either. Felt like someone died there and the room hadn't forgotten. Looking like it belonged to a different era. Two windows, one north, one west, offered strategic views of next door and beyond. No leaves yet, most of next door's garden visible, except for a few spots. Chirpy birds telling spring to hurry up, flying in and out of three nests near the top of one tree. Eventually reminded Colonel Slow-wit of Maurice's tape recorder. So long since it was put there, couldn't remember if it was working or what it could pick up. Went looking for the remote control Maurice had given me. Brat had been playing with it on the attic stairs the day of the chase. Sure enough, still there on the top step. Quietly opened the window, pointed it at the trees and pressed red ON button, mumbling simple prayer. God, make the damn thing work.

Two men in olive green overalls searching the garden, opened wheelie bins, looked under pots and boxes, piles of wood, various bags, containers. Poked short sticks into the soil-only pots. One had an electrical device walking slowly with it, checking readings regularly. Also had long slim poles they stuck into the soil. Worked silently, methodically from house to lane wall. After minutes inside the shed taller soldier tried to open toilet door. Locked. Lit cigarettes and waited.

Third, more senior-looking, soldier went into the house and came back. Handed new key – the Politician had demanded one – to the tallest soldier who unlocked the door, went inside, leaving door open. Came out with wet hands, swinging them in the air to dry. Soldier number three not pleased, directed smaller soldier to go into the toilet. He too came out with nothing but wet hands. Soldier number three then became quite agitated, went into toilet himself, making sure other two stayed to watch. Two soldiers exchanging puzzled looks. For such a small space soldier number three was in there longer than he should've. Also came out with only wet hands and concerned look on his face.

Shrank back from window when he took a good long look around, consigning copious notes in a notebook, including my garden, house, but not me. Took out a phone, made a call, moved away from the others, talked as he walked. All three then went back inside her house. I pressed the OFF button on the remote, sat back for a long wait.

A good hour passed before anything happened. Plenty of time not to want to look around deadbeat room where even dust didn't survive. Faded wallpaper with flowers wilting. Darkly varnished wardrobe creaking autonomously like a crypt. Thick striped cloth covered bare shrunken mattress. Bedside lamp glowed dully with antiquity when I tried it. Threadbare carpet covering most of the floor, except for a wide strip of dark-stained floorboards. No telling whose room it might have been.

Front door opened, banged or was kicked shut. Brat-time. Bag-thud on hall floor, stairs thumping, blissful silence as curtained toilet reached in time. Brat congratulating himself on defeating disaster once again.

"Where are ya?" he shouted after no toilet-flush. "Anyone here?" as feet headed downstairs.

"I'm dead," I shouted hoping he wouldn't hear.

"Where are you?"

Out to the landing shouting, "Up here in the back room, and stop shouting."

"Wha' ya doen up there?"

Couldn't answer, wasn't sure.

Five minutes later door pushed open. In the doorway, in all his Brat-glory, hair like a wild weed, runners with monster lips, loose shoelaces, baggy trousers, T-shirt from 'Kamchatka People's University'. Slurp-sucking on two bent straws from a half-empty glass of watery mint syrup. Eyes me suspiciously, moving the two straws around with his nose as if trying to scratch his nose.

"Wha'ya doen?"

Couldn't answer. Was imagining the missing liquid from the glass spilt on the four flights of stairs from the kitchen. Unfazed by no-answer, he looked around the room, out the window. Slurp, slurp. Knowing well he'd make it up to the attic before I could catch him for much deserved chastisement. Oh yeah, I could see the same thought crossing his febrile mind.

"Stop making noise."

"Wha' ya doen?" he repeated.

Either kill him or take him into my confidence. "Can you keep a secret?"

"Yoo, sailor."

"Shut up, sit down, and watch," I ordered, pointing where he was to sit, on the right of the north-facing window. Within swipe-reach.

"Wha' ya lookin' at? Nothin' there."

Wouldn't in the least surprise him if I said I was up there staring at the sky.

"You have to be patient," warned him. "And quiet, real quiet." Impossible of course, but I liked saying it.

Spotted me moving the remote control out of his reach.

"Wha' tha'?"

Mumbled something even I didn't understand. He repeated the question three times.

"TV remote."

Squinted at it. "No, isn't."

"It's an old one."

"Then wha' ya doen with it? Let me see it?"

"No."

"Wha' ya doen with it?"

"Nothing."

"Ya' must be doen something." Puts the glass down on the floor, thinking could he make a grab for it. Too risky. Sat back, looking out the window, beady eyes searching for clues.

"Any action?" I asked.

"Wha' action? No, wait… Oh, there're guys in Granny's garden. Look."

Peered out from my side of the window. Had to strain my neck. Realised he had the better view.

"They're just standing there in front of the toilet," he said. "Is that what you're… wait." His remarkable brain had finally started working. "Does this have anything to do with… God! Are they checking on the plumbers?" Squeaky voice rising to gosh-levels.

Nodding, put a finger to my lips. "Special army plumbing unit."

"Wha'? Feck off!" He pressed close to the window.

"Just watch and don't let them see you." Picked up the glass and started blowing bubbles into the liquid as he watched. Blub, blub. Noticed me watching him. Blub, blub. Definitely ADHD. He moved back to be sure he was out of swipe-reach.

"There is one thing you could do," I suggested airily. Either that or strangle him with the bloody straw.

"What?"

"You know that sign in the garden?"

"Huh?"

"You know the one about playing football?"

"Huh?"

There'd been war over that sign. I had put it up after all life in the garden had been kicked to death by his blasted football. Sign was in Brat-speak so he could understand, full of Brat-spelling, grandiose proclamations. 'ATENSHUN! FECK OF FRUM FLOWERS. NO

FUTBAL, NO HORSEYPLAY, NO SHOUTEN HERE
OR DERE. BY ORDER.'

When he saw it, he wrote at the end 'OF THE NUT-
KASE'. That and numerous threats worked for a while.
Flowers half-recovered, but then he started using the sign
for target practice. Flowers declined again, sign fell down,
I gave up.

"Would you go down and put it up at the edge there?
You see, where the flower bed used to be?" Stressed 'used'.
"You see, there?" pointed towards the base of tree where I
thought the recorder was, leaves buds having recently appeared. It was the tallest tree in the garden with the most
branches.

"That wasn't my fault."

"You see it?"

"Where?"

"There," I jabbed my finger at the window. God, give
me patience. Opened a new page on the notebook I had
beside me, carefully drew a map of the flower bed, stuck a
big X in the spot where anyone who wanted to climb the
tree would start.

"Why there? Why not... there?" Plonked a grubby finger on the page like picking a horse for the Grand
National.

"Doesn't matter. Just do it."

He didn't move.

"It's to do with the guys next door. I'll explain when
you do it."

"Why don't you do it yourself?" Typical Brat-answer.

"Too big. They'd see me. And don't be cheeky. Just do what you're told."

Still didn't move.

"Look, it's best if a kid does it. Right? And don't let them see you." Looked away to discourage more guff.

Cool watching him bent over scurrying about the garden like a little rat, making sure he wasn't seen.

When he came back up Colonel Magnanimous said, "You can take it down later if you want." Gave me a filthy look, grabbed his glass, forgot to be noisy.

"You keep a look out," I said, leaning back against the wall, closing eyes. "You're in charge while I take a nap."

"Ya can't go to sleep on a stake-out," he complained. "That's not the way it's done."

"Have you a degree in stake-outs? I can do whatever I bloody well like in my house. I'm the commander here."

"It's not your house."

"It is."

"It isn't."

"It..." No, I'm bigger than this.

Quarter of an hour of uneasy peace. Suddenly he shoved my shoulder, whispering excitedly, "Look, look!" Shoved me again.

Three men standing in front of the toilet. One of them new, dressed in civvies, short hair, military bearing... Brat suddenly animated.

"That's him! That's him!" he cried, leaning on top of me. "He's one of them... in the toilet."

"What? Who?"

"That guy. The thin guy with the jacket."

"What thin guy?" Pushed him off me, picked up my camera, angling it into the small gap beside the lace curtain, started clicking.

"There, look!" Brat back leaning on me again, mouth almost in my ear, making it hard to keep the camera steady. "He's one of the plumbers."

New guy. Civilian. Long neck, narrow head, receding hairline, grey-black temples. He stayed outside while soldier number three went inside the toilet and again, came out the same. Empty-handed. I pressed Record on the remote control.

"Wha' ya doen'?"

"Recording."

"But ya said…"

"Shut up."

Crafty Brat-look. "Where's the recorder?"

"Dunno."

"You don't know?" Was pressing down so hard on my shoulders, like he was getting ready to climb on top of my head, then he casually announced, "It's there. Look." Pointed towards a branch near the top of the tree nearest the wall. "You see?"

Couldn't see a damn thing. "How do you know where it is?"

"Just know."

Alarm signals. "What do you mean you just know? What did you do to it?"

"Nothing. Eh, nothing… I didn't do anything to it. You're always blaming me."

Which meant he had. "Did you put the tape back in it?"

Still leaning on me.

"I… one of the guys did it."

"Did what? Oh, shut up and get off me." Tried pushing him away, but he was glued to me with excitement and calculation. I couldn't hit him when he was that close. Civilian crouched down in front of the new lock, ran his fingers over it.

"He's looking at the lock," Brat whispered, pressing again on my shoulder.

Civilian stood up, dialled a number on his mobile. Couldn't hear the faint melodic tones of the different digits. I looked up at the tree and sky. God, please be good to me, make the bloody recorder work. Civilian disappeared into Politician's house.

"Quick," I cried, pressing the OFF button on the remote, throwing the Brat off me. "We've got to go to the front."

Hurricaned downstairs to my bedroom, closely followed by excited Brat trying to get ahead of me. Pulled him back. Got there first, in time to see Civilian talking to the Guard who was standing on her path outside his hut.

"What's happening?" Brat gasped, thrilled by mad rushing around.

Guard didn't look too pleased with the questioning. At one stage he pointed towards my house, both turned, looked.

"Quick, duck!" I shouted pulling Brat down with me. "The bloody fool."

"Wha'? Why're ya cursing?"

"Ssshh." Think fast. What will the guy do next?

"Wha's he asking him?" Brat asked.

"Ssshh!"

"Wait." Brat drew back. "I know what he's doen," he declared, looking pleased with himself. "He's asking about the new lock."

"Bravo."

"But why's he asking about tha'? It's just a lock. Wha's the big deal?"

"Security," I said, wondering would I believe it myself. Guard now pointing at various houses along the road. Civilian writing it down in small notebook. Both went into the house. We dashed back upstairs.

"This is great!" Brat kept saying, hugely enjoying the after-school mystery.

"You don't say a word about this to anyone," warned him, back on either side of the stake-out window. "You hear me? Not a word." Was very firm. "Not one word."

Big round Brat-eyes blinked. I knew what that meant.

Lane door open. Guard pointing at more houses. Civilian still taking notes. Brat nudged me.

"There's Boris," he whispered.

Boris was sitting serenely on top of next door's toilet, eyeing the scene below.

When the others came in, one of the soldiers brought a stepladder out of the house, leaned it against the toilet wall, started climbing.

"Mother of Divine Tulips!" I swore, hardly believing my eyes. "Are they going to arrest Boris? They must think he's a spy?"

"Yeah, sure."

Boris waited until the soldier had his two hands on the edge of the roof before getting up and scuttling off along the lane wall. Soldier got up on the roof, got down on his knees, examined the roof, tapping it in places. Then the whole battalion retreated.

Minutes later, just about saw two of the soldiers in Bernie's garden on the far side of the Politician's. Bernie's washing, large and small, out on the line. Stood protectively beside it, arms folded, watching as they searched her garden. Just about tolerating the intrusion.

"You know what's going to happen next, do you?" I asked the Brat.

Thought a moment, wonderful thing to see, his eyes lit up. "They're going to come here?"

I nodded.

"Yulp!" let out high-pitched squeak of delight, beside himself with excitement.

"Good man," I said, patting him on the head because he didn't like that. "Now, I don't want you around when they call, so go do your homework in the front room."

Looked like he was going to object when his expression changed. Eyes narrowed as he figured out the angle. We both knew he'd be there in the front room listening to every word.

Doorbell sounded like it had been waiting as impatiently as we had. Tone shriller, more piercing than usual. I shouted from the upstairs landing where I'd been sitting, "Coming!"

"Hello," I smiled at the two soldiers on the doorstep.

"Sir. Colonel Corley," soldier number three said respectfully, stiffening which instantly appealed to me. "Sorry to disturb you, sir."

"That's all right, gentlemen. Em," lower voice, "how do you know my name? Did he tell you?" I nodded at the lug still on patrol out in the bushes beside his hut, breaking his active service record.

"No, sir. We know who you are, sir."

In other circumstances I might have invited them in to tell me more about myself.

"Sir, we are doing a routine security check on the Minister's house. We were wondering if you would allow us to check your back garden as well? It won't take long and we will put everything back exactly the way it was."

"The back garden, eh?" Scrunched up my forehead in surprise. "Eh, of course. Of course, but tell me, is there a problem? What are you boys looking for? I might be able to help."

"No, sir. Nothing in particular. It's just routine. We noticed the gap in the wall. That's all."

"Of course," I sighed, leaning closer to him. "You're absolutely right. I've tried to get her to fill it in, but she's never there." Sighed again. "Do you want to close it off? We'd have to get a builder in to do that."

"No, sir. We are not asking for that. That's not necessary. We just want to..."

"Sir," the smaller soldier with fat cheeks cut in. "Have you noticed anything unusual in the area recently? Front and back gardens, I mean?"

"Front and back, eh?" Lowered my voice. "Come over here, lads, and look at this." I brought them over to the back of the trespassing hut. "Now, what do you think of that?" I asked them. "See, it's ninety-two millimetres on my side."

They exchanged glances.

"What we mean, sir, is, well," number three hesitated, "we noticed there is a new lock on the toilet door in the Minister's garden at the back and there was some damage to the door and we wondered what happened to it?"

"You mean a break-in? Into her toilet?" I grinned dubiously. "Come on, lads, what do you take me for? What did they want to do? Steal her toilet paper?"

They smiled uneasily.

"Sorry, lads." I didn't want to be cruel. "You're right. It was me. I got the locksmith to fix it." Put my hands in my pockets. "The lock was smashed and the door was hanging off its hinges. Some ignoramus must have broken in and done a crap. Amazing, isn't it? What people will do nowadays? Not really my job to fix it up, but she's always away and the gap makes it a problem for me as well. So, I called the locksmith and had it fixed. Cost me a fortune too. I'd appreciate if you could make sure she pays me for it." Continued searching my pocket in case the receipt was still there.

"Can you tell us who the locksmith was?"

"I can indeed." Fished the card out my pockets. "Here, you won't have any trouble with Felix. He's a good man and a good actor."

"Can you think of anyone else who might have broken in or... been in there?" Fat Cheeks asked with a hint of impatience.

Put my hand on my mouth. "Hard to say. Could have been anyone. Kids playing in the lane, their friends, visitors, drunks. Sometimes neighbours forget to close the lane gates. And builders, they always leave them open."

"Are there any builders working in the area?"

"Gosh, lads, I don't know everything!" Hadn't thought of this extra avenue of spreading suspicion. "Wait..." I made a face of self-annoyance. "I do remember there was a tortoise in the toilet a few days ago. Poor thing, don't know how it got there, and a lot of the kids went in to look at it. But that must have been after the door was broken... or was it before? Hmm..."

"Are there many kids who play in the lane who saw the tortoise?"

"Loads."

Exchanged glances with each other. "So, sir, can we, erm..."

202

"Of course, yes, sure. Go in through the gap in the wall and please be careful. Haha. Don't want any accidents, do we?"

Slight surprise on their faces as they turned to go. Didn't invite them in the front door.

Fat Cheeks stopped. "Sir, do you own an auburn cat?"

Nodded knowingly. "You mean Boris? I wish I did."

"Boris?"

"A highly intelligent cat."

"And his owner?"

"That would be neighbour Maurice, around the corner." I stopped in fake astonishment. "You don't suspect Boris of breaking into the toilet?" I joked.

"That's great, sir." No smiles. "No, nothing like that. You've been very helpful. Thank you, sir."

Brat and I watched the search from the kitchen window. He got there first, deliberately stood on my favourite sandy-beige tile.

"Get off my place," I told him, pushed him away. He'd take over everything if I let him.

When they got to the sign the Brat had put at the bottom of the tree, they didn't laugh or, more importantly, start climbing.

Chapter 24

Second Security Visit

The sleep of culpable innocence, dreamless, long and restful. Followed by crisp dry air which would get much colder if the wind picked up, as it usually did. Otherwise, carnival of spring in full session. Bird-song competitions all over, more dogs walking their owners than could remember, hordes of school-holiday kids screaming as they played in the playground. Complimented Cecil on the state of his world. Cheered up three auld ones only half-full of grace on their way home from church. Kicked a dog who tried to copulate with my leg. Felt in excellent form. Spring surging, the chase was on, thinking money, and what I could do with it.

Main thing as I walked home was paying for a boarding school for the Brat far away from here and where they played Henry Hurling. After that, it was a toss-up between buying Boris and buying a husband for the young woman.

Turning the corner at the bottom of our street, saw Mrs Hand up at the top of the hill. She was holding the railings outside Tom's house, staring westwards at the road at the top of the hill, shopping bags on the ground. As I came up the hill, she spotted me, waited, when I was closer beckoned me over. Very unusual for Mrs Hand to be so forward. Could see she wasn't her normal self. Was she in trouble? Did she need hydraulic support? I'd always thought that day would come. Hurried over to her.

"They've been in Tom's and in Jim Carew's," she said, breathing heavily, a bit red in the face. "And even Bridget's, searching everywhere. What do you think of that?"

Couldn't think, still processing and wide-eyed as a speechless seagull.

"And they're nearly finished with the Carter's." Fixed me with an eagle eye. "Now," she said again, "what do you make of that?"

An eerie feeling she was blaming me for these strange events. "What is it, Mrs Hand?" I asked, wondering how spring could disappear so quickly. "Is someone injured?"

"Mr Carter told me they've been in there now about an hour, going through everything." She nodded grimly. Why is she the only person I knew who didn't call him Maurice?

"They're not big houses on that street," she added thoughtfully. "But at least the men searching are polite, if that makes any difference. They put everything back where they found it." Looked at me again with an expectant look which said, 'I suppose you wouldn't know anything about it?'

Beginning to dread that look.

Walked up to the corner for a better view. Small crowd of women, children, prams, dogs, wheelie bins had gathered outside Carter's. A policeman was also there. The same green van parked across from the house.

"I wonder what kind of a mess they found in Jim's house," Mrs Hand said. "It hasn't been properly cleaned since his mother died, God be good to her and all she came from," she said, hiking up her shoulders. "If they tidy up a bit, might be the one good thing to come out of this," she added without a trace of irony.

Figure emerged from Carter's house – soldier number three. A shiver of excitement ran through me. Things moving up a gear. They're really worried, pissed off.

"Eh, have they been to my house, Mrs Hand?" Hesitated because just realised I didn't know Mrs Hand's first name. If someone told me she'd been christened 'Mrs Hand' I'd have believed it.

"I didn't see that. Nor to hers," she added inclining her head.

"How do you know?"

"Because that gombeen of a guard wouldn't let them in. The only useful thing he's done since he arrived, the lazy so-and-so. Didn't expect any gumption out of the likes of him. So what do you think of that?"

Shocking stuff coming from Mrs Hand. Had never heard her utter such words about anyone. And, she'd put me on the spot again. Shook my head, actually feeling sympathy for the poor Guard. "But he let them in before."

"Did he now? That would be more like it, alright."

Couldn't help asking. "Do you know the Guard, Mrs Hand?" Had an odd feeling Mrs Hand and the Guard came from the same part of the country. Maybe she resented him because of that.

"No," she said firmly. "He's from the next parish."

"Oh."

Passing train heading west on the nearby track hooted in sympathy and the sound died away. Mrs Hand grew philosophical. "A lot of excitement for our little area, isn't it?"

Still thinking about her guard-antipathy. Concluded Mrs Hand resented outsiders and at the same time would've chatted with the devil and his deputy if they lived locally.

"That it is, that it is."

"Well, I best be getting on," she declared, picked up her bags, heaved her shoulders into position, drew closer for a parting word. "I wouldn't be surprised if it had something to do with herself. What do you think?"

Wanted to reply stop asking me bloody questions but could never show irritation to Mrs Hand. Which made me feel kind of noble. "You could be right. You never know these days, do you?"

"Too true, too true," she agreed, pleased we were parting in agreement.

Off she went, across the road, up the narrow one-way street along the side of the old convent wall. A stoic gait on a tiny footpath overshadowed by high dodgy stone wall. Left me wondering once more where she got this unflappable acceptance of all things human. Next time I'll ask her about the departed Mr Hand.

Tom came out to his front garden, yelping little terrier on a leash, looking dazed. Went over to offer my sympathies. Fine figure of a retired bachelor, an advertisement for the best of the breed. Magnificent head of thick silver hair which belittled my receding wiry curls. Old school, lived with his sister, didn't tolerate fools. We get on well.

"The fuckers," he blurted out, most uncharacteristically. "They just came in, no respect for my privacy, a sick woman upstairs in her bed. You wouldn't believe it. They went into her room and spent most of the time there. They even looked under her bed, the blackguards."

Tom's mouth-dribble, unprecedented, indicated serious upset. Sometimes spoke out of the side of his mouth, my head inclining itself in that direction.

"Terrible, terrible," I agreed, quickly righting my head.

"She told them to get the blazes out of her bedroom or she'd get out of bed in the nip and chase them out or have a heart attack and die on them." Sensing his master's anxiety, the terrier started yelp-howling like it was being mauled by an Alsatian.

"You stay quiet," Tom said to the mutt without turning, "or I'll cut your tail off." Worked too.

"Brilliant answer, that's the spirit."

Looked disapprovingly at me. "I'm serious, Dominic, she could've had one."

"I didn't mean…"

"I called Catherine's office."

Took me a moment to figure out who he was talking about. All Tom wanted was an attentive ear. "Did you? And what did she say?"

"Got her secretary. She's out of the country at the moment, but she promised to tell her as soon as she's back. I said sooner."

Solidarity-nod. My hand accidentally brushing a flake of white paint off his railings. Tom noticed it, said nothing.

"They threatened me, Dominic. Did you know that?"

"No."

"I've worked for the state all my life and they threatened me. Can't believe it. In my own home. I've lived in this street for over seventy years and nothing like this has ever happened."

"What did they say?"

"If I had nothing to hide, I had nothing to worry about. What kind of talk is that?" Hands were shaking, his fine head of hair tousled as if he'd been running his fingers through it too much. "They didn't have to say any more. I knew what they meant." After Tom, I went along the street to Carter's where the search had just finished, small crowd had dispersed, except for the wheelie bins. I went over to Fat-Cheeks sitting in the van.

"What in God's name are you up to?" I demanded, raising my voice. "I didn't think you'd be doing routine searches down here." Colonel Dommo, spokesperson for the neighbourhood.

Looked around, tired eyes, every muscle in his face tight. "Sorry sir, can't talk about it."

"About what? You can't talk about what?"

Didn't answer, stared straight ahead as if I wasn't there.

"Well?" I insisted after a moment, taking my hands off the open van window, "You better come and search my house as well. You've searched everyone else's – Tom's, Jim's, Bridget's, Carter's and, God knows, who else's, so you better do mine."

He didn't react. I tried again, lower voice. "Look, do you know what this makes me look like? What people will say? Do you?" He wanted to be anywhere but here.

"They will say 'Oh, he wasn't searched because of her!' That's what they'll say, and I have to live in this area." Waited, still no reaction. In a louder voice, "So, I demand you search my house and do it now in full view of the whole street. No exceptions."

Of course, highly reckless, but I was learning. The higher the stakes the bigger the buzz. And I liked buzzing.

"Colonel, please, we're almost finished here." He sighed. "It hasn't been an easy day. Sure, we'll search it if you want. We called earlier."

Mollified. "I was out seeing a counsellor from the Shrinkage," I lied. "If you ever need one, I wouldn't recommend him." Leaned closer to his puzzled face. "Complete waste of time, you know." Looked at Carter's open front door. "Yes, I am shocked by all this," I exclaimed louder. "But there must be no special treatment for me. I am a republican," I declared to the wheelie bins huddled on the footpath like penguins. "I believe in equal treatment and equal searching!"

Stared at me, mouth ajar. Then I realised I hadn't asked the most obvious question of all. "So," I cooled down, "what is it you're looking for?"

"Documents, papers that went missing."

"Oh? The Politician's?"

Shrugged his shoulders.

"Right, oh. That sounds serious. Must be very important."

"We don't know. We just have to find them."

"You think someone stole them and hid them here, is that it?"

He rubbed his ample cheeks, impatient with life. "Look, Colonel, you know how it is. I'm just following orders." Looked at his watch. "We'll be over to you in a short while. Excuse me." Rolled up his window. Some neighbours had reappeared. "This is a bloody mess!" I heard him say through the window.

First thing I said to them when they arrived at my front door was, they were free to search anywhere they liked except the basement. That was absolutely off limits and, anyway, there was no chance it was there because I was the only one who knew the code. Meaningful glances exchanged between soldier number three and Fat Cheeks, exactly what I wanted. Also, the front door had to stay wide open so everyone could see what was going on. Felt disappointed no crowd gathered outside my house.

"Well lads," I asked cheerfully when they'd finished after half an hour. All three of us in the kitchen, standing near the guinea pigs' cage. They'd checked under it as well. "Find any of my missing socks?" I joked.

Too tired to smile. "We didn't expect to find anything, sir."

"How about some tea?"

"No, sir. Thank you, sir. We'd better be going. You have been very helpful."

Just as they were leaving, white car pulled up sharply in front of the house. Civilian got out, slammed his door shut, exchanged whispers with the soldiers. Watched them drive off, came up the short path to me standing in my front door. Didn't say hello, just stood there, hands on hips, dark eyes aggressively boring into me. Mouth so firmly closed, his lips almost disappearing. No doubt what he was looking for or trying to do.

"Yeah," I nodded, as if continuing a conversation we'd never had. Thinking it strange, given the conversation we were about to have, I didn't know his name. Didn't seem to matter.

Ignoring his malign rudeness, stepped past him out onto the path, pulling the front door closed behind me. Walked over the grass to the railing, facing downhill, thereby forcing him, if he wanted to continue staring at me, and I think he did, to go out onto the footpath.

Good, our exchanges would be as public as possible. Up and down the street, Guard was still out, looking away but ear cocked in our direction. Tom in his front garden, talking to Grace from further down the hill. Nameless young man who lived in the bottom flat a few doors up was heading for his door. Exactly what I wanted.

Before Civilian could resume his staring game, I took the Package out of my inside pocket, held it up high for all to see – he was on a lower level and couldn't grab it off me – and thrust it at him.

Surprised – you could say that. Slow to react, but his hand took it the way hands do when they react to do something on their own. He blinked, frustrated rage reddening his cheeks as he figured out what I was doing. His eyes quickly swept across the street as he wordlessly shoved the Package inside his coat. Not even a 'Thank you', or 'Where did you find it?' Goodbye Package. "Aren't you going to count it?" I asked. "There's half missing."

His brain refocused on the new information. Shoulders jerked outwards as if limbering up. Finally, he spoke. "You think this is funny, some kind of joke?"

"No, not at all." Though at that moment I did because he had an unlikely high-pitched voice, like he'd had an unpleasant accident as a child. Now I understood why he preferred to be dangerous through his eyes, not his mouth.

"You're messing in things that don't concern you."

"Finder's fee," I simply said.

He nodded a few times in disagreement, shifting his feet so his anger wouldn't ignite and send him rocketing skywards. "All of it, every last fuckin' penny, here, when I come back tomorrow evening or that kid, your grandson," he looked behind me, "has a nasty fall on his way home from school."

"No," I countered immediately. Wrong thing to say. Pushing my face at his.

"You're talking horse-shit." I knew the Brat wasn't there, too early for him. "He isn't my grandson and this isn't his home. He's a, a squatter!"

Deadpan eyes narrowed into swamp-menace. Looked beyond me. "It doesn't matter who you are – just have the money."

Strange, or not so strange, how we reached this existential point so early in a first encounter. Looked him up and down feeling we could have a few things in common, but certainly not our ethics. My silence seemed to irk him. His breathing got louder, probably thinking if I wasn't talking, I wasn't afraid enough. Grunted loudly like a tennis player serving an ace, interlocking his fingers, pushing palms outward in my direction, bones actually cracking.

Rising anger cast aside the envy I felt not being able to do that trick. Not ordinary anger, but anger at being threatened on *my* property. Didn't seem to appreciate how disrespectful that was.

"Do you mind if I ask you a question?"

Muffled grunt. Already stabbing me with his eyes.

"I am speaking in a low voice not to embarrass you in public." Gazed around the street, pleased everyone was still out, watching us. "It's wrong to threaten me in front of my own house. This is a sacred place. It's a kind of temple and threatening me here is like sacrilege." While I was speaking, I scanned his body for hints of hidden objects or what he might do. Decided he was the type who preferred aids – baseball bat, knuckle duster, knife, gun. Didn't have anything on him.

"It's very simple," I explained, controlling my voice, forcing a smile, waving over at Tom across the street. "I have proof you put the Package in the toilet, I know your name and phone number. But don't worry, I don't care what you're up to. But I absolutely will not tolerate threats to me or anyone in my house, even the Brat. So," I paused, worried I had exalted the Brat's welfare too highly, "if you ever come near my house, the neighbours or anyone I know again, you will hear all about it on talk-radio and so will the police. And I don't mean him," I added, nodding at the glum Guard next door. "I mean the real police. And I will come after you. Everyone thinks I'm strange, but you definitely don't want to find out if it's true or not." Waved my non-thumb in his face.

Didn't say a word when I finished. Stared hard at me, weaponised eyes, sneered. Got into his car, screeching off down the hill. Shook my head, well pleased with Colonel Dom Tom. Don't expect to see him again, might miss the excitement, though. Now to concentrate on new life.

Short postscript

Empty tape the Brat handed me next day, when he climbed down from the tree.

"What?" I demanded, glaring at him with kill-or-be-killed eyes in the kitchen when the only bloody sound from the recorder was endless hissing. Probably never any tape there in the first place. Brat probably just fished one out of his pocket. Thought of giving him a good clip on the ear. Could see his mouth forming the words 'No proof'. Before he could say anything, I declared "Proof is for poodles!".

His upper lip jumped in surprise.

"Posh poodles!" I spat out.

PART 1V

Chapter 25

Second Meeting with Retired Detective

Trees in Archbishop's Palace on the far side of the main road alerted me to the peculiarity. Even if it was April the days seemed to be getting shorter, not longer, darkening weirdly. In the early afternoon the massive spreading branches devoured light, burying shadows above ground. Elbow firmly on the table, chin resting on palm, fancied parallels between us. The trees were gaining new leaves. I was shortly gaining my new identity. Their past was written in rings in their trunks, their future was dormant in spring buds, growing in great profusion. My new past, new future lay secluded in the spring-time work of an ex-policeman with a good pension. And no worries about his fee. The slimmed New Package, plastic found in the basement, snuggly stuck in the cistern of the curtained middle toilet, setting down firm roots. Only time I thought of the Civilian was when I patted the lid of the cistern.

Such absorbing thoughts didn't notice the Retired Detective enter the restaurant until he slid into the banquette wall-seat in front of me. Looking satisfied, the demeanour of man on a state pension, houses in bedsits about to earn undeclared income. Finally I said to myself, after waiting far too long. No chance of an apology or explanation. Red and grey lumberjack shirt spectacularly miss-matched with aging puffy face. From the inside pocket of his rain jacket peeked – yes, yes! the top of a folded brown envelope. Was about to learn my new identity. Had to restrain strong temptation to lean across the table, pluck it out of his pocket, give him a deserved smack on the gob for being so bloody slow. Saw me looking at it, grunted indifferently.

"Have you ordered?" he asked with the only show of energy he seemed capable of, picking up the menu, furrowing his face as he read the non-pancake menu. My fingers playing impatient pianos on the table. We were in a new restaurant on the main road, in the hope he didn't like the cuisine and I wouldn't have to watch him stuff his face.

"I'm impressed you have the information so quickly," I lied, to test his detection skills. No response. I chewed my impatience while he chewed his chicken, wondering again why he made me feel he was doing me the favour, instead of the other way around. Not friendly, not hostile, not keen for me to talk until he finished eating. Could he be envious of the Colonel? Who knows the mind of a sour retired detective?

"Before I give it to you," he said in his usual gruff tone, holding up the envelope the way an older kid holds a sweet just out of reach of a smaller one, "You didn't tell me where you wanted to come from or whether you wanted to be Catholic or Protestant."

My feet, which had been tap-dancing under the table to stop my hands shooting across the table for it, stopped suddenly. "What?"

He barely suppressed a belch. "I had to make certain assumptions."

"Oh." I frowned.

"So, I decided for you."

"Oh. Right." Where was this going?

"One of each. It took me longer than I expected. I had to do a lot of searching in different places, but here," he passed the envelope across the table to me. "This is what I came up with."

Three stapled typed pages in the envelope. Mildly disappointed there wasn't more. My eyes crawled greedily over each letter like a centipede attacking a statue. First page listed two names and stated this was genealogical research carried out on commission for private information purposes only. No liability was accepted for anything at all. Hungry centipede started reading the second page.

'John Quick, born 29th June 1949 to Bernard Quick and Dolores Kelly. Only child. Mother died from TB in 1952, father admitted to St Loman's Psychiatric Hospital, Mullingar, shortly afterwards, died in 1966. Both buried in a family plot in Cam cemetery, Roscommon. John was taken in by a bachelor farmer uncle, Tom. At sixteen he emigrated to Boston, USA, where he died in a building site accident in 1968, aged 19. He was buried in a cemetery near Needham, Mass.'

Lot to digest. Looked out the window. How little and how much the few words told me? Retired Detective reading dessert menu. Hmmm. Why include the bit about the psychiatric hospital? If I choose him, I'd have the legacy of a dodgy gene hanging over me. Retired Detective ordered vanilla cheesecake.

Moved on to page three.

'Stephen Adam Knowles Kidney born in Athlone on 29th December 1947 to draper parents, Randal Stephen Kidney and Ruth Knowles Kingston. An only child he went to Summerhill boarding school. Emigrated to England in 1966 where 'he was more at ease with his sexuality'. Worked in a theatre as a cleaner in south London until 1973 and then worked as a care assistant in a hospital in East London until he was killed in a car accident on a short holiday in Morocco in 1984. Parents died shortly after.'

A black coffee was waiting in front of me. The contrasts were stark, my future swinging between two extremes. Looked up, Retired Detective's eyes searching mine for clues. Drank the coffee, forgetting to add sugar. Thinking. Placed both elbows on table.

"I see I'm a flawed person," I said, pursing my lips.

"Isn't that what you want? A nobody? So as not to attract attention."

"Either a nutcase or gay?"

"That's not how people see these things nowadays," Retired Detective said. True, true. Talk radio was full of horror stories about both.

Scratched head. All the same, what a choice? Cowboy builder or glorious queen? On a whim I crossed my legs with a camp flourish, banged my knee under the table, rested my cheek nonchalantly in the palm of my hand. "How's that?"

"Huh?"

"Couldn't you find someone with an uneventful CV?"

Slowly raised his eyebrows. "Take it away with you and think about it. You don't want to rush into a decision."

I looked askance at the sheets, put them back in the envelope.

"Maybe you'll come to be comfortable with one of them."

Frowned, suspicious of his out of character irony. Rubbed my upper lip. "Which one would you choose?" Before he could answer I added, "Just so as you know, I'm not gay."

"You could be retired gay," he suggested.

Restaurant door opened. Two women with a baby in a pram left. A burst
of cold air unkindly brushed my neck.

"Do you have any photos?"

"Not with me, but they fit the profile."

For some reason my initial inclination was towards Kidney. "I suppose… I could change Kidney to a heterosexual? He could have a change of mind."

Gave me a sceptical look. "For your own sake, you better be comfortable with whatever you choose. You'll be acting for the rest of your life." He shifted his chair back a little. "Anyway…" Pay-time, I assumed.

"How did you decide what part of the country they come from?" I was thinking I'd like to be from Sligo.

"I was stationed in Athlone for a few years. I have good contacts there."

"Did you know the families?" I felt like a prospective groom.

"Doesn't matter. It's better you don't ask questions. You chose one and I'll fill in the details."

Waitress cleared the plates, asked if we wanted more coffee.

"Sad lives," I concluded.

"I've seen worse. Three reasons these two stood out – age, height and hair. They're about your size and I think they'd have had a wiry hair like yours, if they'd lasted."

"Curly, not wiry."

Shrugged, his arms on each side of the narrow table as if about to lift it. "You do know, whoever you choose, you can never go anywhere near the relatives or the areas they lived in?"

Nodded unenthusiastically, handed him my envelope, white, smaller. Put it straight into his inside jacket pocket. Another one who doesn't believe in counting money in public.

"You're not going to count it?"

"It would be a lot easier if you weren't living here," he said, almost as an aside.

"What? Say that again?"

"If you're abroad the chances of being found out would be low... unless you were unlucky or careless."

Stood up, took his rain-jacket off the back of his chair, put it on. "Do you speak any foreign languages?" he asked, leaning down towards me.

"I don't think so, but... you never know... No, wait, the women think I do. French." I laughed just to get him to laugh. "Test me. Say something in French."

Ignoring me he said. "Let me know when we move to the next phase."

Chapter 26

Visit Auld One in Nursing Home

My mind was made up before I left the restaurant. Stephen Adam Knowles Kidney. Being named after a body part wasn't instantly appealing, rolled the full name around my mouth, trying it for size like a jumper in a shop, telling myself I had to like it, whether I wanted to or not.

After leaving a message on Retired Detective's phone, I went to the full-length mirror in the upstairs bathroom. "Hi, I'm Kidney, Stephen Kidney.", "No, it's K I D N E Y, not SYDNEY." or "Very funny. It's better than being called Boyle or Ball, but maybe not as good as being Hart and certainly not as good as Hand." Re-combed my hair, putting the almost disappeared split on the right side, got a pair of sunglasses, saying to the mirror, "Originally from Athlone, but I've lived in London for years. Do I have any family left there? No, no family left in Athlone. There might be a distant cousin in Sligo, but, there's no contact with him." Tried putting on a London accent? Couldn't. Would have to work on an Athlone accent. What does that sound like? Will ask Mrs Hand. Could go down there as well.

Over the next weeks, waiting on the Retired Detective's next report, focused on becoming the best Stephen Kidney I could be. Which meant becoming the best care assistant I could be.

That was a challenge. Knew absolutely nothing about that line of work. Didn't think I could bluff it. Knew empathy couldn't be bluffed and I'd have to be endlessly empathetic. Was that possible? Especially after the Brat, the Others and the Shrinkage? Wasn't even sure I smiled enough. OK, I could talk to auld ones, that was a positive, but it wasn't the same. There had been non-nurses around when I was in hospital, seemed like workers, not carers, pushing my wheelchair, never going fast, crashing into other wheelchairs. Sat beside me in taxis with bored faces or collected me from a brain scan or collecting clothes from the laundry. Never chatting, making me laugh which a good carer would do. Realised I needed practice and I knew where to go.

Didn't start well. "No," sharp-nose, narrow-face, sideways fringed head-nurse said firmly. So firmly I can almost hear it echo around the high-ceilinged hall. Below a big painting of brown horses in a daisy and dandelion field. Had come out of her office behind reception after being called by cowardly receptionist.

"You have to be qualified and accredited and have the papers to prove it." Tone said further question futile, would result in security guard being called.

"Is the Auld One here?"

"I beg your pardon," she sniffed stiffly, meaning get out of here. Last chance.

"I've been here before. Is she still here?"

Her hand was under the desk hovering over the security buzzer.

"I need to see her. She thinks she's my mother. It's a bad sad case," I grovelled, going down on one knee in front of everyone.

She made a face. Sensed I wasn't an ordinary visitor. Told me to behave myself and wait over there. Went off to look. After further toing and froing, different faces coming out to stare at me like I was famous. They eventually figured out a name for the Auld One, Millie Corley. For God's sake, half the country could be called that for all I knew. Took another while to find where she was now. Been moved to a nursing home in the country on the edge of a small village, an hour's bus ride away.

Colonel All-Action soon bussing through flat countryside. Low-cut country hedges framed large fields, bus twisted and turned along corkscrew road. Trees were slower decking themselves in leaves, but many gave countryside an elegant promise of summer. Nursing home in long two-storey ex-convent fronted by a trimmed lawn snug in the curve of big road bends. Dodgy toilet smells overlaid with three-quarter-effective perfumed neutraliser hit me when the automatic double doors closed behind me. A real carer is not put off by this.

Told the necessary lie. Couldn't say son, just a distant cousin, lives in Morocco, cold winter, no tan, originally from Athlone. No problem, sir. Smooth, like the Auld One was expecting me.

"Just a moment."

Five-star-smile Gloria brought me to the Auld One's room. Gloria smiled beautifully, irrepressibly, as we walked along the narrow corridor. Great first impression of successful care assisting – white teeth, brown skin, dark eyes, happy Filipino face. Made me feel she knew all about me, liked what she saw. Instantly recognisable empathy role model. Lesson one, smile when there is no reason to smile. Lesson number two followed quickly.

"Tell me again who are you looking for?" Cheerful Gloria asked halfway down the second corridor, after stopping to laugh with two auld ones glaring at each other in wheelchairs while their pushers stopped for a chat.

"Millie."

"Millie!" she exclaimed as if Millie was the most exciting patient anyone could wish for. "Ah, Millie Billie. She a good one."

After that I could have forgotten about the Auld One, followed Cheerful Gloria all day. Second lesson, don't park occupied wheelchairs beside each other.

Cheerful Gloria knocked on a door, opened it when a weak voice called out, "Come in, come in." Announced to the bed, "Millie, you have a visitor."

"Is it John? He said he's going to America and not coming back."

"No, Millie, it's not John. It's a mystery visitor."

"Woooo!" the Auld One went, fake shiver of excitement.

Watched Cheerful Gloria check the pillow, bedclothes, then leave. Wondering should I follow her, forget about the Auld One. Noticed Gloria's hips also swaying cheerfully. Does carer's swagger exist because if it does, I've seen it...

"Are you coming in or what?" the raspy voice demanded, sounding far from terminal, slouched into the pillows, hair recently curled tightly into her skull like bent sausages. "What's wrong with you?" she barked, baring her teeth as if showing what she could do if she had to. "What are you staring at?"

Couldn't figure out if she was the same auld one I'd spoken to before. After a certain age they all look the same. Anyway, didn't matter. "You're looking well," I began as cheerfully as I could.

"Aha, he talks," she remarked, switching tone to observational. "I'm fading away. Where are my glasses?" Stretched out her hand to the bedside table. "I can't see you."

Hurried over, grabbed the glasses before she knocked over a glass of water.

"What are you doing there?" she demanded before I had time to give them to her. "They're mine. Leave them alone."

All this before I'd even introduced myself as Stephen Kidney. Handed her the glasses. When she had them on, she fixed me with a keen stare, eyes had shrunk into their sockets, her skin creased, faded, spotty. Now that she could see, waited for her to accuse me of being an imposter, flexed my mouth for big smile.

"What's wrong with you? Go and see the doctor, haha...."

Guessed she was too embarrassed to admit she hadn't a clue who I was. I introduced myself. "Hi, I'm Stephen, your new personal trainee care assistant." That became my first caring duty every visit, telling her who I was then, who she was. "And you are... Millie Billie," I said with a flourish and a smile. Even if her memory was almost gone, plenty space left for tenacity, temper.

On different occasions told her she was John Quick's mother, Stephen Kidney's mother, the Politician's mother, Mrs Hand's sister. Spoon-fed her whole yarns about the Guard and Mrs Hand, the Civilian and Felix Delahunty to amuse her. She usually listened or didn't interrupt – much the same. Sometimes she suspected I was making it up, but it didn't bother her. Knowing who she was, was the least of her worries.

"Would you like to say a prayer?" I asked, thinking back to the last time she visited me in hospital. Surely a good way of caring.

"No," she retorted bluntly. "I've done enough of that." Like, enough is enough. Lesson three, don't ask them if they want to pray. Lesson three point one, remember to bring a pen to note all lessons for future reference.

Also told her about the trip to Sligo. Then, making conversation, told her about Henry Hurling, which sadly meant nothing to her.

Just getting over this when another carer, Lizzy, arrived with the tea trolley, offering tea and biscuits. Watched Lizzy carefully as she poured the teas, handed out the cups and saucers. Yep, Lizzy smiled most of the time too. When she was gone the Auld One said straight up, "You see, she offered you tea because you gave her the eye."

Spluttered into my cup. Holy moving-statues, are they all like this? Only there to give the eye to whoever I could? Laughed, she looked disappointed.

All this on the first visit. Didn't change either. Never knew what she'd come out with. Kept me on my toes. Caring lessons building up. Nurses said it was the disease talking, that she forgot everything almost as soon as she said it. Cheerful Gloria said it was the birds talking.

Noticed on that first visit no watch or clock in her room. She looked at the ceiling, walls, out the window of her ground floor room, across the car park, often at the office girls smoking outside during their break.

"Does time go slow in here?" I asked when it slowed so much, I began to think it wasn't moving at all. No difficulty coming back from wherever she was.

"If you want it to go fast it goes slow and if you want it to go slow it goes fast."

Lesson four, no matter what they forget, they don't forget they're alive.

"You must be the best starer in the place."

"And you need a good kick in the hole!" she yelled, looking at the window ledge full of flowers, framed photos, postcards. "Was it you sent me that one?"

"Which one?"

"That one."

I picked up a fish-shaped card, couldn't read the writing.

"You sent me that, didn't you?"

"No."

"Was it you?"

"No. It's from abroad, definitely not me. Remember, I am your carer, Stephen Kidney. Maybe I look like someone else."

"Are you sure?"

Could go on like this. "Will I shut up?" I asked. No reply. Lesson five, patients have the right to tell care assistants to shut up, not the other way around, even if you want to.

Asked her could I use her toilet.

"No, you'll have to do it on the floor."

Said to Cheerful Gloria on the way out, "She says she's given up praying." Worrying. All auld ones I knew were addicted to praying.

She laughed. "That one, she thinks she's already in heaven."

Noticed Gloria always wore blue top. Out of respect for her, noted. Lesson six, always wear a blue top when care assisting.

Lucid moments were a great source of care-assistant lessons. Hard to spot, of course, for both of us. She'd look and act the same as always, and I'd only get a sense she was serious if she managed to stay on track for more than one sentence. When she did manage it, it wasn't dying she worried about. It was escaping.

"You know," she'd start off obliquely, "I'm lucky to have my own room." Short pause. "There's plenty of food here," and then, "When am I going back to my own house?" Or, another approach, she'd craftily ask, "Do you have a car?" or "How did you get here?" or "Where's John? He drives me everywhere."

Almost every visit she told me, "You know there's a lock on the front door." Always nodded, always touched, feeling resonated with me. Thought about helping her escape but was learning too much about excellence in care assisting. Did bring her out on the third visit to local café, relishing the responsibility of being the only one in charge. Passed a bus stop, looked at her, ready to stop if she did. Realised neither of us knew where her home was, couldn't trust anything she'd say.

Should a good care assistant reason with a patient against escaping? List all the obstacles. Tried on third visit. She didn't argue, dropped the subject, stared at the wall. Funny, she seemed to lose confidence when we were out too long, wanted to go back.

Yeah, definite parallels. Both prisoners of different sorts. I didn't want anyone trying to talk me out of escaping to my new identity, my new life either. And if it meant counselling her against escaping, so be it. Lesson seven, sympathise but do nothing when they talk about escaping.

On my second visit, snow was hiding in the corners of big fields, she told me she'd been taken out for a drive.

"By whom?"

Looked at me like I was the one who'd lost his marbles. "John. Who else?"

"Where did you go?"

"Don't know."

Five minutes later. "They played music, old music."

I'd seen a brochure for a music centre on the chest of drawers.

"Will you read it out for me?"

"What? You can't read, haha." Lesson eight, never ask them to read.

Should a care assistant talk about money? The Auld One had no difficulty talking about money. She often asked me was I loaded and where was 'Mister Tuppence-h'penny', the man who controlled her money. Money definitely meant lucidity.

"How much do you want?" I asked.

"I'm not telling you." She only took money from 'Mister Tuppence-h'penny' because then she knew it was hers. Fine distinction for a woman with almost no memory. Lesson number nine, if they're able to ask about money, they're lucid.

I wasn't her only visitor. She had others as well, but I avoided them. Why? The usual Onslaught-nonsense. Oh, that's great, you're visiting your mother. Why else would you be here? Eyes would light up even brighter. "But at a deeper sub-conscious level," – they loved 'deeper' – "This must mean you are actually acknowledging the link."

Each time I arrived I checked at reception if anyone else was there or due. Lesson ten, avoid patients whose families call at unpredictable times. Worked fine until I met Mr Tuppence-h'penny.

On the fifth visit she was out of bed, day clothes, baggy dark trousers, colourful jersey, looking for chocolate. Moving slowly around the room, opening drawers, poking at hanging clothes in wardrobe, checking shelves, going over stuff already checked.

"Did you take my chocolate?" she asked suddenly, head stuck in the wardrobe. I thought she'd forgotten I was there. "I hid some here and it's gone."

"No."

"Prove it," she shot back.

"Eh, I'll go across the road and buy some for you."

"No, no, no, you will not do anything of the sort," mother-order-like. "They'll find it and steal it again." She paused, looked at me. "You know they laugh at me when I complain."

Definitely not Cheerful Gloria. "Who stole it?"

"The little ones. They come in and take it."

Never heard this before but was half believing her.

"You know what little ones are like, don't you?"

Gradually I was growing more confident in my care assisting. Still not the real deal. So much to learn, so much

I wasn't let do – wheelchair-pushing, feeding, washing, giving tablets. Suggested a trial spin in a wheelchair a few times, but she absolutely refused to get in one, fighting fierce war against wheels and unused legs. Passing some auld ones in wheelchairs in the corridor, clenched teeth, barely concealing disdain. Taking giant strides to prove legs were better, urged me on, saying, "Use it or lose it, use it or lose it!" Lesson nine or whatever, don't mention wheelchairs to leg-users.

That slow walk to the day room before lunch was almost my only opportunity to experience practical caring. She'd take my arm, we'd shuffle along the corridors. I'd deliver her to her usual armchair, always far too early for lunch, facing the big windows the sun shone through. All the auld ones in a line of wizened faces, synchronised staring. She'd look around disapprovingly. Always reminded me of my own staring out the window, all of us hoping for miracles. When her friend Anne, greeted her, she'd tell me to go. I'd hang around, watching the other carers at work, she'd say, "What are you waiting for? Go." Lesson eleven, don't be jealous of patient's friends. Lesson twelve, don't argue when the patient wants to go for lunch far too early.

Chapter 27

Perplexed Politician

D istortions. Ripples. Near midnight, doing what I often did, standing on my favourite tile in the kitchen, staring out into the darkness. Not aimless, obviously not Boris-waiting. Fascinated by the distorted images of myself produced by kitchen light through the triple-glazed windows, and the few dots of lights beyond the garden wall. Intrigued by the malleability of translucent images, how they were able to distort reality, reveal new ways of seeing myself just by movement, angle. Depending where I stood, how I moved my head, I saw a huge torso, balloon head, tiny legs, that sort of thing. Only tricks of light, but they came from me, were me, and seemed to confirm that, indeed, there could be different versions of myself living inside me. This helped me believe I could have a Stephen Kidney or anyone else inside me. A big help facing an uncertain future.

That evening a bare arm was attached to a bizarre new image hovering towards me out of the black night through the glass. Looked like me mixed with a woman. Moved my bloated head – now man, now man-woman. Christ, am I dreaming? Wait, wait, was this foreseeable? Stephen Kidney just came into my life, Patricia at the school reunion bending lines I never thought bendable. Looked at it again, big nose, next to menacing narrow eyes, not mine. Did Kidney have silty eyes? Horrifying. What did it mean? Was Kidney also a cross-dresser, a half-way house, suggesting Patricia fully detached? Closed, opened eyes. Image now shifting without moving my head.

Bare arm stretched out from darkness, an accusation, and tapped the glass. Not hard. Shrank backwards. At the end of the arm was the face of the ruddy Politician! Air sucked out of my lungs. I wasn't going mad. Relief, embarrassment, anger. Loosened my collar, swept the sweat off my forehead. She'd seen me inside my private space.

Had to readjust quickly. Another midnight visit, that's all. Nothing more. Eh, wait a minute, that's never something to be sanguine about. No wonder I hadn't seen her. Shoulder-less, armless, sleek, strappy, pure black dress. For God's sake, going around like that in the middle of the bloody night. No sparkling jewellery, just big pale face. Sleek material clinging to her like it would die if it didn't hug her skin.

"Dominic, open up. It's freezing out here," muffled voice called out. She rubbed her arms, shoulders.

"What do you want at this hour?" Can guess. Probably to give out to me about anything – the Brat, the searches or some endless monologue about herself. Slid open the door. "It's not convenient now. I'm on my way up to bed."

"That's no problem," she said, smartly stepping in before I had second thoughts. "We can talk in your bedroom if you like."

Outrageous suggestion. "No," I was firmer than Delahunty's locks. "We most certainly cannot."

"Anyway, we need to talk," she announced in an ominous tone, like war could depend on it. I slid the door closed.

"God, it's cold in here. Do you not put on the heating?"

"Can't afford it."

"Nonsense, you never turn it on. I don't know how you can stick it. What were you doing there?" Throwaway question, didn't expect to receive an answer. Marched through the kitchen to the hall, slung one of my jackets over her shoulders, came back.

"I've been at one of those dinners you always liked," she said, rubbed the side of her nose with her little finger. Alarmingly, Harry responded.

She sat at the table, motioned me to do the same. Had pen, notepad in front of her. "Dominic," tapped the table. "Please sit down."

Sat on the other side of the table, wishing the table was longer, wider.

"What's going on?" she asked, puzzled tone. "I'm only back in the country one day and I get a call from Tom. He's been ringing I don't know how many times, and he's up to here," touched the top of her head, "with indignation. He's the only one who's called so far, I think, but I can imagine what they're all thinking and I know the media will be on it soon." She bit the pen. "Thank God, the election is over."

Sympathy nodding. What a dilemma she has. Done nothing to provoke all this, and, here she is, in the middle of it. Welcome, Missus, to the real world.

"I don't know what's going on," I answered truthfully. "It's very strange. They said they were looking for documents or papers."

She started taking notes.

"Have you lost something?"

"Yeah," she replied dryly, "my marbles. Who is they and what papers?"

"They were Army or something, army overalls on. Oh, and," I puffed out my chest, "they knew me."

"Odd, isn't it?" she replied, totally ignoring my fame. "I'm supposed to be in charge of the whole lot of them, and I've no idea what they're doing."

"The Guard knows. He saw their ID. Mrs Hand said it was the only good thing he's done since he arrived. I think she doesn't like him."

"Mrs Hand?" She screwed up her forehead. "Oh, Mrs Hand."

"I think she voted for you."

"OK, OK."

"And so did her husband."

She looked puzzled. "Didn't he die? I think I was at his funeral years ago."

"That's what she said."

"Oh, look, forget Mrs Hand. Stick to the point." She glanced at the unfinished salad abandoned at the other end of the table. I got her a fork. "No, thanks," she said, shivering. "It's disgusting." Didn't agree with peanuts in salad.

Dragged the salad bowl over, started playing with the salad, pushing it around the bowl, eating bits of it, glad to have something to do. "They searched here as well," I added nonchalantly.

"They did what?" she gasped. Genuine shock, so far as I could tell.

"The whole house."

"And you let them?"

"I not only let them, I insisted on it. I couldn't have them searching the other houses and not mine. The neighbours would talk." Plunged my fork deep into the salad. "I mean you're not here, you don't have to live with it."

Staring at me.

"Except the basement. I wouldn't let them into the basement. I won't let anyone in there." She knew that, but no harm reminding her.

Her eyes riddled with disbelief, "Oh my God. Oh my God." New disquiet in her eyes. "Was Thomas here during the search?"

"You mean the Brat? No, pity. He'd have loved it."

"Were there any journalists around?"

"No." I knew what they looked like. Badly dressed, shifty-looking types, usually wearing cheap woollen caps.

Rubbed her nose. "There will be after this." Her shoulders sagged as she emitted a long soundless sigh. "OK, tell me everything. From the beginning."

Strongly tempted to start by saying it was all her fault for not having a proper lock on her bloody toilet door. But if I did that there was no knowing where it would go. Just told her someone had smashed her toilet door for a crap, about the tortoise, the kids, some documents, presumably hers, gone missing. For reason beyond me, I told her they wanted to know who owned Boris. And I would be expecting her to pay the locksmith. Finished by telling her I found the thing they were looking for, at least I think it was, out in the lane under one of the wheelie bins, near the pole they'd been working on, gave it to the Civilian out on the street, everyone saw it. I didn't like his manners. Guessed the envelope fell out of someone's pocket when they were up the pole.

"So that's it. Done and dusted. I'm off to bed…"

"Whoa," she raised a hand. "What was in it?"

"Don't know. Didn't look." Looked at her candidly. "None of my business."

"Describe it to me and who is this Civilian?"

After I finished telling her, I added, "And don't ask me why they are so interested in your bloody toilet."

She spent a while reading over her notes, looked up at me with a fresh frown. "What is going on, Dominic? Something is going on."

"The Guard has their IDs," I reiterated.

"That won't tell us much. My guess is that whoever you saw was following orders but whose?"

As a disinterested observer, I was keen to show I too thought it weird. "What's really weird," I said, "is that

I think they suspected Boris of stealing the documents. That's why they spent so long in Carter's."

"Unbelievable," she shook her head, put the pen down, looked me straight in the eyes. "I shouldn't ask this. You're not seriously telling me they suspected a cat of picking up a plastic thingy and bringing it to the Carter's in his mouth?" She laughed so much I thought she was laughing at me. "Even you wouldn't make that up," she said when she stopped.

"Never underestimate Boris. He's is a very clever cat. You've no idea how clever he is."

"Yeah?" she replied drool-voiced. "Clever with no hands." Tapped the pen against her mouth. "The documents? This is what's so puzzling. I suppose they didn't say what kind of documents?"

"Nope."

Sat back thoughtfully, pushed the strap of her dress back up on her shoulder. "I need to have a good think about this."

Think away, I said to myself, feeling the soft glow of innocence, carried on picking at the remainder of the salad, noisily chewing the vinaigrette-coated peanuts.

"I suspect… I can think of three or four but the organisation and effort that's gone into this is… Can really only be one or two probably really only one… Though, maybe… No, can't be sure…"

Politician on top of her job, she wrote out a to-do list. Mostly phone calls. Stopped in the middle of it, gave me another eyeballing. "You're sure you had nothing to do with any of this?"

Would've liked to swear on my mother's grave, if I knew where it was. Made a face purer than the Brat's before his Confirmation. Shook my head until I felt a little dizzy. "I like that," I protested, stoking indignation. "I solve a problem for you, find the envelope, give it back, and I'm to blame? Thank you very much."

"Dominic?" stern questioning look.

Wagged my finger back at her, said nothing. My innocence, her guilt, about equal.

"Because, you know," she spoke too calmly, "this is serious, even very serious. The Guard will have to be interviewed. You'll be interviewed, so will I and the neighbours. The worst case scenario, I could lose my job."

"No." Intolerable notion. "They can't do that." She'll be around far too much if she loses her job. "Mrs Hand says there's no such thing as bad publicity for a politician."

"God spare me that woman!" Nestled her chin in her palm. Studied her to see where her superior political skills lay, had to have some. "It's going to break tomorrow. We'll wake up and it could be all over the papers and radio. They'll be camped outside on the footpath waiting for me."

"Outside your house, not mine."

"Won't make any difference to them."

"It better. I won't have anyone on my land without my say-so."

"Please, Dominic, no stunts. Just let the guards do their job. That reminds me." She added the local Garda station's phone number to her to-do list. "I'll have to ring Joan to tell Thomas to come in the back through the lane when he comes from school tomorrow." Glanced at her watch. "I mean today. Or, you could pick him up? No, don't. I'll think of something." She looked at me like she'd just thought of something. "Was Thomas there when you gave the envelope back?"

"No."

"That's a relief," she said with heavy sarcasm.

"But," Colonel Big-Mouth couldn't help himself, "he recognised the Civilian because he'd seen him before. In your garden."

"What?" she gasped. She picked up the fork, despite her qualms, dug into my salad. "You promise you will stay well away from the journalists, won't you? Not a word. Not even a hello or I'm fine. Nothing. OK?"

"Sure." Resented being told that when she talked to them every day. Anyway, journalists were a class apart from all decent people.

Scratched her forehead. "I don't need all this now. Really, who would want to do me harm?"

Colonel Stapled-Lips hummed to himself. Divert attention. "And what about the hut?" I asked matter-of-factly. "Don't forget the hut. If you go, the hut will have to go as well, won't it?"

That irritated her. "What are you talking about?"

Know what her reaction was when I told her? Told me not to be so fussy. What did a few inches matter to anyone? Then she burst into a fit of giggles that lasted too long. "What did you do today?" she asked when she calmed down, stretching her bare arms.

"I saw Boris."

"Boris? Dominic, to be honest, you and that cat, you should move in together, then you could gaze into each other's eyes all day long."

Sniffed loudly at the sneer, but realised it gave me an opportunity I'd been looking for. "I'd need to buy him first. Maurice would want a lot."

"Don't you have lots of money?"

"Me?" First I heard of it. True, whenever I went to the Happy-Hole-in-the-Bank- Wall, it never disappointed, but that didn't mean I was rich. It just meant it liked my handshake. Taking money out was one of the first things they taught me when I moved into my house. God, they went on about taking out only small amounts.

"Boris is a thoroughbred. I don't think I would be able to afford him. Eh, would you be able to give me a loan? If I needed it?"

"A loan?" she leaned forward, laughed again, showing too much cleavage. "For a cat? Are you mad? Sorry, I didn't mean that."

"Would you? Would you have enough cash?"

"You're the one with all the money, not me."

"So, you've nothing in the bank or anywhere?"

"No." Mock-laugh. "I have my salary and my pension and some small savings. Politics is an expensive business."

"That's all?" Suppose posters and photographers and hairdressers cost a lot.

Sat up, growing suspicious. "What's this about, Dominic? You're not usually so interested in my money."

Shrugged my shoulders. "I'm not."

Chapter 28

Last Visit to Auld One

My last visit to the nursing home. Last practical in care assisting. Hadn't planned it. Still had some way to go, getting better, but hazy about what that meant. The Auld One hadn't dis-improved or anything like it. Something else entirely.

Pissing rain caught me out on the walk from the bus stop to the nursing home. Had my hat, coat as usual, but the downpour was so sudden and spiteful, got rightly soaked. So agitated when I got inside the building, forgot to ask reception whether any visitors were there or due.

Inside her room she watched impassively as I hurled the wet hat, coat on the floor, rushed to the bathroom, took off my trousers and stuffed them on the radiator in the bedroom, which thankfully was on. The Auld One went, "Agh!" Her hands over her eyes. Rushed back into her bathroom, wrapped one of her towels around my waist. "You're not getting into my bed," she declared when she saw me, her suspicious eyes following me around as I took off my Monday and Wednesday socks, squeezed the drops out of them and shoved them between the radiator bars. One bare foot slid forward on the wet floor and I almost did the splits before grabbing hold of the radiator. Felt I was giving a free panto.

"That'll teach you to swim with your clothes on," she guffawed as I sat down, rubbed my hair with her other towel.

"I have to sit down," I panted, tired after all the exertions.

"Are you pregnant?" she enquired.

"Yes."

She snorted. Her breakfast on a tray on the trolley over the end of her bed, untouched.

"Do you have a good appetite?" I asked, wondering should I force feed her.

"I am a sausage."

"So am I."

"No, you're not. Do you think I came down in the last shower?" Not a welcome pun. But maybe a lucid moment?

"Where's Catherine?" she asked, continuing to look at me.

"Who's Catherine?" Oh, yeah, the Politician's name. What part of her tortured mind had brought that up? Normally we only talked about ourselves and anyone, wasters mainly, who didn't use their legs.

"What I would like to do is to go back to when we lived long ago," she said, distant-voiced, shuffling her feet under the bedclothes as if starting her journey. Nodded in agreement with her, even swallowed, genuine lumpy-throat moment.

"The only way I'll get out of here is in a coffin."

Strange thing was, she didn't look sad or as if she expected it to happen any moment. Twelfth valuable lesson, never molly-coddle a patient who indicates they understand the imminence of death.

Made up another story about Mrs Hand. Dracula had never tasted blood like Mrs Hand's. Made him feel funny, even sanguine. In despair he turned on Irena who he'd been warned to stay away from. After Irena died from lost blood, all cleaners in Romania also died and no one knew how to thoroughly clean blood-stained white shirts. So Dracula had to wear dirty shirts which made seduction harder. Even worse. Every time Dracula was about to bite, his mouth closed in tight smirk. "And that's why there are statues to Irena all over Romania to this day."

"What happened?" she demanded impatiently. She didn't like unclear endings.

"OK. He died of thirst."

"You're not getting my blood," she snorted, making two weak fists of her hands. Lesson thirteen, only tell stories that frighten them.

One leg in the air, doing her exercise, sockless Colonel Bare-Legs copying her from his chair, towel decently arranged. "Lift that leg, higher, straighter," I challenged her.

"Use it or lose it! Use it or lose it!" we were chanting when the door behind me opened.

"Aha," she guffawed loudly, keeping her leg up, "the second gang has arrived."

Lowered my leg, turned to look. In the doorway, tall, thinnish man. Three-piece dark suit, serious-minded, straight silver hair. His eyes already widened, when he saw the towel. He tried opening them more, travelled down to my bare feet and the wet clothes on the radiator. Stood up. Could be the consultant for auld ones. Didn't want to give bad impression. Dismayed to notice his surprise turn judgemental.

"Dominic," he said quietly, without warmth, "what a surprise. How are you?" Shook my hand quickly. "I believe you've been visiting Mammy?" Sound like a rebuke, but wait… Is he saying we're brothers? "Regularly, is that right?" At ease, suave even in his disdain.

He went over to the window side of the bed, leaned over the Auld One, gave her a light hug.

"Ooh!" she went, squirming as if he'd broken her bones. "Don't lean on me. You'll crush me."

"Hello, Mam," he said briskly. "It's John. How are you keeping today?"

"Half dead, half alive." Stock answer. Once asked her what half I was dealing with, 'The one the devil won't get his hands on!' was her reply.

"Look, Mam, I brought you this lovely plant and a card from Alice and the girls." Held the plant in front of her. Showed no interest in it. "It doesn't need much water.

I'll tell the nurse." He made room for the plant on the far windowsill. She stared at the wall as he read the card.

"Wasn't that nice of them, Mam?" he asked. Started telling her about his two grown-up daughters, one married, the other 'too happily single'. Other news which I'd no choice but to listen to. Moved out of his house while builders… blah, blah… yawn. I might as well not be there for all the attention he paid me. Noticed the yawn, though. Finally, he glanced at me as if surprised I hadn't vanished into thin air, and she was now with someone who actually cared for her. Might even have left if he hadn't looked at me like that. But, sitting on the only chair in the room. Wasn't going to let him have it. Besides, I was curious about his antipathy.

"Didn't expect to see you here," he said eventually when he stopped boring her.

Shrugged my shoulders, said nothing, wondering when he'd let it all out. I was well used to hostility and to people thinking they knew me better than I did myself.

"I'm your brother," he said in an irritated whisper, looking at me, kicking away one of my shoes that had strayed over to the radiator beside him. "Your elder brother, not some stranger who's walked in off the street."

The Auld One, who'd been drifting off to sleep, suddenly awoke. "Boys," she cried, "if you're going to fight, go outside."

The notion of fighting clearly disgusted him. Not me. Giving him a poke in the ribs appealed. Checked what shape he was in, nothing to worry about beyond the shouting. Stretched my bare legs, kind of waiting for some remark to get me going, Problem was trousers drying on the radiator near the window. Brief flicker in his eyes told me he knew what I was thinking.

"It's very simple. I'm trying to help," I said.

"Huh, well," he sniffed like he doubted that, "it's good you're visiting your own mother."

She guffawed, as if saying none of this has anything to do with me. We both glanced at her. Yep, with the vibe going on between us across her bed, it was possible to forget she was still there.

"Your last visit when she was in hospital wasn't… good for her."

"Wasn't good for me either."

That seemed to annoy him. "You're not making a fool of her again here, are you?" he asked, looking at my towel which was perhaps showing too much hairy leg. He looked around at my scattered wet belongings. "What were you up to when I came in and, for God's sake, make yourself decent. You look like a joke."

Still said nothing, glanced at the Auld One to see was she still following the exchanges. You could never be sure.

"You better not or I'll have you thrown out of here," he continued cross-voiced, stoking his own anger, nodding vehemently, "and make sure you're not let in again. She's entitled to some respect at this age of her life. Not to be made a clown of for your amusement."

"Seven hundred and three," she said out of the blue.

"See," he said, looking grimly at her. "It's all she has left."

'Laugh, you idiot,' I said without speaking. 'That's what she needs.' Lesson fourteen or fifteen, can't remember – get the patient to make their own jokes. Folded my legs, towel rose too high, didn't care. He'll never make a good care assistant. I knew more about the dignity of auld ones that he'd ever know. Shook my head. Almost asked him to repeat after me, 'Amusement, not respect. Amusement, not …' Couldn't help a quickie smirk. He saw it too, wasn't happy.

"I think you should leave now," he demanded, bristling with indignation. "If you don't know how to behave yourself. It would be best for Mammy. She doesn't need this kind of carry-on." Glared at me as if fully expecting me to hop up and clear off. "And think carefully about coming back if you're going to be like this." Then under his breath, "Unbelievable. Can't cope with rain!"

Amazing arrogance. I'd only just met the man and he was talking to me like this.

"Ask her," I said, nodding at the Auld One who'd stopped moving her head between us like a tennis umpire. I sat forward in the chair, smoothed my towel, in passing wondering if circumstances were conditioning me to become a cross-dresser like Stephen Kidney surely was.

"Who are you anyway?" I asked quietly. "I've never seen you before. What's your name?"

He scowled at the provocation, but his composure held, just. "Oh, no, you're not pulling that one on me, kiddo. I remember when you were a snotty, disobedient, devious little brat who gave Daddy and Mammy a hard time. Don't forget that, because I won't." His hands were moving between rubbing themselves to rubbing his chin.

Wondered how the people who met him every day put up with such a boorish gobshite. But what was even more amazing and intriguing was his use of 'brat'.

"Fuck," he said in a way that suggested he wasn't used to using it. "No one has made me as angry as this in a long time. You haven't changed a bit." He turned his back on me and looked out the window.

The Auld One had fallen asleep. I grabbed my semi-dry trousers off the radiator while he stared out the window, whipped off the towel and put them on.

"Agh!" the Auld One went as if she was being strangled. Eyes wide open, staring at me, acting up. Winked at her. Where did she get this weird sense of timing?

"You should just go," he said, his back still turned to me. "And leave Mammy alone, please. Leave us all alone, for good."

That merited a dig. But I couldn't destroy all I'd learned in the last weeks. I leaned forward, put my hand lightly on the Auld One's cold bony hand lying on the sheet. "I'll see you next week," I said softly. "Keep using those legs." Lesson fifteen or sixteen, suppress all aggressive feelings towards patient's obnoxious family members.

Chapter 29

Henry Hurling

The Brat wasn't pretending. He really wasn't going to do his homework. It was stupid. A project on desert rats? Did I see any deserts around here? I looked out the big kitchen window. "Nope."

"You could do it for me," sly-face suggested, giving me a pretend-friend shove off my favourite tile, as if the absence of a local desert would make any difference to a man like me. "You've been there."

"Me?"

"Mam says you were there in the army."

I looked closely at him. Where did this wide-eyed innocent who asked cheeky questions really come from? Reminded myself to ask Mrs Hand. She's been around here for a long time.

"That's dishonest," I said. "You'll never grow up if you tell lies."

He gave me such a look, like I was too stupid to be called stupid.

Should've shoved him off my tile. Instead, I said, "Right, forget about that. We're going down to the park to play Henry Hurling."

"Henry Hurling?" he cried in horror. "That's for boggers." He defied me, "I can't play hurling. That's for boggers."

"Doesn't matter. We're all boggers. You'll learn, scaredy-cat." I'd told him about the kids playing Henry Hurling in the field in Sligo, but it was obvious Sligo hurling was another undiscovered planet.

"We don't play hurling in our school," he protested.

"Why?"

Gave me the look, pity-coated contempt, he was so good at.

Squared up to him, over a foot above his head, couldn't see him. "I don't give a flying fuck what they play in that snob school your mother sends you to," I snarled. "We're going hurling. Go and get ready."

His eyes bulged at my bad language. I could hear his brain recording it for repetition to his mother. "The teachers say it's dangerous," dainty legs said.

Perfectly obvious trying to provoke me into more incriminating language which his mother had warned me about. I leaned down and shoved my face into his. "What kind of an arsehole school is it anyway? Full of weaklings and snivelling gnomes and tit-suckers, heh?" His mouth ajar, like his tongue was trying to fall out. I nodded in satisfaction. He hadn't heard that one before. Neither had I. "Since when did you become an arse-smelling wimp?

You're going hurling with me and that's that. Now, get ready."

Took him a while to absorb. Still too astonished to be angry. "I've no gear."

A lie, but worth trying. I'd bought him a kid-sized hurley and five sliotars, as the shop assistant called them. He'd soon lose the lot. I'd buy more.

Minutes later, he appeared looking like, I don't know what. Cycling helmet, goggles, elbow, knee pads and what looked like a stab vest.

"I'm going to tell on you," he said, more out of habit than intent, as we made our way goggle-less – that was the limit, down to the park.

"You're always saying that. Can't you think of something else?"

"You're a ... an arsehole!" he cried looking up at me, half running to keep up with Colonel Long-Stride. Guess he felt he had to protest, but not too much in case he liked it.

Well. He took to Henry Hurling like he'd been reared in Tipperary. That first day, his face alive with the thrill of whack-walloping the sliotar. The unrelenting hacking and slashing at each other's hurleys and feet to get at the small ball came later, but his taste for semi-regulated violence was obvious. After that, Henry Hurling in the park became our regular afternoon foray.

What he really buzzed on was hitting the sliotar back and forth across the shallow stream that flowed through the middle of the park. The fool who missed had to go into the cold slimy water to retrieve it. Hiking up his shorts, free to get legs wet up to his thighs, toes covered in gooey muck – hark the moaner-women, was brutal fun. Until he realised it was even better when I missed and had to do it. Then he shouted and pointed at me, wet rolled-up trousers, chasing the bloody ball before the current swept it away, or some dog got it first and I had to run after it. Obviously misses by me were always deliberate to encourage him. Hammed it up too because nothing made him happier than thinking I was even more stupid than he gave me credit for. Worked so well, decided to ask Retired Detective if Stephen Kidney played Henry Hurling.

The Brat made friends through Henry Hurling. Other kids copied us. Some afternoons there could be three, four groups hitting sliotars across the river. Discovered I knew more about the rules of Henry Hurling than I thought. Moved on to organising and refereeing impromptu matches until the damn wimps objected I never blew the whistle. What's wrong with shouting at them, 'Get up, get on with it!'

One afternoon, on a park bench, resting after chasing away three dogs who wanted to play – bothered me, didn't bother the kids, breathless Brat charged over to me, interrupting conversation with random auld one who sat down on same bench after me. Petite, compact, white-hair, black high-ankle boots.

"Granddad, Granddad!" usual fake happy-families mush in front of strangers, "Can I join Na Fianna? Can I? Some of the guys play for them. Derek's dad says I have to have permission. Can I, please?"

Took my time answering. This interruption didn't suit me at all. Had been trialling childless Stephen Kidney with auld one, doing marvellous job of eye-wool-pulling. Lapping it up, she was, like afternoon sherry, then along comes Brat to scupper it.

"Course you can," I replied, also fake happy-families tone with daggers look, adding, "Off with you now and, as they say, haha, do it to them before they do it to you." Apologetic grimace at auld one. "Calls me that all the time. You know the way kids call their parents friends Uncle, same thing. I'm not actually his grandfather." Gazed at Brat getting stuck into a melee of legs and swinging hurleys, no sign of the ball. "A fine lad, but a little," tapped the side of my head. "Sometimes forgets who he is."

"Poor laddie," auld one muttered in strong northern accent, squeezing her hands into each other. "Most be hoird on has poirents."

"They don't care –" Stopped to roar at Brat squaring up to stoneo-faced kid, "Hit him first and run." Was afraid his mother would notice any bruises. Finito Henry Hurling. "No father, you know. Pity, he needs all the parents he can get."

"Aw'll romomber ham in my proyers,' she finally murmured, thin lips barely moving, fingers already working on virtual rosary beads.

"Anyway, as I was saying," Colonel Kidney keen to get back on trial-track, "during my time in the nursing home in London," paused to look painfully up at sky. "Well, some memories are still painful to talk about. There was a lot of dying going on and thinking about dying. You know what auld ones are like" – sudden fit of coughing – "I mean, much older than you, missus. Couldn't get them to think about anything else." Gazed down at my non-thumb, moved it to attract her attention.

"Os it pawnful? Awf yow don't moind me awsking, Mr Kidney, what hawppened tow awt? Awt must've been owful."

"Oh, just one of those things. I'm used to it now. It was in the nursing home, you know. Two auld ones sitting beside each other in wheelchairs in the dayroom. I'd just brought her in, walking, of course, never liked wheelchairs. One accused the other of stealing her dentures – a serious accusation there. She just grabbed a knife off a passing trolley, I saw it, and put my hand out to stop her and… whack, sliced it clean off."

Bench auld one thinking hard. "Dun't worry, sawn. That's Onglawnd for yow. Wauldn't hawppen hure."

Chapter 30

Visiting Neighbour Maurice

The lane at the back of the garden was an open-access cemetery for decrepit, disused, ownerless child-junk. Plastic toys, stolen traffic cones, flash-mobs of wheelie bins, crowd-control barriers, portable goalposts, a one-wheel scooter, bits of wood, deflated footballs, and whatever you're having yourself. Once out there, obedient, parented children form roaming packs of megaphone-voices, fractious, yelping, goading, crying lane-urchins.

Which is why I made my way to the Carter's lane door mid-morning when, by law, the lane-urchins had to be elsewhere.

When Maurice finally appeared, pale and wan as usual – Mrs Hand said he spent all his time on the computer, I had to drag my eyes away from his pale skin before speaking.

"What happened during the search?" I asked, not expecting or wanting to be invited into his small high-walled back garden.

"I had to laugh," he said typically unsmiling, "when they asked to see Boris' teeth."

"His teeth?"

"To see could he carry an envelope. They put a stuffed plastic envelope on the ground in front of him." He snorted. "Tried to get him to lift it. They spent ten minutes at it. Dora wanted to film it, but they asked her not to. They knew well how it would look." Interesting, but Maurice's voice was the best sleeping pill I knew. Nasal, monotone.

"Amazing," I declared. Didn't say it, but would have loved to have been there, wouldn't have been surprised if Boris had picked up the envelope. Just to show he could. If he put his mind to it Boris could do anything. "Boris is too clever to fall for that trick," I said.

"Yeah," Maurice agreed. "He can do things most cats can't do."

"Oh, I know, I know," agreed, Colonel Sycophant. "He's very talented. He's my favourite cat." In the whole world. I barely stopped myself asking if I could buy him.

"It was a howl," Maurice laughed humourlessly. "Hut, hut." Since I admired Maurice, and not just because of Boris, I hut-hutted too.

"It was in the papers."

"About Boris?" I was incredulous.

"No, the searches. Not page one, but it could happen if the story grows legs."

Legs? A spider with a story on its back running up a journalist's leg. Maurice brought out the paper and read it to me. For some reason people often think I can't read. Put my hands in my pockets, shook my head at the right moments, impressed by the madness of the world.

The phone in the hall was ringing when I got back. The only voice I wanted to hear was the Retired Detective's because the bugger hadn't gotten back to me. The damn Politician, wanting to know if anything was happening. "Any news?"

"Boris didn't appear this morning," I told her. "And the lane's still a mess. So is Maurice," I duly reported.

She sighed. "I don't mean that. Any journalists there?" She was always warning me not to speak to them.

"I didn't see any." She told me the Brat wouldn't be coming to the house. She had arranged for him to be collected from a summer camp and brought to the Parliament after-school program. His mother would pick him up from there.

"I did the interview," she announced like she'd been bursting to tell someone. "I think it went alright. I'm so relieved it's over. I still don't know what it's all about."

"How can you do an interview and not know what you're talking about?"

She just laughed to herself. I heard a car stopping outside, put the phone down, opened the front door to check. Only Tom back from taking his car for a rare spin. Returned to the phone.

"Are you there, Dominic?" she was asking when I picked up again.

"Yes," I sighed. "Just spotted twenty journalists getting out of a tiny car."

"What?" she cried.

"Joke." I had a premonition, don't know why, she was going to tell me she'd taken a lover. No problem, all the best. In fact, why only one? I'd say, take two, whatever you want, dear.

"Haha," she said dryly. "You remember I told you about the ceremony in McKee Barracks next week?"

"No."

"It'll be my first time there as Minister and I've been told they'll make a big deal out of it, especially as the French Minister and the French Ambassador will be there as well." On and on she rambled while I looked around the hall for something to look at. Three hats, three coats, three umbrellas, a stand, pile of unopened mail, hall table, two socks, one Sunday, couldn't read the other, chain for the front door.

She went rabbiting on, "...like old women, the generals and colonels, the way they dress up and carry on. Worse than judges."

Jaysus, almost slammed the phone down. Had enough recent references to dressing up like women. How would Kidney look in a Colonel's dress?

"What French Minister?"

"She's a woman," the Politician replied mock-shocked. "That's what they'll all be thinking. Two of us. Must be a record. Oh, I bet they'll trot out every female officer they can find just to show they believe in equality." She paused, small grunt. Sounded like she was multitasking by pulling hairs out of her chin again. "I've been told it's usually the Ambassador who makes these awards on behalf of the government, but she'll be here herself, so."

I'd lost interest, was holding the phone away from my ear, trying to catch the shrieking of a flock of geese flying by, heading for the sea flats.

"What's that noise? Sounds like birds?"

"What noise?" Jaysus, she wants to know everything. How would Stephen Kidney react to this?

"Are you listening to me? Do you know why you're invited?"

"Invited? No."

"To give you a medal."

"A medal? Haha, haha." I always laughed when I thought the Onslaught was trying too hard. That was the silliest so far.

"Isn't that great?"

"I'm tired. I'm going to bed."

"But really, I think," she mustn't have heard me, "it's also about getting us to sign that big contract. There's been so much work done. Wonder what I'll wear. You know what I'm most worried about? That she'll upstage me, make me look like a frumpy old cow!"

Interesting question. What animal does she remind me of? A mongoose? With her nose stuck in everyone's business? Or, a zebra who helped people cross the road and demanded they take a photo of her? Could be amusing to ask the Brat what animal I remind him of.

"I better get Martina to get me a picture of what she looks like, so I'll know what I'm up against. Anyway, I'll have to get a new outfit. Something chic and business-like, but not gaudy or too young. God, where will I find that?"

Monologue suddenly stopped.

"Jesus!" she exclaimed. 'What day is your appointment?" Heard pages rapidly turning. "It's tomorrow. Christ, that's a relief. Did you get a reminder?"

"Eh, no."

"Your appointment with Dr Papp. Frank Papp."

"Do you know him?"

"Do I know him?"

She sounded exasperated. "Dominic, he's the only one who'll still see you."

"He rang to cancel the other day. Said he's going on a holiday to Tahiti. Mightn't come back, who knows?"

She laughed like it was genuinely funny. "He did no such thing."

Tried remembering. Was Papp the idiot who'd pleaded with me to write down on the blackboard every night before I went to bed, 'I want my memory back. Give me back my memory.'

"We'll have to have you spruced up for the ceremony. Your dress uniform, where is it?"

Dress? I have a dress? Did she know about Stephen Kidney? No, not possible. "Jaysus, I don't wear dresses and you can forget about that!"

Chapter 31

TV Interview

The TV was acting up. Taking revenge for being ignored for so long. Still not enough reason to go dead the one time I wanted to use it. Five minutes on my knees fiddling at the back of it, trying to coax it into life. Just as I got it going and found the right channel, the bloody thing went again. Sheer spite. Threatened it with the hurley, started counting. More fiddling. Finally, just as the programme's opening music was fading, it stayed on. Picked up Annabella and Maximus from the top shelf in the closed glass cabinet, thanking God they hadn't scarpered, sat down with them on the sofa, both also facing the TV.

Presenter Miriam, big-boned, girly-faced, sugary blond, wearing peasant-style white blouse big enough to sail a small boat with. Immediately giddy, told Harry to wake up. As ever, he suited himself.

Jolly-Molly-voiced Miriam announced an extra unscheduled item, an interview with the new Minister for

Defence, Catherine Corley TD, over 'recent searches by officials to recover allegedly missing official documents'. Then the programme resumed its scheduled offerings, thirty-five minutes on homelessness in the second city and a plan to build a super-casino in the middle of nowhere. Maximus, Annabella and I wondered was it a joke having such items together.

At the end of these items, Miriam turned to a different camera. "In today's papers there were reports of searches carried out by security officials in the vicinity of the home of the new Minister for Defence over allegedly missing government papers. To discuss this, we have the Minister with us in studio tonight."

Camera turned on the Politician, prepared, false-faced, attentive, unsmiling, further along the same curved desk. Cream jacket, grey blouse, no jewellery. Figured she really was poor if she couldn't afford decent jewellery. Interesting. Lifeless hands flat on the desk, hair coiffed, looking more tanned than last night. Quickly checked my face in the mantelpiece mirror in case I'd sprouted an overnight tan.

"Catherine Corley, I want to begin by asking, what happened on Wednesday last week?"

"Well, first of all, Miriam, I want to apologise to –"

"Me!" I shouted, finishing the sentence for her. "Don't mind the others. Apologise to me."

"– my constituents and neighbours and friends. It's certainly not nice to have your home invaded and searched, is it?"

I practically threw the guinea pigs at the bloody screen. The hypocrisy of the woman. She, the arch-invader of my privacy, preaching to the whole bloody country.

"Indeed, Minister, it isn't," blond Miriam blithely agreed, Jolly-Molly gone. "But what was it about?"

"Well, as you know, Miriam, one of the main planks of this government's policy is of openness and –"

"Yes, Minister, we went through all that during the election. To come back to the searches, can you tell us…"

"There will be three separate independent investigations," the Politician calmly announced, "into what happened." Camera showed Miriam trying not to look dubious. "I will have no part in any of them, except, of course, to cooperate fully."

"That's all very good, Minister, but you would wonder, wouldn't you, why this has caused such a fuss? Three enquiries? What was in those documents?"

"Documents?" I guffawed at the dumb screen. "It was money, lots of it." I shouted, "Go on, Miriam, keep at her. We're with you. No more lies." Even glanced at the phone on a small table beside the sofa on the off chance there was a phone-in number. Miriam at the other end, confessing, 'I can't get anything out of her,' asking me, 'Can you help?'.

"That's a good question and…"

"Ah, that's a cop-out," I shouted, looking out the window, wondering could the blue lug in the hut hear me. "We have a right to know, don't we, Maximus?" Annabella showed me her bum, Maximus went for cover. Maybe I should have sent the Package to Miriam?

"But…"

"I will come back to that in a moment, Minister. But, now, what can you tell us about what happened during the searches?"

"Well, as I said, Miriam," I mimicked her in a falsetto voice, throwing my hands in the air, almost dislodging the guinea pigs.

"I am told the searches were precautionary in case some documents were missing."

"Precautionary, Minister?" arched eyebrows, doubting tone.

"Yes."

"What does that mean, Minister? Was anything found?" Miriam blinked her dark monster eyelashes. Harry stirred. "Was anything actually missing?"

"No, my information is that nothing was missing."

I sat up. The first useful piece of information. So that's how they're playing it. It never happened. Fair fucks to them. I supposed I'd do the same in their boots.

"So," crafty Miriam asked, "if there *were* any missing documents, would they have been missing from your home?"

"I assume so, but they weren't."

"Are you in the habit of keeping official documents at home while you are away? Surely that is…"

"Oh, no, of course not." First time the Politician looked uncomfortable.

"OK, Minister, how can I put this? If some document had gone missing, what, would they be about? Would they be important?"

"Well, Miriam, my officials are checking but…"

"So, Minister," Miriam paused, leaned back as if readying for a knock-out blow. "We have searches over documents which might not be missing, maybe from your house, but we don't know, and if they were missing, we don't know what they might be about, or whether they were important, or who took them if they were taken, is that a good summary?"

"And why," I reminded the screen. "Ask why, it's the most important question."

The Politician looked discomforted, but before she could answer.

"So, Minister," Miriam looked pleased with her summary, "you'll understand if we're confused. What is it all about? Is there more we're not being told?"

"To answer your last point, Miriam. No, as far as I know there is nothing the public is not being told but remember there are three inquiries and we have to let them do their job." The Politician's eyes flashed irritation. I recognised that look. She was going to attack. "This government is totally committed…"

"OK, Minister," Miriam quickly cut her off. "I now want to move on to a different aspect of this story, to the why and the wherefore. I…"

"Yes, of course." The camera caught the Politician moving some papers on the desk in front of her. Looking shifty.

"If you would just let me finish," Miriam's fake smile suited her. Harry was still unsure. The Politician was trying to read what was on the desk in front of her without inclining her head. "Many people will be puzzled by the timing of this. Which issues do you think, in your opinion, could cause all these events which, as you say yourself, you know absolutely nothing about?"

Little flash of you-don't-have-to-put-it-like-that in the Politician's eyes. "Well, there are many–"

"Minister," Miriam interjected fearlessly, wanting to avoid a long diversionary monologue, "there is speculation in some quarters that this whole affair is connected to the government's election manifesto's promise to re-equip the Naval Service and to spend up to five hundred million on new ships."

The Politician's expression didn't waver. "With all due respect, Miriam, I don't know anything about that speculation. The government has always –"

"I see, Minister." Miriam sounded like she was losing interest fast. "We must leave it there. Catherine Corley TD, Minister for Defence, thank you."

The guinea pigs had stopped mooching around in the towel on my lap. My hands had been squeezing them so tight they could've expired. "Moses alive!" I cried in shock, releasing the awesome creatures immediately. Welcome signs of bum-moving. Deeply ashamed, I patted them, but the unfeeling brutes ignored me totally. Went down to the kitchen where I treated them to double portion of fresh cucumber.

Fantasising about being interviewed by Miriam. "Do you like big-boned men?" I'd ask. She'd toss her head back, give a wicked little laugh. "Ah now, Colonel," – she'd call me that, "be serious. We know all about your charm but, what do you think happened and do you have confidence in the Minister?" Quick hand to mouth to hide my smile. But twinkling eyes my downfall. Another question. "Would you vote for her again?" I'd roar laughing, "Again? What do you mean again? Do you know what she's like? Wait 'til I tell you about the gap in the garden wall."

Chapter 32

Shrink Papp

The Shrinkage's office was on the fourth floor. The building near a train station. It overlooked a replanted Jacobean garden laid out in clear ordered lines which seemed to me emblematic of how the Shrinkage saw its role – restoring clear paths in the wilderness of the sub-conscious. Huh! What was wrong with twisting muddy paths, unkempt hedges, bushes? Half the world was the walking lost, the other half the walking dead.

One corner of the office contained the psycho-forest. Meaningful long-leafed greenery which Papp was forever feeling up to assist him help both of us think deeper about my problems – the official Onslaught line. He would stand near his bookcase, which I never saw him use, just beside the wall lined with framed credentials, listening to me or my silence, since he was inspirationally boring. He would move slowly so as not to distract me, towards the end of the window where his long-leafed friends waited.

Some plants had slender young leaves which arched for his touch. He used to take one of them between his thumb and index fingers near the tip and look at it as if surprised his fingers had gone there on their own, run his fingers along its length as if checking for dust. Sometimes he found dust, dropped the leaf, rubbed his fingers. Sometimes taking out a paper hankie and cleaning his fingers. He'd look at me to see if he'd distracted me from the vital business of thinking about myself. Duly let on to being as fully self-absorbed as he wanted.

Papp's neurosis was obvious, but not my problem. If I tried to help, he'd have quickly turned it back on me as indicative of some new feature of my condition. The Shrinkage was perversely good at that.

He was late, as usual. Muttering some excuse I didn't bother listening to. Meekly followed him into his green-light office, determined to resist all devices, stratagems.

Average height, wide shoulders, big head, square face, overbearing forehead, untroubled eyes. His expression, too confident he could not only see through any lies I told him but could actually 'treat' me as well.

"So, Colonel Corley, how have you been?" he began, a posh rural accent, unbuttoning his coat, placing hefty parcel of papers on his desk.

As ever, three possible answers – 'I am fine', 'Why are you always so fuckin' late?' And the one I used, "Actually, it's General now." Deepened my voice to sound General-like. "I've been promoted."

Limp smile, like he feared this was only the beginning.

"How's your hand?"

Held it up, twisted my wrist. "Still there."

"Higher, please, hold it steady."

Took it in his two hands, examined it. "Any pain?"

Shook my head. Occasional pains were none of his business. Only accepted question on the neck up.

Waved me to the usual Shrinkage-chair. Weighty wooden frame, too heavy to throw at him, sturdy armrests for gripping in lieu of his throat. Recording machine sitting in the middle of the low table. Everything was recorded which often made me think I had to be entertaining. I might have been interested in listening back to whatever nonsense I said but suspected it too would be used to 'discover' some further feature of my alleged conditions.

Picked up a folder off his desk. "Your last visit was, hmm, eight months ago? I see you missed your last two appointments?"

Shrugged my shoulders. If he didn't have to explain why he was always late, I didn't have to explain missed appointments. Anyway, he knew well what I thought of his indefatigable inane curiosity about my inner life.

Read for a while. I stared out the window at the garden looking for weeds, signs it was falling apart. Noted small bushes, not let go wild, but hadn't been clipped, in places overhanging the paths, relegating clean lines to the shadows.

"Yes," Papp said to himself. "Normally, we treat post-traumatic stress by getting patients to talk about it in a structured way." Inclined his head like a malfunctioning robot. "In your case, most of my colleagues believe we cannot do that because, as you know, your memory of the key events is not suppressed. It doesn't exist. Period." He almost smiled, clearly enjoying his description. Rubbed his mouth as if excited afresh by such an interesting prestige patient.

Flick, flick, flick, pages turning. "So, what we have been doing is focusing on the symptoms we can see and try to, ah, ameliorate them. That is why we have you living under controlled conditions." Glanced up. "How is that going?"

Shrugged again. At some point I'd switch to saying, "Comme-çi, comme-ça." He seemed content with that.

"Yours has always been an unusual case which, ah," flash tight smile, "I think you rather enjoy. You like being a bit of a puzzle, no?" He wasn't joking either, despite the condescending smile.

"Hrrump!" Good throat-clearance. Christ, did he think I was so thick I'd fall for that? Wouldn't win me over.

Hunched forward, folded my nine fingers into each other between my knees, wondering what it would be like if my left thumb suddenly reappeared without wanting. Would I reject it or welcome it? Good question, worthy of discussion, but I'd have a better discussion about it with the Brat than with him.

"…am more optimistic than some of my colleagues that your pre-trauma memory will improve. Of course, the more time elapses…" Paused to see if I was listening. Inspecting parquet floor for miniscule creepy-crawlies.

"The post-trauma character change is more problematic, though." Backward flicking, page after page, more thoughtfulness. Began thinking this is a reading class. It'll be my turn next. "We suspect..."

Suspect away, Detective Papp. You can suspect I'm from Mars, speak only Martian-English if you like. Examining my shoelaces like a good Martian in case he asks me to un-tie and re-tie them.

He closed his folder, looked at me expectantly. "I am not optimistic on that front." Winked at him, friendly-like. I wasn't optimistic I could keep my hands away from his scrawny throat if he carried on like this.

"Would you like a glass of water or some tea? I have a nice ginger infusion."

Shook my head, Martians don't drink ginger tea. "Do you have any turnip juice? It's very popular on Mars."

He forced a professional smile as he put a glass of water on the table in front of me, seemingly unaware that water can be used for more than drinking.

"Right," show of Papp-enthusiasm, "down to business. There are a number of matters we should get through today." Pulled blinds halfway down, pressed the record button.

"Let's start with the cat. How old is it?"

Big mistake telling him about Boris during previous session. Resented how he thought this gave him the right to ask about Boris. I'd told him about Boris in a moment of pride and weakness. Anyway, who was he supposed to be treating – me or Boris?

"It has a name, Boris, and he's a male and I'd like you to respect him." Being serious when you don't want to be isn't easy.

"Sure, sorry. Now tell me about Boris?"

"What do you want to know?" Boris was none of his business, but to shut him up I told him about his all-seeing, all-knowing eyes, his grace and his patience. I said I'd made Maurice an offer, he was still considering it. If Papp was so good at his job, he'd figure out my lies by himself.

"What will buying Boris do for you?"

"Maurice won't sell him. I know he won't." Big sigh. Had an idea. "Would you help me kidnap Boris?"

No answer. Non-divertible Papp.

"If he did?"

"He won't."

Long Papp-pause. Stopped recorder. Round two to Colonel Mercury. Papp finger-folding on his stomach. Pressed recorder again. "Was Boris wise as a kitten?"

Hmm, had to think about that.

"How old is Boris?"

"No idea."

"Did you know him as a kitten?"

It's true Boris wasn't always plump. His hair wasn't always as long, his rustiness as lustrous. Was more playful too. With an effort I formed a sliver of a memory of a slimmer sprightlier Boris chasing flies in the garden.

"I think I remember him younger."

"Very good. Were you living in the house?"

"Of course. How would I remember him if I wasn't? Where else would I live?"

"Did the neighbours have a cat before Boris?"

Another challenging question, but too hard for Colonel Poor-Memory. Concentration was giving me the beginnings of a headache. There was an image, though. Of a cat in the lane behind the house, but… "Maybe, I'm not sure."

"Good man," he said eventually. "Now, Dominic," he put his notepad down. "Would you like to move your chair back a little, stretch your legs? That's right. Now, please close your eyes and relax, relax. I want you to relax your arms and legs."

Sotto-voce Papp waiting until I relaxed into the closed-eyes position. Why did I tolerate this nonsense? Lingering fear possibly silly, of being returned to hospital, and, I readily admit, a certain relish for the combat with Shrinkage high priest. My wounded wits against Papp wonder-wits.

"That's it, now," mellow-voice Papp. "You are far away… far, far away… feeling very at ease with your body, amazingly relaxed… Every part of you sinking into a softness … All other sounds filter away…"

On and on, wanted to tell him to hurry up. Distant sounds of an orchestra practising rolled up from below, in and out of earshot like someone was opening, closing doors.

"You are back in the lane, Dominic, happy to be out in the open, away from the family. Breathe deeply and slowly… What do you see in the lane?" voice lowered to a whisper.

"Shit," I exclaimed.

"What?"

"Dog shit. Mrs Hennessy's Jack Russell, always reliev-ing himself in the lane." Told him lots about the lane, not leaving out the tufts of wild grass around the man-hole cover beside the telephone pole with all its wires going in every direction like the spokes of a wheel.

"Now, Dominic, you've stopped running. You're standing beside the pole in the lane looking around very slowly. Is anyone else in the lane?"

Ignorant-Papp. The pole is right beside the lane door. You don't run to reach it unless you want to run into it. "Kids. There are a few kids playing in the lane where it narrows. They see me."

"That's great, really good. Now, continue taking deep breaths, Dominic, and hold it there. Keep looking around the lane and remembering everything you see."

Heard his chair creak, the office door open and close quietly. What's this? Not wanting to expire for want of oxygen, I breathed normally, opened my eyes, checked out the garden below for any new weeds along the paths. Faint flush of a toilet, door opened quietly, chair creaked again. Same low whisper which would have made the flies on the window fall asleep. Papp resumed.

"Do you see anyone?"

"A boy." I nodded, eyes firmly closed, drowsy voice, the way he liked it.

"How is the boy dressed?"

"T-shirt, shorts."

"Is anything written on the t-shirt?"

"Eh, no."

"Long shorts?"

"No, shorter."

"What's his name?"

That's when I blew it. "The Brat."

He wasn't happy, my shrink-Papp. Stopped the recorder, tapped the tips of his fingers together, thinking of his next move. A burst of trombones from the practising orchestra blew up from somewhere. Papp was over at the plants, my fault of course, one of his favourites between his fingers, a long slim winsome one.

"Did the image of the boy change after I went out for a moment?"

"We could start again, if you want," I suggested pleasantly. Knock-out in the third round. Colonel Dommo, Papp-slayer.

Chapter 33

Shocking Shrink

H e was gone again to another office. Told me not to leave. Bored-spiteful, sitting there, looking around. Those bloody leaves. What would happen if I cut off a few of his favourites, arranged them neatly on his desk?

Back in his seat with a new folder. Gives me a grudging smile. "I have to admit I admire your stubbornness. It is impressive even if misplaced. It's perhaps your best hope for the future..."

Oh, cunning-Papp! Do you think I'll fall for that? Praise from the Shrinkage? This wasn't admiration. It was a tactic. Everything always for a reason.

"Anyway, we have to move on. I've been asked to show you some photos. Won't take long. You just have to look at them and tell me what you think of them, OK?"

Well, pity me for thinking this would be a dawdle. Smutty photos? Maybe he wanted to assess Harry's interest in the world. Maybe pictures of cross-dressers because somehow he knew about Kidney and Patricia? He was shuffling the photos like a card player arranging his cards.

Boy, couldn't have been more wrong. Nothing smutty. Far worse. Photos of bloody corpses piled beside deep pits in a forest clearing, waiting to be buried. Even said I was in one of those photos. Did I recognise myself?

"Agh!" I bellowed, after seeing three or four of them. Pure horror. Wouldn't have to be a volcanologist to see the smoke rising from my head. Didn't stop him. Quietly slid another photo face-down across the table at me. "No," I groaned, refusing to pick it up. He waited. "That's where they kept you for months."

Stupidly picked it up, examined it. "What are those?" He didn't need to answer. Chains connected to metal rings in the wall. Glanced at him. He was rolling his hands together under his nose, studying me.

"Chains," I said, struggling to stay calm, afraid what I'd do if I lost control. Found myself counting. Five, four, three, two… one. "Why the fuck are you showing me all this… this shit?" I shouted at him, pushing the chair back, standing still for a moment. Was at the door when he called me back.

"Dominic, wait," he said, calm tone, remaining sitting. "Don't go. We're not finished." The fact he didn't budge made it feel like he was still in control, protected by Shrinkage-professionalism.

Only one way to stop this.

Left the door open, came back, heading for him. He stood up, shrank back. Didn't utter a sound. Something in my eyes warning him we were done with words. Backed up against his beloved psycho-forest, long leaves bending around his frame. Stopping when we were almost nose-to-nose, his professional air not fully extinguished.

I tore a handful of his pretty leaves from the plants, gestured for him to open his mouth. His eyes bulged, shaking his head, until I held his nose. His mouth opened like a trapdoor. Without violence, I shoved the torn bits of greenery into his mouth.

"Geeeggghhh!" Gagged a few times, nothing serious. Released his nose, closed his mouth, left the room.

Waiting at the slow lift when he caught up with me. Mouth dripping after hurriedly cleaning it, holding a hand-towel. Breathless, but surprisingly calm, focused. Shock left behind in the office. Had me wondering does the fucker think what I just did was good?

Banged the lift door to hurry it up and warn him to stay clear. Hollow thud reverberated up and down the lift shaft. Christ, deliver me from this maniac.

"There's going to be a trial," he began, "in the Hague and…"

"Doc," I cut him off, refusing to look at him, staring at the grey lift door. Had I been too gentle with him? "Whatever you're accused of," I said slowly, reluctantly, "I won't be a witness."

"No, no, haha! Not me, you. I mean you as a witness." He put his hand on my shoulder, actually laughing, laughing so hard to steady himself. The Shrinkage laughing? Didn't think they were allowed.

"Wow!" he exclaimed as he calmed down. Lift finally coming. "That's a good one. Thanks, Colonel." He patted me on the back. Also, unheard of.

Lift door slid open. Stern-faced young woman inside, hair-bunned, business-suit, white blouse. Moved to make room for me. I pressed G, turned to face the sliding door. Shrink-Papp still there, animated expression, not finished.

"You're a robust chap, Colonel," he enthused. "Very strong internally, great resolve, exceptional resistance."

Swivelled my eyes sideways at the woman. For God's sake, why's he going on like this in front of her? Should I tell her I don't know who this randomer is? She stared straight ahead, steadfastly ignoring us. Pretending she hadn't heard a word.

Lift door began sliding closed. What did the maniac do? Stuck his foot in the way. Door stopped, sliding noisily back.

"I just think you have to ask yourself what you're using it for."

Mortified. Actually blushing. He was saying this in front of a stranger. But sort of adjusting as well. I knew the Shrinkage never wasted time on good-byes. A good-bye was part of the session. Not a budge, not a twitch out of the impassive woman. She'd picked her stare-spot on the wall, wasn't moving.

"I can say things to you I wouldn't say to other clients," he continued, almost palsy-walsy, seemingly oblivious of where he was. Christ, does she think he's coming onto me?

I'll explain when the door closes. Still too astonished to just kick his foot out of the way.

"Something has a hold over you. I don't know for sure what it is." He made a face as if wrestling with the problem, glanced quickly at his shoes. "Your captors weren't looking for information from you so your determination to resist wasn't important, didn't matter to them. Maybe… maybe that's the issue here. Maybe, you haven't forgiven yourself that they took," his mouth widened to reveal a row of even whitish teeth, "that desire, that capacity, that need to resist away from you. Maybe," he paused, looked at the woman but didn't seem to see her, "that was more important than taking away your thumb."

Without opening her mouth. Low growling sound was emitting from the woman.

"That they didn't give you that opportunity to test yourself and to have that dialogue about how important resistance is to you and why." Paused. Smiling apologetically at both of us added, "Think about it." Stepped back, took his foot away, walked off as the door closed.

The young woman held up a firm hand as I turned to apologise when the lift was moving. "Don't say a word," she said through gritted teeth. "That's the third time this week he's done that."

PART V

Chapter 34

Pre-Medal Ceremony

Bed-warmth slipped away as my feet touched the floor. Cold air perused the pores of my skin. Shivering shoulders, stiff legs. Throwing curses at hidden draughts insolently meandering around the room like they had rights too. Running hands through hair, checking wiry curls hadn't left me during the night the way my thumb had. Stubborn curls clinging on to the head-roof. Rubbed skin all over – fat, bones, to be sure all arranged as previously. Not that I dreamt parts of me went AWOL during the night, coming back before dawn, but a certain mood might have prowled around narrow corridors and dark corners while I slept, which made checking necessary.

Silvery daylight peeked along the sides of the blinds. Whiff of percolated coffee, strong, somehow trespassing from next door through the fireplace. Sniffed around the fireplace to find exact way this happened. Only happened when she was there, meaning, she was there. No luck finding it.

Wondered how long the doorbell was ringing before I heard it, why the ringer wasn't giving up. Belted white fluffy dressing gown as I told ringer to get lost. Wondering was it Jean Mc Babe with another photo, shrink-Papp with more photos or anyone with bloody photos. Even Civilian, no photos, just feverish eyes looking for dosh. Carrying gun. Certainly wouldn't be renegade researcher, Retired Detective.

Downstairs, hall mirror telling me to feel pride in my snoozer, rugged features, wiry hair. Slapped cheeks for instant rouge.

"Hi," full-bodied female voice called out too loud for Colonel Delicate-Ears. Only opened the door halfway. "It's me, Martina. Catherine sent me to make sure you're ready." Spoke too fast, decisively. Noted an air that said people don't mess with me. Obviously forewarned.

"Huh?" Unable to compose response, cope with no-nonsense gaze. Scratched ear. "And who would you be?" I objected.

"Did you not hear me? I'm Catherine's assistant." Gave me a withering look. "Will I say it again?"

She was a big girl, short hair, nice eyes, long face, dark trouser suit and buckets of attitude.

"Had a good look?" she remarked dryly.

"I've seen you before," I said. It was all I could get out, still felt ambushed.

"Yeah, I'm famous. I've seen you too."

"Huh?"

"Up there." She nodded up at my bedroom window. "Spying on us."

"Didn't see much."

"Depends what you're looking for." She looked over her shoulder. "Are you going to let me in? This thing is heavy." Hadn't noticed she was carrying a suit or something from the dry cleaners.

"Eh…"

She brushed past me into the hallway, like they all do, and hung the dry-cleaning on the coat-stand.

"Are you going to change here?" I asked, incredulous at her effrontery, miffed at her pushiness. "Why can't you change in her house?"

"Very funny," she said, droll-faced.

"Eh, well, what *do* you want?"

"Do you not know?" Loud sigh. "Do you ever look at your calendar?"

"Calendar?" The way she said it made it sound like a banner hanging from the front of the house.

"Never trust them."

"God help us," she muttered.

By this stage, I admit, was beginning to feel rather excited by this unexpected encounter.

"I'm here to get you ready."

"Is that right? And do you think I can't dress myself?" I looked out. The Guard was out of his hut, hat on, looking officious, pretending to have a purpose in life.

"Casanova is watching you," I said.

"Huh." She knew instantly what I meant. Without batting an eye, she dismissed him. "That fella? Spare me."

"Hey, has he been bothering you?" This was exciting.

"Him? Not a chance."

She spotted the make-believe photos hanging on the wall. Onslaught propaganda that they were family photos, supposed to remind me of who I was to me. Just a different kind of wallpaper. Colonel Jelly-Legs looked at them with her. Most strangers had a good look at them if I forgot to turn them to face the wall.

"What?" she cried. "Are you still here?"

I stayed where I was, tightening the belt of the dressing gown in case it swung open of its own accord. Was admitting to myself that I could enjoy being bossed around by a forceful young woman just as much as the next man. Harry was thinking about waking up. One of his rare days.

Changed tone and tack. "OK," she said. "Let's start again." Faced me. "Hi, I'm Martina," mock-friendly voice.

I copied her. "Hi, I'm Dominic. What's it like working for her? Tell the truth, now."

Laughed, sort of. "Oh, I've had worse." Looked at my dressing gown and bare feet and frowned. "You know what you're wearing?"

Snorted defensively. "I can certainly remember what I put on two minutes ago, thank you very much."

"Can you?" she wondered.

I feared if she stared at me like that any longer Harry would definitely get involved in the situation and possibly stand to attention.

"I mean, for the ceremony,"

"What ceremony? Who's getting married?" Had the Brat's mother finally found a husband? Not before time if you asked me.

"Arrah, stop the nonsense. Come on. Up the stairs with you. And take this." She thrust the dry-cleaning at me. "And put it on. Go on, get moving. We don't have all day."

Was so taken by her commanding tone, I stood on the first step of the stairs and faced her, awaiting more orders.

"Come on!" she cried, clapping hands like a teacher. Turned me around by the arms. With a push in the small of my back, sent me up the stairs. Shouted up after me. "Catherine said there's a shirt hanging on the wardrobe door. And there's a tie with it. And shoes. They're at the foot of the bed. Put them on!"

I looked back down the stairs at this extraordinary and fascinating woman. "Were you up in my room?" That bloody locksmith hadn't given me those extra keys.

"You wish! And do something with your hair. It's a mess. God, a walking disaster!" She turned and walked out the door, shouting over her shoulder, knowing full well I was gazing longingly at her. "You have twenty minutes."

She was right. Everything was waiting for me. Line-free polished-black shoes with a pair of Thursday socks stuck into them. I put them back in the drawer, took out a pair of Friday ones, and put them on. When I was fully dressed slipped a pair of Saturday ones into the jacket pocket, just in case.

The Politician was delighted with me when I got into the car. She declared, "My, you look very distinguished, darling."

"Very smart," Martina repeated, half-mockingly.

I'd put on the uniform like I was going to a posh fancy dress party. The Politician patted my arm almost possessively. "We had it pressed." She leaned forward and moved a stray hair back into place. With all the attention I was getting, I was beginning to feel as giddy as a newly scrubbed boy going out on a trip with a maiden aunt.

The Politician noticed me examining her dark blue dress with medium sized rectangles of red mostly around the shoulders. "You like it?"

Martina in the front beside the driver turned around, ostensibly to hear my reply, but really to give me a warning look.

"Eh, yeah. It's only gorgeous," I said, slipping accidentally into Stephen Kidney.

The car took off and the two women started discussing what the French Minister would be wearing. I tried not to listen and pressed my face against the window, watching the streets and buildings flow by. The car stopped at traffic lights. A stick-cyclist courier in long dark shorts with lean hairy legs stared impudently at Martina through her half open window. I pressed the down button to open my window and told him to clear off. He was so surprised he forgot to move when the lights changed, and we shot off with me giving him the finger out the window. Martina was mine.

"Dominic!" the Politician gasped. "What on earth are you doing?" She looked back at the frozen cyclist in horror. "Did you see that, Martina?"

I defended myself. "Did you see the way he was staring at Martina?"

Martina had seen it through the wing mirror and looked around. Torn, I hoped, between gratitude and embarrassment. My window, as if by magic, started humming back up despite my finger staying firmly on the down button. I could see the silent driver's finger on one of his control buttons.

"Jesus, I hope the visit to McKee Barracks isn't going to be like this," the Politician worried, looking sternly at me. "Dominic, you better behave yourself today. I'm warning you."

I didn't care. I was growing into the role of Colonel-in-Uniform. It fitted well and looked so commanding. I patted my tunic front.

"Ladies," I said looking out the window, talking away from them the way royalty does. "You may call me Colonel-in-Uniform, if you like."

No response, apart from glimpsing Martina's eyes raised at the sky.

The Politician picked up a briefcase from the seat and took out some papers and started reading them. I took one out to read as well, but she took it off me. "None of your business."

What a way to speak to a Colonel-in-Uniform!

"I can't concentrate," she complained after a while, putting the papers away. "God, I hope she's not too stunning and makes me look like a scarecrow."

"You look perfect, Minister," Martina reassured her. "Your dress is gorgeous, really classy. It'll be just as smart as hers. Smarter."

At McKee Barracks the car parked in front of a long red brick building which faced a huge parade ground. A guard of honour was drawn up there. A soldier opened the Politician's door. The female officer greeted her with a salute when she got out of the car and took her off to inspect the guard of honour. I went to open my door, but it was locked. I pushed at it.

"Stop it," Martina whispered fiercely from her seat. "It's only for her. We get out later."

Left there to watch from a distance. The driver went off and Martina stayed in the front seat.

"There she is," she said craning forward over the dashboard to get a better look.

"Who?"

"Who do you think? The French Minister. They're reviewing the guard of honour together."

I couldn't see. "Martina?"

"Ssshh, I'm watching."

"Martina? You can sit in the back if you like."

"Look, it's all right for you to carry on like that. I'm working. She'll ask me all sorts of questions when she gets back."

"But, Martina…"

She turned around unexpectedly. "What is it?" she demanded. "What do you want?"

"Erm, do you want…" Chickened out under that exciting glare. "Do you have a boyfriend?"

"None of your business."

"Go on, tell me. I won't tell anyone." I was copying the Brat and feeling giddy.

When the Politician returned, we got out of the car and Martina said, "Put that on." She took an officer's cap out of a bag she had in the front. I was delighted. It fitted perfectly. Felt like a peacock with bunting on his feathers. Now that I really was a Colonel-in-Uniform I would play the role with aplomb. As the group headed towards the big red brick building, we passed some soldiers who stopped and saluted. Without thinking my arm went into a salute. One of them was so surprised he hesitated mid-salute. I did a second one to encourage him to finish it. It worked. He glanced nervously at one of his colleagues. Oh, the power of a good salute. I was ready from then on to salute anyone who looked like they wanted one.

"Stop it, Dominic," the Politician hissed from the side of her mouth.

"He started it," I defended myself, feeling I'd finally succumbed to Brat-ethics. Besides, am I a Colonel-in-Uniform or not?

"He's saluting the Minister, not you, ya big baluba," Martina whispered from behind, and gave me a sly dig in the side. "Now, I'm in trouble," she muttered.

We were brought into a large first-floor room with long windows which faced the parade ground on one side and mature wide-branched trees on the other. The group had grown into a melee of uniforms, suits and dresses and smart hats. Everyone looked wedding-day smart. I was introduced to loads of people, some of whom claimed to know me and whose names I immediately forgot. Except for Hervé de Gastaud, the French Ambassador, who was called 'His Excellency'. I studied him for signs of excellence and, indeed, he was excellent. His manners were refined. His conviviality warm and discrete.

Some people enquired after my health. I thanked them, told them it was as excellent as the Ambassador's and asked them how they were. Two had scars and naturally we ended up making comparisons. One chap had a scar on his cheek, but it was small. Another had one on his left leg above his sock. I had to insist he show it to us otherwise he couldn't win. My non-thumb trumped them all. This way, no conversation lasted long and I was free to roam around the room, studying the epaulettes and cravats and ribbons of the French officers. I was also on the lookout for someone for Martina, more her own age, to introduce her to.

Spotted a skinny woman at the far end of the room. She was surrounded – no, besieged – by a bevy of codger-officers. They were having such a good time. Laughing and chatting, made my way towards them for a better look. The skinny slight-figure had luscious, streaked brown hair and a narrow, understated face. Cute without forcing me to put on sunglasses. She wore a cream coloured short dress suit which bulked up at the shoulders. It was her laughter though, that caught my attention. It sounded like tickling would sound. Definitely something about this woman that required a closer look. Even the Politician approached her, and the codgers quickly made space in the circle.

From then on, I had eyes only for Skinny Woman. No one else in the big room mattered. Not even Martina. A few times Martina crossed my line of vision, letting me know she was watching me. Watch away, Martina, I am too old for you. This is something that doesn't happen every day. I didn't stare as I usually did when someone or something caught my eye. Oh, no. I moved around the room like Boris on the prowl, pretending indifference, sneaking glances and looking away. Did it so often, her eyes eventually wandered in my direction. I immediately looked away, thrilled she'd noticed me and sure this game of spot-me-looking/not-looking-at-you would go on and on.

Alas, a soldier approached me. I was led out of the room, down a corridor and asked to sit in a waiting room. After a few moments, a French officer entered the room and introduced himself as Emile Thys. He said something in French which to my surprise for a fleeting second, I understood and was going to reply when I remembered I didn't speak French. Strange feeling. He asked me was I well and added that *Madame la Ministre* was looking forward to meeting me and chatting after the ceremony.

"*Mon Colonel*," he continued, "my Minister az a deep admiration for you. She was talking about you in ze plane on ze way over 'ere." Glanced at my left hand and nodded to himself. "And so did I. *Vous êtes un homme exceptionnel et courageux.*"

He didn't flinch as I stared back at him, taking this in. Not sure if this was the Onslaught or a different level altogether. Whatever it is, it feels serious, I thought.

I drank from the glass of water he brought me and studied the lino-covered floor. The idea that this would be another shrink-test was always on my mind, but equally, who wouldn't have been flattered by all this attention? All the great things you're supposed to have done? I liked it. Still, I was drawing on Boris' unflappability not to let them see how pleasing it was.

"You are OK for ze ceremony? Yes? Please be relaxed wiz my Minister. She is very charming, non?"

I knew that look on his face. It said, 'I hope to God we get through this without a scene'.

That look also made it easier for me to ask, "What does your Minister think I did?"

"You 'elped stop barbarism in Europe. That is what she thinks."

Barbarism in Europe? Hm, if this was all a shrink-test, they were really going for broke. This was one helluva claim. Emile went off, returned with an Irish soldier.

"Zey are ready for you now, *Colonel*. Please follow."

Chapter 35

Medal Ceremony

I rish and French flags flaccid behind a podium. At the far end, three soldiers in white putting the finishing touches to a buffet table. In the middle, sofas, tables, armchairs moved to the side to make room for four rows of chairs. About thirty people already seated. Spotted the Brat, his mother and the Politician sitting together. In the row behind them, saw Git John and Beetroot Woman, the woman who'd been with the Auld One when they came to see me in hospital, his wife presumably, and two daughters. Searched for Mrs Hand. No sign of her. Stop the lights. I want Mrs Hand. My eyes went back to the Brat who half smiled at me. I made a note to get big mileage out of this. He'll have to treat me with new respect from here on.

One of the codger-officers with red tabs on his jacket with two others behind him came over to me.

"Colonel Corley. Dominic, how are you? It's me, George, good to see you. You're looking well. How are you keeping? How's the hand? All set? It's a great day, a great honour for all of us and for you. You all set to go?" I couldn't keep up with his patter and just smiled.

"Let me introduce you to Madame Giauffer."

He brought me over to the French Minister standing near the podium. It was her. The skinny woman. Should have guessed. Muted my astonishment. Boris wouldn't have been in the least fazed. Introductions were made. Skinny Woman became *Madame la Ministre*. I smiled politely and stiffly, the epitome of a Colonel-in-Uniform, an exemplar of a bygone era. And, why not throw in the kitchen sink and tell them I'd saved the Politician as well? *Madame la Ministre* was polished and business-like, betraying no trace of the eye-games I had played with her.

Up close she really was a wispy thing. Early warning wrinkle-traces radiating from the sides of her eyes. But that was nothing against the deepest, most compelling, large, inspiring, enigmatic brown eyes I'd ever seen. In the space of a few seconds felt myself drawn into them and was instantly lost. She knew it too, was well used to having that effect on men. She held my gaze professionally while shaking my hand and speaking words I never heard. Not a ripple in her composure. She glanced away for an instant. Just, I felt, to show she could, to show she was not distracted like I was. A graceful put-down. So skilled at diverting male attention away from the person to the position.

The room went quiet. General George stationed himself at the podium and started. Missed most of what he said. Still lost in those eyes and overawed by her closeness. When the General finished, he stood aside to make way for *Madame la Ministre* with Emile behind her. I was behind her to her left, my hands clasped in front of me.

"*Madame la Ministre, Monsieur le Général, Cher Colonel, Cher Collègue, Mesdames et Messieurs,*" she began. "*Depuis longtemps le gouvernement et le peuple français estiment beaucoup… De la part du Président de la République Française…*"

She read from a large embossed scroll, not a word of which I understood, but every syllable and breath flowed in and around my ears like scented air. Don't know how long it lasted, but it would never have been long enough. She read with verve and panache. I soon realised I was also in love with her voice. It had such a fruity, gay lilt. Closed my eyes to bathe in it. If any of the Shrinkage had ever had a voice like that, I'd have been putty in their hands.

Madame la Ministre finished. Emile stepped forward holding an open box from which she took a cross and rosette attached to a short tricolour ribbon. She pinned it above my left breast pocket. Handed me the scroll, leaned upwards, grabbed me by the shoulders and perfunctorily kissed the air above each cheek. She shook my hand, holding it in both of hers and stood back.

The room erupted into prolonged applause. Cameras clicked, smiles everywhere. I beamed. Even a few cheers. Then the room fell quiet. No one took charge. I feared they expected me to speak. *Madame la Ministre* glanced at me and motioned me forward. I took two steps forward and faced the room, sensing a mood of anxiety. Nervousness was written large on the faces of the Politician and the young woman. A few rows back Martina discretely put a finger to her lips and slowly shook her head.

I said, "*Merci, Madame la Ministre.*" Don't know where that came from. Smiled at everyone to show them they had nothing to fear from me.

General George took over then. He invited everyone to enjoy the food and French wine. On cue the waiters circulated, the food and wine were served, the crowd relaxed, and the hum of voices rose. I had a glass of wine in one hand and a *canapé of foie gras and cornichon* in the other, and the scroll under my arm, but wasn't doing much with any of them. Again, wondered how real all this was when someone tugged at my elbow. The Brat wanted to hold the medal.

"It's mine," I said firmly, shaking his hand away. "Not yours."

"Yeah… but I helped you. Remember?"

Was that a threat? "Ssshh, tomorrow," I said. "I'll let you hold it tomorrow. What do you think of it?"

"It's not bad," he said, making a face. He had his reservations, I could tell. "Where are the guns?" he complained. "I don't see any guns."

Called General George over which I don't think he appreciated, his smile thinning as he listened and was maybe fearful, I'd been promoted to General as well. He quickly delegated the task of finding a gun big enough to impress the Brat and was gone. George, I noted, spent a lot of time sitting in the ear of the Politician.

A photographer positioned us for photos. Me and *Madame la Ministre*, best of all. I stood right beside her, couple-like. Our wedding day photo, twelve months hence, surely. Me and General George and some other French general, me and some Irish generals, me with Martina and the sharp-nosed Emile – I insisted on that one. Tried to put Martina beside Emile, but she wasn't having it. I got two of his business cards and gave Martina one. She made a face. There was also me and the Brat and his mother, but not me and Git John. He was hovering in the background, inching forward, and saw him being introduced by the Politician to *Madame la Ministre*. Told Martina, no way was he to be in any photo with me. Nor was there to be any photo with the Politician. It was a sensitive issue, Martina said vaguely. I fully agreed.

When the Brat and his mother were gone, I found myself, not quite by accident, standing beside *Madame la Ministre*. Just the two of us near a corner, her facing me. Gulped some wine to untie my tongue and thought quickly about how blatant I wanted to be.

"Oops," she laughed, and flowers danced around her face as some of the wine dribbled down the side of my mouth. I swept it away with a nonchalant finger. Just couldn't remember any woman ever having this effect on me.

"You were staring at me, Colonel," she said in accent-less English.

I was, I was. The flowers were swaying to the lilting squeak and those wondrous eyes looking only at me. I tried to laugh but sounded like a donkey in pain. "Like every man in this room," I said boldly.

"No, no." She was emphatic and looked away, not to end the conversation though.

"*Madame*," I leapt to my own defence. "I do not usually stare at women."

"And today?"

"I am disarmed," I sighed.

That pleased her. "Here?" She grinned. "In a *caserne*?"

"My mind cannot concentrate on the medal."

"Oh, but it must. You should, Colonel. I want to say this to you personally and I know you are not in perfect health. My government has great admiration for what you did in protecting human rights and innocent civilians against fascism."

As she was saying this, my mind was asking, 'Yes, but what kind of great admiration?'

"You suffer terribly for your bravery—" She broke off, looking down at my left hand. "May I?"

You may, you may, and more. Raised my hand to show her, hoping she'd take it in hers and cure it forever. Miracle touch.

"How do you manage?"

"It's not great for climbing trees."

She smiled but only at what I believed was her decision not to take my hand in hers. "But you try anyway, I hope?"

If you want, I'll become a monkey instead of Stephen Kidney. I grew very bold and cast caution to the winds. "But, *Madame*, would *you* be safe in my hands?" I asked, lowering my voice, bending forward, taking her hand and kissing it. She let me finish and just took her hand back with her trademark composure. Her hand had a musky fragrance. I wanted it back to taste more.

"Colonel," she said in an amused tone. "I see you are still distracted. I must call your wife."

"She's not my wife," I replied a little too firmly, but it meant I could ask the key question. "And you, are you married?"

"Am I married? Hm." Her eyes sparkled and said let me think about that. Definitely playing with me, but was she encouraging me? An exquisite agony. My hopes danced with the petals swaying around her head. "I am not used to being asked that question." When she saw how serious I was and needed an answer, she was bemused. "I am sure it is on the internet somewhere."

We took a pause, sipped our wine, thinking what to say next now that that line of conversation was dead.

"You truly remember nothing, nothing at all?"

"I will remember every second of this conversation."

"Be serious, Colonel," she said not at all seriously.

"But I am. I can't help it."

"Oh, I see I will definitely have to send for your wife." But she didn't.

"*Madame…*" I hesitated at the enormity of what I was about to ask. What is your phone number? Can I see you next week in Paris?

She may have guessed what was on my mind and got in before me. "How strange all this must seem to you? How to connect with the…" she waved her hand trying to find the word.

"Here, here," General George barged in, shoulders and chest aflame with insignia, ribbons and medals, probably responding to a secret signal she'd sent. "Dominic, you mustn't monopolise the Minister."

She ignored him. "Colonel, you do know there are trials going on in The Hague. Some very dangerous men are on trial for crimes against humanity. My government considers it extremely important that the guilty are convicted and that anyone who has evidence should give it."

Was that positive? Changed the subject when George arrived. Not wanting him to know what we'd been talking about. Meant we had something she didn't want to share, didn't it? I thought of whispering in George's ear. "Get lost. Delicate negotiations." In the space of minutes, the world had changed. Goodbye Stephen Kidney, hello Colonel Casanova. There was a new sun in the sky and the thin line I sometimes couldn't help walking between feckless and serious had dissolved. It was all just love.

"You were witness, Colonel, to unspeakable barbarism and your witness testimony can help convict the guilty. We need to get you better."

My look surely told her how she alone could do that, but she didn't let her eyes acknowledge it. In front of General George, *Madame la Ministre* put on her political face, just like I'd seen the Politician do on many occasions.

While I wondered was this a tantalising code for saying we could meet again, the Minister looked around and, as if by magic, Emile appeared beside her. "I am afraid I have to go back to Paris. But before I go, Colonel?"

Yes? Yes? I was like a breathless puppy. Five o'clock next Tuesday in the pancake restaurant? I'll pay and kill the Retired Detective if he appears.

"*Félicitations, Monsieur l'Officier de la Légion d'Honneur!*"

Chapter 36

Love Fever

After that day, what a difference. The world changed so much it shrank. Without help from God, the Shrinkage, the Onslaught. Weeks passed still stricken with the Fever – an up-and-down virus that obeyed no rules, that had no cure, had me swinging so much I didn't know if I was monkey or man. Wild fantasising and glum reality. And based on what? A total of twenty minutes in her company, yet it might as well have been twenty days for all the difference it made.

The Fever began shrinking the world almost immediately. That evening alone back in the house could only think about that sublime smile, that twittery-ikky voice, those eyes like fennel, that lascivious waterfall-hair. All packed into a slight, radiant form. Inspired me to live in fantasy-heaven.

Madame la Ministre would join me on my walks in the city centre. We made a kind of crazy teen-adult-teen couple, teasing, giggling, talking earnestly, stopping, hugging, running. Every hug was a pretext to burying my face in her hair. I sometimes followed young couples, studying their Fevers, adding to the store of Fever-things we did together. She never sat with me on the bus going into the city. She would join me there at unexpected moments. I'd be concentrating on walking in a busy street and suddenly she'd be there, alongside me, smiling at me and studying our reflections in shop windows.

She liked shopping. She brought me into jewellery shops and shoe shops and department stores – places I would never go to on my own. Once we headed for the women's department. I stood near the changing rooms as she tried on different outfits that always suited her. Her manner with the sales staff was exemplary. Gracious, intimate and distant, friendly and formal.

"You know," I told her, "I have a secret place I would like to bring you to. Will you come with me?" She never answered that question. She used smiles and glances instead of words, but that didn't matter. I knew what she thought. I could read the alphabet of her eyes. Then I noticed a scowling sales assistant who kept looking at me and eventually shamed me into scurrying away. I left Madame Giauffer in the changing rooms, promising I would be back.

I didn't know her first name, often tried guessing it. The choice narrowed down to Constance or Isabelle. I choose Isabelle. The look and shape of the name were elegant, exotic, forward-looking. The 'isa' was a head-turner, promising two characters in one name. But I was wrong.

Her name was Beatrice. Didn't matter. It was like falling in love again.

As time wore on, she appeared less and less. Appointments missed. Rendezvous sites reverted to vacant spaces where I scuffed my shoes and felt my thoughts expanding and contracting. Feeling good became the exception. I stopped listening to the radio. It became love-song-radio. I even abandoned talk-radio in case they slipped in some love songs. Too painful. Every love song ever written was, incredibly, amazingly, about me and Giauffer-Fever. Dashed love, unrequited love, secret love, she's-left-me-for-another love, yearning love, hopeless love, doomsday love, doormat love, last-breath love, every-kind-of-unhappy-love love, that's all they ever played. The only thing the songs didn't do was name me, but that didn't matter. I knew who they meant.

One night, at three eleven a.m., going down to the basement for concrete floor-therapy. For the time being I had given up trying to wean myself off that habit, thinking it was no way to live a life, but I was doing it anyway. Going through the kitchen when the *Légion d'Honneur* medal caught my eye, glinting in the light that can miraculously appear in the dark. Lying on the table, all sweet and innocent, where I'd left it. I had been holding and rubbing it and treasuring it like a kind of wedding ring. Suddenly it encapsulated all my woes. If they hadn't given it to me, I'd have never met her and wouldn't be like this. Before I knew it, in a fit of rage, picked it up and flung it at the wall across the kitchen and left it where it fell on the floor.

Chapter 37

Young Woman's Sad News

Phone rang at four sixteen and twenty-one seconds on the morning of the eleventh of July. Time-precision would also be part of Stephen Kidney. He'll never be late for anything. Indeed, he'll often be too early and stand around staring at time until it catches up and stares back at him. And the great thing about time is that it was not Onslaught-owned. It didn't jump around and pretend it was one thing when it really was something else. Obsessing about time could obviously become a tyranny, even a fetish, but that was just another challenge that Stephen would face.

The ringing dragged me back to the nippy-now and I recalled my pre-ringing dream. I was approaching the mouth of a tunnel rapidly. Didn't seem to matter if I was the train or a person. A second or two earlier I'd been watching a younger version of the Auld One walking along a corridor on the arm of Git John. The Auld One was smiling and beckoning me to come over. I was so jealous but couldn't move towards her. Then the corridor became a tunnel and I hit the phone and sent it flying. The blasted thing refused to die on the floor like a groaning animal.

"Dad?" It wasn't Fahy the Retired Cretin, or anyone in the dream, or anyone I feared or wanted a call from, like *Madame la Ministre*. God forgive me for still thinking about that woman.

"Dad it's me. Sorry to ring you so late. Were you asleep?" Sad-voiced, slow-talking young woman. "Dad, I've some sad news."

The Politician has been sacked, imprisoned, water boarded. The Brat has been sent to boarding school. Maurice and Dora were killed by a hit-and-run driver. The Shrinkage got stuck in a lift and died.

"Granny passed away in her sleep at eleven minutes past one this morning." Aha, I like that. She's precise about time. A good habit to have. Could have mentioned the second. I got it straight away. Granny was Onslaught-speak for the Auld One.

"Huh?"

"She died surrounded by Uncle John, Aunt Maureen, Mam and myself. We've already told Uncle Terry. Uncle John rang him, and he said he'd be over for the funeral. That he'd let them know as soon as he could when he'd be arriving from Argentina. We'll have to wait for him."

After this, the young woman fell silent. Presumably waiting for something from me. I'd forgotten to pull down the blinds last night and early dawn streaks were painting themselves into the black. I kicked off the bedclothes, switched on the sidelight to make sure the Politician wasn't hiding in the shadows somewhere, switched off the light again, and tightened all body-cheeks. I levered myself upright in the bed, and finally realised how she must feel. Her granny dies and what does she do? She rings me, the guy who could easily have said it was none of his business, that I wasn't related to any of them, and put the phone down. No, she was brave, and death is death, and, anyway, I too had suffered a loss. That woman had helped me become a care assistant. These reflections extended what I hoped were long moments of respectful commiseration, during which I still had to deal with the irritation of Git John refusing to look at me in the dream.

"Thomas wasn't there," she volunteered, as if my thoughts had asked the question.

"That was a mistake," I said delicately. For all his numerous faults, I knew the Brat could handle it. He would see adults at a weak moment and remember it. Which gave me an idea. I could pretend to be dead some day when he came in. On the kitchen floor, sprawled, ketchup everywhere, knife thrown in the corner, the guinea pigs running wildly around me. After all, Dommo was going to die, only to be re-born as Stephen K. Also didn't mind admitting it, I felt the tiniest bit excluded. With all the Onslaught-talk about being part of their great family and the time I spent visiting the Auld One in the nursing home, well, shouldn't I have been invited too? But these were thoughts the Shrinkage would never hear.

She broke into quiet tears. It was a great shame, she said, that I hadn't been there to say goodbye, that Granny was a wonderful person and she'd really miss her. She was in heaven now with God and Grandad Mathew looking down on us. Grandad Mathew, who is this geezer? Hadn't heard of him before.

More sniffling and my gut started telling me I was feeling kind of fond of her. I even wondered, not for the first time, could I ever just play along with her delusion, for her sake? Just for her sake.

Was I listening? Was I OK?

"I'm grand," I said, rubbing my free hand on the cool sheet, unexpectedly recalling an extraordinary event I saw a few days ago. A blinder, or a half-blinder, was trying to push a bag of rubbish into the open back window of a parked car that he had mistaken for one of the big street bins that was located just beside it, one with an big opening for throwing stuff into. The guy sitting in the front seat of the car got out, not believing his eyes, but calmed down when he saw the white cane. Only a few bits of rubbish had fallen onto the back seat and the driver picked them up himself. Thought of telling the young woman this irrelevant story to cheer her up. Normally she liked a bit of humour, but no, not now. "What? Is there someone with you?" she asked unexpectedly.

"No, absolutely not!" Who did she think I'd be sharing my bed with?

She stayed on the phone a long time. Silent mostly.

"Dad, what are we going to do?"

I let her away with every misplaced 'Dad' that night.

We'd been talking for thirty-five minutes. I'd said everything I could and left unsaid the things I shouldn't say. But would continue the conversation with myself, such as that the Auld One was a bit of a scallywag and wondering had I learned enough about caring from her to be the best Stephen Kidney I could.

"I am sure she is up in heaven at this very moment," I said, raising my head to the ceiling and seeing cracks big enough for heavenly spying lounging across the white plaster, "looking down, smiling, with her husband... Luke, and Mark, and her parents and grandparents and great..." The sniffling escalated.

"It's OK," I whispered into the phone as the darkness fled westwards across the sky. "I'm alive, you're alive, the Brat's alive, we're all alive–" I almost added, 'except for the retarded fat Retired Detective who'll soon be dead unless he gets in touch pronto cause Colonel Thunderclap was losing patience.'

Sniffle. "Yes, it is." Sniffle.

"You're a brave girl," I said. "Thank you for ringing me," and hung up.

Chapter 38

Fishing

The prairie bogs of the East Midlands opened up before us. The car sped west towards the big river that flowed down the centre of the country. The city petered out to farms, fields, and hedges. The opening up of the sky and landscapes as the hedges disappeared and flat, wide-stretching, low-horizon bogs came into view. A totally different kind of world which had somehow escaped me on my bus trip. I was like a child with the window open, my face stuck out and the wind fast on my cheeks, agog at the tawny browns and vivid emptiness. The bog-scape presented the sky as the ultimate glory of the world, unimaginably vast, a sweet to-die-for vastness, that my city eyes couldn't get enough of.

Hankered to be let loose out there and feel my skin buffeted and danced with by the bog-wind. The car passed over a hill and the misty distance spread out like spilled milk. The great river, when we came to it, lapped high against its banks, barely squeezing under the arches of the old stone bridge. It was so glorious in its slow near-flood flow. Told Maurice it wasn't a man's river at all. It flowed too gracefully, too calmly. Neighbour Maurice behind the wheel hutted understandingly.

Thoughts about living somewhere new as Stephen Kidney popped in and out of my head. If I had to leave my house, could I dismantle it in neat stacks of bricks waiting to be loaded onto a big truck to be carted off to Finland. There was a guidebook in the front room about Finland. I'd flicked through it. How about on a coast looking out on the frozen sea and the special ships that cut passages through the groaning ice. Snow lying on the ground for months with people stuck indoors, drinking beer in saunas. An entire country like that, not just one person, overcoming adversity. A country like that would understand a person like me, wouldn't it?

We drove to a small marina just north of the town where the open, small-engined boat was moored. Out on the river, we headed north to where it widened out into a vast lake. We set the modest anchor near the western edge of the lake and Maurice settled down to his fishing. He was as good as his word. He said very little. There was more danger of me talking. Mostly I listened to water slapping against the boat, the sounds of the wild birds, squawks and twitters in the fresh air. Preoccupied Maurice moving about the boat arranging his fishing tackle or gazing at the clumps of trees, and at the odd hillock that peeped out of the flatness all along the eastern edges of the grey-blue water.

Maurice had called to the house before eight, inviting me, just like that, to go fishing with him. I knew nothing about fishing and didn't know whether he did either, but apparently, he did. He had the use of a boat and had said to himself when he got out of bed and looked out the window, 'Hey, why not go fishing today?' Didn't sound like Maurice. He never struck me as the spontaneous type. But it was a clear mild day and I knew I wouldn't be force-fed small talk. So, I said yes. Plus, and this was always at the back of my mind, Maurice might die someday, even today – he could have a heart attack or fall overboard and need a guardian for Boris.

We ate lunch on the boat, which for a man who said he had decided to go fishing on the spur of the moment, was well prepared. I saw Dora's delicate hands behind the prawn pasta salad, the rhubarb and ginger crumble and the flask of decent coffee.

Maurice caught a few small fish and after explaining their names to me and the importance of conservation, immediately threw them back into the water. Horrified by this senseless effeminacy, I felt like throwing him in after them and if Dora had been there, her too. Blamed her for putting such a mushy idea in his head. Then, oh blissful world, I would return to claim Boris for myself. Forever.

The wind picked up and Maurice steered the boat back to its moorings, saying it could get worse. The shadows were lengthening on the motorway bridges as the car sped eastwards towards the huddled city. I was windswept and warm-cheeked and still in awe of the vastness that lived outside the city which I thought I wouldn't be able to live without again, but also knew I'd forget about once I got home.

Back in the city when I realised we were passing the local police station, I shouted, "Stop, Maurice! I have a quick message to do there."

Maurice parked on an empty side-street of redbrick cottages with five for sale signs up.

"Where's Fahy?" I demanded from the guard who eventually came to the enquiries counter. Had heard him opening two doors to get to me. The place was a warren of small spaces for large men. His uncapped, square faced, tunic-less presence looked like it had been interrupted eating his tea.

"How can I help you?" he murmured with frightening calm.

"Where's Fahy," I repeated.

"Fahy who?"

He must have been asleep as well.

"He's not bloody Chinese. Are you a Turk?"

The policeman's eyes narrowed. He growled, "As it happens my name is Burke," he replied primly, "and if you don't change your tone, you'll have to leave."

Looked him up and down, as much as I could to figure out what I was dealing with. Well-built man with an expression that said, 'I've seen it all and it's not pretty, but it hasn't destroyed me'. Moved his hands along the countertop as if he wanted to be closer to the baton just underneath.

"I think his first name is Amen."

"Amen Fahy? Never heard of a name like that."

"He's a recently retired detective and owns a few houses in bedsits."

He almost smiled and waited while I waited too. Eventually he asked, "Are you reporting a crime, sir?" Tricky question to answer and he saw my hesitation.

"I need to find him. It's personal."

"I see, and who might you be?"

I told him my name and where I lived and date of birth. His expression changed, like he just realised something surprising. So did I. Almost at the same time.

"Are you the sergeant who…?"

His look told me all I needed to know. We both now knew who we were dealing with here. Door behind was shoved open. Almost hitting me. An unshaven, slovenly adult ambled in like he knew the place, saying out loud to no one in particular, "The buggers stole me dole."

"Sit down there, Christy, and be quiet now, while I deal with this person," the sergeant said firmly. Derelict Man did as he was told.

"Do ye have a cuppa tea?" he asked counting his fingers.

The sergeant ignored him.

"So," I resumed archly like I had him pinned to the wall, although quite interested in how the two of them reacted to each other, "why haven't you moved that bloody hut off my land? How would you feel if it was in your front garden?"

"The superintendent is dealing with it. You'll have to speak to him," he said like he'd escaped checkmate.

Glared at him, realising we'd reached an impasse. "Look, Sergeant," leaned forward in deal-making mode, glanced around at Christy mumbling to himself, and lowered my voice. "If you tell me how to find Amen Fahy, I might forget about that trespassing hut. Sometimes I have a bad memory or so they say."

He had picked up half a pencil and was tapping it gently on the counter. "An Amen Fahy? Strange name. What station was he?"

"No idea."

"Hmm... Wait," his eyes lit up, "do you mean EAMON Fahy?"

"That's what I have been saying all along." This was taking far too long.

"I do, but I can't tell you his details, but I'll pass on a message if you want."

I would have argued the point, but poor Maurice waiting in the car. "Tell him..." I'll kill him. "Just tell him to contact me urgently because it's urgent, really urgent. OK?"

Dusk was squeezing the living daylights out of the sky as the car rounded the corner at the top of our street. Unusually, all the parking spaces were taken. Strange cars were parked on both sides of the street as far as the bottom of the hill and darkly-clad figures were emerging from them, standing in small groups on the footpath, talking in subdued voices and going up the steps into the Politician's house. The Brat was standing on the footpath waiting for his mother, unusually wearing a dark jacket and a tie. The fringe which usually covered half his face had been swept to the side giving a glimpse of what his grown-up face might look like. Saw me looking at him, seemed surprised, and was about to point at me but didn't. His mother turning around noticed me, as did some others, and while she smiled uneasily, no one seemed pleased to see me and turned quickly to go up the steps and inside the house.

"Don't stop," I said quickly, feeling uneasy. "I think you better drive on."

"I know, I know," Maurice replied, sounding flustered.

"You know what it is, don't you?" I said. "They're just back from a funeral."

Maurice looked back nervously through his rear-view mirror and nodded. He squeezed through the parked cars at the bottom of the hill and turned left to go around the block. He drove so slowly we were passed by a jogger.

"Phew," I said, shifting in my seat, remembering the sharp looks I'd gotten. I didn't blame the young woman. I knew who was to blame. "That was close."

Maurice's face was red which was quite a contrast with his usual pale look.

"Did you know there was a death in their family?" I asked him.

"Yes." He avoided my eyes and pulled into an empty space. Left the engine running, rubbed his face and looked straight ahead as if thinking. He didn't need to explain anything.

"I never knew her. She moved out a good few years ago," he said after a while.

"Nor I, nor I... Well, I visited her a few times in the nursing home."

"Did you?" He seemed surprised.

"But only... erm..." Didn't know if I could trust him with the truth.

"The young woman... you know her? The one who collects the, um, child... she was very upset. You see, it was her Granny." I rolled down the car window for cool air to help me navigate my thoughts. "Rang me in the middle of the night to tell me. She's like that, you know, very... erm, sensitive." I shook my head at the strangeness of it and looked out the window. "I think... I think it..." I was unsure what I thought. "It's very sad all the same. Do you know what age she was?"

I got out of the car, thanked Maurice for a great day and privately bemoaned again his effeminate actions with the fish. When I reached my house, they were all inside next door, curtains drawn, and the street was silent.

The guinea pigs did a freaker when they heard me open the door. There was never anything wrong with their damn ears. Top-gear bleating and olympic-romping around their cage until I lifted them out of it in the towel and settled them on the sofa, the three of us eating cucumber. Fell asleep. Don't know for how long, but when I woke up my hands went instinctively for the towel to stroke the guinea pigs. They weren't there. Sat up with a shock. Whenever they got free on the kitchen floor, they went straight for the smallest darkest holes they could find. Usually behind the washing-machine or in the gap between the fridge and the wall. Took me ages to find the little buggers and get them out with a stick, but once in the towel they accepted captive life and settled down. Yes, they were like that. They loved their little freedom, but it scared them as well.

Chapter 39

Funeral Visitors I

Not long after midnight, knocking on the big kitchen window. Heard the resonating thud from the front room. The faint hubbub of voices through the wall from next door had died away and was spying on the mourners as they departed. Suppose could have forgotten about what was going on next door and gone to bed but had left most of the lights on. Months ago, I'd have definitely gone to bed and left them at it, not thought any more about it. But now I was better at figuring things out for myself. If they really believed I was part of their family, and should have been there, maybe they'd want to come and visit me, if only for appearance-sake.

So, I wasn't too surprised by the knock and didn't rush down to the kitchen to open the sliding door. Waited a few moments, letting them chill in their guilt.

Opened the door and stood aside, examining the three darkly clad figures who followed the Politician. Two men and Beetroot Woman. Git John looked around as if he knew the place, walked over to the table, lifted up the tablecloth, ran his fingers over the wood as if looking for an indent of some sort. He wandered over to the blocked-up fireplace, stood a moment studying the bric-a-brac on the iron ledge of the fireplace, lifted the lid of a tiny ornamental copper pot on the ledge, and put his finger inside it. Noticed me staring at him, put the lid back on the pot, came back to his wife. The stranger too looked like he was curious. I even had a sense they would have liked to see the rest of the house, but their looks were too searching and proprietorial and the tour guide was off duty. Something about the stranger hinted he wasn't from the Shrinkage. I never allowed the Shrinkage into my house. I had a good Shrinkage-radar and it showed no blips this time.

Beetroot Woman veered towards the Git. The stranger didn't veer towards anyone, though from appearance he might have faintly resembled the Git. Something different about him though, took me a few moments of staring to figure it out. He was tanned, too tanned, and the grey jacket and open-necked white shirt made it look like he'd come from a day's sailing in the sun.

"I heard you were fishing today," the Politician started, chattily enough. "Catch anything?"

How did she know? "Were you speaking to Maurice?"

Smiled like she was admitting a secret and I began to guess what had happened.

"Yes," she said, wanting me to know it was a lie.

"The place was full of mermaids," I said, glancing at Git John who was again walking around the kitchen, examining things, showing far too much curiosity. Cheek of him. That's all he'll see. Noticed me watching him and stopped.

"Maurice said we had to throw them back in the water," I told the Politician.

"I've brought some visitors to say hello. This is John." He came over and put out his hand. I ignored it. I may have a bad memory, but what I remember I don't forget. He took it coolly. Acted like it made no difference. Politician didn't seem put off either.

"This is Maureen, John's wife." Beetroot Woman was short and squat. Her jacket had padded shoulders. She had trimmed hair, big lips, and red blemished cheeks. An impressively ugly person and oddly desirable, and just then full of hurt pride that kept her hand by her side.

"We've met before," Beetroot Woman said as if it pained her to admit it.

"Good." I said, sensing that death by stoning was all she thought I was good for.

The second man seemed embarrassed by the icy atmosphere. He grinned when the Politician introduced him as 'Terry, your other brother'. Used both hands when shaking mine and unexpectedly gave me a hug.

"Dom," he said with real feeling. "Long time no see. It's me, Terry."

I hugged back. Why not? It was a friendly gesture and I hadn't had many of them lately. Did it matter if it was with a total stranger? Hoped the Git was looking and learning.

"We were at the funeral," the Politician said.

I nodded. "Please, take a seat everyone." Remembered the duties of a host, waved them towards the kitchen table.

"Mammy's funeral," Git John added almost vehemently, as he sat down, looking at the others.

"Of course," I said, unsure whether offering condolences would be well received.

An uneasy silence. Hands flat on the table like we were sharing a silent prayer that God was good. I looked at The Politician. Usually she's the one who starts and finishes the talking, but she was avoiding my eyes. Her body language said she was taking a back seat.

"Will I make some tea?" she finally suggested.

"That would be grand, Catherine," Beetroot Woman said.

The Politician got up and started to make the tea. Of course, she knew where everything was, but I felt she could still show common civility by asking me just to let on she didn't.

Looked at the faces around me, not impressed by the silence, sensing they were here for a reason but reluctant to start. Didn't think much of that. They troop into my house, sit at my table, drink my tea, and say nothing? It was just as well I still felt an inclination to be sociable.

"Eh, would anyone like something stronger? A whiskey or…?" I'd nothing else.

Terry nodded, "Please, Dom." Git John shot him a glance like he was fraternising with the enemy.

Came back from the front room with the bottle and three glasses and invited them to help themselves.

"Nothing for me," Beetroot Woman said and stood up and went over to help the Politician.

"You're looking well," Git John said.

"Me? Eh, thank you. You can't beat fresh air. I had a very invigorating day's fishing with a neighbour."

"Did you?" Git John's eyes flashed like I'd said the wrong thing. Clearly Maurice's invitation wasn't all that spontaneous. No, rather, it made sense to have me out of the way, if they were afraid I'd make a scene. Shouldn't have felt annoyed but I did.

"Sad," I said, thinking of the trick. "Very sad."

"It was so sudden," Terry said.

"What was? Oh, yes." Nodded quickly. "Yes. I visited her, well, you probably know that. She was a… feisty character."

Git John's eyes darkened again. He was now seriously getting on my nerves. He had been like this since he came in. Could see it made Terry uneasy and the women behind were in no rush to come back with the tea. As long as he was like this there was no chance of a sociable chat. Didn't see why in my own house in the middle of the night I should have to put up with this. Sipped my whiskey and made a decision.

"John," I said trying to sound polite, but maybe not succeeding. "Do you have something on your mind?"

The question caught him off-guard and his look for once was uncertain. Didn't give him time to think. "Because," I continued. "I am getting these vibes, you see, that a volcano has entered my kitchen." I paused. "And that it's waiting to explode." The more I said, the angrier I became. "So, either erupt now, and get it over with, or fuck off out of here."

The shock of the words ran across all their startled faces like a Mexican wave. I heard Beetroot Woman gasp behind me. Terry's jaw dropped. He was about to say something when Git John got in first.

"How… How dare you!" His fists did a little dance on the table. His cheeks bulged and his eyes widened so quickly I noticed hairs from his eyebrows hanging down. If he didn't get words out fast, he would explode. "I will not let *you* speak to me like that," he hissed icily, keeping his voice steady. "Especially on this day, of all days." He glared around the room like it would help him recharge his anger. "I am not a stranger in this house," he said ponderously. "None of us are." He glared at me. "I grew up here. In this house. In this kitchen." He tapped the table twice with a pointed finger. "Just like you. This was my seat." He tapped the table in front of him. "That was Terry's." He pointed to where Terry was sitting. "And that was yours."

To my horror he pointed at the very seat where I was sitting. I was so amazed I almost stood up like I'd had an electric shock.

"I am your brother," his voice boomed, "and so is he. Younger by eight years. Yes?" He looked at Terry. Terry nodded. "So, don't you talk to me like that, you… you…"

Even in a tense situation, I am capable of rising above strife. Ignoring his anger, I started studying their faces for resemblances, glancing from one to the other with the mad notion of suggesting all three of us go and stand in front of a mirror.

Table creaked. Git John's elbows were pressing hard on it. He had long arms and a double chin which he had no reason to be proud of. Checked my own chin, only one, rubbed it, trying to give him a hint. He saw me alright and his look said he thought I was mocking him. I suppose I was.

"Dominic," Beetroot Woman called from behind the kitchen island. I looked around hoping she was bringing the tea over to the table. "Do you realise what happened today?"

Just looked at her blankly, not expecting any compliments.

"No?" She put what she was holding down. "Well, let me explain." Couldn't keep the sarcasm out of her voice. "Today was a very sad day for the family. We buried your mother, Mammy. Your mother, the person who brought you into this world, who reared all of you, who loved you, who never stopped loving you until the day she died. Do you realise that?"

Heard what she said, but was watching him, thinking what to do if things got out of hand. Put my hands under the table in case they noticed my tight fists.

"She is buried in the same grave as your father and," her voice wavered, "and we couldn't take the risk of having you there. And... and we simply can't believe it," her voice rising three octaves as she made it to the finishing line of what was a short race.

It was like good cop, bad cop. But this wasn't a police station and I wasn't a prisoner or a suspect. It was my kitchen after all, my house, and this was only happening because I allowed it. If it hadn't been such a sensitive time, I'd have thrown the pair of them out. Might still do it. But the bereaved live in a strange place and are entitled to charitable latitude.

"We could not take the risk of you being there," Git John had taken over, repeating the accusation as if more would be gained that way. I was not going to shame myself into saying you never, em, invited me. Boris wouldn't have replied either.

"May she rest in peace," Beetroot Woman added, as if to mark that she hadn't finished her role in the conversation.

Still resolutely composed, I was going to propose a conciliatory toast to the Auld One's memory, but Git John wasn't finished.

"To her very end, to her last breath," he intoned like a man used to others having to listen to him. I readied my glass for the toast. "Mammy believed you would regain your memory. She thought if you could only…"

Terry was nodding. I proposed my own toast to myself. To auld ones with a sense of humour.

The Politician finally arrived with the tray. They made space in the middle of the table. The tray – my property, all of it, mugs, milk, sugar, spoons, crackers, blue cheese and biscuits, all mine – was unloaded and the table set. I watched this with mixed feelings. I hoped it would ease the tension but knew I might have been adding to it a little. All this stuff was mine and no one had asked me could they use it. Even if I said nothing about it, it was still robbery. All I'd offered was the whiskey.

Terry put a mug in front of me, added some milk. "No sugar."

"That's right." I looked at him. It took a moment to register.

"I remembered," Terry said almost shyly.

I noticed he had a slight accent.

"Well?" Git John said in a tone which indicated the tea had no effect on him. "Do you have anything to say?"

My mouth was stuffed with the cracker and cheese. "To whom?" I mumbled.

"To whom!" he repeated, his hands crushing the cracker he was holding into small pieces. He looked at his wife as if saying forgive me for what I am about to do.

I continued eating. I love blue cheese. I think I had stopped taking him seriously.

He practically shouted. "Your mother!" He threw his arms in the air.

The suddenness of the gesture disturbed me. I felt an urge to react. I told myself, 'Sit tight. Do nothing.' Throwing his arms like that was, for the moment, a substitute for attacking me. Which was just as well. He didn't look in great shape for a confrontation and I wouldn't have minded seeing his face as he looked up at me from the floor, surrounded by cracker crumbs. Terry was looking at the Politician, almost pleading with her to do something. But she remained determinedly passive.

"She is dead," I said when my mouth was empty, naively hoping that stating the obvious would stop them.

It was too much for Beetroot Woman. She stood up and exclaimed, "Dominic, you really are a disgrace. A disgrace to your family, your wife and your daughter and… and so ungrateful for all that's been done for you. How do you think you are able to live like this? Do you think it just happened? That it's a miracle? It's because… and the state of you… I won't talk about it, no, I won't…" She broke off to catch her breath, noticing her husband's questioning look. "No, John, I'm sorry. It has to be said. Someone should tell him. What's gone on here for months with no one daring to say a word because we were all scared of a relapse… is a joke. A sick joke… A sick joke which cannot continue." She produced a paper hanky and blew into it. "Your joke, which you played relentlessly on your poor mother, never mind your wife and daughter, and Thomas, for far too long. Far too long. No wonder Thomas won't be…" She shook her head. "How dare you!" She broke off again, turned around and sped out of the kitchen into the dark night.

The Politician gave me a dirty look, got up, reluctantly I sensed, and hurried out after Beetroot Woman. Perhaps to stop her committing suicide or coming back with a hatchet. I thought the Politician might have shrugged her shoulders when I looked at her, as if to say, well, she's always been like that. After a moment Git John too got up, sighed loudly and followed his wife. Good riddance, I said to myself, wondering only what I was supposed to have done to the Brat, happy to ignore everything else she said.

"Drink up," I said half-cheerily to Terry, lifting my glass and pushing the bottle towards him. The evening could only get better. Maybe now I could learn more about him.

Chapter 40

Funeral Visitors II

"We are all a bit tired and stressed, Dom," Terry said in a neutral tone. No hostility there, just regret. "It's been a long day. I only arrived last night." He yawned. "I think I'm still jet-lagged."

He did look tired. Behind the tan, he was at that point where mid-life begins to face real ageing. His hair was thinning and had tinges of grey at the temples. When he smiled, the foundations of future wrinkles danced in and out of view. But he still carried a youthful air and, I have to say, he made me feel good. For one thing, he let me stare at him like he understood my need to do so.

"Where did you come from?" I asked when I finished my staring.

"Rosario in Argentina."

"But you're from here?"

He nodded. "Left twenty-three years ago. Didn't plan it, met a girl…"

I was going to ask him what he thought of all these crazies claiming they were related to me but thought better of it.

"Argentina? That's a long way away, isn't it?"

He smiled gently. "It sure is. More than sixteen hours by plane."

"Rosario? What's that like?"

Put his hand in his jacket pocket. "I have some pictures here. Look," he said, taking out a small camera. "Have a look. There's a bit about the funeral and then about Rosario. You'll see the family." He started re-winding a video.

I was so glad he didn't say *your* family. "You have a family?"

"Graciela and three kids, Cristina, Karen and... Dominic."

"Go away," I said, genuinely surprised. "Dominic?"

He laughed. "Yeah, you're not the only one called Dominic."

"Wow." That hit some unexpected spot.

"I can skip the funeral if you like?"

"No, no, leave it. I'll watch it."

He handed me the camera. "There, it gives a little flavour of the place. I asked Thomas to film in the church. There's about eight minutes of the funeral. I took it for Graciela and the kids. It's a pity they weren't able to come."

"Thank you, thank you very much. Rosario? I like the sound of it."

"It's in the Pampas. It's beautiful. You should visit us. They'd love to meet you. They've never seen you."

The coffin was being taken from the hearse and rolled into the church surrounded by pale-faced dark suits. A priest's voice could be heard above the metallic clatter of the ambient noises. The mourners watched the coffin move up to the front of the church. Sitting in the pews nearest the altar on both sides of the aisle were the Auld One's family. A lot of them, faces I didn't know, pious, attentive and solemn. Some disliked being filmed. Others glanced nervously at the camera and looked quickly away. Others gave a level I-don't-care look.

Lead solemnities, Git John and Beetroot Woman, sat nearest the aisle in the front row, exuding dignified grief that couldn't be bought. Beside them were a younger couple with two demure girls between them and beside them an older woman around the same age as the Brat's mother, who could only be the Git's daughter. Long dark wavy hair framed a bony face with a significant snoozer.

Terry stood out like a tiger in a bed of swans, his tanned face, smart jacket and open-necked shirt making the rest of them look ill. It was the only time he appeared in the video. Behind him sat the young woman, the Brat and the Politician, together and apart, separated by the Chinese walls of every church. The camera lifted itself up to the high wooden ceiling and came down on the sparsely occupied nether pews at the back. Recognised many neighbours, surprised and pleased they were there, in spite of the house searches.

"There's Mrs Hand," I exclaimed, pointing at her.

Terry leaned over. "I don't know her."

I would have to compliment her the next time I saw her on how well she looked and how she didn't let the solemnity of the occasion mar her keen interest in everything around her.

"There's Dora," I pointed at the little face towards the back. "Where's Boris?" I asked in spite of myself.

"Who's Boris?"

"The cat." Saw that look, but in my house would not hide my feelings. "Boris is my best friend," I said turning back to the screen. "Do you have a cat?"

Paused the camera when the video showed the Auld One's face. Composed, powdered and restful. She looked more alive than any time I'd seen her. Like she might wake up and say something outrageous like, 'Whose funeral is this, anyway?' Still felt only the regret of a learner carer who hadn't finished his course. All the same, was conscious of my feelings for unexpected reactions, not wanting to fool myself or anyone else, and completely respectful of the mute grief she inspired.

Terry was sitting there doing nothing, like a small child sitting beside a bigger child. Just happy to be there, no matter what I said or did. Which struck me as quite agreeable. A man without an agenda.

Fast-forwarded to the burial to watch the Brat at the graveside. These days he was becoming more a person than a pest. Henry Hurling was making a man out of him. The camera caught him taking his mother's hand, unprompted. No fidgeting, slouching, yawning, looking around for something more interesting. He'd held my hand once before as well, hadn't he?

I gave back the camera and Terry fiddled with the controls, handed it back. Suddenly I was there. Rosario. It said it in light print at the bottom of the small screen. The screen filled with sunlight and leafy trees, wide streets and a big lake and tall buildings and green spaces. It was like being transported to a planned paradise. I watched open-mouthed, not believing a place could seem so perfect and it sent my skin line-dancing on my shoulders. The mini-Manhattan skyline seemed to rise up out of the sparkling water. The sailing boats on the lake were like languid swans moving hither and thither in no pattern. Boats and skyscrapers made of the same stuff, realised human hopes and dreams, first cousins. The lake was lorded over by a wondrous long, slender bridge as if God himself had stretched steel beyond what nature could do.

I saw a detached low red-roofed white house in a suburban street and a brown-haired thin-faced woman with deep tired eyes stopping her gardening as the camera approached. A tall, long-haired, almost-woman girl came from the side and reluctantly stood beside her, taller than her, and made a face at the camera. The camera moved along a flower bed to a clear-skinned boy in shorts whose Terry-like smile left no doubt who he was.

"Tell me more," I said when he stopped the camera. Too many thoughts running around my head. Could anywhere be as nice as this?

"Rosario is…" Terry's soft accented voice, as he described Rosario, awakened a hunger in me. What kind of hunger, I didn't know. My mind leapt into the unknown and made new connections. Stephen Kidney in Rosario, on a boat, walking a street. And then it all sort of fell flat when I remembered Flabby Fahy, the key to my future, sitting on his arse, eating his pancakes, forgetting about me, blocking my progress. If he'd been beside me then I'd have wrung his wretched neck.

"…nothing to be done."

Regrettably, Git John was back, resuming his seat at the table, finishing a sentence started somewhere else, his voice bringing me back to the antagonistic present.

"Nothing."

"Dom?" Terry spoke with new urgency, as if he knew his time was running out. "I only come home every few years. I have to get back, back to work. But I want to get to know you again. I mean... as you are now, but it's very difficult being so far away." He moved his empty glass backwards and forwards on the table. "But if you ever wanted to come and visit us in Rosario, you'd be more than welcome. We'd love to have you. You do travel on your own, don't you?" He glanced at Git John as if that Git would know anything about me. "Graciela and the kids would love to meet you. You could stay as long as you liked. We have plenty of room." He paused and looked at the table. "Because no matter what's happened... you are, you always will be my brother, no matter what you think." He smiled at his boldness and so did I, but Git John emitted an impatient cough. "That's it," he said shyly, raising his eyebrows and standing up.

Looked up at him, not wanting him to go but feeling if he had to, he had to. I stood up too, thinking he was the nicest person I'd ever met. "That's… Thank you, Terry. And you're always welcome here too in my house, I have plenty of room too." I added, wanting to be symmetrical.

I wondered how difficult it really was to fly from Rosario to Dublin. Brother or no brother, there was no doubting his feelings for me. Terry threw his arms around my shoulders, hugged me again and left.

"Nice guy," I said, watching him disappear into the darkness of the back garden and pass through the gap in the wall.

"Too nice," Git John grumbled, stony-faced as ever.

"Why don't you go as well?" I asked him, still staring into the dark. Pleasantries long since finished between us. I remained standing, hoping this would add umph to the message. Time alone with him was the last thing I needed just then or any time. But he stayed in his seat like he hadn't heard me. He had some papers on the table in front of him. I reluctantly sat down again.

"She appointed me her executor," he said, managing an almost civil tone.

"What?"

"I'm the executor of her will."

"Eh … fine." So what? I was slow picking up his thread. But a small worry-ball was already forming in my stomach.

"She left you the house."

"Sorry… say that again. She did what?"

He repeated himself louder. "This house." His expression said he wasn't going to repeat himself a third time.

I leaned back, stroking my chin, trying to figure his angle. Was this just to annoy me? If it was, it could only end badly. For him. On this of all nights and with no witnesses?

"It is hard to believe, I know, but that's what's in the will. It's her wish and we respect it."

I put my hand to my temples, scratching fast, realising he was deadly serious. "But... Are you sure? This is *my* house. Not hers." How could she leave something to me which was already mine?

"It isn't yours. Well, it is now or will be soon."

"What... what the fuck are you saying?" My eyes were bulging wider than a crocodile who's had its dinner taken away from it. This guy should not mess with me. I pointed an accusing finger at him. "Are you saying that the house, this house *isn't* mine?"

"Yes, I am." He sounded like a patient teacher explaining something to the class dunce. He'd better get rid of that tone soon, I thought, or I'll get rid of it for him.

"But..." Not in a million years did I ever expect to hear something like this. "I don't believe you."

His expression said he didn't care what I believed.

"This is *my* house," I repeated, my voice rising, ready to shout if he contradicted me again. Ready to stand up and speak directly to the house, tell it not to listen to this liar. So annoyed, near ready to go for him.

"My house has feelings. Same as I have. Are you trying to mess with my head?"

The briefest just-what-I'd-expect-from-you look flashed across his eyes. "You can look at the legal documents if you want. It won't make any difference. It doesn't matter what you think."

I banged the table with both fists. "Hold on a minute, what do you mean it doesn't matter? It sure does matter. It matters a huge deal to me." I was jabbing the table with my forefinger as I spoke, getting really annoyed. Clearly, the man had no idea how angry he was making me and how fundamental the house was to everything in my life. My sanity, my happiness, my neighbours, my friends, Boris. And the god-awful implications only coming into view now.

If he was right, it meant I had been wrong all along – as wrong as anyone can possibly be, since I had come out of hospital, about the very basis of my life. And it also meant they had lied to me. Lied about something too serious to be lied about. Incredible. They had said I was going into my own place and that was a lie. My anger was near out of control. The fact that he'd taken away and given back in the same breath didn't matter a whit.

"You can check with the solicitor if you want."

"I will, I will. Did you want it?"

"I wouldn't have left it to you, if that's what you're asking. You don't deserve it."

"Do I not? Do. I. Not?" He wouldn't have spoken like that if he had any idea what I was thinking.

"That's all she left you. The rest goes to Terry and me."

I didn't care what she left to anyone else.

He stood up and put his hand inside his suit pocket and tossed a thick envelope on the table. "That's your copy of the will if you're interested. And the solicitor's contact details. Good night."

He had to walk by me to get out. I was on my feet, itching to do something. As he walked by me, I pushed him hard backwards, savouring the shock, the stunned look of disbelief on his face. He stumbled against a chair and almost fell over it. I was up against him before he knew it, grabbing his nice suit by the lapels and shoving him against the wall. I couldn't hit him as long as my hands were occupied, and I consciously kept it like that. I didn't trust what my hands would do if I let go of the lapels. I hung onto them like a drowning man clinging to a bit of wood. A lot of stuff was criss-crossing my mind. I snarled into his face and slapped him hard twice on the cheeks with an open palm. Just to humiliate the smarmy arrogant Git, not hurt, nor leave any marks. Sensed I knew how to hurt without leaving traces. I was ready for more if he said the wrong thing, but he heeded my warning finger wagging under his nose. Fear in a bully's eyes is sweetness itself.

When I was sure there was no fight left in him, I let go his lapels and stood back. "Go on, get out of here. Get out of my house and never come back."

Chapter 41

Checking with Solicitor

The mattress made its intent clear. It didn't want me lying on it, which was pretty bizarre because I used it every night. Tested different parts, different positions, made no difference. Bumps, lumps, inclines, hollows I hadn't noticed before which seemed to move whenever I did. Was it saying I didn't own it? That I had no right to sleep on it? That it would never let me sleep peacefully again?

Got out of bed, took off my pyjamas, got out the hurley from under the bed and started beating the mattress. Methodically, ritually. Held the hurley up with two hands. Thumbless pain helping my rage. Hesitated before each blow. Wham, bang, wallop. Anger into energy into flattened mattress. Grunted like a tennis player and sweated like a sprinter. Wham, wham, wham. The bed jumped or moved a little with each wallop. Soon it wasn't only the mattress. I was also beating my instincts. Had trusted them implicitly, guided my life by them, and they'd let me down. Badly. Not that I fully believed what Git John said but was in a strange frame of mind. After the funeral, Terry and what he'd made me feel, then taking away my house and giving it back to me – I wasn't in the same sceptical space I usually occupied.

The mattress-beating wasn't the start of it either. After they'd left, turned off the lights and stood in the dark in the kitchen for a long time. The adrenaline subsided. My feelings caught up with me. Realised was in some kind of shock, but the dark and absence of noises gave it a surreal edge which allowed a measure of calm. At some point I started moving around the kitchen. I touched everything. The sink, the taps, the fridge, the table and chairs. I opened drawers and presses and ran my hands over crockery and cutlery, afraid to look at them directly because of my betrayal of them. I had always told them they were mine. Emptied the cutlery drawer onto the ground just to show that I could. No one would stop me. Even so, everything tangible in the house now had two dimensions, the surface and the hidden.

In the bedroom I went over to the wardrobe and touched, not the wood, but the clothes hanging there. They were all I could still be sure of. It meant the clothes and the wardrobe now belonged to different categories. The always-mine and the recently-mine. Held up the leg of a hanging pair of trousers, cut it off above the knee with scissors and stuck it back on again badly with safety pins and studied it. Was it like having a leg amputated and put back on while you slept?

Rang the solicitor as soon as it was nine. A reticent voice answered. "Yes?" Its owner was clearly not paying attention to how he sounded.

"What did you do with my house? The Git said it wasn't mine and now it is or will be. How is that possible?"

"Pardon?" Rapid change of tone. "Who is this?" the posh sure-of-itself voice asked.

"I'll answer that when you answer mine. Come on, what did you do with my house?" I heard voices behind him. Things happening. Is he going to hang up? If he does, I'll come straight around. I had his name and address. "I'll give you my address. You'll have to manage with that."

New tone. "I see. Just let me note that down. Hang on, I'll be right back."

While he was gone, I was imagining what a posh crook's face looked like, but all I kept seeing was the Retired Pancake's face.

The voice was back. "Ah, I think I have it now. Would you please just confirm your identity?"

I did.

"Would you be related to Judge Corley?" An embarrassed short laugh.

"No, I don't know any judge."

"No? Are you sure?"

"Course I'm bloody sure. Are you sure who you are?"

Muffled sounds. Could be laughter, or gasps. Couldn't tell.

"Right, now, get on with it."

"OK, sure. Just let me get the papers out."

While he was doing this, I asked, "Who is this judge guy?"

"He's the executor of Mrs Corley's will."

Was this guy another dope? "I mean, is he really a judge?" I was laughing. It was too ridiculous – the Politician defending the country and the Git filling the jails. "What does he judge?"

"He's a very eminent judge of the criminal courts. I used to brief him when he was still in practice."

"Well, he wasn't very eminent the other night when I had to slap him for being a gobsh–"

Muffled gasps. Sudden burst of coughing at the other end of the line. "I didn't hear that," the solicitor said, "and please don't repeat it to me. Now, about the will–"

"Did you take my house off me and give it back again, you grimy toad?"

PART V1

Chapter 42

Growing Curious

Hard to tell, but suspect I began changing around this time. Before then, true, I coped, I processed, I resented, acted tactically. But aside from wanting to become Stephen Kidney, the big picture escaped me. Might have helped me see better what was fast approaching.

One morning, not long after the phone call to the solicitor, came down the stairs, saw the usual pile of unwanted mail on the floor under the letter box, and... didn't snigger or ignore it. Instead picked it up, brought it down to the kitchen table, sat down, spread it out, studied how the envelopes were addressed, started reading. Felt ordinary, no big deal.

Sure, enough junk to convince anyone that half the world would do anything to get into my letterbox, but there was also stuff that was newly interesting. For instance, for all the bills I'd ignored, never thought about, they still got paid, automatically I soon discovered, without any fuss. Who paid them? Apparently, I did. After comparing bills and bank statements, it appeared I had been doing this for ages. Nothing wrong with that, I thought. Except didn't remember ever setting it up. And where did the money to pay the bills come from? Soon discovered payments into my bank account every month, more than enough as far as I could see, from mysterious Code-Person. Learned how much electricity and gas I used, how much I paid for health insurance. Health insurance? Fast thinking. Was I paying the Shrinkage? Oh my God, better not.

Immediately rang insurance number, barely able to contain bubbling outrage. Helpful lady told me, no, but maybe I paid by direct debit from the bank. Ring the bank. Did so, immediately. Bank-voice wanted all sorts of numbers from me before they could even fart. Told them I was blind, had one leg which I was standing on in a public phone box, with five people queuing outside and would topple over if they didn't hurry up. Never mentioned non-thumb in these situations. It worked. Eventually got through to fast-talker who wouldn't admit failure if he was in a plane hurtling towards the sea.

"Yes, sir, the three payments over the last, eh, twenty-four months went to a Doctor Canoe and a Doctor, eh, Papp."

"Cancel them immediately," I ordered tersely. Someone would pay for this.

"Yes, sir. Right away, sir." Liked this guy. But, he couldn't. Already paid.

"Then cancel any future ones."

"Yes, sir."

Christ, they've taken me for an absolute bloody ride. "Someone's going to swing for this," I muttered. "Not you, lad, you're doing grand." Loud huffing and puffing sounds into the phone, had it practically stuck to my mouth. Must've sounded like a gale force eight.

"Of course, sir. You just have to send us the completed cancellation form with the two signatures. You can get the form in your local branch."

"Bloody Beelzebubs!" I swore. "A form and two signatures? What's wrong with one?"

"Yours and, ah, the signature of a… Mrs Catherine Corley."

"What?" I spluttered. "Who the hell put her name there? She's not my wife, trust me. That woman is a fraud. What's she got to do with it?"

"No, sir, I don't think so. That's in accordance with the instructions you gave when you sent it up. I have the document here in front of me."

"Oh, for God's sake," I banged the kitchen table. I'd signed a ton of stuff just to get out of hospital. Of course, hadn't looked at one of them. Would've signed Lucifer's canonisation form if it would've helped. Should've killed her when I had my hands around her neck. Drummed fingers on the table. No point asking a banker how to forge a signature. Fiddle figures, yeah, but not signatures. Still, it wouldn't be hard. Damn signature on every election poster.

Chapter 43

Sad Brat

N ext time I saw the Brat was the last time for twelve years. Didn't know it at the time. Had I known it, would've sat him down, made him listen to a speech full of good advice for a long modest non-political life. Would've contained many cautionary words about interfering women and many encouraging words about phlegmatic women of rural backgrounds. Would've advised against searching in toilet cisterns or relying on retired detectives for anything. Would've praised Henry Hurling as a manly de-stressor and counselled against lying on concrete floors when things got tough. And much else besides, but by then I'd have gone on so long he'd have been off on some space-cloud.

For a good while Brat hadn't appeared either at the house or in the park for Henry Hurling. The hurleys and sliotars were cleaned and ready. Even put a towel in the small rucksack he used because I thought it was time I hit another ball into the stream, so he could jump about and crow how useless I was. Could see it wouldn't be long before he refused to play with me and would only play with kids his own age. Bag all ready and packed beside the radiator in the hall.

That last time, Brat was sad. Strange, I know. Didn't know he had real sadness in him. I was at the back of the garden, among the bushes, studying the spread of spiders webs across the bushes. Felt sorry for the hard-working spiders who seemed to have only one plan of action. Keep spinning out the same web and hope for the best. Admired the spiders timeless optimism but wondered why they couldn't make better webs.

Heard the front door banged shut. Aha, the Brat's here, I thought. Mixture of foreboding, anticipation, moderate irritation. Someday, he'll learn how to close a door. Waited for the thud of his school bag on the hall floor, the rapid pounding on the stairs and then sweet silence. Defeated nature once more. Resumed my study of the spiders webs swaying in the mock light of the overcast afternoon. Whole swathes of bushes covered in net-like, fly-catching web. If all spiders webs are the same, could I invent a new better one? A more proactive one that could reach out for the flies instead of waiting for them.

Brat lounging on the sofa in the front room, turning thick red plastic wheel with a small hole in the middle, over and over in his hands. School bag unopened on the floor, no pretence at doing homework. Tapped the sliotar on the hurley in my hand without saying a word, hoping he'd get the message. Quite a while since we'd last played in the park.

Brat didn't react. Didn't even look up at Colonel County-Hurler or tell him he was mad or definitely stupid which would have been quite acceptable. Just stared at that stupid bit of plastic in his hands, looking subdued and dejected.

"Hurling sucks," he muttered.

I knew he didn't believe that. "What is it?"

"Nothing."

"Are you sick? Will they not play with you?"

"No. It's nothing."

"Well, it must be a big nothing… Been in a fight and lost? I can show you a few…"

"I don't want to talk," he muttered firmly.

Unheard of talk. Left the room, came back wearing the *Légion d'Honneur* medal on my shirt. Sat on the ground in front of the white marble fireplace, said nothing, waited. Eventually looked at me, saw the medal. It annoyed him.

"Take it off, will you?" he demanded. "Why… why the…?"

Put it on the mantelpiece, sat down again on the floor, staring and waiting. I can spot distress when it stares me in the face.

"Stop staring at me, will ya?"

His nasal breathing the only sound in the room. Turned his face more towards the wall so I couldn't see it clearly. Don't know how long it took, but finally looked at me, sad expression.

"Why can't you remember anything?" His voice wavered. Was he close to tears? Not possible. "In school they all think I'm from a mad family."

Speaking for myself, I could only agree. "Just give me their names," I said matter-of-factly, "and I'll…"

"It's not funny," he shouted.

Shifted my legs to avoid cramp. "Did you see the video?"

"No. What video?"

"The one Terry had at the funeral. Of Rosario. Did he show it to you?"

"Rosario? What's that?"

"It's a… blue cheese."

Wasn't listening.

"He has a son about your age. Want to know his name?"

No answer.

"Dominic," I declared with pride. Big smile.

"So what?" red-cheeked Brat gulped. Had to wait a moment before he could continue. "Leave me alone."

I didn't move. He needs me, I know he does. Some practical caring from Colonel Almost Professional Carer. He just didn't know it. "Was your Dad at the funeral?"

"I don't have a Dad."

"Everyone has a Dad."

"You don't," fierce-toned Brat-retort.

True. "Do you… miss the Auld One who died?"

"Dunno."

Would go on like this unless I did something. Could slap him on the face, let him slap me. Brat could take it, fundamentally robust. Or, a tickle-attack. Heard a stifled sob from the corner. Drew his legs up to his chest, turned more towards the wall.

"You miss her?"

Loud sniffle. "Stop asking stupid questions."

Got up off the floor, lumbered over to him. Looked up at me looming over him, watching me warily with moist red eyes.

"Get away from me," he blurted. "Get away!"

That was good. "Easy, soldier," said soft-voiced Colonel Insightful.

He didn't know what I was doing. For once I did.

"I'm not afraid of you. You can't tell me what to do."

"Ssshh!" Put my hands on his soft cheeks, held them gently, searched his eyes. Couldn't say I knew what I was looking for, except I'd know it if I saw it. Didn't struggle or scream. Just looked up at me, blinking.

"Thomas," I said quietly.

He blinked again, this time astonished, swallowed hard. That was enough. Took my hands away, went back to sitting in front of the fireplace. Probably as confused as he was over what had just happened.

"Mam was crying. She's upset," he said. "And Granny says I can't come here anymore after school. They're sending me to boarding school. Your school."

"My school?" Didn't know I had one. Wasn't mentioned in the post or the will. What kind of nonsense were they telling him? "Why did they say you're not to come here anymore?"

Shrugged his shoulders. "Dunno. Mam is always telling me not to stress you out and... and she doesn't want me playing hurling."

"Huh… now, *that* is crazy." What does she know about Henry Hurling? Never saw her playing it. "So, why'd you come here today?"

"No one picked me up."

"You did the right thing," I said.

He sniffled again. "Granddad, why did she die?"

"Who?"

"Mammy's Granny."

Gave it to him straight. "She was an auld one. All auld ones die. It'll happen to us too."

Very satisfied with my answer, leaned back too far, banged my head a good wallop against the side of the marble fireplace. "Fuck!" Rubbed head. Bloody sore.

"You're not allowed say that," he shot up quick as a bullet, rubbing his eyes to enjoy the spectacle.

Sensed a possible change of mood. "OK, OK," Colonel Magnanimous said, holding up his hand. "Time to break a rule. I am declaring a fuck-amnesty. You can say it once, no, twice without any consequences." Held up two fingers.

He laughed. "Can I?"

Nodded a get-started nod. "Three times. That's all."

Well, he spent at least two minutes saying it every way he could. On its own, before a word, after it, in the middle of a word. Spelt it repeatedly, real fast like he was racing himself, shouted it out like there was a chorus behind him. Made rhymes with it, used every 'uck' sound known to man. Ending up singing it. Amazing inventiveness and how filthy his little mind was. Certainly got him out of his rut.

When he realised wasn't going to stop him, he stopped himself.

"I won't tell if you don't," he said sheepishly.

"Good man." Was on the verge of saying Thomas again, but twice in one day was too much. "That's the spirit. Want to hold the medal?"

He looked up at the mantelpiece, nodded. "Hey, it's got a bang on it," he exclaimed when holding it.

"Show me."

Came over, leaned against me as I looked at it. Hmm. Must have thrown it harder than I thought. "Did you do that?" I asked accusingly, time to re-establish combat-relations.

"Granddad," he said cheekily ignoring the charge, "tell me what you did to get it."

"Killed thousands in single combat," Colonel Machine-gun answered, straightening up, hoping the figure was big enough, wondering how much more of this 'Grandad' I could take. Aside from everything else, it made me feel old.

"Go on, tell us."

Wanted me to be serious so I was.

"No idea. Did your mother not tell you?"

"Yeah, but..." Wanted the gory details from the hero's mouth. Sat up on the sofa, waiting.

"I've no idea."

He sniffled again.

Jesus, what am I supposed to do? Invent a story just to stop him whimpering? No. "Have a good cry," I suggested. "You're entitled to it."

"I'm not crying."

"There's nothing wrong with crying. I've seen men cry." Which felt true.

"Yeah? Do you cry?"

"Sounds really ugly when a man cries."

Chapter 44

Deafers, Blinders and the Retired Detective

November weather grew bored repeating itself, was now trying to fool everyone. People went out ready for rain, got sun, ready for sun, got rain. Overdressed, underdressed. Umbrellas in the sun, sunglasses in the rain. Whereas I, in new long dark padded raincoat with rolled-up collar hood – bought on one of our shopping trips to stop the staff staring at me, was always rain-ready.

That day the sun quickly dried the footpaths. Warm breeze blowing up from the south, everyone sweating, carrying coats, jackets on arms, umbrellas in hand. Solitary shopping held no attraction for me. No-plan walking, going with the flow, happy in any moving crowd, on the look-out for a purpose.

Blinder ahead. Five metres. Now had my purpose. One of my favourite sights. Real deal too. Full-length white cane, not the effete cut-off one, roller-balling its way, broad side-to-side sweeps, head erect, arm autonomous.

Fell into step behind him, as ever finding solace in the conquest of adversity, ready, if needed, to offer protection. Blinder walked, as they all do, in an uncannily straight line. Oncoming crowds parted like the Red Sea, as if the white cane was hotwired to heaven for miracles. In the presence of both fortitude and beauty. I walked in his slip-stream like a car following an ambulance.

At traffic lights impatient crowd waited. Some broke ranks, crossed among the stalled traffic. Readied myself in case the blinder moved at the wrong time. On my right, hand-gesturing two men making discreet signals to each other, mouthing words. Deafers. Deafers and blinders together. What luck! Like winning the Lotto. God being good to me today. Didn't understand deafers as well as blinders. Different ways of conquering adversity. Lights changed, crowd surged forward, blinder and deafers as well, ignoring each other as they do, blinder strutting his stuff, deafers engrossed in silent conversation. Followed in good order, tail-end of a medieval daisy chain of the infirm.

As a rule, deafers walk too fast. Maybe it's the rhythm of sign language or they're forever challenging each other to walking races. Anyway, they soon overtook the blinder, neatly side-stepped a café sign badly placed in the middle of the narrow footpath. Blinder heading straight for it. Raced forward and just before blinder got there, kicked the sign out of the way. Collapsed with a loud clatter against the café window. Blinder stopped, only as if changing gear, started short sweeping of the ground in front of him.

"It's OK," I said, going over to him, careful not to touch him – they're not imbeciles, slightly breathless but pleased with myself. "There was a sign in your way. It's gone now."

"Thanks." Voice had a far-off quality which told me he just wanted to continue on his way. Again, as a rule, blinders don't say much in these situations. Stood aside as he re-orientated himself and walked off.

Door of the café pushed open. Overweight youngish man in a tight white shirt, narrow green tie emerged.

"Hey," he called out, looking up and down the street. "Who did that?" Eyes landed on Colonel Demolition. "Did you do that?" Too slow answering. "Oi, what're you lookin' ah?"

"The blinder couldn't see your sign. He'd have walked into it."

"The what? What's a bleedin' blinder?" Let out a sneer-laugh. "Course he couldn't. He's fuckin' blind, isn't he? Shouldn't be out walkin' on his own." Came up close to me, forehead up to my nose, heavier.

"Did you knock it down?"

Smell of fried onions. I didn't move, said nothing. Suddenly on the brink of a fight, demanded full concentration. Rapidly calculating, how would the Colonel react? First time thinking like that. Didn't mean I was the Colonel, becoming like him, just that by thinking like he might, I might gain something. Ordinarily confusing, not then.

Looked around me. Two guys, mid-thirties, shabby clothes, stubble few days old, watching us, still talking to each other in foreign language. Looked used to rough living.

"Are you deaf?" café-lout demanded, still glaring at me. "I told you to clear off."

Eyeballed him, tone too insolent, felt that close to hitting him if he said another word. Noticed it too, didn't like what he saw, backed off, re-set his sign at his window, went inside, motioned me to clear off.

Another café down the street, decorous little tree in a pot outside, enticed Colonel Befuddled inside. Needed to sit, settle, calm down. Banged a couple of empty chairs on my way to a table. Table so narrow if I looked at the little plastic flower dangling its head out of a mini vase, it might fall off the table. My body sagged into the seat, unused to sudden tension. Almost toppled over, pulled chair right into the table. Studied the menu. Halfway down the starched page, realised where I was. A pancake restaurant. Lots on the menu, most people eating them. For God's sake, a bloody pancake restaurant. Thought of getting up, leaving.

Gazed around at the customers, you never know, idly thinking what I'd do to him if I found him. Have to order something. Back to the menu, stir myself, something stronger than pancakes. Ordered coffee. Listening, not listening to the chatter and clatter, one voice sort of separated itself from the rest. Where's that coming from?

Looked over at a table around the counter which I hadn't seen when entering. Two men facing each other.

Didn't know face I could see. Other guy, back to me, hunched forward, shape of the head, shoulders…

In an instant I knew who it was. Fahy, the Retired Detective. No doubt about it. Jesus. Looked away quickly. Looked back again. No mistake. After waiting forever, almost giving up on Stephen Kidney, out of nowhere, who flies into my web like a fly from God? Staring at spiders webs not a waste of time.

Sudden anger an antidote to tiredness. Snap decisions. Hands gripping sides of the table to stop me going straight over, grabbing him by the throat. Didn't have to read out the charges against him. Two words. Kidney killer.

My decision? If Fahy went into the toilet, I'd go in after him. If he didn't, I'd leave him alone. Let fate decide. I am not a brute. Or… maybe I am. Waited, had a second coffee, drank a glass of water. Now I could hear his voice, laughter clearly. Never laughed like that with me. Always sour, grumpy.

Leaving coat on the chair, hurried downstairs to check out the toilets, hurried back up. Still there. Five minutes before the fly stood up, said something to his companion, went downstairs to the toilet. Put on my coat, had already paid, quickly followed him. Downstairs got the cleaning sign out of the cupboard beside the toilet door. Said, 'No Entry. Cleaning in Progress'. Put it outside the door of the men's toilet, went in quietly.

Two urinals, two cubicles. Only one cubicle occupied. No one else. Checked lock and door of empty cubicle, pressed hot air hand dryer. Lock wouldn't withstand good kicking. And that's what I did. Gave his door a right kicking, Loud violent bang. Door sprang inwards on an astonished Fahy, sitting on the toilet, trousers around his ankles, one hand holding a roll of toilet paper and the other a piece he'd just torn off.

Before he uttered a sound, I hit him hard on the cheek. Head jerked back against toilet cistern, he slumped sideways on the toilet bowl becoming wedged between cistern and wall. Dazed, not out, just as I wanted. Knew I was saying goodbye for ever to Stephen Kidney.

"You fucker!" shouted at his glazed eyes after I dashed over and restarted the hand-dryer. A trickle of blood coming out of his mouth. Already the makings of a good bruise on his cheek. But his eyes were rapidly focusing. I could see him adjusting to the new situation. He put up a hand to feel his cheek. I pulled his trousers and pants over his shoes so he couldn't kick me. I picked up the plastic bottle of toilet cleaner with the big red X on it. I'd found it in the cleaning cupboard. pointed at the big X and opened the bottle. Watched me with bulging eyes and gaping mouth. Quietly filled up the large red cap and held it over him. His genitals were exposed and one of his hands was trying to pull his shirttails down over them.

"Hey, you're… you're not –"

"Shut up, you pancake-eating dustbin. If you move at all, Fahy, or shout or try anything, you could knock this out of my hand and look where it'll fall." Let a few drops fall onto the front rim of the bowl near his genitals.

"Aaaah," he groaned, squirmed to get away from it. I pushed the door three quarters closed behind me.

"Now, talk. And don't waste my time. You've wasted enough already." He did talk. Which I admired. Saved both of us more bother. He was furious, of course, indignant, but knew he was rightly fucked, half-naked with Colonel Maniac looming over him in a really tight space. Told him not to waste his or my time threatening me. He could take it, I was rightly threatened. In the same vein, I didn't list the people who might hear about our arrangement if he complained to anyone. I assumed he took that as given too.

Spat some blood out of his mouth before continuing. He'd never intended going any further. The Politician and the Shrinkage knew about it all along. Hadn't put him up to it. He'd told her himself and she'd told the shrinks and they decided to go only as far as the first stage, to wait and see what happened. Well, now they'd know what happened, wouldn't they? Hurt me more than I let on to hear that. Played for a fool again. Now I had the clearest proof who my enemies were. If I'd had the Shrinkage there in the cubicle with me, I'd have poured the whole bloody bottle over their shrivelled goolies. Instead left him, taking his trousers and shoes with me, throwing them in the urinal. On my way out approached Fahy's companion at his table.

"I think your friend had an accident in the toilet. He needs some help. You should go down to help him." Guy looked at me in surprise and was still looking at me as I left the restaurant.

Chapter 45

Politician's Announcement

E ven outrage can't stop time. Months passed. Was supposed to be spring. But spring wasn't doing its job, still trying to suck the guts out of winter. Winter fighting back. Buds in the trees were raw. Droning bees didn't sound revved-up. Daffodils were confused. Time to open or not? Spring-breezes in cardiac-care. Spring showers didn't feel like it. Ducks, ducklings staring forlornly at each other in the river, flies withdrawing into the shadows. As if nature decided spring had been too hasty, should be punished like a footballer who takes a free kick before the ref's whistle. Spring marking time, awaiting instructions.

So was I. So was the solicitor. All through autumn and winter been sending letters to call into his office to sign papers. Didn't go. Why should I? The house was mine. Always had been. They could say what they liked. Yet each reminder was like taking a brick away, grinding it into red dust, blowing it into my face. As if the more they told me it was mine, the less it was. And Stephen Kidney? Down the toilet with Fahy's pride. Never went into a pancake restaurant again. Maybe he didn't either.

Late afternoons wandered in the Botanic Gardens. Sun's weak rays fought their way through the colander clouds, caressing life in the Garden's many glades. I avoided the glass palaces for obvious reasons. Often watching decline of the sun and its fading streamlets shooting across the grass like angled arrows. Some days the brief luminosity was so startling it cast the trees in the grassy landscape like bedraggled old men, touching their heads, astonished so little hair was left. More than once I stood among the trees in my long coat, stretched out my arms and stood on one leg. More than once took off my hat, ruffled meagre curls. Knew who I was, but it didn't feel enough.

The Politician was abroad. The Guard in the hut told me, that's why he wasn't around. Thought about blaming him for Fahy's Gross Betrayal but said nothing. Nor did I ask again about the hut. Had grown used to the irritation. Brat was away in boarding school with a whole new world to annoy, and his mother kept telling me she was very busy with work. Seemed the Onslaught was in hibernation too or losing interest. Remained suspicious of course, on-guard.

But calm is never innocent. It's always calm before something. Near the end of March, was woken up one morning by a car engine running and voices out on the street, including Martina's loveable siren. Pronto, out of bed, pulled back the blinds. Ah, there she was, my lovely Martina, white blouse, dark trouser-suit, short hair, mischievous eyes, staring right up at me with a I-knew-you'd-be-spying-on-us look. Sent such a shiver through me I threw on the dark green bathrobe, dashed downstairs and threw open the door, hoping for more deliciously stern rebukes. She wasn't at the door. She was on the far side of the car. Saw the Politician coming out of her house, descend the steps in a brisk walk, carrying a bag full of files. When she saw me, she stopped, put the bag in the back of the car and came over to the railings of my front garden. Tanned and a slightly different air about her. I smelt an unknown foreign perfume. We'd hardly spoken since the night of the funeral. The way she looked at me I feared a renewal of Onslaught-denial.

"Dominic, erm…" She hesitated, looking at the car and at Martina standing on the other side. Then she noticed the V-shape of hairy chest on display for Martina. I feared she'd get the wrong impression, primly drew the sides together. And, yes, I did think of throwing them open and shouting 'Voila!' But that was too flighty a thought for Colonel Serious.

"Martina," she turned around. "I need about half an hour with Dominic. Erm, can you ring ahead and say I'll be delayed for half an hour, please? Thank you. Is it alright to go inside?" she asked me. "For a short chat."

Glanced wistfully at Martina like a schoolboy being brought in for extra study as I followed the Politician into the front room.

"Dominic," she began, standing in the bay window, holding a creaky new brown-leather handbag. She wanted this to be quick. "I didn't come here straight away when I got back. I wanted to wait a few days… see how I felt before I came over to see you." She stopped, her expression uncertain, as if remembering she should first enquire after my health. "How… how are you keeping?"

When an Onslaughter asks that question, it's time to head for the trenches. And the way she asked didn't sound very wifely. In the past, I might have answered with a shrug, but now felt easier to give a simpler response. "Fine."

She placed the crease-free bag on the ground beside an armchair and sat down, folding her long legs into a demure position. I was distracted by the bag. How long before she picked it up, put it down, and picked it up again? Another foreign purchase? I tightened my mouth. Whatever she had to say I would be Boris-like in my serenity.

"I've heard all about what you've been up to. Sergeant Fahy showed me what you did to him and…" She shook her head in resigned disbelief. "I honestly wasn't surprised. For a few months now I've noticed… No, wait, let me finish. I'm not here to give out to you or lecture you. That's over for me, though God knows, you need it. I just want to note certain things and to tell you something important." She paused and looked out the window. I did too. Martina and liberty. Colonel Boris said nothing. He was working on his composure, fixing his eyes to be inscrutable.

"So, please don't interrupt."

My mouth opened involuntarily and closed again. Not very Boris. The wail of an ambulance howled by on the nearby main road frightening the traffic.

"I will listen to what you have to say when I'm finished and then we will part like sensible adults." She glanced around the room as if picking out things she had claim over. The sofa lamp, a row of gilt-edged books in the bookcase, the fender surrounding the fireplace. I was studying her finely shined dark shoes and dug my toes further into my slippers.

"I'll get you some water," I said with commendable generosity. Came back with two full glasses and handed her one.

"Thanks. I also know you were taking Thomas out to the park to play hurling." Her mouth tightened. "Against our express agreement to never leave the house with him on your own. Yes, we had an agreement about that even if you want to pretend you don't remember. And what you did to John, the way you treated him and then, yes, there's the on-going investigations into those... documents. I suppose I should call them that. They are asking whether you had more involvement in the missing... documents than you let on." Looked me right in the eye. Like daring me to speak up. "So far they're not blaming me. Now, I don't want to hear what you were up to. The key point as far as I'm concerned, is you lied to me." Her tongue curled around 'lied' like it was licking it. "That's what you did and, Dominic, and that's..." she said lowering her voice to a whisper, "unforgiveable. That threatens my career and I won't let that happen. You know me when I'm like that." She shook her head, her voice stronger. "I won't. I want to be very clear about that." Extracted a paper-hankie from the bag and wiped her sweaty hands.

Silence after a threat is as pure as the threat itself. Two silences fighting it out while words took shelter. Sage Colonel Boris, head above the parapet, beyond the urge to prick political pride with certain facts, marvelled how three realities were grinding against each other like tectonic plates. Her armchair creaked when she stood up, picked up the shiny handbag and took a final sip of water, carefully placing the glass beside the sofa lamp. "I won't be calling here again," she said almost as an afterthought. "I will have the gap at the back filled in. I… I am separating from you, Dominic. After a few months, I will seek a divorce. Please pay attention to the papers when they arrive." She moved to the door. It had taken only ten minutes, not half an hour.

Stopped at the door without opening it, like she wasn't quite ready to go. "I know you've never considered we were married since you came back from Yugoslavia. Well, we were, we are." Took a document out of her jacket and handed it to me. Her voice shook a little. "That's our marriage certificate. It proves we were married for thirty-three years." She sniffled and blew her nose into the paper-hankie, looking sad and sour. "It doesn't mean anything now." Her eyes moved around the room again, as if for old-times-sake. "Sorry for being… like this." She firmed up. "In a few months, I will start divorce proceedings. I suggest you get legal advice for yourself." I was going to tell her she'd already told me that, but she continued. "That is all I have to say."

Colonel Boris still in the ascendant. Wise inscrutable-eyed.

"Well, have you anything to say?" she asked with a trace of impatience, sitting down on the edge of the sofa near the door, as if giving me one last chance. "After thirty years?" She asked, "You're happy to leave it like this?" She spread her hands as if appealing to me. I thought of the Brat and the young woman, the surrogate family I would lose, had already lost.

I stood up, telling Boris-in-my-head to take a stroll.

"Well?" she asked looking up at me, her eyes searching my face to provoke some response.

Then, out of the blue, I don't know why I said, "There's a finder's fee for the Package. It's already been paid."

Stared at me blankly for a long while, sighed quietly and left.

Stood in the bay window, watching her car start, turn right and disappear. Looked hopefully down the street in case a clutch of auld ones came staggering up the hill, all in need of a smile and a chat. Or just Mrs Hand and her reassurance that nothing in the world is unpredictable or surprising. Only eight twenty-two. Perhaps a bit early for her, though sometimes we caught each other out at odd times. Hadn't seen her for a while and hoped she hadn't changed to home delivery.

Picked up the marriage cert and studied it, looking for signs of forgery. Was she as good at forging my signature as I aimed to be at forging hers?

Chapter 46

The Miracle of Mrs Hand

I cebergs calve in different ways. They don't just stop in the middle of the ocean, hunker down and push. During our fishing trip Maurice droned on and on about bloody icebergs in the car. No idea why, maybe the colour because his face was so pale. Anyway, it stuck with me. Calving happens below the waterline, unnoticed above. The iceberg looks proud and upright, but warmer surface or sub-surface currents eat away at the iceberg's outer layer, waves sweep away the debris. The buoyancy of the water raises more of the iceberg above the waterline, bringing more of the base into contact with warmer water, the process begins again. The deeper the warm currents, the more the iceberg is undermined. Until the iceberg has calved so many times as it floats through increasingly warm waters nothing of its former glory is left. Calving at the surface is not usually seen until the very end. Only later I realised I was an iceberg who'd already started calving.

A few days after the Politician left me, bumped into Dora on the street. Had run out of the house after a long fruitless spell of Boris-waiting for Boris eye-zapping. Because of a phone call I didn't answer. Because when it stopped ringing, Colonel Wistful Idiot decided it was *Madame la Ministre* calling. Uneasy at making me wait so long, finally having the courage to pick up the phone. She thought I'd understand. Was I angry? Wanted me to know how hard it had been for her, how busy she was, meetings, traveling, campaigns and shopping. Had tried to forget me. Made no sense. Didn't fit into anything, her life, my life, anyone's life. Did I fit into her dreams, I asked? She hesitated, her voice throaty, tense. She'd never met anyone like me, hadn't felt like this since she was a teenager...

Aah, I slammed my palm against the thick glass of the triple-glazed window. I had to get out of the house.

"It's very sad, isn't it?" said well-dressed Dora, not known for her conviviality, on the footpath alongside the high stone wall surrounding the old convent. Just where the ivy engulfed the wall. Face as well-pressed as her clothes. I sometimes wondered if she ironed them while wearing them. Air-hostess scarf and long heavy dress.

"What is?" I asked, always competitive for abruptness, and smiled because Dora part-owned a certain four-legged russet-haired font of wisdom.

"Oh," she went, taken aback by my impressive abruptness. "You don't know?" A hand darted up to her mouth. "I don't know if I'm the right person to tell you. Maurice would be better. Oh dear..."

"Know what?" Ready to strangle her with the bloody scarf if she carried on like this.

"Oh, dear!" She looked flustered, but I couldn't tell if it was genuine or put-on. "Oh golly, no… I don't think I can."

"Yes, Dora, you can. Maurice is too busy."

"Oh, well… You promise you didn't hear it from me, Dominic? Well," she licked her lips, now determined to enjoy it. "I suppose… you'll find out anyway." She took a big breath. "Mrs Hand died."

"What?" I can be very slow taking in bad news. Expected something like the new neighbours had parked their car in front of her house two nights in a row.

"Two weeks ago." Her eyes were the biggest I'd ever seen them.

"No, that's not possible," I said, face frozen, mouth agape.

"Oh, it is, Dominic. Terribly sad." She nodded a condolence nod. "Dead and buried up in Glasnevin," she said emphatically and then softened a bit. "I wasn't at the funeral. I was over in Scotland visiting my sister."

"Your sister?" Who gives a toss about your effin' sister? I leaned back against the wall, not far from hoping it would fall on top of both of us. My God, this can't be happening.

"Maurice represented the family. They asked him to come to the afters in the pub up at Cross Guns Bridge." She said more too, her mouth kept on moving, but I have no recollection what she said. My mind had stopped processing any new information. I turned and leaned my head against the wall. Heard a flock of noisy geese flying overhead towards the sea.

"Are you all right, Dominic? You seem... Sorry to be the bearer of... We were all upset over it."

Turned back towards her, a little breathless. "Do you mean to say, Dora, she's really dead?"

Patted my arm and nodded. Looked at her watch and moved to leave. "Dominic, I have to go. I have to get to the library before it closes. I'm late with these." Held up two books. "Sorry, bye."

If I had a lighter or matches with me, I'd have snatched the ruddy books off her and burnt them on the spot. Jesus! Watched her walk along the wall and around the corner, the day collapsing around me. Dora was too serious-minded not to believe and I'd never suspected her of being part of the Onslaught. Christ, I felt devastated, obliterated, numbed and lonely.

"She's dead," I said to the footpath. "Dead. My closest ally against the Onslaught... But... but she can't be dead." Looked around, tried to recall when and where I'd seen her last. A young guy in jeans and belief in the world skipped onto the road to avoid me. Glared at him wanting him to challenge me to a mad fight. Did bloody Dora have any idea what Mrs Hand meant to me? Did anyone? I looked at the gates. Frantic, not anxious, not in front of me. I wanted Mrs Hand herself to appear instantly to stop the slander.

I ran after Dora and caught her down at the bottom of the hill. She heard me shouting and turned.

"My God… My God, what happened to her?" I demanded, the words jumping out between gasps.

Dora looked worried and disapproving of her name being shouted out across the street, but she was also pleased her news had such an impact.

"She was coming home from the supermarket and apparently – I wasn't there you know, and she just fell down dead on the street. A stroke, I believe." She looked around. "Somewhere around here too, eh, I think there." She pointed across the road, at the redbrick wall in need of repair with overhanging bushes. "Somewhere along there, I think. I'm in a rush," she smiled guiltily and walked off, not knowing she was carrying so much of my life with her, so much of my hopes for happiness. I knew she thought I was mad and that I coveted Boris. But still.

Crossed the road between the parked cars to where she pointed. On my own street? Unbelievable. Walk along here every day. Looked down at the darkish concrete where I stood. I could be standing on the very spot where Mrs Hand breathed her last breath. Remembered seeing flowers against the wall a while back, gone now, and assumed it was one of the auld ones. There hadn't been any writing on the flowers, and I'd forgotten about it. People died or were killed in our area all the time.

The crime of not attending an important funeral. This is what I now accused myself of. How dare I miss such a major event? I'd no right to not pay my proper respects to a great woman. Well, there was only one thing to do. Right the wrong straight away.

On the way to the cemetery, got more information from neighbour Tom coming out of the church. Not a known churchgoer. I wonder had it put the wind up him too.

"Ah, the poor woman. She collapsed near Grace's house," he said with his usual don't-look-me-in-the-eye humanity. As usual I was lost trying to find a spot on his head to look at instead of his hair. I settled on his right ear, only a short distance from his eyes, noting the few hairs that sprouted there.

"What?" I shouted at him. He almost recoiled at that.

"Hold on there, Dominic. I'm not deaf."

What had Dora been saying? It wasn't the same place at all. Same stretch, but across the bloody road. She'd died even closer to my house.

"I don't know who found her," Tom said. "It wasn't Grace anyway. The ambulance got here quick, but I think she was already gone." Tom was always to-the-point, was always able to say the right thing, but I could never tell if he actually felt anything.

"I only just found out," I said, telling myself to be calm. "I can't believe it."

Tom was too polite to say, 'What kind of an eejit are you that you didn't hear about it?'

"She was carrying too much. Two heavy bags of groceries and she had only herself to feed. No idea what she did with all the stuff she'd been carrying for years. I told her plenty of times she didn't have to carry all that stuff. You know the supermarket deliver it to your house for you."

I agreed.

"God rest her soul."

"Amen." But I didn't pray she'd rest in peace. I prayed that she wasn't resting, that she was entertaining the angels with her wry observations about heaven and carrying light grocery bags for St Peter.

Tom fixed me with a cool look. "Haven't seen you around for a while."

"The rain, Tom," I lied. "Too much bloody rain."

Before I left him, Tom told me where Mrs Hand was buried in the cemetery. He also told me the enquiries into the searches had started. He'd received two official letters inviting him to an interview. Had I gotten them too? I said sure. I'd have to check when I got home.

Reached it in fifteen, saying to myself, 'It can't be true, she can't be dead,' and, 'If you are dead, Mrs Hand, what will I do? How will I manage without you?' Of course, I was in shock, denial. But closer and closer to the cemetery I was saying, 'If I'm going there, if she's in the cemetery, then she must be dead.'

Inside, the cemetery was so quiet, felt like a good place to die as well as be buried. Found the grave quickly. Amazingly, already a headstone there. First sign of divine intervention. An upright wide-shouldered slab of unpolished granite. The inscription was hewn in dark lettering. It was apt.

"Cherish the memory of Eleanor Hand, mother and grandmother, wife of Able Hand, died 29th of March 2002, aged 76 years."

So pleased it didn't say something kitsch like, 'Devoted wife', or 'Pray for the repose of the soul of'. Wouldn't have been Mrs Hand at all. She didn't need prayers. She would take God and St Peter and the whole shebang as she found them. Leaning against the pearly gates to catch her breath, she'd fix Peter reckoning her sins with that gaze and say, 'Aye, that'd be right… alright, fifty-five years ago, and that too.' And 'Are you busy today?'

Took off my hat, shoved it into my pocket and placed the large bunch of flowers bought in the cemetery flower shop beside three aging bunches already there. Told her I would never forget her and that people like her were rare. Even told her she was better than any Shrinkage I'd ever had the misfortune to meet.

While sad, I was also uplifted by the well-tended condition of the fresh grave, the aptness of the headstone and the suitability of the inscription. Maybe in her death she might transfer some of her wisdom to me.

So deep in contemplation, it was a while before I realised my head was wet. It was raining lightly, and I didn't feel panicky. Shook myself, surprised I wasn't running for shelter. Touched my hair, amazed I was still in the same spot and not hyper. Lord above. What's going on? Felt just the same as before I'd noticed the rain. Resisted rising excitement and urge to leap and shout, "It's a miracle. It's a miracle!" Instead walked back and forth along the tarmacked path beside the grave, testing the discovery in the open drizzle, closely examining my state of mind for signs I was imagining it. There were none. It was no lie.

Put my two hands on my head like a prisoner of war, walked back to her grave, and stood there, awestruck, still wanting to declare a miracle. And who made the miracle? Who had a word in the ear of the man himself? She hadn't forgotten me. What was her first name again? Eleanor. Now Saint Eleanor. Said it out loud, "Saint Eleanor." First person in the world to say it. She'd told St Peter about me and, wise man that he was, he'd done what she asked him. Thanked Saint Eleanor profusely. Sat down on the ledge around the grave, told Able he was one lucky guy, and looked around to spread the word, sad and happily wet.

Chapter 47

New Beginnings

I t wasn't a two-minute wonder. Drizzled the whole way home and I didn't cover my head once. The feeling was exhilarating. Raindrops didn't sink inside my head and cause a commotion. They just dampened the bits of curly hair I had and added freshness to the rest. Walking by the church I was dancing in the rain.

What a few days! The 'wife' leaving me. Mrs Hand dying and Saint Eleanor curing me. I just felt great. No disrespect to the dead or departed. The shock and sadness weren't gone, but nothing beats a miracle. Who knows, maybe more where that came from.

Back in the house by six forty-two. Colonel Special-One got a bottle of champagne from the basement and put it in the fridge. While I waited for it to chill, I took a big chunk of semi-conscious cucumber from the fridge and settled on the kitchen sofa with Annabella and Maximus on my lap. Told them the story of the day and when their agitation increased – speed-nudging and butt-following, knew they shared my excitement. Wanted to share our joy with Boris as well, but it was already dark.

Reflected that the secret of a miracle is in not asking for it. But, how could I wish for the next one and not ask for it at the same time? Would take a lot more figuring out. Still it felt like I was at the dawn of a new era of miracle-making. Not as Stephen Kidney, but, yes... as any Dominic Corley I wanted to be. With Saint Eleanor to guide me. I saw myself, Dommo the Man, sitting under a blue sky which didn't know what clouds were, surrounded by friends, talking nostalgically about my injuries from playing Henry Hurling, my belief in miracles, and remembering my rural primary school and how we used to pick blackberries in September and throw snowballs in February and cycle along country lanes in summer.

Humming to myself popped the cork of the chilled champagne – not easy holding two guinea pigs and only one thumb – filled the most elegant glass I could find in the house. Also filled a saucer for the guinea pigs. Took each one in turn on my lap and held it close to the saucer. If I had put the saucer on the ground in their cage the silly rogues would have trampled over it. Maximus liked the taste, Annabella only wanted to dip her bum in it.

When they were back in their cage and I was on my third tasty sparkling glass, sunny images of Rosario started drifting in front of me. Lay back on the sofa, closed my eyes and pictured myself out on the lake, sailing with Terry and his son, admiring from afar the sleek exalted bridge and the fluttering flags along the shoreline. Saw myself asking Terry's son whether sharing a name with someone counted for anything, telling him about the Brat and explaining the rules of Henry Hurling to him. That reminded me how the afternoons had grown much longer since the Brat stopped calling after school.

The doorbell rang. Fourth glass in hand opened the door, ready to greet whoever it was and drag them in to share my bonhomie. Neighbour Maurice. Aha! Was about to drag him in for some champers when the look on his face stopped me. The only part of his face that was expressive was his eyebrows and they looked… nervous. Wished I was in better shape to react.

"Boris is missing," he announced, simply and directly in a droll tone, the kind a bored newsreader uses to report the Russians have landed. "Since this morning. You haven't seen him?"

"What? No, no," I stuttered, afraid I sounded shifty, un-empathetic. This was so un-Maurice. Was he mildly or madly upset? Impossible to tell. "I haven't. I was out today." To be honest, it didn't seem that big a deal to me. Everyone knew Boris wandered. I'd once seen him coming out of the church grounds.

Then I got it. If Maurice was out looking for him at this time of night something major was up and he wanted me to help. Me, the greatest Boris-admirer in the world. My boozy spirits began a slow slide into cold storage.

"Come to think of it, I haven't seen him for a few days," I said. I'd have liked Maurice to know I was always on the lookout for Boris and how long I'd waited for him this morning, but it wasn't the moment. "He didn't come into the garden this morning," I added, getting nervous myself, wondering whether Maurice's eyebrows harboured a suspicion I had something to do with it. Was he waiting for me to deny taking him?

"Dora is very worried."

"Is she? I met her earlier. Didn't mention Boris. She told me about Mrs Hand. First I'd heard of it. Very upsetting."

"Yeah," Maurice agreed, but that was all. "She was out looking for him then."

"Was she?" As well as going to the library? But then I knew of her indifference to my feelings for Boris.

Maurice had lapsed into silence but was still looking directly at me. He glanced at the glass of champagne in my hand. Knew what he was thinking. "One second," I said, putting the glass on the hall table and getting my coat, but not my hat, and felt thwarted I couldn't tell him about Saint Eleanor's rain miracle. "I'll help you," I said and switched off the light and joined the search.

"We let him out this morning," Maurice was saying as I closed the gate behind me. "Just like every day and he hasn't come home. He's usually back by noon."

"That's not like him. Did he have the bell on?"

Maurice shook his head. A delicate matter. "No, I didn't want him handicapped any more. Dora wasn't too happy." He sighed. Could well imagine that battle took a lot out of him.

"We have six people out looking for him."

Even in extreme stress, Maurice couldn't hide his pride in Dora's organisational skills. I guessed those skills would extend to post-search refreshments in the house.

"It's terrible," I sympathised as we hurried down the street, fighting to subdue the champagne-gaiety that might break out any moment and I'd say the wrong thing. "What do you think might have happened?"

"I don't know. But you have to be suspicious. The neighbourhood seems full of dodgy characters these days."

A black cat emerged from between two cars parked about fifty metres ahead under a streetlight and scarpered across the road, spooked by an on-coming motorbike, and disappeared.

"Pity we can't ask him if he's seen Boris," Colonel Foot-In-Mouth said. "I suppose we'll see every cat in the neighbourhood now except Boris."

"I would miss Boris if anything happened to him," Maurice said in a gloomy voice.

"Don't be a worrier," I said, trying to check the side of a house. "He'll come home, 'wagging his tail behind him'. You'll see." But the gloominess was catching. "We would all miss him," I said looking into the dark distance and thinking there's no hope of finding him tonight.

We reached the church and split up. Maurice went down towards the park. I went up around Cross Guns Bridge and along the canal, yes, sweeping everywhere for small orange-gold furry creatures. Under cars, between cars, sitting on top of cars, walls, sheds, wheelie bins, door-steps, everywhere. Without knowing a thing about what cats did at night. I hoped Boris' distinct colour would stand out in the dark. No point calling out his name. Never answered anyway. I gave it a good go, even searching as far as Broombridge along the canal, but Boris would need to have been off his head to wander that far.

Didn't take up Maurice's invite to join them back at his house for post-search refreshments and planning of tomorrow's campaign. Didn't want to get sucked into long discussions about him. As far as I was concerned, no one, apart from Maurice and myself, had any right to real feelings for Boris. I also feared a long discussion about which photo of Boris to use in the lost-cat posters I was sure were already being worked on. Knowing Dora, the poster would be up on every lamppost by midday. I had a thing about posters on bloody lampposts staring at me for weeks on end.

"Aye," I could hear Saint Eleanor saying. "That's what they did all right. On every second pole. They must think we're blind. Maybe we are."

"And what do you think of the poster?"

"Oh, a bonnie cat, alright. The five or six left in the house are surely jealous."

Before we split up at the church Maurice had revealed the depth of his pessimism to me.

"Dora has a bad feeling about this… and so do I. I don't see how he could just disappear like that. Boris wouldn't get lost. He knows the area too well." He shook his head. "I don't know if we'll ever find him."

The idea of never seeing Boris again was an awful one. "We will find him," I insisted. "Maurice, don't worry."

Wanted to call on Saint Eleanor for help, but just thinking about it meant I couldn't. Started repeating to myself, 'I don't want to find him, I don't want to find him,' hoping she'd get the message.

When I got back to my house, went straight to the back garden and sat on a garden chair. The black sky was suffused with a thin film of yellow city light. Wanted to feel close to Boris' spirit and to reflect on the day's momentous events. If it was cold, didn't notice. Was afraid, with all that was happening, I wasn't thinking enough about the cumulative effects of the abrupt departure of Mrs Hand on top of everything else and especially what the Politician said. In other words, the future. But being alone in the dark in my back garden, chair square in the middle of the grass facing south east where there were no overhanging branches, somehow, I could only think about Boris and what he was doing right then. If anything happened to him, if he'd wandered off and gotten lost or been run over by a car, could I ever again look out the kitchen window from my observation tile? There were other cats, but they were all ungainly, all clodhoppers… Would I have to spend years looking for another Boris?

My arms were aching from gripping the armrests of the chair. It was as if part of me was anticipating something terrible. Stood up, shook myself rid of these gloomy thoughts and stretched my legs. Might do some gardening. Looked around for the rake or broom, start sweeping the earth at the back of the garden. Needed to urinate first. Inched my way among the bushes and the low branches and dead leaves to the gap in the wall. Left foot stubbed against something soft. Used my toe to poke it to see what it was. Seemed small, compact, heavy enough, easy to move. One of the lane kids must have thrown someone's teddy bear over the wall.

Bent down to examine it. The hair of the small creature was wet, matted and sticky. My fingers found a snub nose, whiskers, a small rigid open mouth. Below that a gooey slit in the throat, two inches long, the knife didn't go deep, didn't need to. Shifted position so the weak light from the kitchen showed the hair to be less dark than the surroundings. Closing and opening my eyes made no difference, I knew who it was.

Before daybreak I was gone. Before the posters of Boris went up on lamp posts in the area, I was sitting on an aeroplane high over the Atlantic. Ticket paid for in cash. Doing something I never thought I could or would do. It should have been the hardest night of my life after a difficult day, but I was too busy to think. The fright I got in the back garden dislodged something inside me and I became energised like I'd woken up after a long sleep. Got no sleep. Hours after midnight, when the street was deserted and the traffic on the main road had died away, left the house by the back lane. Slipped six envelopes containing one thousand euros each into the letterboxes of Tom, Maurice, Jim, Una, Bridget and Bernie. No one saw me, not even a cat. If they had, I'd have been stuck for an explanation, but I knew what I was doing. It was Santa Claus came early, dates mixed up. Nothing in the envelope I put in my own letterbox. Reckoned they would figure things out when word got around I'd gone, not fled.

Thought about killing the two guinea pigs but couldn't. Put two whole cucumbers on the kitchen floor and let them out of their cage. Now free to wander wherever they liked. Watched their tentative first steps to freedom. They looked around suspiciously, as if not believing they were free. Uncomfortable with the freedom that also made them easy targets. They scurried over to the wall because it narrowed the sources of attack, and hurried along it, looking for dark small spaces to hide in. Told them they would not have to worry about Boris anymore.

Took the rest of the cistern money, the medal, the red plastic wheel the Brat had played with on the sofa, the two hurleys, two sliotars, and a taxi to the airport.

Please Review

Dear Reader,

If you enjoyed this book, would you kindly post a short review on whichever platform you purchased from? Your feedback will make all the difference to getting the word out about this book.

Thank you in advance.